D0120477

WITHDRAWN

993384601 9

The Hanging Wood

By Martin Edwards

LAKE DISTRICT MYSTERIES

The Coffin Trail
The Cipher Garden
The Arsenic Labyrinth
The Serpent Pool
The Hanging Wood

HARRY DEVLIN NOVELS

Waterloo Sunset

a&b

The Hanging Wood

MARTIN EDWARDS

First published in Great Britain in 2011 by
Allison & Busby Limited
13 Charlotte Mews
London W1T 4EJ
www.allisonandbusby.com

Copyright © 2011 by Martin Edwards

The moral right of the author has been asserted.

*All characters and events in this publication,
other than those clearly in the public domain,
are fictitious and any resemblance to actual persons,
living or dead, is purely coincidental.*

This book is sold subject to the conditions that it shall not,
by way of trade or otherwise, be lent, resold, hired out or
otherwise circulated without the publisher's prior
written consent in any form of binding or cover other than
that in which it is published and without a similar condition
being imposed upon the subsequent purchaser.

A CIP catalogue record for this book is available from
the British Library.

10 9 8 7 6 5 4 3 2 1

13-ISBN 978-0-7490-1054-6

Typeset in 11.25/16 pt Sabon by
Allison & Busby Ltd.

Paper used in this publication is from sustainably managed sources.
All of the wood used is procured from legal sources and is fully traceable.
The producing mill uses schemes such as ISO 14001
to monitor environmental impact.

Printed and bound in the UK by
CPI Mackays, Chatham ME5 8TD

Dedicated to the memory of Joan Edwards

GLOUCESTERSHIRE COUNTY COUNCIL	
9933846019	
Bertrams	22/07/2011
AF	£19.99
TY	

CHAPTER ONE

'I must talk to Hannah Scarlett, it's a matter of life and death.'

Orla shaded her eyes from the July sun. Her right hand trembled so much that she dropped her mobile into the shallow ditch and had to reach down to fish it out. In front of her stood the hedge marking the boundary of her father's farm.

'Life and death,' she hissed into the phone.

'May I have your name?'

'Orla . . . Orla Payne.'

A long, long pause. 'You spoke to DCI Scarlett yesterday afternoon?'

The detective constable sounded young and sceptical. Orla pictured her, pursing her lips, searching for a politically correct way to say *get lost*. A gatekeeper, tasked with making sure her boss wasn't disturbed. She'd written Orla off as a drunken time-waster, just because her voice was too loud and she'd slurred her own name. So what if she'd downed a few cans? This was supposed to be a free country, it wasn't against the law to drown your sorrows.

'That's right.' Yesterday's call had gone badly, but she'd summoned the nerve to try again. The last chance saloon.

In the hedgerow, a linnet sang. The summer air tasted sweet, and she could smell the fields. But her head ached; she couldn't do this. It was too difficult.

'Ms Payne. Are you still there?'

Legs swaying, Orla grabbed the handle of the car door and steadied herself. She'd parked next to the ditch. On the way, she'd cracked the wing mirror against a drystone wall, but who cared? People would say she was unfit to drive. Yet here she was, calling the Cold Case Review Team at Cumbria Constabulary. She wasn't afraid any longer. Fear had become as pointless as hope.

'Ms Payne?'

'Just put me through, will you?'

'I'm sorry—'

'Am I talking to myself?' Orla was trying not to scream with frustration.

'DCI Scarlett is on leave today.'

The woman spoke with exaggerated patience. Orla's cheeks were moist. Despair made her guts churn.

'Can I help, Ms Payne?'

'Too late,' Orla mumbled into her phone. 'It's just ancient history to everyone else. Nobody cares about justice.'

People never listened to her. The warning she'd been given was true: nobody would believe what she had to say. She had no proof; talking to the police was a waste of time. The energy had drained out of her, like oil trickling from a leak in her car. She had no fight left.

'Ms Payne?'

Orla killed the call.

She tried to crush the mobile in her hand, but it was impossible, so she hurled it over the hedge. The phone struck a black tank squatting on top of a small trailer, and fell into a trough filled by the tank with water for the cattle to drink. The trough was an old enamel bath, and her father hadn't bothered to take the taps off.

Contacting the police was a stupid idea. She should never have listened to Daniel Kind. All he knew about murder came from books and dusty archives. He'd advised her to talk to Hannah Scarlett, but yesterday afternoon Orla's brain was even fuzzier than it felt right now. She'd made a fool of herself when she was put through, and in the end, Hannah lost patience.

Orla kicked the car door, wishing it was the head of the detective constable. Her boots had steel tips, and they dented the paintwork. Didn't matter. She'd never drive that old banger again.

The lane led to Mockbeggar Hall, and she saw its turrets poking up above the copper beeches. As a child, she'd dreamt of living in the Hall. In one of her favourite fantasies, there had been some mix-up, and in the end she proved she was no farm kid, but an unacknowledged daughter of the Hopes family, who had owned the Mockbeggar Estate for generations. But now the Hall belonged to the Madsens, who had made their money through selling caravans. Her father reckoned the Madsens always got what they wanted in the end, and he was right.

She walked to a point where the hedge gave way to a fence. In the field, a trio of plump Friesians grazed, each with a yellow tag in its left ear, bearing a number inked in black. Their eyes were dark, with no discernible pupils. They looked mournful, as if someone they knew had died.

Orla ripped off her headscarf and threw it into a clump of nettles. A splash of red and gold among the green. She no longer felt self-conscious about her bald head. The cows weren't embarrassed, and neither was she.

A red sign stapled to a fence post said *Danger – electric shock*. She heard a faint tick-tick-tick. Throughout summer, the strands of wire were live. As she levered herself over the fence, her leg brushed the wire. The impact from the current felt like a blow from a mallet. It was years since a farm fence had shocked her, and she landed on the ground in a heap.

Swearing, she clambered to her feet, vaguely aware that the booze had deadened her senses. She stumbled away from the fence in the direction of the farm buildings. Sometimes she kept to the tractor tracks, sometimes she veered over the grass. A single cow, black with a white blotch on its belly, trudged towards her. Its lumbering tread hinted at menace, but Orla wasn't scared. She'd grown up with animals, and found their smells comforting. Cows don't hurt anyone, unless you are stupid enough to let a dog scamper around and frighten their calves.

As she passed, the cow made a crooning noise. It didn't take much imagination to believe the animal was pleading with her. Orla had never lacked imagination; she and her brother Callum shared that in common.

Lane End Farm stood four hundred yards ahead. On this side of the old higgledy-piggledy house was a long line of cattle sheds and outbuildings, along with a slurry tank and the grain silo. The back garden where she and Callum once played was overgrown. Most of the windows were at the front of the house, facing in the opposite direction. She remembered peering through each of them, gazing at the horizon, trying to make out the contours of Blencathra through the morning mist.

She'd come full circle; Lane End was where it all began. Her mother had given birth to her in the kitchen – her waters broke suddenly, and there was no time to drive to the hospital. Orla's earliest memories were of playing hide-and-seek with Callum around the sheds and machinery while their father barked orders to his men and their mother stayed in bed with what she called a migraine and Dad called a hangover. Orla used to shut her eyes so tight they hurt, counting to one hundred and then calling, 'Coming, ready or not!' Callum always made it hard for her to find him, taunting her for the eternity it took to track him down.

Callum's voice rattled around in her brain. The last time she saw him, he'd been so pleased with himself, teasing her by refusing to let her into a secret, laughing fit to burst when she ran off with tears in her eyes, saying she didn't care.

Her foot caught on a hook protruding from a lichen-smeared stone cheese press long ago abandoned in the grass, and she lost her balance for a second time. This time her ankle wrenched, and she sat down to massage the tender flesh. For an instant, she had an impression of a flash of light, as if the sun had glinted on a pair of field glasses.

When she picked herself up, not a soul was to be seen. These days farms needed fewer people to do all the work. An engine roared into life behind the stone-built shippons;

a tractor must be heading out into the narrow lane.

The grain silo loomed in front of her, linked to the farmyard by a dirt track rutted by huge tyres. The silo was forty feet high, a finger pointing to Heaven. A memory swam in her head of the silo's arrival at Lane End Farm; it came in component parts, arched sections of steel. She and Callum watched the crane lifting the sections into place as their father yelled instructions, and waved his arms like a human windmill.

'Silos are scary,' Callum said. 'We won't be allowed in.'

Orla had dreamt of bathing in the harvest, letting the grain run down in rivulets over her face, breathing in the aroma she adored.

'You're lying to me!'

'No, I'm serious. It's too easy to become trapped. When the conveyor pumps the grain in at full blast, it works so fast, it can overwhelm you. There's no way out. If you call, nobody would hear. Too much noise.'

Callum possessed curiosity by the wagon-load. He loved finding things out just as he loved to parade his superior knowledge, drip-feeding titbits to his sister to keep her hanging on his every utterance.

The back of her neck prickled. *Was* someone watching her? She glanced around, but if someone was hidden in the wych elms of the Hanging Wood, or lurking behind the buildings, she could not tell. Perhaps this sense of someone observing her every move was caused by feeling so alone. Loneliness was a cancer, eating up your confidence. After Callum vanished, she had nobody to turn to. Mum was wrapped up with her new husband, Kit Payne, who worked for the Madsens at the caravan park. The children were pawns in a bitter divorce, and Mum messed Dad about so he didn't get the access she promised in court. Orla didn't set eyes on him for weeks after Callum disappeared. By the time she was allowed to go back to the farm again, they had become strangers.

Before the silo tower was built, she loved to join Callum in the grain piled high in the barn. The pair of them took turns to swing on the rope that hung from the rafters and jump into the heap, where they would roll about, laughing without control as they pretended to bury each other. More fun than a seaside holiday and getting buried in sand. Sometimes they showered in the grain as the conveyor sprayed it down. As daylight faded, they emptied it from their wellies, squirming because it itched and had slipped down their shirts. The smell of dry grain fresh from the combine was the smell of summer. Not like when it was wet and fermented, and smelt like the beer her father drank.

The building of the silo tower ended the game, as Callum forecast. The children had to find other places to go, new stories to dream up. But Callum was never at a loss. They were like Hansel and Gretel, he announced. Their uncle's cottage in the Hanging Wood became their very own gingerbread house.

She gazed at the silo. It might have been a religious monument, eerie yet inspiring awe. A shaft of light fell upon its walls as if a miracle were about to happen. For years, she'd disclaimed any faith, but now she had a fuzzy image of herself as a pilgrim, a devotee lured by the mysterious landmark. It wanted to draw her into its clutches.

Her boot crunched on something, and she came to a sudden halt. A scattering of tiny white bones lay beneath her feet. She peered at the skeleton for so long that her eyes began to water. The remains of a heron, chased to destruction by ravens or crows. She'd heard rumours that red kites were coming back to the Lakes, but if they returned, they too would be mobbed by birds determined to guard their territory.

'Birds are like people,' Callum once said. 'They hate trespassers.'

Orla forced herself on. The closer she came to the farm, the more it resembled a surreal graveyard. Remnants of old farm machines were strewn around. Some must have lain here for years, dirty spikes and shards of metal like a parody of some weird work of art.

A wail from a small shed chilled her spine. The cry of a calf, distressed by the absence of its mother. It sounded hoarse, and she supposed it had been wailing for hours. She remembered teaching the calves to drink from buckets so the cows were not distracted from producing milk for market. The smell of stale milk from the calf-pen lingered in her sinuses.

She limped up to the half-door at the base of the silo. Another memory slithered into her head. The first harvest after the silo was built, the weather was wet for weeks on end, and the grain became stuck. One afternoon, Dad took his shotgun out of the cupboard, and Callum and Orla followed him to the silo. He shouted at them to stand back when he opened the grain door. Holding her breath, gripping her brother's arm, Orla watched as their father raised his shotgun and fired into the mass of damp grain.

The blast deafened her, and she clamped her hands to her ears with a wail of dismay.

'What are you mithering about?' her father demanded. He'd turned round grinning, as if expecting applause, and her feeble reaction annoyed him. Callum's face was a sly mask, as usual. 'That's how you do it. Moist grain bridges, and it needs to be loose.'

Most farmers loosened grain with a pole, Callum told her later, but that wasn't thrilling enough for Dad. He relished the sense of power. It felt like a drug coursing through his veins. Shooting turned him on, Callum said.

A bolt was fixed to the grain door, a nod to safety regulations, but it was rusty from lack of use. Orla wondered about crawling into the bottom of the silo. No, she had a better idea.

The ladder up the side of the silo was covered by a safety ring, a tube made of fibreglass. A belated safety measure, added after one of Dad's men fell off the ladder on a windy day and broke his ankle.

Once you were inside the ring, nobody could see you mounting the ladder, until you reached the top of the silo. Orla surveyed the fields. Her only witnesses were the cows, and even they were losing interest.

She wriggled into the tube, and started to lever herself up the rungs of the ladder. Her head and ankle throbbed with pain. Those cans of lager had made her so woozy she found herself dreaming that someone had begun to shin up after her. What did it matter if she took a tumble? She managed to cling on to the cool metal all the way to the top.

Orla hauled herself from the ladder ring into the sunshine. At the top of the silo was a metal platform, and she sidled behind the pipework through which the grain was blown. Until the last moment, she wanted to be concealed from anyone who might emerge from the buildings and stare up at the silo from the farmyard.

A hatch on the platform led down to the inside of the silo. The hatch wasn't padlocked, there was no point. A rubber seal kept the grain free from moisture, and the hatch was closed by wing nuts. Orla fiddled with the wing nuts, and slid them across.

Crouching by the side of the open hatch, she peered down into the silo. The grain was deep, a darkly golden mountain. Forty tons, minimum. Cattle needed feeding all year – that was why the silo was half-full at the height of summer. Inhaling, she sucked the smell of the grain into her lungs. The odour made her think she'd stuck her face into a barrel of bitter beer.

It was like gazing into a tunnel. The sun fell on the grain, casting light on darkness. What might you find at the end of such a tunnel? But her brain was a junkyard, and she didn't want to guess. Better find out for herself.

Peacefulness enveloped her, warm as a blanket. No question, her instinct was right. Only one way to go.

Orla stood up straight, lifted her arms, and put her hands together. Her lips moved as if in silent prayer. The sun burnt her scalp but she felt no pain.

She thought she heard a hoarse voice. Was that someone close by, hissing her name? Too late to take notice. No second thoughts.

I'm coming home.

CHAPTER TWO

'Don't you *care* about justice?'

Hannah Scarlett took a sip from her mug as the question echoed in her brain.

The coffee scalded her tongue, but Hannah didn't notice. All she felt was the sting of Orla Payne's scorn.

Crazy, crazy, crazy. A summer morning on a rare day off, and she was sprawling on the sunlounger; yet she couldn't stop thinking about work. She never should have taken that call yesterday. Over the years, she'd interviewed rapists, paedophiles, and murderers who felt no flicker of remorse for the harm they caused. So why succumb to guilt when she'd done nothing wrong?

If Marc were here, he'd roll his eyes and moan that the job mattered to her more than anything, and certainly more than he did. She'd insist he was exaggerating, refuse to acknowledge that he might be right.

Anyway, she was on her own now, out at the back of Undercrag, the sun warming her as Marc hadn't done since the depths of winter. They had bought the house last year, before everything fell apart and he moved out. Six weeks ago, she'd lugged the garden furniture out of the shed, but this was the first time she'd found time to laze. Meadow browns and dark-green fritillaries flitted among the shrub roses; she heard the plaintive cry of an invisible lapwing. The wildlife garden of Undercrag was turning into a wilderness, her failure to do any gardening just one more shortcoming to prick her conscience. But there was nobody around to see the evidence of her neglect. A tall holly hedge and half a dozen huge horse chestnut trees afforded complete seclusion from the neighbours' houses. Marc was keen on the privacy; knowing him, he'd had half an eye on the potential for al fresco sex. No chance of that now, mate.

She was wearing only the T-shirt she'd slept in and a pair of shorts. Soon, she must figure out what to wear for her meeting with Marc. Dress up or dress down? Remind him of what he was missing, or impersonate a bag lady, in the hope he'd abandon interest in winning her back?

She bit into a slice of toast, telling herself not to obsess about the job. Yet police work offered escape, and when she wasn't on duty, thinking about it helped her to dodge decisions about what to do with the rest of her life.

Better stop beating herself up about Orla Payne. The woman had been pissed, but Hannah shouldn't have let her temper fray. Blame it on Marc; she'd been psyching herself up for the challenge of seeing him again. Yet Orla wasn't a routine time-waster. She'd been drinking, but the muddled desperation in her voice sounded genuine.

'He deserves justice,' Orla said. '"*How could you do that to your own brother?*"'

'What do you mean?' Hannah asked.

'Those were Callum's words. Our uncle was a scapegoat. He wouldn't hurt a fly, let alone Callum. He loved us both. Why does nobody understand?'

'I don't understand.'

'You'll say that Callum hasn't been seen for twenty years,' Orla muttered. 'But I'm only asking for justice for my brother. Is that too much to ask?'

'Your brother's name was Callum Hinds, and he disappeared all those years ago – is that what you're saying, Ms Payne?' If this was a cold case, it was slap bang in her territory – but very, very cold after a couple of decades. 'Ms Payne, if you want my team to consider looking into a case, we must have something to work with. Can you provide new evidence? Facts not available until now?'

'He said you would listen,' Orla muttered.

'I am listening.' Teeth gritted. 'But I'm not clear what you're telling me.'

'For God's sake. How many times . . . ?'

The woman's voice trailed away.

'Ms Payne?'

'He was wrong. I should have realised. You're not interested.'

Ever-decreasing circles. Impatience gnawed at Hannah.

'*Who* was wrong?' she demanded.

'Daniel Kind.'

Hearing Daniel's name out of the blue snatched Hannah's breath away. For a moment, she could not think what to say.

'I'm wasting my time, aren't I?'

'Ms Payne—'

'Don't you *care* about justice?'

The line went dead.

Leaving Hannah to wonder about Orla Payne, her brother's disappearance, and Daniel Kind.

A grey squirrel crouched on the grass in front of her, its eyes bright and inquisitive. Hannah offered it a small piece of toast, but the squirrel took one look and scampered off up a tree trunk, leaping from one branch to another before disappearing into the thick mass of leaves. Oh well, so much for bonding with nature. When she and Marc first looked round Undercrag, he said the grounds would be lovely in the summer months, a haven of peace and quiet two miles from the traffic jams in the tourist trap of Ambleside. They mustered the purchase price and cost of renovations thanks to money Marc had inherited, yet he hadn't set foot inside the house since early January. His fault, so why did Hannah feel a pang of remorse? That was as stupid as fretting because a boozed-up woman she'd never met accused her of not caring about justice.

After Orla's call, Hannah asked Chantal, the team's latest admin assistant, to dig out the file on Callum Hinds. He'd disappeared when Hannah was still at school. The name rang a bell – no doubt she'd seen it in the papers or heard it on the TV news, but she couldn't recall any details. In her mind, his story was blurred with those of all the other teenagers who went missing, never to return.

Once she started reading, she became so absorbed that she took the buff folders home and trawled through each and every one of them, staying awake till the early hours. Callum Hinds' parents were divorced. Niamh, his mother, had remarried a man called Kit Payne, but Callum kept the surname of his father, who ran a dairy farm near Keswick. One day, his mother raised the alarm when she discovered that he had gone missing. A search was mounted, but no trace of Callum was ever found.

Soon after the police were called in, his uncle – Philip Hinds, brother of Mike, the farmer – committed suicide. His body was found dangling from a branch of an old elm tree, a stone's throw from the cottage where he lived.

'He died somewhere called the Hanging Wood,' Chantal had said, unable to resist a nervous giggle at the irony.

'So how old was Orla Payne when Callum vanished?'

'Seven.'

Only seven. Had life treated her roughly since then, had drink or drug addiction led her to fantasise about her brother's fate? The call gave the team nothing to latch on to; there was no reason for Hannah to feel wounded by the jibe that she didn't care about justice.

Gulping down the rest of her drink, she stretched out on the lounger. But the caffeine made her nerve ends tingle, and she had plenty to do. Forget Orla Payne. This was meant to be decision day, when she finally summoned up the nerve to tell Marc they were finished.

'You're looking fantastic,' Marc said.

She shrugged, determined not to respond to flattery, even though she'd experienced a zing of triumph when she first pulled on her jeans. Trophy jeans, a pair she'd kept long after she'd last been able to squeeze herself into them. Over the past six months, she'd lost half a stone. Living on her own must suit her.

She closed her eyes, listening to the water crash over the weir. They were lunching out at the back of Marc's second-hand bookshop. He'd cordoned off a space that overlooked the stream. Hannah had suggested meeting elsewhere, on neutral ground, but he'd persuaded her to come here. The bookshop was his kingdom – but not, these days, exclusively his. He'd gone into partnership with Leigh Moffat, who ran the cafeterias here and at Marc's other shop in Sedbergh. Food and drink lured more customers than the stacked shelves of books. All over the country, second-hand bookshops were closing their doors as customers migrated to charity shops and online buying, but Marc was contrary. Besides, even people who hated reading needed to eat. Earlier in the year, when the bank manager started to make menacing noises about cash flow and overdraft limits, Marc had sold a half-share in the business to Leigh. Years back, Marc had had a fling with her sister, but he insisted this relationship was about business, nothing more. Would she care if he was lying?

'Busy at work?' Marc was determined to keep trying.

'Uh-huh.' Hannah tasted her soup. Carrot and coriander, seasoned with garlic and a touch of black pepper. Warm, sweet and spicy.

Marc smeared low-fat spread on a wholegrain roll before passing it to her. Talk about buttering her up.

'Still flogging yourself to death, I suppose.'

'We're short of staff. You must have read about the row over cutbacks.'

'Yeah, don't the newspapers reckon that twice as many Tesco supermarkets open twenty-four/seven as police stations? But I see that congratulations are in order. Your team has been shortlisted for an award. Isn't the ceremony tomorrow?'

Hannah almost choked on a mouthful of bread roll. Give him credit, he was making an effort.

'You've done your homework.'

'I'm interested, believe it or not.'

Then why leave it so late?

'It's nothing to get excited about.'

'Typical Hannah. Underselling yourself.'

'No false modesty – we aren't going to win. I've been tipped off that we finished as runners-up for the Contribution to the Community Award. The girl who types for the judging panel fancies Greg Wharf. She told him that we lost out to a bunch of litter collectors.'

He laughed. 'Don't tell me – the Cleanliness in Cumbria Partnership?'

'Yeah, their press releases get everywhere. They emptied more bins than we solved rapes and murders, I think that's how it works.'

'Hey, it's not about winning, but the taking part.'

She couldn't help grinning. 'If you believe that, you'll believe anything.'

'Any major cold cases on the go?'

'Only if you count a miserable old sod in his seventies who lives in Lancaster, but spent most of his life in Barrow. We spent six months searching for a match to DNA from a rape at Millom thirty years ago. The victim has been in and out of mental hospitals ever since. Eventually, we found our man, but the CPS are digging in their heels, they don't want to prosecute. He has advanced Parkinson's disease, and the medics say he's unfit to plead.'

'Frustrating.'

'Life's rich tapestry.'

'No more murders?'

'I needed a break from murders.'

He nodded. At the start of the year, he'd found himself mixed up in one of her cases. They'd reached a tacit agreement not to speak about it again. The wounds were too raw.

'I guess so.'

'Matter of fact, I took a call yesterday. A woman whose brother disappeared, his name was Callum Hinds. Their stepfather managed Madsen's caravan park, up at Keswick.'

'The caravan park?' He pondered. 'Aren't Madsen's the people who sponsored your award?'

'The award we didn't quite win, you mean?' Of course, that was why she knew the name. 'As a matter of fact, you're right.'

'Successful company. I've bumped into the Madsen brothers at Commerce in Cumbria events. Bryan Madsen is a big wheel in local politics, and once upon a time, Gareth was a racing driver. If they can afford sponsorship money in the current economic climate, they must be worth a packet.' He paused. 'As it happens, I do recall a boy going missing somewhere near the caravan park.'

'Your memory goes back that far?'

'There's nothing wrong with my memory,' he murmured. 'My parents talked about the case, because they'd discussed buying a caravan at Madsen's. In the end, they settled for a timeshare in Majorca. Kept it for five years and went out there only twice. The lad and I were much the same age. You don't expect to die in your teens.'

'No trace of Callum was found. There's nothing to prove he died.'

Marc pushed a hand through his thicket of fair hair, a habitual gesture. As she finished her soup, it struck her that this was one of his mannerisms that she found appealing. She'd actually missed it.

Weird, very weird.

He looked into her eyes, and she averted her gaze, focusing instead on sheep traipsing across the fells. She understood how much effort he was making to appear relaxed, indulging her with small talk. Marc fizzed with nervous energy and, beneath the surface affability, his insides must be knotted with tension. He was as photogenic as ever – she'd felt familiar stirrings of desire, unwelcome but undeniable, when he greeted her – but there was no masking the dark rings beneath his eyes. The legacy of a sleepless night, fretting that he was about to lose her? He hated losing, something else they had in common. No way would she let him soft-soap her. Her heart was hardened. At least, as much as it ever could be.

When it dawned on him that she would not break the silence, he said, 'How's your new sergeant shaping up?'

'Greg Wharf? An old hand by now. Smart guy. Almost as smart as he believes he is.'

'Not as smart as Nick Lowther, though?'

Nick had left the force and emigrated with a new partner before last Christmas. Marc had been suspicious of their relationship for years. If only he knew how wrong he'd been. Before that, he'd imagined she lusted after her old boss, Ben Kind, though their relationship was never more than platonic. This winter, Marc had got it into his head that she'd started an affair with Ben's son, Daniel. His jealousy tore them apart. That, plus his pathetic swooning over a girl who had worked for him, downstairs in this very shop.

'There's no comparison. Nick was quiet and thoughtful. Greg is noisy and relies on what he calls his "gut".'

'Not your type?'

She frowned. 'I'm not sure I have a type.'

He knocked back the rest of his wine and said, 'Thanks for coming, Hannah. I wanted to apologise to you.'

'You apologised before.'

'And you said you accepted my apology. But I don't think you did.'

She focused on the grazing sheep. What were apologies for? They were empty words, devalued currency. Spouted by politicians who were keen to say sorry for sins of the distant past, but lacking the courage to admit mistakes of the here and now.

'I meant to ask your forgiveness.'

She'd never heard him speak with such humility.

'What for?'

'For everything. The way I treated you when we lived together. Spending too much time on the shops, not enough on you. Accusing you of shagging Daniel Kind.'

He lowered his voice. A couple of elderly women in raincoats, who had spent too long living in the Lake District to be fooled by sunshine and a cloudless sky, plonked themselves down at a table on the other side of the chain, and he was desperate not to be overheard. He didn't want witnesses to his mortification.

A wild instinct seized her.

'What if I did shag him?' she whispered.

She'd never before said anything to him that was meant to hurt. Grief was scrawled all over his face, as plain as if a vandal had sprayed it with paint.

'I . . . I wouldn't be surprised.' His voice was hoarse. 'Good-looking successful man. Good-looking successful woman. Both let down by their lovers. Who could blame them?'

On the drive from Undercrag, she'd rehearsed this conversation, expecting resistance, bitterness, anger. Conceivably, for he was an emotional man, a torrent of tears. Self-abasement wasn't in the script. She didn't want to humiliate him, or lie about her relationship with Daniel.

'For what it's worth, we haven't done anything.'

One of the women at the nearby table brayed with laughter, enjoying a bit of salacious gossip. Marc's hands shook. He was unsure whether to believe her.

'You don't have to say that.'

'It's true.' She hesitated. 'Well, he kissed me once. In the car park of The Tickled Trout, not the ideal spot for a romantic tryst. If you must know, I haven't seen him for months. The last time we bumped into each other was at a lecture given by a professor of criminology at the University of South Lakeland. All about the narratives that criminals weave, to justify their behaviour to themselves. Daniel was with his sister – she teaches law at the uni, remember? The three of us had a chat over a glass of orange juice, and then went our separate ways. All right?'

Marc swallowed a mouthful of baguette. 'You can see whoever you like. Specially a good friend like Daniel. As a matter of fact, I got you something.'

She stared as he reached into a shoulder bag that he'd dumped on the decking underneath their table. He pulled out a parcel in gift wrapping and put it in her hands.

She tried to hand it straight back to him, but he'd folded his arms and it was impossible.

'Marc, I can't accept—'

'Don't be so hasty. Unwrap it and have a look, before you turn it down,' he said.

Unwilling to be churlish, she tore off the wrapping. Inside, the present was packed in tissue paper. She slid out a slim hardback book, with gold lettering on the front and spine. The title was *Hidden Depths*, the author D.B. Kind.

'Is this by Daniel?' she asked. 'I've never heard of it.'

'You won't find *Hidden Depths* mentioned in his bibliography. I think he prefers to forget about it, but he's too modest. It's a collection of poetry that he published when he was a student. Not exactly Coleridge, but definitely not McGonagall, either. Quite a few of the verses deal with rifts between parent and child – read into that what you will. Maybe he needed to put it down in black and white to get the bad stuff out of his system. And writing poetry doesn't pay the rent – you can see why he gave it up for popular history.'

She opened the book. 'A first edition?'

'Yep, it was never reprinted.' He gave the engaging grin she'd always liked. 'The publishers went out of business shortly afterwards, but I'm sure it wasn't Daniel's fault.'

'You shouldn't give this to me.'

'This copy took a hell of a lot of finding, trust me. I tracked it down to Manitoba. After all that effort, you have to accept it. No way am I planning to flog it on the Internet.'

She shook her head.

'Peace offering,' he said. 'No strings.'

'Whenever anyone says there are no strings, there are strings.'

'Put it in your bag, Hannah.'

She considered him. He was pleased with his coup, and it would be childish to spurn the gift. He'd been riven by jealousy, first of Ben, later of Nick, finally of Daniel, and people didn't change. But he'd striven for generosity, and the little book was worth more than any protestations that the leopard had changed spots.

'Thank you.'

Again the grin. This was more like the old Marc – low-fat spread wouldn't melt in his mouth. Hannah pictured her oldest friend, Terri, a self-certified expert on the opposite sex, warning her it wouldn't last – it never did. Terri ought to know, after three marriages and half a lifetime deluding herself that she could transform some of the most unsuitable men in Cumbria, possibly in the western hemisphere, into a cross between Mr Darcy and George Clooney.

Time to seize back the initiative.

'So what about you and Leigh?' she asked.

'Nothing to tell. She made it very clear when she put up the money, it's an investment, because she believes we can make it work. Books and food, nourishment for brain and body, a magical combination. We're partners, sure, but it's only in business.'

The cynic in Hannah wondered if that meant Leigh had rebuffed his overtures. Whatever, their teaming up didn't offer her an easy escape route.

Time to look him in the eye.

'I don't want us to get back together again,' she said.

'I know.'

She'd steeled herself for a protest, perhaps an eruption of fury.

'So, there are things to decide. Arrangements to be made.'

'Hey, not so fast. We're not married, remember?'

'I haven't forgotten,' she snapped.

'Well, then. There's no question of a divorce. No legal stuff. We can take our time.'

'Marc, it's more than six months already.'

He leant across the table, putting his face close to hers.

'I've counted the days. I can give you the calculation in minutes and seconds if you like.'

'That won't be necessary.'

Her cheeks tingled. The two old women had stopped talking. Out of the corner of her eye, she saw them studying her with thrilled curiosity.

'Half a year of numbness,' he muttered. 'What happened was terrible, it was bound to take an age for us to get over it.'

'I'm over it,' she said. 'I've moved on.'

'Bollocks,' he hissed. 'You need more time.'

'The great healer?'

She meant to strike a sardonic note, but her voice sounded scratchy and she felt embarrassed. The old women were loving this. Lunch in the sun, with free reality entertainment thrown in. Who needed daytime TV?

'I'll give you all the space you want,' he said. 'There's no rush.'

She was about to say: *forget it, I won't change my mind.* But the words stuck in her throat. How could she be so sure?

He bent forward, and brushed his lips against hers. As her body tingled, he sprang to his feet. Crushing his paper napkin in his fist, he hurled it into the bin on the edge of the decking. His eye was good, it was a perfect shot. She wondered that their audience didn't break out into applause.

'What we have is precious,' he said. 'Don't be in such a hurry to chuck it away like a piece of litter.'

With the same lithe ease that so often set her pulse racing in their early days together, he moved past her, and disappeared down the stairs and into the darkness of his shop.

As she stood up to go, her eyes met those of one of the elderly women. She waved towards Hannah's table.

'Don't forget your book!'

CHAPTER THREE

Daniel Kind swung off the lane at the entrance lodge. On either side of the narrow drive, oak trees spread branches to form a tunnel with a roof of green. Daniel slowed the car to walking pace. It felt like passing through a portal into a different world. He loved travelling back in time, even if only in his head; for a historian, the past was a perfect destination. The drive curved, and through the thick leaves, he glimpsed the mysterious bulk of his destination.

The magic of the extraordinary building lifted his spirits. In his imagination he was transported to fifteenth-century France, approaching a strange chateau, hiding place of treasures and countless dark secrets. St Herbert's was constructed of freestone, tinted a greenish grey that seemed dour even on the brightest morning. The slate roofs were dark and austere, the design eccentric. The architect had let rip with flights of Gothic fancy, a confection of steep mansards and conical turrets jostling on the skyline with the parapets of a huge square tower. Above the tower's battlements, a wrought-iron balustrade ran around the cut-off top of a roof in the shape of a pyramid. In the middle of the front elevation, a carriage porch had been elaborated into a two-storey gatehouse flanked by octagonal pilasters, with an oriel window jutting out above the arch. This was a residence fit for a marquis, viscount or duke.

A grubby white delivery van shattered the illusion, tyres screeching as it hurtled around the building from the loading bay by the kitchens. It headed past him to its next drop-off in the real world, and Daniel spotted a slogan scrawled in the muck on the rear doors: *I wish my girlfriend was as dirty as this*. Not the level of literary sophistication associated with St Herbert's Residential Library, but it brought him down to earth. Appearances were deceptive; this wasn't the Loire Valley – St Herbert's was English, through and through. The freestone came from Low Furness and the slate from Westmorland quarries.

Daniel reversed into a marked space at the end of a row of parked cars. No sign of Orla Payne's rusty old banger. Taking a second day off work in succession, by the look of things. Had she mustered the courage to speak to Hannah Scarlett? God, he hoped so. If anyone could make sense of Orla's ramblings about her lost brother, it was Hannah.

Lifting his laptop case from the passenger seat, he flicked the remote fob to lock the car. The Mercedes was a new toy; he'd treated himself after his agent sold translation rights to his next book throughout Europe. All he needed to do now was to finish writing it. Deadline only three weeks away. Fifteen thousand words and who-knew-how-much revision to go.

As he'd sweated over the manuscript, he found it

suited him to work at St Herbert's. He was writing a study of Thomas De Quincey's influence upon the history of murder. The library kept a small archive of De Quincey's correspondence from his time living in Dove Cottage, together with a collection of nineteenth-century manuscripts so obscure that the online monoliths had neglected to digitise them. Each time he came here, Daniel found himself not wanting to pack up as darkness fell and set off home to Brackdale. St Herbert's possessed a unique charm, a residential library where you could read by day, sleep by night, and then wake to stroll through gardens boasting some of the finest views in Britain. He'd stayed over a couple of times, sharing Laphroaig and conversation with the principal in front of a log fire in the drawing room before resuming work until the small hours.

He wanted to fill his lungs with fresh air before finding a table in the library. Such a gorgeous summer afternoon was too precious to squander. A path curled past a yew hedge to the rear of the building. Beyond a neat lawn and a fountain with a cherub lay a walled garden. A wooden door in the middle of the stone wall was kept open during daylight hours. Gertrude Jekyll had presided over the planting, and the bulk of the garden was devoted to dozens of rose cultivars, sequenced by colour from red, through pink and white, to yellow, apricot and orange. Where the cross paths met in the centre stood a rondel of timber posts covered in climbing roses and clematis, alongside a tiny pond inhabited by fat goldfish.

Daniel inhaled the fragrance of the blooms. The garden was deserted, and he imagined himself striding out like Sir Milo Hopes of Mockbeggar Hall, taking a morning constitutional around the monument he had built to celebrate his love of literature. Sir Milo, who fancied himself as a man of letters, had compiled an archive of memoirs and other family papers, as well as trying his hand at fiction. Having skimmed a couple of the historical romances which the squire of Mockbeggar had privately printed and expensively bound for display in the library, Daniel understood why Sir Milo was remembered for his munificence, not his plodding prose.

'Daniel!'

He spun on his heel. Above the wall, the upper part of the building was visible. On a narrow parapet, outside a first-floor window, a tall lean man with a wild mane of thick black hair and a flowing beard stood. His arms were held aloft, forefingers pointing to the sky. He might have been a demagogue in mid rant, intent on whipping up a frenzy in a raging mob. Or a zealot about to make the ultimate sacrifice.

Jesus, what is he doing?

The man's dark eyes stared down and met Daniel's.

'Aslan!' Daniel bellowed.

He burst into a run, desperate to avert disaster. The man on the parapet stood motionless, as if deciding what to do, before relaxing, as if the tension had been squeezed out of him like paste from a tube.

He shook his mane, and let his arms fall.

'Sorry!' he called. 'Did I give you a scare?'

'How did it go?' the voice on the phone asked.

Hannah switched off the ignition of her Lexus. Even though Terri was her closest friend, it had been a mistake to confide, in a moment of weakness, that she was planning to make the break with Marc.

'We talked, which is progress.'

'And?'

'We'll talk again, I suppose.'

'So he's fighting to keep you?'

'I didn't say that.'

'It's taken long enough for him to realise what he's throwing away.'

Hannah's head was starting to hurt. She hadn't realised how much she'd been building up to this face-to-face encounter with the man she'd loved for years, the man she thought had loved her. It shouldn't be a spectator sport, and she wasn't in the mood for a bout of post-match analysis.

'Listen, I've got to go. Sorry, things to do.'

'You're still OK for tomorrow?'

Hannah had forgotten they'd arranged an evening out together, listening to a folk band. The last thing she needed was a bunch of amateur troubadours serenading her with songs about heartbreak, but Terri was not to be put off.

'Sure.'

'Try not to be late for once. You never know, that hunky Polish barman might pick me up, and you'll wind up listening to the band on your own while Stefan and I make wonderful music in his bedsit.'

'Be careful what you wish for.'

'What was all that about?' Daniel demanded.

They were outside the rear entrance to St Herbert's, in front of the mullioned windows of the deserted dining room. Aslan Sheikh had shinned down to the ground by way of an iron drainpipe. Shades of Spiderman; agile and fit, he'd not even broken sweat. The sight of him standing on the ledge had left Daniel's stomach weak and his knees feeling like mush. A flashback took him to the day his partner Aimee fell from the Saxon tower in Oxford's Cornmarket. Daniel had arrived too late to save her, but he was haunted by a picture in his mind of the young woman, teetering on the brink, before she took a last breath and jumped.

Aslan was not to know that. He was indulging in high spirits, not twisting the knife.

'It began as a fag break, would you believe? I came out for a smoke, and it occurred to me that I hadn't climbed for years. I was curious. Wondered what the view was like from the parapet.'

'Curious?' Daniel shook his head. 'You could have borrowed a key and taken a look from inside one of the offices up there.'

'Where's the fun in that?' Aslan pulled a pack of cigarettes out of the pocket of his jeans, and lit up. 'Hey, I'm a creature of impulse. It was a spur-of-the-moment thing. A break, a chance of excitement.'

For a creature of impulse seeking excitement, choosing to work at St Herbert's was pretty counter-intuitive, Daniel thought. Aslan's shock of hair, beaky nose and swaggering gait, coupled with his olive skin and handsome cast of features, suggested he was cut out for somewhere much more exotic than St Herbert's. But he worked here as a part-time conference and events organiser. He'd explained to Daniel that he was half-Turkish, accounting for his unusual first name, and that he'd spent the last few years travelling, working in tourism and on cruise ships as well as having a spell in the United States. His late mother had once worked in a Keswick pub, and although they had deserted the Lakes for Istanbul when he was a baby, he'd vowed one day to make a pilgrimage back to the place of his birth.

'So was the view worth it?'

'Need you ask? You can see Mockbeggar Hall, the farmland owned by Orla's father, and the fells in the distance. The caravans are the only blot on the landscape. They are supposed to blend in with the landscape, and priced to match, but it doesn't quite work. The Hall is due to reopen any day now as a leisure complex, would you believe? Old Sir Milo must be revolving in his grave.'

'Speaking of Orla Payne, I didn't see her car. Is she around today?'

Aslan clicked his tongue in mock disapproval. 'It was my day off yesterday, but Sham tells me she didn't show up then, either. Yet she hasn't called in sick. AWOL two days running, naughty, naughty. The principal won't be a happy bunny.'

'I bet.' Professor Micah Bridge could never understand how the conscience of any member of his staff allowed them to show less dedication to the library than his own. People management gave him palpitations. 'She hasn't been in touch?'

'Sham hasn't heard a peep from her. Nobody has any idea what's up. Let's hope she isn't lying behind a pile of garbage down some back alley in a drunken stupor, eh?'

'I thought the two of you are friends?'

'We're not seeing each other, if that's what you mean.'

Aslan sniggered. 'As communications manager, she showed me the ropes, and we went out to a pub in Keswick once or twice, nothing heavy.'

An unexpectedly brutal denial. Orla was a nice-looking woman, but perhaps Aslan had his eye on Sham Madsen, with her anything-goes grin and very rich parents.

'Uh-huh.'

'Don't get me wrong, I really feel for Orla, you have no idea. Nothing can replace the loss of a brother or sister. Nothing in the world . . .' Aslan's voice trailed away for a moment before he collected his thoughts. 'Saying that, it's no solution to obsess about stuff. And you must admit, she does have an obsession. I've noticed her buttonholing you in the dining room.'

'You've heard the story about Callum, then?'

'Hasn't everyone? As a matter of fact . . .'

'What?'

Aslan seemed to change his mind. 'I don't mean to sound harsh, not knowing what happened to her brother was horrible. But for goodness' sake, it was twenty years ago. The world goes on, you know?'

'Sure.'

Daniel moved towards the main entrance, but Aslan stubbed out his cigarette, and caught him up with quick loping strides.

'Hey, she's making a mistake to dwell so much on the past, don't you agree?'

Daniel halted under the archway. 'I'm a historian, remember? Dwelling on the past is what I do.'

'Yeah, right. I only meant . . .'

Daniel pushed open the double doors. He was worried

about Orla, and he didn't want to show how much. If Aslan was distancing himself, she needed all the friends she could muster.

Behind the welcome desk perched Sham Madsen. Her given name was Chamois, but everyone called her Sham. She had an elder sister, Perdita, always known as Purdey. Sham reckoned their mum picked the names of heroines in her favourite Mills and Boon novelettes for her daughters, and their father indulged her whim. Along with his brother Bryan, Gareth Madsen ran the caravan park, and Sham exuded the self-confidence that comes with glamour and wealth. With dark shoulder-length hair and a glamour model's figure, she'd taken advantage of the heat to sport a top so skimpy that Daniel feared for the principal's blood pressure.

'Hiya, Daniel.'

She beamed in greeting before treating Aslan to a flirtatious wink. Daniel noticed his companion respond with a sly smile.

Close to the desk, a grand staircase swept up and out of sight, leading to the main offices as well as the residential quarters. To the right of reception, a corridor led to the dining room and the principal's suite. Daniel turned left down the passage that led towards the main library, but there was no escaping Aslan, who fell into step beside him. He could smell smoke on the man's breath and on his clothes.

'Orla trusts you, Daniel. Can you persuade her to seek help with her booze problem?' Aslan spoke in a rush; did he regret his earlier tone? 'Medical advice, counselling, whatever works. I pleaded with her, said she'd go the same way as her mum if she didn't watch out, but it made no impression.'

The door to the Old Library opened, and a stooped bespectacled man ushered a companion ahead of him, making a courteous gesture with an age-spotted hand. The principal of St Herbert's and a woman Daniel recognised as Fleur Madsen. Her picture appeared on the St Herbert's website. Fleur was Sham's aunt, and six weeks ago she'd been appointed as chair of the board of trustees of St Herbert's.

Fleur and Micah Bridge made an odd couple. What little remained of the principal's hair was white, the top of his head bald and shiny. He wore a tweed jacket, yellow-and-red-striped MCC tie, twill slacks, and brown lace-up shoes that might have been bought from a charity shop. Fleur Madsen was elegant and elfin, a sort of blonde Audrey Hepburn in a blue linen jacket that matched her eyes, an ivory top and trousers, and a big buckled belt chosen to show off her tiny waist. At first glance, you'd think the pair belonged to different generations, though Micah Bridge was no more than five years Fleur's senior. His entire wardrobe probably cost less than her statement necklace.

'Daniel!' the professor exclaimed. 'Just the chap! Here is someone you really must meet.'

Aslan coughed. 'I'd better get along.'

He sprinted away to the offices. Daniel noticed Fleur Madsen cast a thoughtful glance at his retreating back as the principal effected introductions. Next moment, he had her full attention. The full-wattage smile revealed inevitably perfect teeth.

'How lovely to meet you – may I call you Daniel? I've

been dying for our paths to cross ever since the principal mentioned you were working here. Of course, I adored your TV series. I'm a history junkie; I really can't get enough of it, can I, Micah?'

The principal's well-scrubbed cheeks turned pink as he murmured assent. Fleur was a member of the landed gentry, the genuine article, with posh vowels picked up from some expensive private school to prove it. Mockbeggar Hall had belonged to her family for years before she teamed up with Bryan Madsen, elder son of the man who had bought a slice of the Hall's estate to found a caravan park and make millions out of it. A smart lady, in every sense.

'I've given up on television,' he said. 'Better than waiting for it to give up on me.'

'Far too modest. And what a shame you abandoned your university teaching. Though I do admire a man who quits while he's ahead.' A teasing smile. 'No regrets?'

'None.'

'Glad to hear it. How marvellous that you've agreed to give our Founder's Lecture in September. I can't wait.'

Daniel stepped through the doorway. The lovely smell of the Old Library assailed him, the aroma of thousands of books packed tightly together blending with a whiff of leather upholstery and the tang of furniture polish. Shelves reaching ten feet high were separated by narrow aisles that twisted and turned like a labyrinth. A spiral staircase curved up to a gallery from which you could see the pattern of the maze. Behind the balustrades lurked desks with shaded lamps, where a handful of people read. But for an occasional fluttering of pages, the library was silent. To step inside was like entering church.

Fleur Madsen pointed to a fresco on the wall showing a bearded ancient, complete with halo and beatific smile, and bearing the legend *St Herbert of Derwent Water*. Beneath it hung a mahogany board on which the Venerable Bede's remarks about Herbert's spiritual bond with St Cuthbert of Lindisfarne were recorded in gilt letters.

'Funny, isn't it?' she murmured. 'A library taking its name from a seventh-century hermit who spent years cut off from the world on a tiny island in the middle of a lake.'

'I am sure,' the principal said, 'we still cherish St Herbert's ideal of thoughtful contemplation, far removed from material concerns.'

'Of course, Micah, but we need more than thoughtful reflection if we're going to patch up the black hole in the staff pension fund, let alone refurbish the dining room and make sure all the windows fit their frames.'

Daniel winced. Sounded like a debate in which there could only be one winner. 'I have to admit, I'd barely heard of St Herbert's before I moved up here. The library is a hidden gem.'

'Exactly! Hence why we need to bang the drum more loudly.' The principal cringed. 'I was saying so to Micah five minutes ago when he took me up to the gallery. The lighting needs to be rewired, and I daren't guess at the cost. We can't put up the prices of our accommodation, there's too much competition from bed-and-breakfast places around Keswick. Our being the Lake District's best-kept secret doesn't pay the bills. The auditors insist we keep a closer eye on cash flow.'

The principal sucked in his cheeks. He had more in

common with the anchorite of Derwent Water than with any accountant. Micah Bridge lived for books, and his worst nightmare probably involved St Herbert's Residential Library metamorphosing into a literary theme park for caravan dwellers.

'Our communications strategy is almost finalised.' The principal cleared his throat, as if in distaste at having to embrace such a tawdry concept. 'I shall let you have it as soon as Orla is back in harness, and we're able to tidy it up.'

'Orla, yes.' A frown disrupted Fleur's features. 'Do we know what is the matter with her?'

'I'm afraid she hasn't done us the courtesy of letting us know.'

'If that girl doesn't watch out,' Fleur said, 'she'll go down the same slippery slope as her mother.'

She spoke loudly, and Daniel noticed heads turn up on the gallery, in wordless disapproval. There was a blunt edge to her voice that the pricey education hadn't smoothed away. That resemblance to Audrey Hepburn was no more than skin-deep.

The principal stepped back through the doorway, leading them away from the literary temple. 'I shall ask Sham to enquire when we can expect her back.'

'Good plan.' Fleur closed the door behind them and turned back to Daniel. 'Marvellous to meet you in the flesh. I can't wait to tell my husband that I've met a television star.'

Exactly the sort of reaction he'd come up to the Lake District to escape. 'I gather yours is one of the biggest parks in the area?'

'Oh, several have more pitches, but size isn't everything, is it?' A sleek smile. 'My father-in-law always drummed into Bryan and his brother that quality counts. You need to understand people's expectations, and then exceed them. Which is why I'm so glad my family home is about to enjoy a new lease of life as part of the park.'

The principal struggled to suppress a cough of disapproval at the prospect. It didn't faze Fleur Madsen.

'Buildings can't stay the same, Micah, just as people can't. It's true of St Herbert's, and it's true of Mockbeggar Hall. My family couldn't afford to invest on upkeep after the Second World War, and it went to rack and ruin. How much better, Gareth said, if we reinvented the place as part of the park. It seemed like one of my brother-in-law's more hare-brained ideas, but really it's turned out to be a stroke of genius. The project has taken five years to complete, but believe me, it will be worth it. We've not only refurbished the entire building, we've built a new link road from the main park, across the beck. Planning permission was a nightmare, of course, always is in the National Park, but nobody's as persuasive as Gareth, and my husband has some political clout.'

And so the rich keep getting richer, Daniel thought. He gave an ambiguous smile.

'I wonder,' Fleur said, 'are you free to come over for dinner with us at the Hall? We would be honoured to have you as our guest. Together with your wife, or partner, of course.'

'I live with my sister.'

'Ah, shades of the Wordsworths!'

The teasing smile returned. Somehow she'd created a

moment of intimacy. It was as if the principal had ceased to exist.

'Not exactly. I bought a cottage in Brackdale with my ex. We split up, and then Louise's own relationship came to a sudden end, shortly after she moved up to the Lakes. We decided to share until she found a place of her own. Six months on, she's still looking.'

'I don't blame her for staying on. Brackdale is lovely. Though the Northern Lakes are even further from the madding crowd. Now, do say you'll come!'

'Thanks . . .' Daniel was about to mutter something about checking Louise's availability, but Fleur was too quick.

'Splendid! Shall we say Friday evening?'

Before he could reply, the crash of heels along the parquet floor of the corridor made them all turn round. Sham Madsen was running towards them at full pelt, her cheeks pale, strands of hair flapping over her face.

'Professor Bridge!'

The principal stretched out a hand. 'What is it, my dear girl?'

'The police are on the phone!'

'What do they want?' Fleur demanded.

'It's about Orla. Oh my God, it's so awful!'

'What about her, Sham?'

The girl stared, wide-eyed, as if unable to credit what she had been told.

'They say she's dead. Her father found her body.'

'Oh my God!'

'It's horrific,' the girl mumbled.

Fleur's face was ashen. 'How did she die?'

'She suffocated in a tower of grain.'

CHAPTER FOUR

'Suffocated?'

Hannah's heart jolted. She grabbed the arm of her swivel chair, as if to check that she wasn't dreaming and this wasn't some nightmarish hoax. The walls of her tiny new office seemed to be closing in on her. She closed her eyes and tried to imagine sinking head first into the clammy embrace of tons of thick beery grain.

'In the farm silo,' Linz Waller repeated. 'Like I say, she must have climbed up and jumped in.'

So Orla Payne had given up on life.

Shit.

Opening her eyes, Hannah glared at her surroundings. No pictures on the walls, only a year planner, charts, and a list of phone numbers. She kept forgetting to bring in potted plants, and no way was she putting up a photograph of Marc. A fortnight in her new domain, and the smell of paint still lingered. The team had been shifted without a fig leaf of consultation to the other side of the Divisional HQ building. Lauren sold it as a change for the better, on the basis that the windows gave a view of the fells rather than the car park, but the true rationale was workspace planning. By trimming the Cold Case Review Team's head count, and cramming those who remained into half as many square feet as part of a package of dextrous manoeuvres, Lauren had kept office overheads below budget for the current financial year. Despite the cutbacks, Hannah had heard the ACC singing in the corridor first thing that morning. An off-key rendering of 'I'm a Believer'. No wonder she was pleased with herself. Keep the politicians and the accountants happy, and the sky was the limit. The smart money said that if she carried on like this, she might even become the first woman commissioner of the Met. Give her two years in charge in London, Les Bryant maintained, and the capital's police force would boast the highest number of PR apparatchiks in Europe, and the fewest front-line officers.

She wrenched her thoughts back to Linz's bad tidings. 'Tell me about the call you took from Orla yesterday.'

'Listen to the tape, if you like.'

'Later. First, you take me through it.'

Beneath her expertly applied make-up, Linz's cheeks were pallid. She'd rung a mate in the Keswick neighbourhood police team to fix a night out. Her friend had just come back from Lane End Farm to make a start on the paperwork about the death of a woman whose corpse had been discovered by a farmer that morning. The body was buried in the grain. The farmer, Mike Hinds, had identified the deceased as his daughter, Orla Payne. She didn't live on the farm, and he claimed he had no idea why she would have come there to die. They hadn't spoken to each other since a brief telephone conversation a couple of days before had ended in a quarrel. He said she was drunk.

'The woman must have been an alcoholic.' Linz cast her eyes to the heavens. 'I only took the call because Chantal was on her break.'

Hannah leant across her desk. 'We're not playing a blame game.'

'Will the IPCC need to be involved?'

Every police officer dreaded becoming the subject of an investigation by the Independent Police Complaints Commission. Once the IPCC started to crawl over your career, even the best CV could turn into a train wreck.

'One step at a time, huh? What did Orla have to say?'

'She was pissed out of her brain, you can hear it for yourself on the tape.' Linz folded her arms tight across her chest, hugging herself for comfort. 'All I could make out was that she had to speak to you, and nobody else would do. When it finally sank in that you weren't around, she rang off.'

'All right.' Hannah exhaled. 'How did they find the body?'

'While Hinds was out in his fields, he caught sight of the top of a car parked in a lane at the back of his land. It was so unusual, he went to investigate, only to see it was Orla's motor. On the way he spotted a brightly coloured headscarf, caught on a bramble. He recognised it as Orla's. She wore headscarves all the time.

Hannah blinked. 'Even in the height of summer?'

'Yeah, seems she'd lost all her hair. Stress-related, apparently.'

'She suffered from alopecia?'

'I guess.' Linz shrugged, a healthy young woman who didn't know much about illness. 'When he found her mobile in a drinking trough, panic set in. He and a couple of his men started searching the farm. It was Hinds himself who looked inside the grain tower.'

'And there she was?'

'Yeah.' Linz's face twisted as she pictured the scene. 'God, what a way to go. And his own daughter, too . . .'

'Suicide?'

'Or accident.'

'Strange accident. What else do we know?'

Linz's expression said *Isn't that enough to be going on with?*

'All right, make sure the tape of the phone call is on my desk in five minutes. Once I've listened to it, I'll decide if we need to make a report to the PSD. Chances are, we will.'

'Yes, ma'am.' Linz bowed her head. The Professional Standards Department would liaise with the IPCC. 'I suppose I may have been the last person she spoke to before she died.'

'You weren't to know.'

As Linz scuttled out, Hannah slumped back in her chair. If only, if only – her life sometimes seemed full to bursting with 'if onlys'. If only she could have persuaded Orla to talk sense to her, the woman might be alive now. Allowing her a chance to answer that contemptuous question, 'Don't you *care* about justice?'

'I must talk to Hannah Scarlett,' Orla Payne said, 'it's a matter of life and death.'

The muffled voice of a woman about to die. DC Maggie Eyre paled, listening in silence until Orla rang off, and Hannah stopped the tape machine.

'She may not have intended to kill herself, ma'am,' Maggie said. 'Jumping into a grain silo isn't a sure-fire way of killing yourself, and if she'd grown up on a farm, she'd know that.'

Maggie, a member of the Cold Case Review Team since its inception, was the same age as Linz, but they had little else in common. Square-jawed and down to earth, she came from a family which had farmed in the county for generations, while Linz was a townie to the tips of her painted fingernails. Linz came up with flashes of insight that Maggie, for all her sturdy common sense, could never match, but the combination of their talents helped to make the team effective despite being starved of resources. This afternoon, Hannah wanted to pick Maggie's brains. Investigating Orla's death was miles outside her bailiwick, but she couldn't bear to wait for information to seep out from Keswick.

'No?' Hannah raised her eyebrows. 'Haven't I heard stories about farm workers being asphyxiated by grain?'

'It can happen, but if you're hell-bent on committing suicide on a farm, plenty of methods guarantee the right result, no messing.' Maggie looked as though she was about to mount a soapbox. 'More than one farmer I've known has killed himself. Call it an occupational hazard. The work is stressful and tough, the financial pressures can be horrific.'

'From what I've read, the average farm is a death trap. All that dangerous machinery, countless heavy vehicles roaming the fields.'

'People on the outside don't have the faintest idea how many farmers take their lives in their hands seven days a week, fifty-two weeks a year. It's the nature of the job.'

Maggie's scrubbed cheeks turned pink whenever she spoke from the heart. Hannah knew her joining the police hadn't gone down well with her parents, and guessed Maggie still felt a pinprick of guilt for turning her back on their way of life.

'So if Orla Payne chose to die on her father's farm, she picked an odd way to set about it?'

'It wouldn't be my choice. But the cushioning effect of the grain would break her fall. It's not quicksand, ma'am. More like ordinary sand. You can walk on it, or lie on it. It's only if you find yourself deeply buried in it that you're likely to have a serious problem.'

'So she wouldn't necessarily be buried in the stuff?'

'No, though she'd probably find it difficult to haul herself out of the silo, even if she tried to climb up by way of the bolts holding the steel sheets together. She might be able to make her way up to the top by treading through the loads of grain whilst the silo was being filled. Not so easy if she was drunk. If she couldn't get out, she'd run the risk of dying of thirst. Definitely not a nice way to go.'

'What if she banged on the walls of the silo and called for help?'

'Depends. If the silo was being filled, the noise from the machinery would drown her cries. And she might not have been conscious, and able to make herself heard, if she hit her head on the way down and knocked herself out.'

'Is that likely?'

'Absolutely. If it didn't, do you know how far the silo is from the farm buildings, and the spot where the grain is loaded on to the conveyor?'

Hannah shook her head. 'I'm just trying to get an idea of what might have happened before I break the news to the ACC that the dead woman called us twice before she died.'

'On the day of the awards dinner?'

'Mmmm. Not ideal timing.'

'Rather you than me, ma'am.' Maggie was no fan of the ACC.

'You said it.'

'I can put out feelers if you like. In the farming world, everybody knows everybody else. You say this farm belongs to a man called Hinds? I bet my dad has come across him.'

'Would you mind having a word? It's not our case, but I'd like to learn more about Orla's background. In particular, any feedback on this story about the brother who disappeared twenty years ago.'

'Will do.' Maggie nodded. 'So the farmer lost both his children?'

'Yes.' Hannah could not comprehend what it must be like to have both your kids die young. 'Unlucky man, Michael Hinds.'

Gaby Malcolm, in the PSD, was one of Hannah's favourite people in the Cumbria Constabulary. The keepers of the force's conscience were never likely winners of any popularity contest, but nobody could dislike this small bird-like woman from Bermuda. Her manner was so calm that ten minutes in her company felt as soothing as a session with a skilled hypnotherapist.

'I'll talk to the IPCC, but there's really no need for Linz Waller to get her knickers in a twist,' Gaby paused. 'Or you, come to that. Ten to one, they won't want to get involved. You know the drill. As long as nothing improper seems to have occurred, and there's no hint of the force sweeping the crap under the carpet, they will pass it back and tell us to decide what to do for ourselves. I doubt there will be a need for a local investigation, so we can make a short report to stick in a file, and everything will be sorted.'

'And if they insist on a local investigation?'

'Whatever happened to looking on the bright side, Hannah?' Gaby smiled. 'Look, you've acted immediately, and from the tapes of the two conversations, there's nothing much more that could have been done. The woman was obviously drunk. There's no way the IPCC will want to investigate themselves, that's only if the shit really hits the fan with a bang. Local enquiry? I'd be very surprised.'

Back in her room, Hannah told herself Gaby was right. She needed to lighten up. The clock never stopped ticking, no time to waste in wondering what might go wrong. Time to make the most of life.

Which led, inevitably, to Daniel Kind. He'd encouraged Orla to call Hannah about her brother's disappearance. He ought to be told what had happened.

Hannah's hand hovered over the telephone on her desk. She didn't need to double-check the number of his mobile. By a bizarre trick of memory, it had lodged itself in her mind.

Just do it.

The phone rang out for twenty seconds and then Daniel's disembodied voice asked her to leave a message.

But what could she say? 'Sorry, the friend you put in touch with me is dead'?

The phone bleeped and for a split second she thought Daniel must have been blessed with ESP.

No such luck. Lauren Self's name flashed up on the screen.

'Ma'am.'

'You haven't forgotten that we need to arrive in very good time for the drinks reception, I hope?'

'Certainly not, ma'am.'

This evening's awards dinner, down the road at the Brewery Arts Centre, was the last thing she needed. She'd toyed with the possibility of wimping out of it, but the only viable substitutes were Les Bryant, who had come out of retirement to provide his expertise to the team on a short-term contract, and Greg Wharf, a Jack-the-Lad sergeant transferred from Vice after taking one chance too many. Cynicism was embedded in their DNA, and they regarded the team's recognition in the award judges' rankings as cause for hilarity rather than celebration. Lauren couldn't bear either of them.

'I don't suppose you've changed yet?'

Hannah checked her watch. 'Not yet, ma'am.'

'That makes me feel better, at any rate. Suppose we meet in reception in an hour's time?'

'Certainly, ma'am.'

She banged down the receiver. Lauren's face smirked at her from the rogues' gallery that bordered the Cumbria Constabulary year planner, along with advertisements from 'carefully chosen partner organisations'. Immaculate coiffeur, glistening lips, perfect cheekbones. The camera loved her. Mind you, the camera didn't have to work for her.

Hannah stuck her tongue out at her boss's pretty, unblinking image. The childishness of her small act of rebellion supplied an instant pick-me-up. She intended to *do* something.

Without a second thought, she dialled Daniel's number. His voice message greeted her, asking her to leave her number, saying he'd call back as soon as he could.

Should she just ring off?

Sod it, no.

'Daniel, this is Hannah. I'd like to speak to you about Orla Payne, if you don't mind. I'm out this evening, but hope to hear from you soon. Bye.'

She leant back in her chair. OK, then, Daniel Kind would have to wait. Never mind.

What mattered was doing Orla justice.

As bad luck would have it, Hannah bumped into Greg Wharf the moment she'd changed into her glad rags. The DS had spent the afternoon giving evidence in court, and as he bustled through the double doors that led from reception, his expression was pensive. Gruelling cross-examination, Hannah supposed. But at the sight of her, he broke into a smile.

'Well, good evening, ma'am.'

'Greg.'

Predictable to a fault, his gaze locked on her cleavage. She'd agonised about the lowish cut of this dress in the shop last Saturday, but she'd decided to hell with it, she was going to take the risk. The plan was never for Greg to get an eyeful. A poster on the wall advertised a Federation talk about *The Surveillance Society*; Hannah felt like a target of it.

'You're gonna wow them, ma'am, no question.'

Hannah ground her teeth. Greg had this talent for catching her off balance.

'It'll be a miracle if I stay awake.'

'Too many late nights?' He treated her to an all-innocence smile that, she knew instantly, he'd bestowed on a hundred women before. 'Believe me, I'm devastated that I can't be there. VIPs only, of course, it's to be expected. No room for the humble spear carriers.'

Sarky bugger. 'Don't pretend you're heartbroken. Especially after what you and Les said when we found out we were on the shortlist.'

'Churlish of us, ma'am, on reflection. It was no mean achievement; now I see it all.' He allowed himself another peek down the top of her dress. 'Obviously, I'm not suggesting for a moment that Les is a bad influence, but the truth is, I've recognised the error of my ways. I reckon I could have found this a very enjoyable evening.'

'Oh yeah?' She made a move to go, but it was difficult to stride past him in the corridor without brushing against him.

'Don't do anything I wouldn't do, ma'am,' he said, and with a last lingering leer, he stepped aside.

As she shoved open the double doors, it struck her that his banter no longer annoyed her as it once had. Crazy, really. Greg Wharf was a sexual harassment claim waiting to happen, the sort of officer she'd loathed from the earliest days of her career. But she'd also come to realise that beneath the bravado was a very good detective who didn't mind putting in extra hours when they were short-handed. To her astonishment, she felt almost sorry she wouldn't be able to chat to him at the dinner.

'Congratulations, Detective Chief Inspector.'

Bryan Madsen had limped through the hubbub to join her the moment the final award was presented, the final words of gratitude gushed. The Malt Room buzzed with a hundred voices, the conversations lubricated by generous quantities of alcohol served throughout the five-course dinner. Bryan struck Hannah as strong and vigorous, even if his paunch and florid complexion suggested overindulgence in fine food and wine. Tall, with expensively cut steel-grey hair, he might have passed for a brigadier, or a leading man in a 1950s British black-and-white movie, sporting a stiff upper lip and a gammy leg caused by a shrapnel wound. You wouldn't cast him as a bloke who had spent a lifetime trading static caravans. During the longueurs of the presentations, Hannah had kept awake by studying Lauren Self's companions on the top table, and she'd recognised the Madsen brothers from newspaper photographs. They were accompanied by good-looking and expensively attired wives. Bryan often featured in the local press, though never in stories that held the slightest interest for Hannah. A businessman with a taste for politics? She'd stereotyped him in her mind as a boring old fart.

'It's an honour to have been in the mix.'

Scary, how the lie sprang to her lips, but she was bound to get away with it. How many captains of industry with a passion for politicking had a built-in irony detector?

'Your cold case team ran the winners desperately close, I can assure you. Your people did a first-rate job with that dreadful business up at Ambleside last January.' He mopped his brow with a monogrammed handkerchief, and fiddled with the window to let in a breath of air. 'Boiling in here, isn't it? As for the judging process, I suppose what tipped the balance is that your profile in the community only rises every now and then, while the Clean Cumbria Campaign is never off the advertising billboards.'

'They deserved it.' She resisted the temptation to simper – better not go completely over the top. Though she couldn't resist adding, 'Cleanliness is next to godliness.'

'Absolutely right.' He snapped his fingers and a young woman in a short glittery dress materialised by his side. Her sinuous and silent movements reminded Hannah of a magician's assistant, her smile was cool and enigmatic. 'Purdey, another glass of Bolly, if you don't mind. This is Detective Chief Inspector Scarlett – Purdey Madsen. Now I promise I'm not driving, Chief Inspector! But what will you have?'

'Nothing for me, thanks.'

'Please, I insist. You sat with the patience of Job through all our speeches.' An appraising smile. 'Surely even a senior police officer can let her hair down once in a while?'

Hannah wondered what he was after. 'An orange juice, please.'

'Thanks, Purdey.' As the girl melted into the chattering crowd, he said, 'Lovely kid, took a degree in psychology last year; such an asset in her father's team, marketing our holiday homes. I absolutely dote on her.'

And get her to fetch and carry for you. 'She's your niece?'

'That's right. Gareth and Sally have two daughters; it was a great sadness to my wife and myself that we never . . . Anyway, past history, long gone, forget it. Do you have a brood of your own, Hannah?' When she shook her head, he said, 'Never mind, you're only young. Plenty of time yet.'

Hannah was saved from the need to reply by Lauren Self, timing her arrival to perfection for once in her life. The ACC was enjoying her second champagne, or possibly her third, to judge by the flush on those taut cheeks. Body-swerving through the crowd like a footballer followed a man she'd seen chatting to Lauren during the dinner. Unmistakably a Madsen, but younger than Bryan and with an athletic build; this must be Gareth. Not even a hint of grey at the temples, but if his light-brown hair had been coloured, he got away with it. He moved with the self-confident swagger of a man accustomed to getting away with things.

As the ACC and Bryan effected introductions, Gareth Madsen glanced at Hannah. In an odd moment of complicity, his lips twitched with suppressed amusement, though she wasn't sure what he found funny, his brother's self-importance or Lauren's photo-opportunity smile. Both, she hoped.

All of a sudden, the ACC was her best friend. 'Gareth was fascinated by your work on cold cases.'

'I did vote for your team, cross my heart and hope to die.' He gave a cheeky grin that tested Hannah's own irony-detector. 'Bryan let me down, to his eternal shame. I mean, binning litter is extremely worthy and all that, but your department puts away serious criminals. As good as something off the telly. Finding DNA matches to help you solve old crimes! Bringing people to justice years after they thought they'd got off scot-free!'

'I'm afraid DNA testing is horrendously expensive,' Lauren said. 'The current funding crisis means the generosity of partners like Madsen's Holiday Home Park is more important than ever.'

'Our commitment to giving something back to our local community is a core aspect of our mission statement.' Bryan might have been reading an autocue. The legacy of too many speeches, no doubt. 'We hope the constabulary thinks of us as a friend in need. Delighted to do as much as we can to help.'

Hannah could imagine. The rules allowed every police force in the country to garner up to one per cent of its annual budget from sponsorships and other business ventures. It was supposed to offer a good way of funding equipment that the government was too tight-fisted to provide. The bait for private businesses was a higher media profile, a chance to brag about their commitment to corporate social responsibility. Nobody ever hinted that the quid pro quo for funding might be a blind eye turned to questionable business practices. That was forbidden. Any suggestion of dodgy dealing would be met with outrage and threats of legal action. Naturally.

'I'm guessing you're not a poker player?' Gareth whispered in Hannah's ear, as Lauren engaged Bryan in a cosy chat about shared values. 'Your face is a picture.'

'Never said a word,' she murmured.

'You don't need to, Hannah – may I call you Hannah? Obviously you don't approve of the forces of Mammon currying favour with the forces of law and order.' He narrowed his eyes, mimicking a stage villain. 'Pity, I hoped our largesse would get me off with a slap on the wrist next time I'm caught speeding.'

'Forget it, the fines are an even more important source of revenue.' She placed her empty glass on the window sill. 'So, do you play poker . . . Gareth?'

'I'm an entrepreneur, that's what entrepreneurs do. To do well, you have to gamble. Business is all about taking risks. As I keep telling my esteemed chairman.'

'I hear you used to be a racing driver.'

He grinned. 'Your sources are impeccable, as I'd expect of Cumbria's finest. I'm afraid I never made Formula One. In my youth I totalled a Porsche and a Ferrari in quick succession and walked away without a scratch, but that kind of luck doesn't last for ever. Ask Bryan, he never drove so much as an open-top sports car, but when he drove into a tree years back, he nearly died. Can you wonder that we settled for life as businessmen? Not so much fun as racing cars, but you live to draw your pension.'

Purdey arrived bearing drinks. Despite the crush at the bar, she'd managed to get served in record time; no doubt she'd inherited her father's *savoir faire*. With her snub nose and long chin, she might not be a raving beauty, but her skin was fresh and her legs slim, and what was that line of Greg Wharf's – there's no such thing as an ugly heiress?

Gareth helped himself to the champagne. 'I think your uncle had better go easy, don't you?'

'Cheeky whippersnapper,' Bryan brayed.

Purdey's eyes misted over. 'I can't believe it, really.'

'What's that, sweetheart?' her father asked.

'Here we are, out enjoying ourselves, and yet poor Orla . . .'

Bryan said, 'Orla's death is an utter tragedy, but quite frankly, she inherited her mother's weakness. The poor girl couldn't hold her liquor, that's the top and bottom of it.' He turned to Hannah. 'Lauren tells me that you've heard about this dreadful business?'

Hannah nodded. She'd briefed the ACC about Orla's calls to the Cold Case Review Team, and her family connection with Madsen's. It was the last thing Lauren wanted to hear, as a prelude to schmoozing wealthy captains of industry, but she found a crumb of comfort in Gaby Malcolm's confidence that the IPCC wouldn't be looking askance at the handling of the phone calls.

'She rang me two days ago,' Hannah said. 'While I was out yesterday, she tried to contact me again.'

Bryan stiffened. 'Good Lord. Not wanting you to reopen enquiries into her brother's disappearance, for goodness' sake?'

'Had she discussed what happened to Callum with you?'

Before Bryan could reply, a jovial fat man from Commerce in Cumbria slapped him on the back and asked how the hell he was doing. As Bryan disengaged himself, Gareth checked his watch.

'Come on, we've done our duty here. Why don't we say cheerio to the mayor and then nip round to Mancini's? It will be quieter, and there will be more oxygen.'

'Good plan.' Bryan was in avuncular mode. 'If you like, Lauren, we could talk some more about whether we can find a way to contribute to these DNA-testing costs.'

Hannah opened her mouth, about to make her excuses, but Lauren was having none of it. 'We'd love to join you, wouldn't we, Hannah?'

The ACC smiled at Bryan, and he beamed back at her. Hannah cringed inwardly. Easy to guess what was going through Lauren's mind.

Don't get your hopes up, chum. It's not your body she's after, it's your wallet.

CHAPTER FIVE

Mancini's was tucked away in a courtyard off Kirkland. It called itself a jazz bar, and a lonely saxophone wailed from hidden speakers. The walls were adorned with moody photographs from films noirs, and Gareth Madsen made straight for a table beneath a shot of Lana Turner making eyes at John Garfield in *The Postman Always Rings Twice*. Hannah recalled watching it on a movie channel late one night with Marc. Realising that the two of them would never see another film together gave her an unexpected pang of regret. Lauren seated herself between the two men, arranging her rather short skirt with care; when it came to ruthless pursuit of her objectives, the ACC could give Cora Smith a run for her money. As for Bryan Madsen, he was much smarter than Frank Chambers. Presumably.

Fleur and Sally Madsen showed up as Purdey was despatched to the bar. 'Your favourite spot, Gareth?' Fleur asked, nodding to the photograph. 'I'm starting to think you fancy yourself as a twenty-first century John Garfield.'

'Do you mind?' Sally said in mock indignation. She patted her husband's knee with a bejewelled hand. 'That chap isn't half as good-looking as my feller. He still reminds me of Paul Newman in his *Butch Cassidy* days.'

Her husband raised his eyebrows but smiled, as though his wife's admiration was his due. And Hannah had to admit that he had blue eyes to die for. Gareth Madsen wasn't her type, but if Terri were here, she'd never be able to keep her hands off him.

'I spoke to Kit,' Fleur said, as if bored by the display of marital bliss. 'He's stunned by Orla's death, keeps reproaching himself for not realising the extent of her depression. Sally's had a word with Mike Hinds, to offer condolences.'

At first sight, the Madsen wives contrasted as much as their husbands. Sally was raven-haired, mid forties, and plainly determined not to surrender to the ageing process without a fight. Hannah suspected her lips were Botoxed, while her curves screamed implants. The grace of her movements made Hannah suspect she'd once spent time on a catwalk. Fleur, though, was a natural born lady of the manor. Even if the manor had been subsumed into a caravan park.

'Change your mind and stay for a drink,' Gareth said. 'We can ask the driver to wait for an hour and take us all back home together.'

Sally opened her mouth, and seemed about to say yes, and hers was a Bacardi and Coke, but after a moment's hesitation, Fleur shook her head. 'It's been a long day. We'll send him back after he's dropped us off. You two can concentrate on helping the police with their enquiries.'

Gareth grinned at his sister-in-law. 'We'll try not to incriminate ourselves.'

He blew his wife a kiss as Fleur pecked Bryan on the cheek and said, 'See you later, darling.'

Purdey brought the drinks, and told her mother she'd come back home with her father and uncle. As Sally and Fleur headed off, Hannah turned to the girl and said, 'So were you close to Orla?'

'To be honest,' Purdey said, 'I'm not sure anyone was that close to her, poor thing. God knows what made her tick.'

'Surely as a student of psychology—?'

'Believe me, Sigmund Freud would have found Orla a challenge. We sort of grew up together, because the Paynes lived nearby, but she was older, so I didn't know her well. Over the past few years, I've seen her around the park occasionally, visiting Kit. The last time we spoke was when I called in at St Herbert's one day on an errand for my dad. A quick exchange of pleasantries, that was all. She seemed OK, but you can never tell what's going on inside someone's head, can you?'

Hannah wasn't convinced that was the right attitude for a psychology graduate. 'Where did she live?'

'In a small flat on the outskirts of Keswick. Kit and her father gave her money to help her to put down the deposit after she came back to live in the Lakes.'

'When was this?'

'The end of last year. She went to uni in Newcastle, but she dropped out after a couple of years, though she stayed in the North East. I don't think she ever truly settled. She had a string of jobs in marketing, but none lasted long. I heard she had a bit of a breakdown.'

'Did Orla's stepfather consider fixing her up with a job at the . . . uh, holiday home park?'

'She never showed any interest in caravans.' Purdey made it sound like a character flaw. 'I didn't expect her to move back here. Not many youngish people do.'

No arguing with that. Local children often moved away from Cumbria for good once they left school. Good jobs were easier to find in the cities, and so was cheap accommodation, given that house prices in the Lakes kept being driven up by middle-aged incomers who sold their swish detached homes in order to live the dream up in the rural north. Purdey was lucky, with a successful family business ready and waiting for her to step into.

'Why did Orla come back? To follow a boyfriend?'

'None of her blokes stuck around for long, sad to say. She is – oh God, was – quite attractive. Or could be. Though between you and me, she never really did herself justice, and it didn't help when she lost all her hair.'

'What caused that?'

'Alopecia, brought on by stress. She never had much luck, didn't Orla.' Purdey hesitated. 'I hate to sound cruel after what has happened, but I think Dad is right. One of his favourite sayings is, you make your own luck. If Orla was unlucky, in a way she brought it on herself.'

'How do you mean?'

'She could be clingy and persistent. Once she got an idea in her head, she didn't like to let it go.'

Lauren's mobile sang – her ringtone was 'Pretty Woman', what else? – and she moved away to take the call. Gareth turned to Hannah, and she sensed he'd been paying as much attention to her conversation with his daughter as to Bryan and the ACC.

'Orla found it hard to accept that Callum was dead. Understandable, since there was no proof that his uncle did kill him. Though topping yourself is pretty good circumstantial evidence, I'd say.'

'Suicide isn't necessarily an admission of guilt,' Hannah said.

'Your colleagues twenty years back thought it as good as.' Gareth turned to his brother. 'There were no other suspects, were there, Bryan?'

'None whatsoever.'

Hannah said, 'I suppose the people living in your caravans were all checked?'

'Thoroughly.' Bryan's cheeks reddened, thanks either to the champagne or the provocation. 'It was established that none of our customers had any record of misbehaving with children. No surprise, I can assure you. There's a good deal of mindless snobbery about caravans, but you only need take a look at our visitors' car park. You'll see plenty of BMWs, even the occasional Porsche. We don't cater for oddballs.'

'Unless they're loaded.' Gareth gave a mischievous grin.

'By all accounts,' Bryan said, 'Orla became irrational on the subject of Callum. Kit was quite concerned about her.'

'Concerned?' Hannah asked.

'About her mental state. He worried that if she didn't pull herself together, she might need to be sectioned.'

'That bad?'

'I'm afraid so. Kit felt he owed it to Orla's late mother

to do his best for the girl. It wasn't enough, but he can't be blamed for that. She was a loose cannon. You could never be sure what she might say or do next.'

'I suppose that's what led her to do such a ghastly thing,' Purdey said. 'She simply lost the plot.'

'Assuming she did kill herself,' Hannah said.

Gareth's eyebrows shot up. 'Is there any doubt?'

'Until the inquest verdict, who knows?'

Purdey said, 'It's awful for Kit. I feel so sorry for him. After everything he went through when Callum disappeared and then during Niamh's long illness. Now this.'

Bryan said, 'He was due to join us today, but of course, in the circumstances . . .'

'He's rebuilt his life,' Purdey said. 'New wife, new family. Glenys gave him a son; they dote on little Nathan.'

Bryan nodded. 'The chap deserved some happiness after Niamh drank herself to death.'

'Were Kit and Orla close?' Hannah asked.

'He made sure she was never short of money.'

Not an answer, Hannah thought.

Gareth seemed to read her mind. A disturbing knack. 'You have to understand, he wasn't her real father. Once Niamh was dead, there wasn't much to keep Orla and her stepdad together. But he did his best for her.'

'What was the state of her relationship with Mike Hinds?'

'Uneasy. Mike's an old mate of mine, and it cut him to the quick when she took Kit's surname. Callum refused to follow suit, though I suspected that was as much to piss Kit off as to please Mike. Orla was younger, and when Niamh remarried, she went along with what her mother wanted.

There were furious arguments about access. But Orla never lost touch with Mike.'

'Though she never went back to live at his farm?'

Gareth shook his head. 'No, she stayed with Kit on the park until she started at university. By then, Kit had remarried, and so had Mike.'

'She told me once she felt there was nowhere she could truly call home,' Purdey said. 'No wonder she suffered from stress. First she lost her brother, then her mum, and both her dad and her stepdad began new lives that didn't include her.'

Lauren was still gabbling into her mobile, no doubt bragging about the dinner to her husband, an insurance broker whose fat commissions kept her in haute couture. She was standing in front of a shot of Gene Tierney in her most famous role as the eponymous Laura – she probably thought that movie about the seductive woman who drove a detective wild with desire should be remade as *Lauren.*

'What do you think drew her back to Mike Hinds' farm yesterday?' Hannah asked.

Bryan shook his head. 'Who knows what goes through a disturbed mind?'

'My guess is,' Gareth said, 'they had a row and it was a childish kind of payback on her part.'

'What makes you think that?' Hannah asked.

'Mike hated the way she drank so much, it reminded him of Niamh. And he couldn't bear her raking up the past. He'd accepted his son was dead, he'd moved on. It was up to Orla to do the same.'

'He told you this?'

'Mike wears his heart on his sleeve.' Bryan grunted

scornfully to make clear he didn't share Gareth's charitable assessment. 'Snag is, he has a shocking temper. If Orla got the wrong side of it . . .'

'She might have taken it so hard that she felt life wasn't worth living?'

Gareth downed the last of his champagne. 'If that's the way it was, I pray that he can cope. Bad enough to lose one child, but to lose two . . .'

'Poor Hansel and Gretel,' Purdey said.

Three heads turned towards her.

'Hansel and Gretel?' Hannah asked.

'Yes, that's what they called themselves.'

'Who?'

'Orla and Callum. She told me they thought of themselves like the kids in the fairy tale.' Purdey gave a theatrical shiver. 'Except that neither of them had a happy ending.'

'So what did you make of Orla Payne?' Louise Kind asked.

Eyes closed, Daniel stretched to soak up the warmth of late evening. This was the life, lazing on a vast and colourful Mexican hammock. He'd set up the stand beside the path that wound around the garden of Tarn Cottage. The cipher garden, he called it, secluded and secretive grounds that stretched to the foot of Tarn Fell. The hammock had room enough for three or four, but his sister hadn't joined him. She lounged in a deckchair with canvas decorated with artwork from *Evil Under the Sun*. Their glasses and the empty wine bottle stood on the paving. The alcohol had done its job, and blunted his sorrow at the death of a woman he'd liked.

'She was an unhappy woman.'

'Sounds like it, if she's killed herself. This story that her uncle didn't murder her brother, was there anything in it?'

Louise's tongue was as sharp as her spiky new haircut. A lawyer to her fingertips, she kept asking questions until she prised out an answer. Years ago, she had left private practice for academe; at times Daniel felt a pang of sympathy for her students.

'She convinced herself, for sure. I felt sorry for her.'

Louise gave a theatrical sigh. 'I bet the moment she knew who you were, she latched on to you. Another lame duck you took pity on?'

He tried to shrug, tricky in a hammock. Louise had never hit it off with Aimee; after their first meeting, she'd caused a row by asking Daniel if the woman was always so neurotic. Maybe that's why he'd scarcely mentioned Orla to her until now. Orla reminded him of Aimee, if only because they were guided by instinct, not reason, and their instincts drove them to self-destruct.

'Not fair. Orla and I talked once or twice when I took a break from writing. She told me she loved history before she knew I was a historian; she described herself as a failed history undergraduate. There was something unworldly about her, which appealed to me. Eventually someone recognised me, usual story, and before long the principal came and said hello.'

'Goodbye to anonymity?'

'He urged me to become involved with the library, and asked Orla to talk to me about ways of publicising St Herbert's and raising cash. Her job was to improve the library's profile in the region and further afield, but she didn't seem cut out for it. She preferred mooching through books to hitting the phones. The principal brought in an events organiser to help, so Orla could focus on public relations while he packed the guest rooms with conference attendees.'

Louise stretched her arms, soaking up the last of the sun as it set behind the Sacrifice Stone on the top of the fell. 'Was Orla afraid of losing her job?'

'I can't imagine the principal firing anyone. No, getting the sack was the least of her worries, even though she told me that before she came to the Lakes, she'd been unemployed following a period of illness.'

'What was wrong with her?'

A heron flew across the garden, and perched at the far side of the tarn. Daniel contemplated its elegant form before answering.

'I gather she had some kind of breakdown, and her drinking didn't help. Booze had killed her mother – maybe neither of them got over the loss of Callum. Orla was emphatic that she never felt uncomfortable with her uncle, quite the opposite. He used to tell her fairy tales and she adored that, said it gave her a lifelong love of the stories.'

'He might have been more interested in boys than little girls.'

'And perhaps she blanked stuff out, who knows?'

'So she committed suicide on her father's farm? Did she talk about her relationship with him?'

'It was difficult, I gather. Like everyone else, he reckoned his brother killed Callum. But Orla was adamant that there must be some other explanation for what happened.'

'Such as?'

'She didn't say. The last time we spoke, she was in a state. Not making much sense.'

Louise clicked her tongue. 'Hey, you're the one who claims that historians make great detectives. Didn't you ask?'

'It wasn't healthy, this dwelling on the tragedy. I tried to steer her off the subject of Callum, but without any success.'

'You always say that to understand the present, you have to understand the past.'

'Yeah, yeah, hoist with my own petard.'

Louise narrowed her eyes. 'I suppose she fancied you.'

Orla's eager face sprang into his mind as his gaze settled on the Sacrifice Stone, its dark bulk outlined against the sky. What she liked, he thought, was the fact he listened to her without passing judgement. She'd spent a lifetime being ignored.

'It wasn't like that.'

'You didn't fancy her, by any chance?' He shook his head. 'Not your type?'

Louise had this habit of turning conversation into cross-examination.

'I don't have a type.'

'How about Aimee and Miranda?'

'Are you kidding? They couldn't be more different.'

'Only on the surface. You're a sucker when it comes to needy women.'

'Thanks for that.' Better not remind her that she kept falling for selfish bastards who did their best to mess up her life. 'Orla was fixated, desperate to unravel a mystery everyone else thought was solved twenty years ago. Her stepfather was unhappy about it, she told me; he thought it was doing her no good.'

'And her father?'

'I sensed she was afraid of him. I even wondered if she thought she bore some kind of responsibility for his disappearance herself.'

'How?'

'Something I heard her mutter to herself on Friday, the last time we met. She'd been working in the library, rather than her office, and we had lunch together. She wasn't with it, frankly. It was as if something in her life had changed, but don't ask me what.'

'What did she say?'

'"*How could you do that to your own brother*?"'

'Meaning?'

'Dunno. When I asked what was bothering her, she brushed me off. At first, I thought she was quoting Callum. But perhaps in some way she thought she'd betrayed him. If she started torturing herself, that might be why she committed suicide.'

'Where's your evidence for that?'

'If I'd known what she meant to do, I could have asked—'

Louise interrupted. 'If you are even thinking you may be partly at fault because of what happened to her, I will scream. Please, Daniel, forget it. People are responsible for their own actions, OK? You did your utmost to help her, I'm certain.'

'On Friday, I suggested she might talk to the police.'

'There you are, then.'

'I gave her Hannah Scarlett's name.'

'You did?' Louise sat up in the deckchair.

'Callum's disappearance is a cold case. Right up Hannah's street. Orla may have been obsessive, but she wasn't stupid. Suppose she was right, and the uncle didn't kill Callum? If anyone could make sense of whatever was whirling round in Orla's brain, Hannah could.'

'And?'

'And what?'

'Don't tell me you haven't spoken to Hannah yet.'

'I haven't spoken to Hannah.'

'Daniel, for God's sake, what are we going to do with you?'

'Don't start.'

His sister insisted that he and Hannah were right for each other. But he'd decided he wasn't ready for another serious relationship. He'd fallen for Miranda on the rebound after Aimee's death, and it had been a big mistake. Besides, things with Hannah were complicated. By Marc, for a start. And there was something else. Hannah had been close to their father, Ben. Daniel couldn't help wondering if her interest in him was driven by curiosity, because he was his father's son.

'I'm just saying.'

'I'll phone her tomorrow.'

'Terrific.' Louise mimed applause. 'Faint heart never won, et cetera.'

'Calm down, it's nothing to get excited about. All I'm doing is returning a call. She left me a voicemail message this afternoon.'

* * *

Night had fallen by the time the cab dropped Hannah back at Undercrag. The bulb had gone in the so-called security light that Marc had fitted, and in the darkness, the dour old house seemed lonely and uninviting. Not at all like home. At this time of day, the bustle of Ambleside's shops and cars seemed to belong to a different world. Undercrag was the last of a group of five buildings that had once formed a cottage hospital, and Hannah often thought about the patients who had come here in the hope of a cure, only to die.

God, she needed to loosen up. It wasn't as if she had drunk enough to induce melancholy. As she unlocked the front door, she reminded herself for the hundredth time to beef up the security around the house – the box fastened high up on the front wall of the house had no alarm inside it – but this was another on the long list of jobs which she never seemed to reach. Better sort it out soon. How embarrassing would it be as a senior cop to find yourself burgled because of a failure to take the simplest precautions?

In the hall, the light on the answering machine was flashing. She swallowed hard. A return call from Daniel, even though she'd said she'd be out this evening? She pressed playback, to be greeted by the voice of her old friend Terri.

'Hiya, just ringing to confirm timings for tomorrow. See you at seven-thirty? And if you arrive first, mine's a pina colada. Lots of love.'

Hannah deleted the message and headed for the living room. Kicking off her shoes, she poured whisky into a tumbler. Lately, she'd got into a routine of having a drink on her own before going to bed. It helped her to get to sleep. She never had more than a couple of glasses, but she knew it was a bad habit. She ought to break it, but for this evening, never mind. Just savour the alcohol.

Curling up in her favourite armchair, she closed her eyes and thought about Hansel and Gretel. Two kids with a wicked stepmother, they had ventured into a wood, only to encounter death and destruction. What prompted Callum Hinds to make the comparison? Was it possible that he suspected Kit of wanting to abandon them, just like the horrible woman in the fairy tale?

On the short drive back from Mancini's to HQ, Lauren had told her Bryan Madsen had asked if Orla's death might prompt a fresh look at Callum Hinds' disappearance.

'Bet he doesn't fancy that.'

'Look at it from his perspective, Hannah. The Madsens are in the leisure business, like so many other people in the Lake District. It doesn't help if there's a suggestion that a boy who lived on their park was murdered, and the culprit wasn't found. That sort of thing can deter potential visitors.'

'Yeah, Philip Hinds' suicide was a real stroke of luck for them.'

'Don't be sarky, Hannah, it really doesn't help. We both know the odds are that Hinds did kill the boy. But Bryan Madsen is a reasonable man, he realises we can't simply ignore Orla's calls.'

'So you're happy for my team to take another look at Callum's disappearance?' Hannah had expected resistance. Talk of financial constraints and the need to prioritise. 'Do the Madsens understand that?'

'Absolutely; they strike me as very constructive. They're keen for things to be cleared up, if only to set Kit Payne's mind at rest. But don't waste too much time and resource on a wild goose chase, Hannah. All the Madsens ask is that we don't drag our feet.'

'It will take as long as it takes.'

Lauren shook her head. 'In fairness to everyone, we need a quick outcome. Can you make sure your report is on my desk by this time next week?'

So that was it. A box-ticking exercise, a low-cost means of proving that no favouritism was extended to business partners. The Madsens' reaction was shrewd. No attempt to stifle her by insisting that sleeping dogs must lie. For all Gareth's jokes, he and Bryan realised they couldn't dictate how the police handled their enquiries. They'd done their best to bond with the ACC, and the head of the cold case team whom Orla had contacted. Their aim must be to come over as law-abiding folk with nothing to hide, and she'd rather taken to Gareth, though experience warned her to be wary of rich men who oozed charm. As for Bryan, she wouldn't care to spend long in his company, but the bottom line was that if the brothers were sweating, they were smart enough not to let it show. Even after a few drinks.

Seven days to pore over a case that reached a sudden and melancholy conclusion twenty years ago. Not enough time, it went without saying. But she couldn't ask for more, given the apparent lack of fresh evidence. Orla probably was a sad obsessive, as the Madsens reckoned.

And yet.

Daniel Kind believed Hannah should hear what Orla

had to say. He wouldn't waste her time, Hannah was sure of that.

She needed to talk to him.

So Orla was dead.

Aslan Sheikh lay on his bed in his underpants as a rapper boomed from his iPod dock. A tap never stopped dripping in the washbasin, and the music drowned the sound. Even at the height of summer, this scruffy little bedsit in Crosthwaite was draughty, the breeze from the fells sneaking in through the cracks in the window frame. A yellowing house plant festered in a beige pot, a perfect advertisement for botanical euthanasia. The place smelt of damp and last night's curry. He'd smoked a couple of joints in quick succession to calm his nerves. Funny how Orla had refused that time when he brought her back here, insisting that she didn't do drugs. Naive to a fault, for what was alcohol but a drug that had killed her mother?

The sun's rays caught the blade of the small knife on his bedside table. When it shone so brightly, he barely remembered the damage it could cause. It was a silver butterfly knife, or 'balisong' as the Filipinos called it, and he'd picked it up in London after he'd had to leave its predecessor in the States for fear of arrest at airport security. This little fellow was over a hundred years old and counted as an antique. It fitted snugly into the pocket of his jeans; he carried it everywhere. A balisong had helped him extricate himself from some of the tight spots he'd got himself into. He'd made a few mistakes over the years; he supposed his mother was right when she said he was too headstrong, too wild.

He couldn't get over Orla's death. Suffocated in grain, what a shitty way to go. Sham Madsen had shaken uncontrollably as she broke the news, and he'd thrown an arm around her by way of comfort, but when she clung closer to him, he managed to disengage. Her tears were self-indulgent, and he knew enough about phoniness to recognise it when he saw it. She seldom had a good word to say about Orla when she was alive. The spoilt rich kid, scorning the stepdaughter of her father's right-hand man. Surely not even she could be jealous; a bald woman with barely a penny to her name was no competition for one of the heirs to the Madsen millions.

Sham was gorgeous – more so than Purdey, with her unfortunate chin and micro-boobs – but she was a drama queen whose sole topic of conversation was herself. He humoured her, but the endless stream of *me, me, me* became a bore. She didn't disguise her lack of interest in St Herbert's, and he was sure she'd only taken the job because she wasn't keen to play second fiddle to Purdey at the caravan park.

He'd no experience of sibling rivalry, let alone everything else that had happened here since his arrival. Even though he'd spent so little of his life in Britain, he liked to think of the Lakes as home. How many times had he dreamt of this homecoming? He'd never settled anywhere for long. The first place he could remember was in Istanbul, and then his mother had moved to Germany, where her cousins lived, and they'd lived in a cramped flat in Berlin before moving out to Rostock, eventually finishing up in the small coastal resort of Warnemünde, where his mother worked in one of the bars that served crew members coming ashore from the big ships. When she entertained at home, he'd make himself scarce and go to watch the cruise ships sailing out of the harbour and beyond the lighthouse, into the wide blue yonder. At sixteen, he took a job with one of the cruise lines, lying about his age and what he could do, and over the next few years he moved from ship to ship, but he never found what he was searching for. Perhaps the truth was that he didn't know.

He'd travelled far and wide before drifting around the States, but he'd never bought a share of the American dream. Women, drink, drugs, he tried them all, but none of them meant much. He'd as soon smoke a cheap fag as a joint, and the money he earned or stole never lasted long. In the end, he persuaded himself the way to change his life was to come back to England. This was to be where he finally discovered himself.

But he'd never expected things to turn out like this. Orla was dead, and the Lakes didn't feel anything like home.

CHAPTER SIX

Half a year without Marc should have acclimatised Hannah to waking up alone, but as the radio woke her, she still put out an arm, an instinctive searching for the warm body that had lain by her side for so long. Instead, her fingers clutched at emptiness.

The weather forecaster said today promised to be the sunniest of the year so far. After a cold shower – not from choice; the hot water system was on the blink – she dressed hastily so as not to keep Maggie Eyre waiting. A true farmer's daughter, Maggie was an early riser, and the doorbell rang as Hannah swallowed her last mouthful of toast.

'How was the awards dinner?' Maggie asked as her little Citroën bumped over the potholes of Lowbarrow Lane.

'I managed to stay awake. In fact, it wasn't a complete waste of time.' Hannah told her about meeting the Madsens. 'Even if they aren't thrilled about the prospect of our looking into Callum Payne's case, at least they didn't put any roadblocks in the way.'

'They are convinced the uncle killed the boy?'

'A neat solution is best for their business. The ACC has given us the green light, but wants an outcome by this time next week.'

'A week?' Maggie nearly swerved into the path of an oncoming tractor. 'A proper investigation takes months. Sometimes years.'

'She's taking it for granted nothing new will turn up. It's not as if we have any DNA to retest with the benefit of improved technology. Her thinking is that if we talk to the main witnesses who are still around, we'll have done the necessary. She's not worried about the IPCC complaining about Orla Payne's calls to us. So the game plan is, we give the file a quick once-over, and move on.'

'And if we find something worth investigating?'

'The ACC would say, let's cross that bridge when we come to it.'

Eyes on the winding lane, Maggie said, 'Surely we wouldn't give up if there was evidence that Philip Hinds wasn't guilty?'

Hannah gave her a sidelong glance. 'Let's find the evidence before we worry about that, shall we?'

Enough said. Maggie fell silent until they reached the main road.

'My father reckons Mike cast Philip as a scapegoat.'

'He knew the Hinds family?'

'It's not surprising. Farming is a close community, everybody knows everybody else. People bump into each other at shows and markets and National Farmers' Union events – can't avoid it. By the sound of it, my dad prefers to avoid Mike Hinds, that's for sure.'

'They don't get on?'

'Dad says he's a maverick, always arguing the toss, whether about bovine TB or compensation for foot-and-mouth disease or anything else. Thinks he's clever because he won a scholarship to Cambridge, even though he soon dropped out. I suppose he sees Dad as a pillar of the establishment because he's held office in the NFU. And Mike doesn't think the union does enough to protect its members' interests. Dad said, if it was left to Mike Hinds, tractors would be parked permanently across Whitehall, in protest about the way the government has wrecked the industry.'

'Does your father know much about Callum's disappearance?'

'Only what everyone knew. Of course, I didn't go into detail about why I was interested in the Hinds family, confidential police business and all that. Dad never met Philip, but said he felt sorry for him. For Mike Hinds too; it is terrible to lose your son like that. Dad heard that Philip was simple, but decent enough. People were too quick to jump to conclusions, in Dad's opinion.'

'If their conclusions were wrong, we'll find out,' Hannah said. She couldn't forget what Orla Payne had said about justice. 'If Philip was innocent, we'll clear his name.'

Daniel and Louise breakfasted in the garden, looking out to the reed-fringed tarn and the fell beyond. The water was still, with no breeze to rustle the leaves of the oaks and the yews. The air smelt fresh, and they heard the piping call of a wood warbler hidden in the trees. No mist clung to the upper slopes, the merest scraps of cloud drifted in the sky. Already walkers in shirtsleeves were striding along Priest Ridge, their voices drifting down from the heights. The Sacrifice Stone gleamed in the sun, for once benign, not sinister.

'No regrets about abandoning the rat race, then?' Louise asked.

Daniel's eyes followed a flash of yellow as the warbler emerged from a tall oak before flying off towards Tarn Fold.

'Need you ask?'

'At first, I thought you were mad to give up your career,' she said. 'But now . . . this place is addictive, and I'm hooked too. All I need is to find a place of my own, so I can get out of your hair.'

'Stay as long as you like.'

She grinned. 'No, better quit before we start bickering all the time, like when we were kids.'

'We've grown up.'

'You think so?'

As soon as she went inside to get dressed and stiffen her sinews for a renewed onslaught on the local property market, Daniel fished out his mobile and dialled Hannah's number.

'Is it convenient?' he asked when she answered. 'If not, I can call again.'

'I have a briefing scheduled in five minutes, but no worries,' she said. 'Great to hear from you.'

'And did you hear from Orla Payne?'

'I spoke to her, yes. And then she rang again when I was off work. I'm assuming you met her at St Herbert's, where she worked?'

'Yes, I've spent a lot of time there lately, trying to finish the book.'

'You know what happened to her?'

'She suffocated in a grain silo on her father's farm,' Daniel said. 'That's all I've heard. So she talked to you about Callum?'

'I didn't get much sense out of her. Certainly no clue about her brother's fate. Linz Waller got nowhere either, when Orla called again. Each time, she sounded drunk.'

'Sorry I've added to your burdens, but she was so screwed up about Callum's disappearance, and I thought it qualified as a cold case.'

'How much did she tell you?'

'She talked a great deal, but if she had any firm evidence about what happened to Callum, I didn't hear it. She rather liked to be mysterious. But she was emphatic that their uncle didn't kill the boy.'

'Was it wishful thinking? She was fond of her uncle, and didn't like the idea that he was to blame.'

'Possible. But . . .'

He hesitated, trying to put into words the intuition he had about Orla, and her quest for the truth about Callum.

'Yes?'

'Orla's life was a mess. She reminded me of someone who has the pieces of a self-assembly kit, but doesn't know how to put them together.'

'I know that feeling,' Hannah said. 'My garage is full of segments of a kitchen trolley, and instructions written in Japanese with illustrations that make no sense to me.'

He wondered if she'd ask Marc to stick the pieces together, but said nothing. He heard someone speak to

Hannah, and her muffled reply that she'd be along in a moment.

'Daniel, I'm sorry, but I need to conduct this briefing. Can we speak again?'

'Love to.'

Story time.

Hannah's mentor, Ben Kind, was a grizzled teller of tales. As she stood and waited for Greg Wharf – as ever, the last to arrive – while Les Bryant chewed the fat with Maggie Eyre, and Donna Buxton nagged Linz about becoming more active in the Federation, her thoughts drifted back to her early days in the CID. How the briefing room fell silent as Ben took his team through the sequence of events leading up to the latest murder. How she listened, spellbound, as he highlighted scraps of information culled from page after page of witness statements, suggesting fresh lines of enquiry, and ideas about the culprit's motive and MO. By the time Ben finished briefing you about a case, the victim was no longer a name, always a person. That cold corpse in the mortuary had once been flesh and blood. Ben made you care about the victim's fate, strengthened your resolve to see justice done.

'Sorry I'm late,' Greg said, marching into the room like a chief executive greeting members of his board. Donna, an arch-feminist recently drafted into the team, threw him a withering look, but Greg smirked in response, pleased to have provoked a reaction.

Hannah breathed in. She'd soaked herself in the old statements, and reckoned she had a handle on the main facts, but there was no denying that the mood today was so different from that at briefings from Ben. From the moment murder was done, every hour that passed reduced the chances of a result. Statistics proved the need for speed. Everyone felt an adrenaline rush. By definition, cold cases were rarely time-critical, and Hannah's team knew it. They knew, too, that each of them was there for a reason. Most were misfits, as far as the brass was concerned. Some folk, and not just in the hierarchy, reckoned that cold case reviews were cushy and only fit for underachievers. Others regarded transfer to the team as a form of exile or punishment, the Cumbria Constabulary's very own Gulag Archipelago. All of which meant the pressure was on her to motivate people to get results.

'The body of Orla Payne was found buried in a grain tower at the farm of her father, Michael Hinds, near Keswick. An apparent suicide. She had been in touch with us about a cold case, the disappearance of her brother Callum twenty years ago.'

'Is murder a possibility?' Les Bryant asked.

'Nothing is being ruled out, pending the inquest. Mario Pinardi up in Keswick is looking into the circumstances surrounding her death. He's waiting on the results of toxicology and urine tests. Our focus is on the cold case. What happened to Callum Hinds?'

Hannah nodded at a black-and-white photograph on the whiteboard. A dark-haired boy with a hooked nose and deep-set eyes, reluctant to smile for the camera.

'Callum's mother came over from Donegal as a student. After she took a degree in Lancaster, she stayed in England. She was called Niamh, and her first husband was Mike

Hinds. Three years before the boy went missing, the couple split up.'

'Why?' Greg asked.

'Niamh's story was that she wasn't suited to being a farmer's wife.'

'It's a vocation,' Maggie said.

'And the husband's story?' Greg was a city boy, scornful of the so-called pressures of rural life.

'You can almost taste the bitterness when you read his statement,' Hannah said. 'He scarcely had a good word to say for her. She drank too much, cared only for herself. He blamed her for the boy's disappearance. Obviously pissed off that she'd landed on her feet. Before the divorce was finalised, she'd moved in with Kit Payne, a manager at Madsen's.'

'The caravan park?' Donna Buxton asked. 'My uncle and aunt used to have a pitch there. We stayed with them when we were kids.'

'They call it a holiday home park these days,' Hannah said. 'One of the biggest in the Lakes. The site borders Mike Hinds' land. In next to no time, Niamh and Kit Payne were married, and instead of slaving away all hours cooking and cleaning, she had a husband with a well-paid job and free accommodation thrown in. Even if it was only a glorified log cabin.'

'How did the stepfather get on with the kids?' Greg asked.

'Kindness itself, according to Niamh. There weren't any issues between him and Orla, or so it seemed. Yet Callum resented the new man in his mum's life, and refused to take Payne's name.'

'He stayed close to Hinds?'

'The divorce was acrimonious. Niamh played games over Hinds' access to the kids. Arrangements would be made, and at the last minute she'd come up with some excuse for cancelling. But Kit Payne tried to act as a peace-broker, and Callum made it clear that he was determined to stay in touch with his dad. Since the farmhouse was a stroll away, Niamh could hardly stop him.'

'How about the prime suspect?'

'Philip Hinds was older than his brother Mike, and they had nothing in common. He was single, and seems never to have had a girlfriend. Or a boyfriend, that we know of. He enjoyed the company of his nephew and niece, but for all anyone could prove, it seemed perfectly innocent.'

'Oh yeah?'

'Yeah, actually. Everyone agreed he was devoted to Orla and Callum. Mike Hinds discouraged them from spending time with their uncle, but Niamh was fond of Philip, and didn't mind the kids visiting his cottage. Hinds said it showed she was a bad mother, letting them walk through the wood on their own. His argument was that, never mind Philip, the caravan site was nearby; you couldn't be sure who might be lurking around, on the lookout for kids.'

'You can see his point of view.'

'Sure, but does it do any good to wrap kids up in cotton wool?'

As she spoke, Hannah wondered if she'd ever face that dilemma as a mother. The closest she'd come to parenthood was when a miscarriage had put an end to an unplanned pregnancy. Marc had said all the right things, but he reckoned he wasn't ready for fatherhood, and he'd hardly been able to hide his relief that a baby hadn't complicated their relationship even further. Perhaps that was the moment she should have decided he wasn't the right man for her.

Greg shrugged. He didn't have kids, either. At least, none that Hannah knew of.

Aslan had the habit of coming and going as he pleased at St Herbert's. What was the worst that could happen? The principal wasn't made of the right stuff to sack anyone, and why get rid of a spare pair of hands, even if they belonged to someone as bolshie as Aslan?

He strode down the corridor towards the main entrance. With Orla dead, St Herbert's' publicity efforts were on hold. No point in twiddling his thumbs. It was time for a visit to Lane End Farm. He could not delay it any longer. Yet his stomach churned, and his skin was all gooseflesh. He would go the long way round to the farmhouse, along the meandering lanes rather than taking a short cut across the fields. He needed plenty of time to work out what to say.

'Penny for them!'

Sham, in breezy mood. A deeply cut pink top fought a losing battle to contain her breasts. She'd made a rapid recovery from the trauma of learning that Orla was dead.

He smiled. 'If you knew what I was thinking, you'd never believe me.'

She giggled and leant back on her chair, revealing a skirt so short that it was more like a belt. 'You reckon?'

'I reckon,' he said, and strode out through the door.

'How did Philip Hinds earn a crust, ma'am?' Greg asked.

'Odd jobs around the caravan park, a bit of joinery here,

mending a fuse there. Bryan Madsen had little time for him, so he reported to Gareth, who by reputation is more easy-going. In the middle of the wood was a tumbledown cottage. It was built a hundred years ago and occupied by a succession of gamekeepers who worked for the Hopes family until the cash ran out and the wood was sold, along with the land for the caravan park. Philip lived there for a peppercorn rent. The deal suited both sides, though Philip's handyman skills don't seem to have extended to upgrading the cottage. It was in a shocking state of repair at the time of his death.'

'Who reported Callum missing?' Linz asked.

'Niamh Payne. It was the start of the summer holidays. Callum had finished at school and she'd gone shopping in Keswick. Orla went with her, but Callum refused to tag along. He was fourteen, and she took the view that it was fine to leave him alone in the house.'

'Caravan,' Greg said.

'Log hut, whatever. It wasn't unusual for her to leave the boy to his own devices. Her ex-husband moaned about it, but nobody suggested there was serious neglect on Niamh's part. She and Orla were back by half three. Callum wasn't around. He'd muttered about calling on his uncle, and when he was still nowhere to be found at six, she went to the cottage in the wood. Take a look at the map and you'll see the lie of the land twenty years ago.'

All eyes turned to a sketch map on the whiteboard. The Hanging Wood was in the centre, crossed by two diagonal footpaths, with a cottage close to the point where the two paths intersected. To the east lay the caravan park, occupying the greater part of the area shown, its borders shared at different points by Lane End Farm, the wood, the Mockbeggar Estate, and St Herbert's Residential Library. A stream ran along the boundary, with the estate and St Herbert's on the west side, and Madsen's on the east, before veering off just before the Hanging Wood and threading its way through the caravan park towards the River Derwent.

Greg Wharf grunted. 'Typical Lakes, eh? Orla Payne grew up at the farm, moved to the caravan site, worked at the library, and then went back to the farm to die. And you can fit them all in a small-scale map. Claustrophobic, or what?'

Hannah reached into her case, and unfolded another sketch map which she pinned on the board. 'Compare past and present – spot the difference?'

'The Mockbeggar Estate has been swallowed up by the caravan park!' Linz was never afraid to state the obvious. 'How come?'

'Mockbeggar Hall was owned by the Hopes family. The last of the line, Fleur, married Joseph Madsen's elder son. At the start of the nineteenth century, the Hopes owned this whole area on the map. In the late Victorian era, Sir Milo Hopes gave away a chunk of it for this private library to be built, where Orla Payne worked. Come the twentieth century, and the family fortunes plummeted. Death duties, bad investments, spending too much for the sake of appearances. The farm was sold to Mike Hinds' grandfather. The land to the east became a caravan park, the Hanging Wood was flogged off for good measure. Fleur Hopes' grandfather and father were useless with money, and so was her older brother Jolyon. She was last of the line, and when Jolyon died, there was nobody left to live in the Hall.'

'Fleur, Jolyon?' Linz frowned. 'The names ring a bell.'

'You're thinking of *The Forsyte Saga*. Their mother was called Irene, maybe she was a Galsworthy fan. Though the father's name was Alfred, not Soames. Fleur's solution was to marry into the Madsens, and her husband Bryan has run the business ever since his father suffered a stroke. Jolyon Hopes was a bachelor who broke his neck fox-hunting twenty-one years ago.'

'Serves him right,' Linz said. 'A sick way to pass the time, killing animals for pleasure.'

Maggie gave her a dirty look. The two of them often argued about country sports. Hannah's worst nightmare was that one day, budget cuts would cause the ACC to insist that the Cold Case Review Team be roped into policing hunts.

'Fleur inherited the Hall and estate, but also the Hopes debts. Jolyon lived for a decade after his accident, but his nursing fees cost a fortune. Once everything was paid off, the Madsens set about transforming the old Hall into a new centrepiece for their park. They built a new bridge over the stream to link the Hall with the business headquarters. No expense spared. The official opening is due soon, and most of Cumbria's VIPs will be there.'

'Funny, that,' Les Bryant mused. 'My invitation must have got lost in the post.'

'In all their publicity, the Madsens emphasise that the park is carefully managed and secure. They have never allowed their caravanners access to the Hanging Wood. Philip spent most of his time in the wood alone, apart from when Niamh's children visited. It wasn't frequented by locals, and even poachers gave it a wide berth.'

'Niamh didn't find Callum in the cottage?' Linz asked.

'No, Philip said he'd dropped in during the morning. He spent half an hour climbing trees around the cottage, a schoolboy letting off steam, if his uncle was to be believed. Philip was supposed to mend a fence on the site that afternoon, and Callum didn't stop for lunch, though they often shared a bit of bread and cheese. According to Philip, the boy didn't say where he was going afterwards, just said he had stuff to do. Philip helped Niamh search the wood, but there was no sign of Callum, so she ran back and phoned Mike Hinds. When he said he hadn't seen his son, she rang the police. Within half an hour, the search spread further afield. First to the caravan site, then the farm.'

'What about the grounds of Mockbeggar Hall?' Maggie asked.

'Eventually – much to the disgust of Alfred Hopes, who thought an Englishman's hall was his castle. He sounds like a cantankerous old bugger.'

'Could Callum have hidden in the cottage?'

'It wasn't until twenty-four hours had passed, with no trace of Callum, that Mike Hinds suggested to the police that his brother might be responsible for the boy's disappearance. There was a tiny cellar under the cottage, and he said Philip might have put Callum there. Dead or drugged. Philip flew into panic mode when he got wind that he was a suspect. Said he'd rather die than harm a hair on the lad's head, but barricaded the door and refused to let the police inside. In the end, they obtained a search warrant and forced their way in, but all they found in the cellar was a pile of wood chippings and a few ancient porn magazines.'

'Heterosexual porn?' Inevitably, it was Greg who wanted to know.

'Old naturist magazines called *Health and Efficiency*, with black-and-white pictures of people playing volleyball and wearing only a smile, that sort of stuff. There was no evidence Philip had ever had any kind of sexual relationship, whether with man, woman or a child.'

'Christ.' Greg's mind boggled at the very idea of lifelong celibacy.

'Poor sod,' Donna said.

'The enquiry team was becoming desperate. They put Philip under a lot of pressure. It wouldn't happen today.'

'You don't think so?' Greg muttered.

Maggie asked, 'Had Callum run away from home in the past?'

'Niamh said not. She admitted that Kit had been cross with him, but that wasn't unusual, and insisted his disappearance came out of the blue.'

'Girlfriend?' Les Bryant's tone suggesting that he blamed most extraordinary male behaviour on trouble with the opposite sex.

'Not as far as anyone knew.'

'He could have kept her existence secret. A lot of kids do.'

'One possibility was that he'd become involved with a girl on holiday with her family in one of the caravans. The Madsens had a rule that staff weren't allowed to fraternise with holiday visitors, and Kit Payne insisted his stepchildren didn't mix with them, even though they all lived cheek by jowl on the site. Callum was supposed to have been shy of girls.'

'Yeah,' Greg said. 'Mums often think that about their lads. Mine did, that's for sure. Little did she know.'

'The team didn't take Niamh's word for it. Everyone on the site was questioned. The only clue was in a statement from a girl of sixteen, who said that she'd spotted Callum watching her as she stripped down to her bikini.'

'What happened?' Les asked.

'She shouted at him to fuck off or she'd fetch her dad, and he ran for his life – if she was to be believed. The officer who took her statement reckoned she was looking for her fifteen minutes of fame. But that didn't mean she was lying.'

'Was this on the day he disappeared?'

'No, a couple of days earlier, so it wasn't thought to be of major significance.'

'Unless he went back for another peep, and the girl's dad caught him.'

'The father was a police officer.'

Greg said, 'Not all of us are lily-white.'

'As a matter of fact, he was a DCI.'

His teeth flashed. 'They can be the worst of the lot.'

'Don't push it. Everyone was quizzed, including the girl's family. There was no proof that Callum ever went near their caravan again. He wasn't the bravest soul, it seemed. Not your typical devil-may-care teenage lad. If the girl screamed abuse at him, he was probably scared stiff, as well as humiliated.'

'Did anyone see him after he supposedly left his uncle's cottage?' Maggie asked.

'No, and that turned out to be a huge problem for Philip. There was no trace of Callum's movements after he visited the cottage. Of course, we had the usual crop of false sightings, everywhere from St Bees to Robin Hood's Bay. All faithfully investigated, all dead ends. He'd vanished without trace. The press got excited, and the gossipmongers went into overdrive. Philip kept a pig, and that disappeared as well. All grist to the rumour mill. Soon, the received wisdom was that Philip had sexually assaulted his nephew, then killed him to keep him quiet. How to dispose of the remains? Simple – a snack for Porky.'

'Was the pig found?'

'No, what happened to it, nobody ever knew. Almost certainly, it made its way out into the countryside and tumbled down some gully or ravine. Unfortunately for Philip, there was nobody else in the frame as regards Callum's disappearance. He was hauled in for questioning, and didn't do himself any favours by buttoning his lip and refusing to cooperate. He became upset and confused and his brief made ominous noises about police brutality. Laughable, considering that the senior officer was Will Durston, whose reputation was more tabby cat than Torquemada.'

'Was Philip represented by a duty solicitor?'

'No, a sharp-suited lawyer from the biggest criminal practice in Leeds. Joseph Madsen footed the bill.'

'Didn't he want the truth to come out?'

'Joseph's story was that he felt obliged to see that Philip was properly defended. Bryan Madsen was furious, he wanted them to distance themselves from the man. But there was no proof Philip had harmed Callum, and the solicitor's presence ensured there was no confession, so he was released. By that time, his cottage had been daubed with red paint. Obscene graffiti saying he was a child killer and a paedophile. Some people thought Mike Hinds was responsible, but of course he denied it.'

'Wasn't the place put under guard?' Linz asked.

'The Madsens were afraid that Callum's disappearance would damage their business. Parents wouldn't take their kids to a caravan site where a boy was missing, presumed abducted. So they persuaded Durston and his superiors to keep the police presence low-key.'

'Typical,' Linz grunted.

'The Madsens carried a huge amount of clout in the district. Important employers, with plenty of friends in high places – you can't ride roughshod over them. Philip insisted on going back to the Hanging Wood, and nobody could talk him out of it. An Englishman's home is his castle and all that. Even if it is a semi-derelict ruin.'

Maggie wrinkled her nose. 'And that's where he committed suicide?'

'Yes, Kit Payne found him dangling from a rope he'd tied to an oak branch at the back of the cottage.'

'So it really did become the Hanging Wood,' Linz said. 'Why did Payne go to the cottage?'

'Joseph Madsen had asked him to keep an eye on Philip. Neither Kit nor Niamh were baying for the man's blood. They didn't want to contemplate the possibility that Callum was dead. They preferred to think he'd run off through some misguided spirit of adventure. Out of character as it seemed.'

'Did Philip's death change their minds?'

'Everyone took it as an admission of guilt. It suited the

Madsens to draw a line under the case fast, and Kit Payne was pragmatic. If people stopped visiting the caravan park, he would be out of a job. For Niamh, it was different. She couldn't face losing her son. Or the suggestion that she was partly to blame, through allowing her children to visit their uncle without a chaperone.'

'You can understand it,' Maggie said.

'She made a scene when the investigation was wound down. The press loved it, but once new stories cropped up, the journalists lost interest and there wasn't much else she could do. Her husband tried to calm her down, but it took gin to do the trick. Although she was a grieving mother, the more she hit the bottle, the less credibility she had when she insisted Callum was still alive and the search for him shouldn't be called off.'

'When did she die?'

'Ten years ago. She'd been ill for a long time before that, but Kit Payne did his best to look after her as well as his stepdaughter.'

'Quite a paragon,' Greg said with a grimace. 'Did he have an alibi for Callum's disappearance?'

'Not entirely. He spent much of the day in question looking round the caravan park, supposedly checking work done by a firm of maintenance contractors whose bill was in dispute.'

'So he could have slipped into the Hanging Wood and done something nasty to his stepson?'

'Correct. You can see from the map, the cottage is within walking distance of the Madsens' offices.'

'Were the Madsens around that day?'

'They gave statements, but they were never suspects.

Will Durston was careful to keep on their right side. I never knew Will, and he died not long after he retired from the force, but I'm told he didn't like to make waves. Joseph was away from Keswick. He was a cricket fan and spent the day watching a Test match at Headingley. Bryan had been injured a fortnight earlier, when his car came off the road at a bend on Castlerigg Hill. He broke his leg badly, and was lucky not to be killed. He'd just started going back into the office on crutches for half an hour a day, the rest of the time he was recuperating at home. His wife was out at a fashion show with brother Gareth's wife, so there wasn't any corroboration, but nobody could see him as a one-legged murderer. Gareth was at the caravan park, keeping an eye on things in Bryan's absence. No solid alibis, then, but Durston was satisfied they wouldn't have dreamt of harming the boy.'

'What about Mike Hinds?' Greg asked.

'Working on the farm. Again, he was moving around, at various times of the day he was on his own. So he had the opportunity to bump into Callum, and if they argued about something, who knows? On a farm, there are countless ways to dispose of a body. But what could drive a man to murder his own son?'

'To spite Niamh?'

'But why Callum, who kept the Hinds name even after his mother took him to live with Kit Payne?' Hannah asked. 'That was why all roads led back to Philip. If he wasn't guilty, who else could possibly want to make a fourteen-year-old lad disappear for ever?'

CHAPTER SEVEN

Begin at the beginning. The first person to see was the father of Callum Hinds. Tactful handling was vital any time, but all the more so given his latest bereavement. She rang Lane End Farm to arrange an appointment; to progress the review in line with the ACC's timescale, she couldn't leave the grunt work to admin staff. Hinds' wife Deirdre listened in silence as Hannah explained she was looking into Callum Hinds' disappearance, not his sister's death.

'Routine, I suppose?' she said at last. 'That's what the police always say on telly, isn't it?'

She sounded numb. Shock, more than grief, Hannah supposed. Orla was not her own flesh and blood, but the discovery of her stepdaughter's corpse buried in grain was enough to stun the sturdiest soul. When Hannah asked for a word with Mike Hinds, his wife said he was out in the fields, too far away to be summoned to the phone.

When Hannah expressed surprise, Deirdre Hinds' patience frayed.

'This is a working farm, Detective Chief Inspector. Life goes on, there is no choice. We have livestock to look after. This sunshine is too precious for Mike to waste after the rotten spring we had. Anyroad, he's not the type of man to sit inside and feel sorry for himself.'

But she agreed that her husband would make himself available at the back end of the afternoon – 'Might as well get it over with' – and Hannah rang off before she had time for second thoughts.

Hannah was determined to lead the key interviews herself. One compensation of being shunted into cold case work – Lauren had sidelined her after a major prosecution turned sour – was the chance to work as a proper detective again, rather than sinking forever into the quicksand of management. Whenever the chance to escape bureaucracy and desk work came her way, she grabbed it. She was so much keener on meeting witnesses than targets.

Better not take Maggie, lest old antagonisms between Hinds and Mr Eyre complicated the discussion. She'd bring Greg Wharf along. Mike Hinds might be one of those old-fashioned blokes who didn't take women police officers seriously. Pick one maverick to deal with another.

Her next call was to Kit Payne. She made it as far as his PA, who insisted he was in conference, and couldn't be disturbed, but booked her in for the following day – 'Only an hour, mind. He has an important meeting with a delegation from the Bulgarian Holiday Home Association.'

In between lunch and an interview for the force blog

about the previous evening's award ceremony, she tried ringing Daniel, but his phone was on voicemail. Oh well. At least she had a date with Mario Pinardi.

'How could you do that to your own brother?'

Orla's voice jangled in Aslan's brain. He'd roamed the country lanes hour after hour, losing track of time. His shoes were pinching his toes. Tomorrow, he'd have blisters, but so what? Anything to put off the moment when he came face-to-face with Michael Hinds.

Of course, he should have been kinder to Orla, but now it was too late. He'd never done regrets, and now wasn't a good time to start. Once she'd come back to his squalid bedsit, and he'd shocked her by offering to share a joint the moment they stepped through the door. She made it clear she wanted to talk, to reminisce about her childhood with Callum, and the days leading up to his disappearance. He was sure she'd dreamt that he was Callum, come back to find her – it was her very own fairy tale. She'd detected a resemblance, something in the shape of his head, and the way he walked, not to mention the almond colour of his eyes. The line between fantasy and reality was hard to draw.

It didn't help that she was pissed. When she took off her headscarf, he saw her bald head for the first time. Her features were pretty, but the smooth scalp turned him off. He gave her a can of beer, while he had a smoke. When he dropped a few hints about his past, she didn't seem to take it in. He'd assumed she would be happy, but instead she was bemused. They talked for a while, but when she sat herself down on the side of his bed and asked for a cuddle

– for comfort, she said, that was all – he drew away. She must have seen the distaste in his eyes, for a tear trickled down her cheek. This infuriated him, and when he'd said something cruel, her face twisted in pain. She jumped up and ran off down the stairs. Of course, he didn't follow.

What was it about women? The easier he found it to attract them, the sooner he wanted them out of his sight. His mother had doted on him, had given everything she could and asked him for nothing in return, but a heart attack had taken her away from him at a stupidly young age, while he was on board a ship in the Adriatic. At her funeral he'd wept, but no woman since had stirred his emotions.

A muck spreader thundered down the narrow lane towards him and he pressed against a hedge to allow it to pass. For a nanosecond, he understood the strange impulse that had caused Orla to take her own life. How easy to leap under the heavy wheels at the last moment, and put an end to everything. A cop-out, yes, but at least he'd be rid of his baggage for good. No more complications, no more crushed expectations.

How long had he dreamt of making his way back to Lane End Farm? Across three continents, and for as long as he could remember, yet now he saw the fields in the distance, he felt a chill that the sun's warm rays could not dispel.

His nerve ends jangled, pins and needles pricked his fingertips. He patted the butterfly knife in his pocket, but for once it didn't give him the warmth of reassurance. He wasn't spoiling for a fight. But he was afraid.

DS Mario Pinardi was tall, dark and handsome. Unfortunately, as far as his female admirers in Cumbria

Constabulary were concerned, he was also married, to a stunningly lovely lady, a fellow Scot of Italian descent. Hannah's best friend, Terri, had met Mario at a Cumbria Constabulary charity dance years ago, and still asked after him, but she was wasting her time. Photographs of Alessandra Pinardi, along with young Roberto, Davide and Claudio, festooned the walls of Mario's cubbyhole in the police station in Keswick. His family-man image might have been tedious if he were not such good company. Hannah liked him enough to push to one side the sneaking suspicion that he was in the same mould as Will Durston. Insufficiently driven to make a first-rate detective. She was prejudiced by her apprenticeship with Ben Kind. The job came before your private life, was Ben's creed. Mind you, Ben had messed up his own private life, and hers was going down the pan as well. Mario was wiser than both of them.

'Horrible way to go, drowning in grain,' he said. 'Fancy a cup of tea?'

Hannah and Greg shook their heads, and he grinned. 'Good decision, it's out of a machine and tastes like weasel pee.'

'Any words of wisdom from the pathologist?'

'Orla cracked her head on the side of the tower on her way down. Nasty gash, the blow probably knocked her unconscious. Otherwise, she might have been able to climb back up.'

'If she wanted to,' Greg said.

'True, but the deputy coroner is a softie. If she can find a way of turning this into an accident, rather than suicide, she will. Easier for the family to bear, especially the father. Bad enough to find your one remaining child lying dead in a heap of grain. Worse if you torment yourself over whether you could have done anything to persuade her not to jump.'

'You're sure she did jump?'

'If anyone wanted to do away with her on a farm, there are plenty of easier murder methods. You couldn't drag an unwilling victim all the way up to the top of a grain silo.'

'Might someone have talked her into making the climb?' Greg asked.

'To take a look at the interesting grain? I don't think so. She'd been boozing, there were empty cans on the passenger seat of her car. God knows what was in her mind, but she wanted to climb that tower. The only reasonable assumption is, she intended to jump.'

'She grew up on the farm,' Hannah said. 'If she had suicidal thoughts, she'd know there was no guarantee that she'd die. The cavalry might have ridden to the rescue. In the shape of her father, or his labourers.'

'If they saw her go up there, or heard her yelling for someone to drag her out. If not . . .' Mario made a throat-slitting gesture.

'Might have been a cry for help,' Hannah said. 'People weren't taking her seriously. She wanted Callum's case reopened, nobody was listening . . .'

Mario winced. 'Do you really want to go there, Hannah? I heard about those calls she put in to you and your team. Let's not encourage the IPCC to get excited, eh? When those guys go off on a wild goose chase, you never know how long it will last, or where it will lead. Keep it simple, that's my recommendation.'

He meant to be supportive, but her stomach wrenched

with frustration. If she'd wanted an easy life, she wouldn't have joined the police in the first place.

'Orla didn't give us enough to enable us to take any action. She was unhappy, and she'd had too much to drink . . .'

Greg said, 'You don't haul yourself up a grain tower just to enjoy the view from the top.'

'Her father says she and her brother used to love playing in the grain,' Mario said. 'Once the silo was built, he put it out of bounds. Maybe she was reliving childhood memories. The mind can play strange games.'

He said it as though he'd read the phrase in a book. Hard to imagine sensible, uxorious Mario allowing his own mind to play games. Yet his theory was persuasive, if obsessing over Callum meant Orla wanted to relive their shared past. 'How is the father? You'd think he'd be prostrate, but when I rang the farm, he was out working as usual.'

'That's farmers for you,' Mario said. 'On duty twenty-four/seven; it's not so much a job as a way of life. Doesn't mean Hinds isn't gutted. But he'd never show weakness. Strong man, very proud. We offered him a leaflet about bereavement counselling, and he ripped it up without a word.'

'Didn't he realise Orla had come to the farm?'

'He says not, it came as a total surprise. And nobody seems to have seen her climb into the silo.'

'Do we believe that?'

'Lane End isn't swarming with workers, like most dairy farms these days. Hinds has cut back on headcount to keep turning a profit. His labourers are Polish, and they were scattered far and wide over two hundred acres. Given the path she took from the rear of the farm to the silo, it might have been more surprising if somebody had spotted her.'

'Unless they were looking out for her?' Greg suggested.

'Nobody seems to have had the faintest idea she meant to come to the farm. The pathologist thinks the time of death was not long after she dived into the grain. We'll know more once the PM is completed.'

'The gash on the head,' Greg said. 'Any chance it might have been inflicted by someone else?'

'There are blood traces on the inside of the tower, where we believe she banged her head,' Mario said. 'Indications are that the impact was severe enough to knock her out, and when she came round, she was up to her waist in grain and unable to free herself. It would have been dark inside, and the noise would have prevented her from attracting attention. The next load probably buried her. The one after that would have been fatal.'

'Open-and-shut case?' Greg asked.

'Trust me, she killed herself. That's the reality of what happened; whether she changed her mind when she recovered consciousness is academic. We don't need to overelaborate, it's simple. Same as your cold case, I guess.'

'We'll see,' Hannah said. 'I want to ask Michael Hinds if he still thinks his brother killed his son.'

'Better wear your body armour, then.'

'You think so?'

'I'm sure so. Orla tried to persuade him that Philip didn't murder the boy, and their conversation turned into a furious row.' He lowered his eyes, as if struggling to comprehend why some families could never be happy. 'Pity – that was the last time she and her father ever spoke to each other.'

Until now, Aslan had always found it easy to take decisions. Go there, say this, pretend to do that. Perhaps the secret was that none of it seemed to matter. Once he'd arrived at the Lakes, decisions became harder to take. In the past he'd scoffed at ditherers, people who were afraid to act. But did they hesitate simply because they cared too much?

Outside Lane End Farm, he'd encountered a couple of labourers who had sneaked out for a crafty smoke. The men exchanged a few words in a foreign language, and wandered back into the farmyard. Maybe they thought he was an undercover snooper from the Border Agency, checking up on migrant workers. If only they knew his own visa was phoney, bearing a made-up name, and that his knees were knocking with apprehension.

So far he hadn't caught sight of Mike Hinds. He knew what the man looked like, he'd memorised his appearance thanks to Orla. A sentimentalist, she'd kept dog-eared photographs of her parents as well as Callum, and she'd shown them to Aslan over a drink in a bar. For once, he hadn't needed to fake interest.

No matter how many times he rehearsed what he might say when they came face-to-face, it never sounded right.

You don't know me, but . . .

I know this will come as a shock . . .

Sorry to disturb you, but we need to talk . . .

Please don't slam the door in my face, please . . .

Shit, he was no good at this. He hated his own weakness. People who knew him would never believe it; everyone thought he was brash, so why had confidence deserted him, when he needed it most?

He heard a car with a quiet engine, coming down the lane. Even before he set eyes on it, instinct told him the police were coming. Surely they could not be on to him?

His stomach felt queasy. This was all too difficult. He wanted to run away and hide.

Hannah smelt the farm before she set eyes on it. She had the sunroof open, making the most of the weather. Sitting behind her, Greg had spread notes about the Callum Hinds case over the back seat and was studying them in uncharacteristic silence. The lane traipsed around a forbidding hawthorn hedge, and petered out in a tight turning space. North of the lane, woodland stretched towards the slopes of the fells. The caravan park was masked by trees. Lane End might have been in the middle of nowhere, rather than five minutes' drive from the centre of Keswick.

Crumbling stone pillars guarded a dirt track leading to the stone farmhouse. Ugly single-storey extensions had been added on either side of the building, as if to remind visitors that this was a workplace, not the setting for some rural idyll. No front garden, just an open space where a mud-spattered estate car and a couple of farm vehicles were parked.

As Hannah reversed in the turning space, she caught sight of someone in her rear-view mirror. A tall man with a thick mass of hair and a beard, standing next to one of the stone pillars. He wore a T-shirt and shorts, and she'd have assumed he was one of the myriad walkers who swarmed over the Lake District, if he'd had a rucksack on his back.

But there was no rucksack. As the car swung round, the man stared at them, before turning on his heel. Within moments, he rounded the hawthorn hedge and vanished from sight.

'What do you suppose he was up to?' Hannah asked.

'I've heard of trainspotters.' Greg shrugged. 'But farmyard spotters?'

The only greenery this side of the fields was the thick ivy curtain around the entrance porch. A cobbled yard separated the house from a slurry tank, a straggle of steel-framed sheds and a two-storey L-shaped brick outbuilding. Two swarthy labourers watched from behind a tractor as the two detectives got out of the car. They muttered to each other in a language that Hannah recognised as Polish. You heard it spoken a lot in the Lake District nowadays; the place was a magnet for people who wanted work and didn't expect to be paid the earth. She caught the word *policja*, and for a moment she thought they were about to come up and buttonhole her. But one of the men put a restraining hand on his companion's wrist, as if he'd had second thoughts. Before Hannah could approach them, they hurried off towards the sheds.

'Ever get the feeling that people are avoiding you?' Hannah said as she locked the car.

'All the time,' Greg murmured. 'Cold Comfort Farm, eh? They're not exactly rolling out the red carpet.'

'Maggie has a favourite phrase,' Hannah said. '*Every farm is unique*. Each has its own design, but more than that. Each has a distinct personality.'

'Yeah, well, what does that make Lane End?' he asked. 'A surly recluse?'

A muck spreader roared in the distance as they rang the doorbell. Deirdre Hinds kept them waiting a whole minute before she opened up. In her early forties, she was short and squat and carrying too much weight. Her cheeks were pasty, and her eyes red-rimmed. Distress due to her stepdaughter's death? Her hands were covered in flour, and she didn't offer to shake.

'Inspector Scarlett, is it? He'll be somewhere around the yard. You'll have to excuse me, I'm busy baking.'

The door banged shut in their faces before they could utter a word.

'Charming,' Greg said. 'And there was I, hoping she'd offer us a traditional farmhouse tea.'

'Wonder what she made of Orla?' Hannah said as they headed for the yard.

'She doesn't look like a wicked stepmother to me. Downtrodden, yes. I bet her old man wasn't happy that she arranged this meeting.'

Hannah pointed to the top of the silver tower, visible in the distance above the roof of the barn. 'That must be the silo where Orla died.'

Greg made a face. 'I can think of better places to finish up.'

'What would be your choice, then?'

'Easy.' He smirked. 'A nightclub, surrounded by lap dancers. Expiring happily at the age of ninety-seven.'

'In your dreams.'

'You did ask, ma'am.'

Insidious, how working alongside someone changed your attitude towards them, for better or worse. She'd heard a good deal about Greg before he joined her team, most of it bad. Lauren Self loathed him, which explained his banishment to Cold Cases. Yet although he had an ego the size of Blackpool Tower, she'd begun to warm to him. In her head, Ben Kind growled, 'For Christ's sake, don't get soft in your old age.' Good advice. Given an inch, Greg would take a mile.

Their path took them towards a tall building with a corrugated roof. Inside stood a fearsome metal contraption with a conveyor belt and a huge circular saw with teeth sharper than a shark's. On the ground at the far end of the machine was a big sack filled with poplar logs.

'DIY wood cutter,' Greg said. 'Naughty, naughty. Bet he makes sure it's out of sight when the health and safety people come round to inspect. Lethal, by the look of it. If Orla Payne wanted a quick exit, she could have squatted on the conveyor and switched on the saw.'

'Nasty way to go.'

'Hey, a few nanoseconds of agony, and it's done. As compared to – what?' He pretended to squirm. 'Trapped in a pile of grain, waiting for the loader to dump the next batch. Think about it. Knowing the stuff will suffocate you, and able to do bugger all to save yourself.'

Hannah swallowed. 'Point taken.'

The barn loomed before them. Stone steps led up to the haylofts; calves squealed in the bays below. A spade and scythe leant against one wall. At the sound of unfamiliar voices, a broad-shouldered man in a faded black T-shirt and grubby jeans came out of the nearest bay. Hair grey and close-cropped, face weather-beaten, arms muscular. A line of sweat gleamed on his brow. He considered them rather as he might weigh up cats caught in a hen coop.

'Mr Hinds? My name is Detective Chief Inspector Scarlett, and I head the Cold Case Review Team. This is DS Greg Wharf. Thanks very much for sparing us a few minutes.'

'My time is money.'

Mike Hinds had a strong local accent, which he seemed to be laying on with a trowel, as if he liked to play the horny-handed son of toil. But there was more to him than that; he'd spent a year studying natural sciences at Cambridge before giving up and going back to the family farm. Bloody-minded, yes, but intelligent.

'We understand that, Mr Hinds.'

'Then hopefully you won't cost me more than a few quid, Chief Inspector. I've already spent a long time talking to your people about Orla.'

He stood on the cobbles, legs wide apart, hands thrust deep into his pockets. His sceptical tone made her rank sound like proof of declining standards, as if she'd been promoted because she was a thirty-something woman, not a proper detective. Hannah ground her teeth, unwilling to give him the satisfaction of provoking her temper.

'We'd like to ask you a few questions about Callum's disappearance.'

'When my wife told me you wanted to talk about my son, I thought she must have got her wires crossed.' Hannah guessed Deirdre had felt the rough edge of his tongue. 'What has Callum got to do with this? He died twenty years ago.'

Were his eyes glistening? Could be the sunlight, rather than tears.

'I'm sorry, Mr Hinds, I understand this is a difficult time for you.'

'Oh, you understand, do you?' He took a stride forward, and for an instant, she thought he meant to grab hold of her and wrap his meaty fingers around her throat. 'A boy dead, twenty years back, and now his sister? You've got dead children of your own, have you? Do you really *feel my pain*?'

Hannah remembered the unborn child she had lost. *Don't go there.* He didn't know; he was a wounded animal, lashing out in a confusion of grief, rage and self-defence.

'Might be easier if we went inside, Mr Hinds,' Greg said. 'This doesn't need to take long.'

All of a sudden, her DS had morphed into Mr Nice Guy, affable as a saloon bar chum. It was like watching an alien bodysnatcher assume the appearance of a harmless human being. But Hinds wasn't shifting.

'Don't worry, Sergeant. It definitely won't take long, you can bet on that.'

'Orla contacted the Cold Case Review Team this week,' Hannah said. 'She wanted us to look afresh at what happened to her brother.'

Mike Hinds flexed his muscles. Habit, or a warning sign? 'She knew bloody well what happened.'

'She discussed the case with a variety of people after coming back to this area. It's clear she wasn't satisfied that her uncle was responsible for Callum's disappearance.'

'She didn't have a clue,' Hinds said. 'As a kid, she preferred fairy tales to reality, and she never got them out of her system. Things got worse once the booze started to rot her brain. Just like it rotted her mother's.'

'Niamh didn't believe Philip killed Callum either, did she?'

'Her state of mind depended on how pissed she was. After Callum went missing, she was in . . . what do you call it?' He glared. 'Denial?'

'Philip didn't leave a suicide note, or any confession. There is no proof he harmed a hair on your son's head.'

'Hanged himself, didn't he? What better evidence do you want?'

'He'd been interviewed by the police, he must have been scared witless. A man with learning difficulties, under intolerable pressure, who had never learnt effective coping skills.'

'He was pathetic. So fucking weak.'

Mike Hinds spat out the words, and Hannah saw in his eyes that nothing, in his book, was more contemptible than weakness. He must have despised Philip for as long as he could remember.

Greg said, 'After the divorce, Niamh made it hard for you to see Callum. Women do that sometimes, don't they? The law's in their favour, and they use it to their advantage. Driven by some sort of thirst for revenge.'

'She was a mean bitch.'

Greg nodded towards the barn. 'Couldn't hack it, I suppose. Farm life doesn't suit everyone, eh?'

'Farmers marry farmers' daughters, it's the best way, but I met an Irish girl with big tits at a club in Carlisle and let myself get carried away. Biggest mistake of my life.'

'Often let yourself get carried away, do you?'

'Not by women,' Hinds said. 'Least, not for a long while.'

He fixed his eyes on Hannah. She was wearing a cream trouser suit and open-neck blouse. Lauren had issued fresh 'standards of expectation' a month back, as part of her campaign to smarten up the force's image, and as a DCI, Hannah was expected to take a lead when it came to dress code. In the age of austerity, the emphasis was on looking sober and businesslike – no earrings for men, no tattoos likely to offend, no violently coloured hair. And certainly, nothing too revealing. Hinds didn't look impressed.

'You did better second time around,' Greg said.

'Deirdre? Yeah, she's not quite such a pain in the arse as Niamh.'

Don't go overboard with the compliments, Hannah thought. Spare a thought for what it's like for a woman, trying to make a life with you. But she kept her mouth shut. Greg was doing fine, talking man to man.

'You got to know her before Callum went missing?'

'She was only young at the time. Training to be a farm secretary; we met at an NFU do. Her dad had a sheep farm, a few miles this side of the Scottish border. Thankless task – poor sod went bankrupt six months before cancer got him. Deirdre was one of five, the baby of a family that didn't have two pennies to rub together.'

'Until you provided a roof over her head?'

'We didn't live together until we'd been courting for eighteen months. Things were different in them days, and I bided my time. Once bitten, you know?'

Greg said with feeling, 'I do know.'

'Deirdre would come over here to visit, then go back home. Bit by bit, she started staying the night.'

'How did Niamh react?'

Hinds snorted. 'She got wind I was seeing Deirdre, not that it was any of her business after she'd run off with Kit Payne.'

'I bet it didn't stop her grabbing her pound of flesh in the divorce settlement.'

'You're not wrong. She tried to say it wasn't good for Callum, hanging around here.'

Greg chuckled. 'When you might be occupied with your girlfriend?'

'He caught us at it once, admitted.'

'You're kidding!'

'Nah, we were on the sofa in the back room.' Hinds had his eyes on Hannah. The idea of shocking her appealed to him, she thought; he couldn't resist the temptation to talk. 'I couldn't wait to get her upstairs, and we suddenly realised he was watching us through the window.'

'Bloody hell.' Greg sounded almost admiring. Hannah realised, not for the first time, that she was very glad not to be a man. Talk about basic instincts. 'What happened?'

'Told his sister, the daft sod, and of course she opened her trap to Niamh. I think he'd guessed what he was going to see, but there you go. He wanted an eyeful, and by Christ, he got it. She was a bonny lass, Deirdre, before she started eating too much chocolate cake. Anyroad, that's teenage lads for you.'

Greg nodded. 'Yet Niamh reacted badly?'

'Too fucking right. Hypocritical cow – she was the one who started shagging a businessman whilst she was still married to me. Talk about one law for the rich.'

'How did she get to know Kit Payne?'

'I've known old man Madsen and his family all my life. Bryan's stand-offish, doesn't care to mix with riff-raff like me, but Gareth's not so bad.'

'You were students together, weren't you?'

'For a year, that's all. I couldn't stick the place. Full of posh folk who talked through their arses. They made me sick, but Gareth had a whale of a time. He loves being cock of the walk. Anyroad, he introduced Niamh and me to Payne. I would never have guessed she'd fall for Payne – he's as ugly as sin. But she hated being a farmer's wife, and he lent a shoulder for her to cry on.'

'Money talks, eh?'

'Yeah, when she broke the news she was running off with Keswick's answer to Quasimodo, I didn't know whether to laugh or cry.'

'And she used the incident with Deirdre as an excuse to prevent Callum visiting you?'

Hinds' face darkened. 'There was no cause for her to take it out on the boy. To stop him from seeing his dad was pure malice.'

'He kept your surname. That says a lot.'

'He was made of sterner stuff than Orla, she just wanted everything to be happy ever after. Niamh liked to have things her way; why do you think the kids were given Irish names? I wanted Callum to be christened Eric, after my dad, but she wouldn't hear of it. But she couldn't watch over the boy twenty-four hours a day. She and Payne only lived across the field; no way could she stop us seeing each other every now and then.'

Greg nodded. 'When was the last time you saw your son?'

Hinds frowned. 'You'll have read my statement?'

'At the time Callum disappeared, you said you hadn't seen him for some time. But was that right? Niamh is dead now, it can't make any difference.'

'If it makes no difference, why ask?'

'We need to be clear about Callum's movements in the period leading up to his disappearance. The more accurate our information, the better our chance of making sense of what Orla was saying.'

The farmer kicked at a pebble, and sent it skittering across the cobbles. 'So what if he did come and see me? Where does that get you?'

'It's simply a question of building an accurate picture of his movements.' Greg's tone was so soothing, Hannah half-expected him to start crooning a lullaby. 'Did he come here before he visited your brother?'

Hinds scowled. 'If that's in your mind, think again. All right, the last time I saw him was the night before he disappeared.'

Well, well, a result. This was what Hannah liked about cold case work. Sometimes, just sometimes, you unearthed treasure trove. Important evidence that had lain buried for years.

Greg's expression didn't flicker. He was too smart to give away the excitement he must be feeling. 'What happened?'

'I used to make my own beer in those days, and Callum slipped over here after Niamh gave him his tea. He told her he had a headache, and wanted a breath of fresh air. As soon as the coast was clear, he scooted over and we knocked back a few glasses of home brew. He loved the stuff, it had a bit of body to it. Not like the bat's piss you get served nowadays.'

'He was only fourteen,' Hannah said.

Shit, why did I open my big mouth? She should have

bitten her tongue. Greg gave her a pained look, and no wonder, after he'd got on to the witness's wavelength. She edged backwards, in tacit apology.

'So what? His mother may have been a drunk, but I'm not. It's all about knowing your limits. He came to no harm with me.'

'Deirdre wasn't around?' Greg asked.

'After that time he saw her starkers, she made a point of checking when Callum was likely to show up. Not that she's easily embarrassed, but she drew the line at having a teenage lad gawping at her knockers.'

'Yeah, well, that's women for you.' Hannah felt she had become invisible. If it was punishment for her indiscretion, she could scarcely complain. They were like two mates, bad-mouthing the opposite sex over a pint. 'Did he tell you he was going to see Philip the following day?'

'Never mentioned it.'

'Did Niamh object to him seeing your brother?'

'Not on your nelly. Shows what sort of a mother she was, uh? Refused to let him visit his own father, yet happy for him to call on an oddball with a brain like mashed potato. Always had a soft spot for Philip, reckoned I was too hard on him.'

'So what did you and Callum talk about?'

'Usual sort of stuff. England's crap batting in the Test match. Carlisle United's prospects for promotion.'

'Bonding, eh?'

'Whatever you like to call it. Father-and-son stuff.' Hinds glared. He was angry about life's unfairness, Hannah thought, far more than their intrusion. 'The boy had his whole life in front of him. He'd had time to forget school and start enjoying his summer holiday. No wonder he was excited.'

'Excited?'

'Yeah. It's how I remember him. Pleased with life. And himself.'

Hannah couldn't contain herself any longer. 'Any particular reason why he would be excited?'

Hinds glared at her. 'Such as?'

'Was it about a girl?' Greg asked. 'He'd met a teenager on the caravan site.'

'That was a load of bollocks, for a start,' Hinds said. 'The girl's father tried to say that Callum was spying on her. Chances are, she made the whole thing up. Who knows? Maybe she'd led Callum on, and then got cold feet and was afraid of her dad going ballistic.'

'Did he have a girlfriend?'

A shake of the head. 'He was only fourteen.'

'I had girlfriends before I was fourteen.'

'Look, he was interested in girls, yes, but I told him there was no hurry.'

'And did he take your advice?'

'What are you getting at?' Hinds' face reddened under the sunburn. 'My boy was no peeping Tom.'

'Despite watching his father at it with his lady friend on the sofa?'

'A young lad's natural curiosity. You can't read anything into it.'

'The girl's story makes him sound like a voyeur.'

'The little cow lied.' Hinds balled his fists, struggling to control his temper. 'It's what women do. Just like my bloody stupid wife, when she told me you'd not bother me for more than ten minutes. Come on, I've answered your questions fair and square. Time's up.'

He waved beefy hands at them, indicating the way back out of the farm. He might have been shooing animals through a gate.

'Had Orla discovered something about Callum?' Hannah asked. 'Did she mention it to you the last time you were together?'

'I said all I've got to say about my daughter yesterday.'

'Finding her like that must have been a terrible experience, Mr Hinds. We only want—'

'Didn't you hear me?' he yelled.

'Take it easy, eh?' Greg said.

For answer, Hinds bent and lifted up the scythe. 'Get off my fucking land.'

'Mr Hinds.' Hannah's voice sounded thin in the silence. 'You have been cooperative so far. Please don't do anything you will regret.'

The farmer's face had blackened with fury. With the scythe in his right hand, he advanced towards them. He'd come to within two or three strides of Greg. Five yards further back, Hannah froze.

Stomach churning, she exchanged glances with her DS. He gave her the faintest nod and mouthed: *Run for it.*

No way was she abandoning him. She shook her head.

Sunlight flashed on the curve of the blade. Hannah fought the instinct to retch with fear. The wrong move now . . .

'All right, Mr Hinds.' Greg must be wetting himself, though you'd never guess from his relaxed tone. The scythe was within striking distance of his neck. 'Thanks for speaking to us.'

'You should never have come here,' Hinds muttered.

Hannah heard the door of the farmhouse open. Out of the corner of her eye, she spotted Deirdre Hinds. She stood on the doorstep, shaking with fear. Not knowing what her husband might do.

He took another pace towards Greg, who raised his hands to shoulder height. Whether to calm the man down or for self-protection, Hannah couldn't tell.

'Mike!' Deirdre screamed. 'Put it down!'

'Piss off back inside,' he shouted back. 'This is nothing to do with you.'

'Mike, this won't solve anything! What do you think Orla would have said, if she'd seen you like this?'

The farmer stopped in his tracks. In a swift and smooth movement, Greg jumped forward, seized the man's wrist, and twisted it. Hinds let out a cry of pain and dropped the scythe. Greg kicked it over the cobbles, out of reach.

Hinds spat at Greg. The DS wiped his face, gave Hinds' wrist a final jerk, and dropped it. Turning on his heel, he strode back to join Hannah and they both hurried off towards the drive.

'You shouldn't have done that, you scumbag,' Hinds roared. 'Next time, I'll be ready for you.'

They strode past the farmhouse. Deirdre stood motionless on the doorstep, hands clasped as if in prayer.

'I'd get him to a doctor double quick, love, if I were you,' Greg muttered over his shoulder. 'A psychiatrist is what he needs. I've heard of people with anger management issues, but your old man's a powder keg, waiting to explode.'

'Do you really think I don't know what he's like?' she hissed.

Hannah glanced back at the cobbled yard. Mike Hinds winced as he rubbed his injured wrist. Shit. If Greg had fractured it, they had a problem on their hands. Next stop, the IPCC.

'If you need help, dial 999. We can have backup here in minutes. Support is available, trust me.'

'Trust you?' Bitterness made Deirdre Hinds' voice grate. 'Ask the police for help? Don't you think you've helped enough for one fucking day?'

And she ran towards her husband.

CHAPTER EIGHT

The door to the Old Library creaked open, and Daniel glanced down from his eyrie as Fleur Madsen walked in. Short rapid strides, this woman knew what she wanted. Cool and chic in white shirt and trousers, designer sunglasses dangling from a small hand with orange fingernails, she didn't look as though she'd turned up for an hour or two of quiet scholastic research.

Daniel watched her scan the ground floor. Today he'd faced no competition for his favourite corner table. The sunshine was tempting, but his book wouldn't write itself. No climate control system cooled St Herbert's, and although the mullioned window behind him fitted its frame imperfectly, there wasn't enough breeze to make the pages of his typescript flutter. The reek of leather and calfskin filled his sinuses. Readers came and went, only the books stayed for ever.

Looking up to the gallery, Fleur caught sight of him. She signalled with the sunglasses, and hastened towards the spiral staircase. Stiletto heels clicked on the metal treads as she climbed, cracking the silence like warning shots. What did she want?

Fleur arrived at his side, and bent her head. He caught a strong whiff of Chanel as she whispered in his ear.

'Sorry, I know you're working. Please tell me to go away if I'm a nuisance.'

She said it as though no man in his right mind would ever tell her to go away.

'Great to see you again.'

'Difficult to work in this heat, isn't it?'

He smiled, said nothing.

'Could you spare me five minutes? We could have a word outside in the garden if that suited you?'

He shut down his laptop and followed her down the staircase. Her figure was gym-toned, her movements lithe. She was in her fifties, but you'd never guess. An intelligent well-bred woman who had married a millionaire, Fleur Madsen had it all. So how come he detected a restlessness in her that hinted at discontent?

On the ground floor, she swept past the catalogues and the desk where the librarian sat, through folded-back double doors into the rear of the building. Daniel had bumped into Orla here, the last time he'd seen her, and they'd agreed to grab a bite together. She should have been working, but he sensed she'd lost interest in her job and preferred to browse through collections of old papers. Here the De Quincey correspondence was stored, along with Sir Milo Hopes' extensive archives; thousands more volumes were packed into towering book presses.

'I told Micah to put more warning signs on the presses,'

she murmured. 'If you were crushed between them, you'd end up as flat as a dust jacket.'

Done to death by books? There were worse ways to go, even if you weren't a bibliophile. Like suffocating in a mountain of grain.

Beyond the last book press lay a steep flight of stairs and a door marked *Private*. Fleur fished a key from her trouser pocket and, with the gentlest touch on his shoulder, guided Daniel through the door. Grey blinds masked the windows, and even on such a bright day, she had to switch on the lights. Gilt-framed portraits of solemn dignitaries, along with a scattering of landscapes, covered each of the oak-panelled walls. A dozen chairs were grouped around a mahogany table. There were no bookshelves, but a drinks cabinet squatted in one corner. Daniel's throat felt dry and dusty. In the heat of the afternoon, the darkness of the wood and paintings was claustrophobic.

'The trustees meet here. Even the principal is allowed to enter only by invitation.' Fleur indicated the largest painting. 'That formidable old chap with mutton chop whiskers is Sir Milo Hopes, founder of St Herbert's and first chairman of the trustees. That is the house I was born in – and there you see the Hanging Wood in autumn.'

Two landscapes faced them. In fading light, Mockbeggar Hall was all flaking stonework and shuttered windows, a study in grandeur tainted by decay. But his attention was seized by the other painting, captioned *The Hanging Wood*. So this was where Orla's brother was last seen alive, and their uncle committed suicide. At first glance, the woodland scene, with dense foliage glimpsed through morning mist, seemed tranquil, if sombre. Dew glistened on bracken and ferns, a bird drifted between the branches. But the fallen leaves were curled and dead, the small pond looked stagnant, and a fox sneaked through the undergrowth with something in its mouth.

'The style is familiar.' He pondered. 'Not Millais, by any chance?'

She clapped her hands in delight. 'Brilliant, really well recognised! This pair of pictures are not at all well known. I'm not a fan of his work, too often it seems cloying. But he must have been reading 'The Fall of the House of Usher' when he painted the Hall – it's as if he anticipates our family's financial downfall. And *The Hanging Wood* haunts me. Not his best work artistically, you can see he rushed it. But I like the lack of sentimentality.'

He suspected Fleur Madsen didn't have a trace of sentimentality in her DNA. How could she, if she'd annexed her ancestral home to a caravan park?

'I haven't ventured into the wood.'

'Not many people do. It's fenced off to deter trespassers, but frankly there are plenty of pleasanter walks on the doorstep. Even on a day like this, the Hanging Wood seems gloomy. When I was a child, I didn't play there, and to this day, I've never walked through it on my own. Millais stayed at the Hall a few times as a guest of Sir Milo. He was a dog lover, and he paid Millais a small fortune to paint the family pets. Those pictures are hack work in the style of his chum Landseer, but Milo proudly hung them in the dining room. I prefer these, which he dashed off and presented to Milo as a gift.'

'This was after Millais ran off with Ruskin's wife?'

'Oh yes, forty years later. You know the story? Ruskin

never consummated the marriage, although Effie was a lovely woman. They say he couldn't cope with the sight of her pubic hair.' She smiled and tapped her forehead in a parody of belated awareness. 'Doh! Of course you will know, you're a famous historian.'

He pointed to a door at the far end of the room. 'Shall we?'

'Of course. There aren't many perks for trustees, I'm afraid, but at least we have our own private garden.'

They moved outside into a tiny knot garden, crammed with herbs and screened from the rest of the grounds by a tall box hedge, into which was set a small bolted door. An aroma of marjoram wafted through the air, strong and sweet. She sat on the solitary wooden bench and beckoned to him. He joined her, keeping a few inches between them. She wanted something from him, and experience had taught him to be wary of attractive women accustomed to getting their own way.

Fleur smiled. 'Very Frances Hodgson Burnett, don't you think?'

'A secret garden, yes. Designed by Gertrude Jekyll, like the walled garden?'

'Actually, no. There's a rural legend that Beatrix Potter organised the planting, though I haven't found any evidence to back it up.' She put on a wistful little-girl face. 'I yearn to find some truth in it. The Blessed Beatrix is a much bigger draw than Gertrude. Tourists are so besotted with Peter bloody Rabbit, we could fill our accommodation with pilgrims from Japan.'

'Would the trustees be willing to sacrifice their privacy?'

'A price worth paying,' she said. 'Anyway, the sacrifice would be mine. I'm the only regular visitor to this little haven. It's so close to home, and believe me, if you live on a caravan park, you need to escape, every now and then.'

She made it sound as though she inhabited a dilapidated mobile home surrounded by washing lines and snivelling toddlers. Perhaps even a luxurious architect-designed mansion in a secluded enclave in Madsenworld represented a comedown from the splendour of living in a stately home, however dilapidated.

'Now Mockbeggar Hall is renovated—'

'It belongs to the company. And it's not a home anymore. The ground floor and part of the grounds will be opened to the public. Soon, visitors will be roaming around the nooks and crannies I loved as a child. I've spent years planning the project together with my husband and brother-in-law, but now it's almost complete, becoming involved with St Herbert's has made a refreshing contrast. Which brings me to why I interrupted your afternoon.'

She leant towards him, closing the gap that separated them.

'After we met, I started wondering if you . . .'

She paused, and he knew she was teasing him. He waited.

'Yes, I wondered if you would care to become a trustee of the library? I'd love to have you on board. We have to make sure St Herbert's is fit for purpose in the twenty-first century. Lottery funding for building maintenance and more acquisitions is an option, but we need a higher profile. An eminent historian, working here on his latest book – what could be better?'

Daniel murmured something non-committal. Ungrateful to refuse on the spot, but there was no way he wanted to join the great and the good of Cumbria. He'd sat on too many committees in Oxford and London; he was determined to remain his own man. He temporised, hoping she was smart enough to realise he didn't want her to push it.

'Of course, you need to think it over,' she said. 'But I do hope I can tempt you.'

When she looked into his eyes, he felt again the magnetic force of her personality. Fleur Madsen didn't take no for an answer.

'I promise to get back to you next week.'

'Fine, thank you.'

She touched him on the arm as they rose from the bench. As they retraced their steps, his eye was caught by a flash of sunlight on a window looking out on to the parapet on which Aslan Sheikh had stood the previous day.

'The staircase outside the trustees' meeting room,' he said. 'It doesn't lead to the gallery of the Old Library, does it?'

'No, it's another route to the offices and guest accommodation.'

Daniel indicated the window glinting in the sun. 'Fantastic views of the walled garden from a room like that. And of this garden too.'

'Yes, that was poor Orla's office, actually; it's next door to the room I use for St Herbert's business when I'm over here. She said she found the view quite inspirational – pity it didn't inspire her fund-raising work.' Sensing Daniel's disapproval, she added, 'Sorry, I don't mean to be unkind. Her death was a ghastly tragedy, but I have to say, I've always regarded suicide as a selfish act. Poor Kit was stunned by the news.'

'He was close to his stepdaughter?'

'He had a great deal to cope with because of Niamh's alcoholism, but he never let either Niamh or her daughter down. After Niamh died, he put Orla through university, and made sure she wasn't short of money, even though he'd started a new life with Glenys.'

'Do you know any more about how Orla died?'

'No, it's such an extraordinary thing to do. On her father's land, as well. None of us can quite believe it.' And she did sound bewildered, although he also sensed that something else was bothering her. 'Of course, we're desperate to find out more about what happened. Mike Hinds must be beside himself.'

'You know him well?'

'We grew up together, but we have never been close. His father had a chip on his shoulder about the Hopes family, even though we'd become as poor as church mice. As Mike grew up, he had a reputation as a ladies' man, but he never exercised his charm on me.'

She feigned a rueful expression, and Daniel shook his head in polite disbelief.

'Besides, Bryan asked me out on a date not long after my eighteenth birthday, and after that I was pretty much spoken for. Mike always gave me a wide berth – he and Bryan have never been pals. Poor Bryan assured me that one day he'd be prime minister, though I never got to see inside ten Downing Street. But we've been together for over thirty years. Through good times and bad, so to speak.'

'Mostly good, I'm sure.'

She raised her eyebrows. 'Oh yes, I'm very fortunate. Bryan was never cut out for the national political stage, and he was badly injured in an accident ages ago, which didn't help. But the combination of his business acumen and Gareth's salesmanship and flair is hard to beat. The park has gone from strength to strength, while farming is a struggle these days. Mike isn't an easy man, but he works damned hard.'

'Orla gave me the impression she and her father weren't close.'

'There were bound to be tensions after Niamh left the farm to live with Kit.' Fleur paused. 'Sham tells me you spent a lot of time talking to Orla.'

'We chatted, yes.'

'She saw the two of you munching baguettes together the other day. Orla's last at work, I think. She seemed upset, and you were trying to calm her down.'

Orla underestimated Sham, he thought, when she dismissed the girl as just a pretty airhead with rich parents, who played at working nine-to-five until she found a man she wanted to settle down with. The pretty face included a pair of lynx eyes.

'Orla told me about her brother who went missing.'

'Callum? That was heartbreaking. But . . . it was twenty years ago.' Fleur's brow furrowed. 'She never seems to have reached closure; it was such a shame.'

'I told her that if she had any concerns, she should talk to the police.'

'Surely they want hard evidence, not wild speculation? The case was finished once Philip hanged himself.' Fleur breathed out. 'Poor Orla, she must have been depressed.

She loved fairy tales, and I can't help thinking she made one up for herself about Callum.'

'So you believe Philip killed his nephew?'

'Absolutely, no other explanation made sense. Callum was a strange boy, but he'd never run away from home. I can't believe he is still alive, that he's stayed out of touch for all these years. Why did Orla torment herself, when the passage of time made it *more* certain that Philip was responsible for his death, not less?'

'She seemed to think someone else murdered him.'

'But that's ridiculous! Who else could have killed Callum?' Fleur shook her head. 'A passing tramp? I don't think so. You're not saying she had a suspect in mind?'

'If she did, she never told me. I had the impression she was flailing around, trying to make sense of stuff she didn't understand. Which is why I encouraged her to talk to the Cold Case Team. The woman who's in charge of it is a friend of mine; I thought she'd give Orla a fair hearing, and see if there was anything worth investigating.'

Fleur arched her eyebrows. 'You have friends in the Cumbria Constabulary?'

'My father used to be a police officer here.'

'I didn't know you come from the Lake District?'

'I don't. We lived in Manchester, but he left my mother for another woman and came up to the Lakes with her.'

'And now you've followed him?'

'He died some time ago.'

'I'm sorry, Daniel.' Fleur considered. 'Perhaps Orla was seeking attention. You're a well-known person, and if I may say so, a bit of a catch for anyone, let alone a girl like her. She probably wanted to make a big impression.'

'She was genuinely interested in history. And I am sure about one thing.' As he spoke, Daniel's intuition hardened into certainty. 'Orla had good reason to believe that Philip Hinds didn't kill her brother, even if she wasn't sure who did.'

Aslan knew the man and woman he'd seen at Lane End were police officers. They didn't have to be in uniform or to be driving a Panda car; he'd had enough to do with representatives of law and order to recognise that mix of watchfulness and assurance common to cops the world over. Ironic, deeply ironic. He'd taken so long to make it to Mike Hinds' home, and the moment he arrived, he'd needed to beat a hasty retreat to St Herbert's.

But nothing was lost. On the way back, he'd kept thinking about Orla, and some of the fuzziness in his mind was clearing. It was like groping your way through the mist as it cleared from the slopes of the Langdale Pikes.

Orla's muddled thinking and lack of coherence, coupled with the fact that in her last few days alive she'd rarely been entirely sober, meant that people paid little attention to what she said. Her habit, no doubt learnt from Callum, of keeping cards close to her chest, made matters worse.

Now he was getting somewhere at last after a false start the other day. He'd taken it into his head on a whim to break into Orla's room at the library while she was off sick, and see if he could find anything of interest. He'd committed a few petty thefts in his time, and never been caught, even though he'd had a few narrow squeaks; the secret of success was not worrying too much. Orla's door was locked, and when, in his frustration, he climbed up on to the parapet outside, and began to prise open an ill-fitting window, Daniel Kind's unexpected appearance in the garden, which was usually deserted in the morning, forestalled him. But once again, he'd got away with it. Daniel suspected nothing.

He'd toyed with the idea of picking Daniel's brains, seeing if he could cast more light on what Orla had told him. It might be worth the risk. Or it might just be a big mistake.

With hindsight, he was unlikely to have found anything worthwhile in Orla's room. She wasn't the type to write stuff down, she just let things whirl around in her head, as she struggled to make sense of fragments of knowledge.

The last time he was with her, she'd talked about Callum, and Castor and Pollux. He was bored rigid with her fondness for talking in riddles; she only did it to make herself seem interesting, and the moment he showed any interest, she'd retreat into coy evasion. Typical Orla. Once she had your attention, she never made good use of it. As for Castor and Pollux, he didn't have a clue who they were. But he meant to find out.

Orla was right about one thing: a library was the perfect place to learn stuff. He did a Google search the moment he got back to St Herbert's, and supplemented his knowledge with a glance at a couple of reference books. Within minutes he discovered that, in Greek and Roman mythology, Castor and Pollux were twin brothers who had the same mother but different fathers. One boy was mortal, and the other immortal. One destined to live with the gods, another doomed to lie among the dead.

The librarian, a rotund woman in her sixties, had,

since his arrival at St Herbert's, formed a deep distrust of his lack of interest in the literary treasures under her care, and watched him conducting his researches with ill-concealed suspicion. When he bestowed a charming smile upon her, she scowled like a gargoyle. The ungrateful old cow was impervious to charm. He found himself patting the butterfly knife in his pocket. Orla's reference to the old legend didn't make any sense to him, but he found it strangely disturbing.

'Provoking a deranged farmer to attack us with a scythe,' Greg Wharf said as Hannah accelerated away from Lane End. 'I'll be honest, ma'am, when we were discussing suicide, that particular MO never occurred to me.'

'Yeah, well, a close-up encounter with a wannabe Grim Reaper adds a touch of excitement to our tedious lives. What do you reckon to him?'

'Bad, bad news. Went to Cambridge, did he? Makes me thankful I screwed up my A Levels. Don't worry, his wrist won't have broken, but with any luck he'll sport a nasty bruise.'

'It's his wife I feel sorry for.'

'She doesn't have to stay with him.'

'Might not be easy to escape. He'll keep tight hold of the purse strings. More than likely, Deirdre would rather stick with the devil she knows. The question is whether that temper of his will get him into big trouble one day.'

'You suppose he knows more about what happened to Callum than he's let on?'

'He never mentioned the boy's last visit to him before today. But why would he want a cover-up?'

'He's not stupid. He wouldn't incriminate himself so casually.'

'What if he wanted to protect somebody?'

'Can't see it. Why help someone who has done away with your child?'

Hannah slowed the car, and nodded towards a high fence and clump of beeches to the right. 'See the big houses through the trees? That's where the Madsens live, and Kit Payne.'

'Hinds was right – not far for Callum to go. From Payne's house, he could have nipped over to Lane End and got back home inside a couple of hours, with plenty of time to sink a couple of pints of his Dad's home brew.'

At a fork in the lane, they halted at a large sign for Madsen's Holiday Home Park. A steel security barrier barred the way in. Visitors were told to report to a reception lodge in the style of a Swiss chalet, occupied by two smart men in uniform.

'Not so much a caravan site as an exclusive gated community, by the look of it,' Hannah said.

'I checked their prices on the website before we came out,' Greg said. 'My eyes haven't stopped watering. You could buy a three-bedroom semi in Kendal for less than one of their top-range caravans. Amazing. The Madsens must be rolling in it.'

'Not a business you'd want associated with the publicity surrounding a teenager's apparent abduction.'

'He might have done a runner, you know. Happens every day. His parents had split up, he wasn't on the best of terms with stepdaddy.'

'But to disappear completely, for ever . . .'

They drove on past a recently created second entrance to Madsen's park, close to its southern tip. Again, the way in was barred, but a large signboard proclaimed the glories of a 'State-of-the-Art Leisure Complex in Historic Mockbeggar Hall'. The new route linked in with the original service road to the site, and crossed a bridge over the stream that once divided the Hopes' estate from the caravan site. All this land had once belonged to a single family, and now it did again. Only this time, the owners were business people, not the landed gentry.

'I bet the Madsens shat themselves when they heard Callum was missing,' Greg said. 'Lucky for them that Philip was so quick to top himself.'

'You don't suppose they gave him a helping hand?'

'Hanged him and staged it as a suicide scenario, you mean?' Greg sucked in his cheeks. 'Difficult to achieve, easy to foul up. Too much of a risk.'

'Gareth Madsen is a risk-taker, even if his brother isn't. It says in the file that not only was he once a racing driver, he also had a spell working in a casino in Las Vegas.'

'Nah, why would he chance it? Philip Hinds' death was investigated through a microscope. Having a suspect hang himself the day after you've given him the third degree is never easy to explain away. The inquest verdict was suicide. If there was any evidence of murder, surely the truth would have come out.'

Hannah put her foot on the brake and brought the car to a standstill. A small brass plate on a wall, as discreet as the Madsens' signage was garish, announced that they had reached St Herbert's Residential Library.

'So that's where Orla worked.'

'Yeah, how long before the Madsens turn it into a pleasure palace, with rides and interactive fun days?'

'They don't own it, thank God. Milo Hopes set it up as a charity.'

'Fleur Madsen is Chair of the trustees, isn't she? That's how people like that operate. They call themselves networkers. I call them control freaks.'

'The rich are different, didn't someone say?'

'Yeah, like someone else said, they've got more money.'

Hannah squinted through the trees, trying to make out the library building. 'This is so close to where Orla grew up. It must have felt like coming back home.'

'Why would you want to come back, if home was Lane End Farm?'

'She never found happiness anywhere else, so why not?'

Greg shook his head. 'That's what baffles me about the countryside. All these open spaces, yet it's as claustrophobic as a broom cupboard. So many lives intertwined, it's worse than a soap opera. No wonder *The Archers* has kept going so long.'

'I like it,' Hannah said.

'What, *The Archers*?'

'When do I get the time to listen to the radio? No, the countryside.'

'Come on. It may look pretty, but the beauty's only skin-deep. There's more poverty in Cumbria than in most urban areas. And fewer places to shelter from the rain. What's so good about it?'

'The sense of community, for a start. That's what brought Orla Payne back, I guess. She was sick of being alone in the city.'

'Her father and stepdad had both remarried and moved on. Coming back to the country killed her.'

Hannah pressed the accelerator. 'Let's take a look at where she left her car. It's only half a mile away as the crow flies.'

'Not expecting to find clues, are you, ma'am?'

'I want to get into her mind. Try to figure out what drew her to that tower of grain.'

The lane wandered past the grounds of St Herbert's, and the edge of the old Mockbeggar Estate, before Hannah dived off on a short cut along a narrow track, with barely room enough for a single vehicle, no passing places, and half a dozen bends. To her relief, they reached Mockbeggar Lane without a close encounter with a tractor coming the other way.

Mario Pinardi had shown them photographs of Orla's car, prior to its removal, and they soon identified the flattened grass where she had parked. Hannah jumped out of the Lexus and walked up to the fence, Greg following behind.

'She wasn't keen for her father to see her,' Hannah said. 'Otherwise she'd have taken the same route we did, to Lane End, and approached the grain tower from the other side.'

'So she did mean to jump into the grain.'

'Must have done.'

Hannah swore to herself. She moved towards the electrified fence. Putting herself in the shoes of the young woman, who threw away her mobile phone, and contact with the outside world, followed by the scarf she'd worn to disguise the loss of her hair. Orla had given up. In her mind, life had nothing more to offer her; the abortive phone call to Linz Waller was the last straw. Not Linz's fault, but the accumulated failures had become too much. For everyone else, Callum was history. Nobody would listen.

In the distance, she spotted movement. A brown bird with pointed wings, hovering fifteen feet above the ground. A kestrel, with a field mouse, grasshopper or vole in its sights. As it swooped for the kill, she heard a rustling noise as Greg Wharf approached. She had a sudden awareness of his physical presence behind her. For a moment, she thought he was about to wrap his arms around her body.

'Are you all right, ma'am?'

There was a concern in his voice that she hadn't heard before. No trace of the laddish cynicism that she regarded as his default tone. And thank God, he didn't lay a finger on her.

She didn't turn straight away, needing to compose herself into the customary competent Hannah. She saw the kestrel rising, some small mammal caught in its beak. It whirled in triumph, as if expecting applause, before dashing for the trees to devour its prey.

'Yeah, I'm fine.'

'Hot, isn't it?'

'Uh-huh.'

'My throat's parched; I'm not used to so much sunshine in the Lakes. I don't suppose you've got time for a drink before you get back to Ambleside?'

She hesitated, aware that he was studying her. Weighing up his options, or simply waiting for the boss to make a simple decision?

'Thanks, but I'd better drop you off soon. I'm seeing a friend this evening.'

'Right.'

She guessed from his tone that he assumed the friend was a man. Tempting to let him think so, it was better to make it clear she wasn't available. Just in case he might be wondering. Mixing work and pleasure was never a good idea, no matter what the temptation. She'd never succumbed with Ben, whatever private thoughts had whirled around her mind, and any fool could see it would be a colossal mistake to get too close to Greg Wharf. Verging on the unthinkable.

However.

'She's my oldest mate, we were at school together. As a matter of fact, she met Mario Pinardi years ago, and ever since she's been a member of his fan club.'

Greg smiled an enigmatic smile.

'Aren't we all, ma'am?'

'Daniel!'

He turned to see Aslan Sheikh walking towards him across the car park from the main entrance to St Herbert's. Aslan's shoulders were hunched, making it look like he'd lost a couple of inches in height. Mud covered his shoes, as if he'd returned from a marathon yomp through the countryside. His face looked pale beneath the tan.

'Horrible news about Orla,' Daniel said.

'I never dreamt she would do such a thing. What could have possessed her?'

'You knew her better than I did,' Daniel said. 'But who can tell what goes through another person's mind?'

'When we talked yesterday, I didn't mean to put her down, please believe me.'

'Uh-huh.' Was Aslan feeling guilty, or just trying to redeem himself in Daniel's eyes?

'She was just . . . hard work. I had no idea she was desperate enough to do something so terrible. If she'd given me a clue of what was going through her head, it might have been—'

'Might-have-beens are a waste of time,' Daniel said. 'You said it yourself, you were just colleagues who went out together a few times.'

Aslan chewed his lower lip. 'You're right. I mean, we absolutely never slept together or anything.'

Too much information. Daniel flicked his key fob to unlock the door of his car.

'I haven't been able to concentrate.' Aslan moved closer, reluctant to let him go. 'I went for a long walk, trying to get my head straight. I finished up at the farm. From the lane, I saw the silo where she died. Imagine, Daniel, deprived of your breath by the sheer weight of the grain.'

'Better not to dwell on it, it won't help.'

'But how can I get her out of my mind?' Aslan exhaled. 'I can't stop thinking of Orla. She was fascinated by . . . by siblings.'

'Hansel and Gretel, you mean?'

'Hansel and Gretel.' A faraway look came into his eyes, reminding Daniel of a gambler contemplating a last throw of the dice. 'And Castor and Pollux.'

'Castor and Pollux?' Daniel frowned in puzzlement. 'That's not a fairy tale, though, is it?'

'You're right.' Aslan closed his eyes, and Daniel sensed he was playing a game, but didn't intend to explain the rules. 'Sorry, my head is spinning. There's too much to take in, it's not easy to make sense of things.'

Footsteps came clip-clopping over the gravel, and Aslan

spun round. Sham Madsen aimed an infrared key at the door of her sports car. It bore this year's registration plate. A present from Daddy, no doubt.

'Too nice to work overtime!' she called, gesturing to the cloudless sky. 'Fancy going into Keswick for a drink, Aslan?'

'I'm not—'

'Oh, come on. It'll do us both good. We deserve a pick-me-up after what's happened.'

Daniel watched the pair climb into the natty yellow car. Sham gave him a cheerful wave as she revved the engine, shattering the quiet of St Herbert's. Not everyone was in deep mourning for Orla Payne.

'The folk singer reminded me of Marc,' Terri said, as she returned from the bar to rejoin Hannah at their table under the spreading branches of a willow tree. 'Are you going to ask him to do a request after the interval?'

They'd come to listen to a folk singer perform in the beer garden of a pub-cum-hotel in Windermere. He wasn't exactly Paul Simon, and not simply because he was fair-haired and flat-voiced, but while the sun shone and the wine flowed, who cared?

'Marc's taller, and he doesn't have a cleft chin.' The wine was dry and strong. Already her head was starting to swim. 'And this guy is way less gorgeous.'

Terri squealed so loudly with merriment that a couple of heads turned. She never had many inhibitions at the best of times, and she'd got stuck in to the pina colada while waiting for Hannah to arrive. Just as well they'd booked cabs home.

'Tell you what, if you really are serious about giving up on dear old Marc, would you mind if I gave him a call?'

'Are you kidding?' Hannah almost choked on her drink. 'I thought he wasn't your type.'

Terri smirked. Three marriages and countless other relationships had ended in tears, yet her faith remained unshaken that Mr Right was waiting for her out there. Preferably on the deck of his own private yacht or beside the drawbridge of a baronial castle, but she wasn't that fussy, over and above her golden rule of getting rid of all her underwear every time a relationship broke down: *new man, new pants*. Hannah loved her relentless optimism, even though there were moments when she could understand why she drove so many people to distraction.

'Hey, I couldn't misbehave with a bloke who lived with my best friend, could I, now? So I covered up. But if you're moving on . . .'

'Jesus, I don't believe this.'

'Honest, kid, if you let him go, there will be plenty queuing up to take him off your hands. I'm asking for a head start, that's all.'

'Do me a favour.'

'Hannah, you don't realise. Good-looking bloke like that? Intelligent, with oodles of charm. Did I mention he reminds me ever so slightly of Hugh Grant? I might as well stake a claim.'

Flowering jasmine spread over a small pergola close to their table. Hannah breathed in the perfume before fumbling for her dark glasses. Not so much to keep out the sun as to disguise any trace of mistiness in her eyes.

'You're welcome.'

'Seriously?'

'It's more than six months now. No sign of these frantic women battering down the doors of his bookshop to get their hands inside his dust jacket.'

'He's fobbing them off, I bet. Waiting for you to give him the chance to make amends.'

'It will take more than making amends.' Hannah swallowed a mouthful of wine. 'We've been through this before.'

'All right, then, where are you up to with Daniel Kind?'

'Not seen him for ages. We bumped into each other at a lecture about criminal narratives, and that's about it.'

'But?' Terri would have made a good prosecuting counsel. She could spot the slightest gap in a witness's testimony. 'Anything planned?'

Hannah groaned. As if her own labyrinthine romantic entanglements were not enough, Terri was addicted to matchmaking. 'Well, he referred a cold case to me.'

'He's definitely interested.' Terri pronounced her verdict with the supreme assurance of an agony aunt. 'Just cautious, if you ask me. I'd say he's been hurt in the past, and doesn't want to make himself too vulnerable.'

'Maybe. By the way, you didn't tell me about your blind date with that bloke from the driving school?'

Terri's face was a picture. 'When I first saw his stomach, I thought he was eight months pregnant – enough said. And don't think you can get away with changing the subject, Hannah Scarlett. I know what you're like. So when are you seeing Daniel again?'

'Listen, he's a friend, no more than that. Right now,

friendship is all I want from any man, believe me.'

Terri became solemn. 'This isn't just about Marc straying off the straight and narrow, is it? The miscarriage knocked you back more than you realise, Hannah. It takes a long time, believe me, I know. But—'

'The miscarriage is nothing to do with it.'

Apart from Marc and Terri, nobody else knew about her miscarriage. Oh, and Daniel, she'd mentioned it to him in a moment of weakness. But she hadn't made a big deal of it, and he'd probably forgotten. Might Terri be right? From day one, she'd tried not to dwell on her loss, but once or twice it had featured in bad dreams. Invariably she awoke in a cold sweat of fear and self-loathing, for the inadequacy of her mourning for the child that never was. Would she ever have a baby of her own? Time kept moving, the odds against lengthened with every year that slipped by.

'OK, OK, keep your hair on.' Terri adopted a confidential tone. 'Anyway, Marc isn't the only show in town. Stefan, that hunky Polish bloke behind the bar, was telling me about Krakow, where he comes from. Sounds fabulous. Maybe he's hoping to whisk me off for a mini-break.'

Hannah let her friend's chatter slosh over her as the folk singers made their way back through the crowd. Was she being too harsh on Marc? They'd been together a long time, it might be a mistake to throw away all those shared memories. Out of the corner of her eye, she spotted Stefan the Pole emerge from inside, carrying a tray of drinks to a table of his fellow countrymen. He cast Terri's bare legs a very frank glance, and Terri treated him to a coquettish smile without pausing for breath in the midst of an account of the latest idiocy of the girl she'd just hired at her make-up studio.

Chances were, Terri might find a reason to cancel her taxi home tonight. Oh well, good luck to her.

The singer who looked a little like Marc cleared his throat and tapped the microphone.

'And now we'd like to do one of our favourite songs from the Fifties, "Bye, Bye Love". Maybe it's one of your favourites too.'

Yeah, Hannah thought, you're singing my song. And I didn't even need to put in a request.

The early hours, and Aslan staggered off the pavement and on to the road that led to his bedsit. At last, he'd shaken off Sham; he wasn't in the mood to take her back, and they'd both had so much to drink that they'd probably have fallen fast asleep the moment they climbed into bed.

A car hooted from behind and he ducked out of the way. Once again, he thought how easy it would be to stumble into the path of a passing vehicle. But suppose you didn't die? Some people were maimed for life, and he didn't fancy that. Sham had talked endlessly about her family; she wanted him to be impressed that on one side she was descended from the landed gentry, on the other from successful business executives. Money turned her on; she said her father always said that money was power. But famously, it didn't bring happiness, and it gave Aslan a rush of pleasure – much more than when she let her legs brush against his while they were drinking – to hear that even the Madsens were not as content as they seemed. He'd never figured out what he really wanted from life –

apart from loads of money and no-strings sex, obviously – and it made him feel better that other people hit the same snag. He'd hate to think of himself as some kind of sad loser.

According to his daughter, Gareth Madsen felt twinges of envy, because his brother had control of the family company. Bryan resented the fact that he'd never made a mark in national politics, while Fleur was, in her niece's eyes, an older woman who flirted shamelessly with younger men, but never got up the nerve to do anything about it. Sham was right there; during his fleeting encounters with the chair of St Herbert's, he'd felt conscious of her appraising stare, and when they talked, she never allowed him enough personal space. But she gave the impression she was just amusing herself. Perhaps she guessed that he didn't fancy shagging someone old enough to be his mother.

Weird though it was, Purdey appealed to him more than the other Madsens, something he'd had the tact to conceal when Sham persisted in running her sister down. Maybe it was just Purdey's ruthless determination to succeed that he envied; she must have inherited it from their dad, as their mother, an ex-model, was apparently no Einstein. Sham was better-looking, but she was jealous of Purdey. Not a bit like Orla, who idolised Callum, even though he'd treated her with disdain.

Aslan found himself on the doorstep of the whitewashed cottage converted into bedsits and fumbled with his key in the lock. He meant to get up early tomorrow when his head had cleared, and follow through on what he'd gleaned from Sham. In the end, it had been just as well he'd agreed to go out with her. Orla had made no sense with her drunken hints about Castor and Pollux, but tonight Sham had unwittingly given him a glimpse of the truth. He'd have kissed her, but she'd only have got the wrong idea.

CHAPTER NINE

Ugliness was in the eye of the beholder, but Hannah had to admit that Mike Hinds had not been too unfair to the man who had taken away his first wife. Kit Payne's face and body seemed lopsided, as if the result of inexpert do-it-yourself. Tall, with an egg-shaped head and hunched shoulders, he had a large nose, a receding chin, and teeth as crooked as Chesterfield's church spire. There was a mournful light in his grey eyes, and the corners of his mouth drooped, as if apologising for his lack of photogenic appeal. Whatever Niamh Hinds once saw in him, it wasn't good looks.

His office, on the first floor of Madsen High Command, was airy and spacious, reminiscent of an upmarket hotel room, with a leather sofa, plush chairs, and a balcony overlooking the park's lovingly tended gardens. A shelf next to his desk was crammed with awards and certificates bestowed upon the park by tourism and environmental bodies. Half a dozen photographs showed a woman with dyed red hair, a toothy smile and lots of bronzed flesh. In one picture, she'd posed on the deck of a yacht in a tiny pink bikini. Niamh's successor, no doubt, someone else able to see past Kit's lugubrious appearance to the man beyond. Or at least as far as his bank balance.

Once his secretary had supplied bottles of water, he led Hannah and Greg on to the balcony and waved them into wooden chairs. When Hannah expressed her condolences, the egg-head bowed.

'Poor Orla.' Kit chewed at a fingernail. 'I'm not sure she was ever truly happy.'

'You've known her all her life?'

'Pretty much. I started work here before she was born, although I began in the offices, assisting the operations director. When he retired, I was promoted, and I became friendly with Bryan and Gareth. In those days, the old man was still in charge – Joseph Madsen, I mean. Gareth and I are much the same age, and he's always been good to me. He was friendly with Mike Hinds, and through him I met Niamh. That was when Orla was a baby.'

'So, before you began your relationship with her?'

'Of course.' Kit's sallow cheeks suffused with colour. 'At that time, we were acquaintances, nothing more.'

'How come Gareth and Mike Hinds were chums?' Greg asked. 'They don't have much in common, do they?'

Kit raised his eyebrows. 'You've met Mike, then?'

'Yesterday.'

'Hard work, isn't he? But Gareth is brilliant with people. Like Mike and Niamh, he and Sally both had young children, it was a bond. Besides, Gareth always believed it is vital to have good relations with the local community. It's the secret of our success.'

And Bryan Madsen married the lady who inherited the stately home next door, Hannah thought. No wonder the brothers were rich; even their social life was a masterclass in strategic planning.

'When did you become involved with Niamh Hinds?'

'Gareth told me their marriage was on the rocks. It saddened him. He liked Niamh, as well as Mike, but it was a match made in Hell. Mike was a womaniser, who had a string of affairs with local girls he picked up in the bars of Keswick, while everyone saw that Niamh wasn't cut out to be a farmer's wife. She was lovely and vivacious, but making sure the cows were milked was never a priority for her. I understand why Mike found her frustrating. She was never the easiest woman.'

'But the two of you . . . ?'

Kit coughed. 'She and Mike had a blazing row one night. He'd been messing about with some girl in Keswick, not for the first time, and she consoled herself with a retail-therapy binge at the expense of their joint account. He's never been the sort to seek forgiveness for his sins. Instead, he threw her out of the house, when she was only wearing a nightdress. I used to go for a walk around the park every night, checking that everything was as it should be. I still do, even though we now have state-of-the-art CCTV. I was on my way home when I saw Niamh. Running from Lane End towards Gareth's house – though I knew he was away at a conference.'

'Did she ever have a fling with Gareth?' Greg asked.

'Certainly not!' Kit's voice rose, and a couple walking along the path below glanced up in surprise. If his outrage was faked, Hannah thought, he was in the Charles Laughton class as an actor. 'Gareth's a handsome chap, and he's never been short of female admirers, but he's not like Mike.'

'Meaning?'

'In his younger days, Mike Hinds was pathologically unable to keep it in his trousers. I'm not saying Gareth behaved himself before he met Sally, either, but Mike was reckless. He has a self-destructive streak, if you ask me. Poor Niamh was faithful to him despite the provocations and the mistreatment. At least, until . . .'

'Go on,' Hannah said.

'That night, we talked. She'd drunk a couple of bottles of Rioja, but I persuaded her to return to the farmhouse and make her peace with Mike. Not a sensible plan, but I didn't have much experience of marital discord. To be honest, I didn't have much experience of women, full stop.' He hesitated, but Hannah's sympathetic expression encouraged him to continue. 'I'd only had one significant relationship, and that ended when my girlfriend decided to become a nun. Niamh went home, but she and Mike started arguing again. In the end, she hit him, and blacked his eye.'

Hannah noticed Greg fighting a losing battle to keep a straight face. He loved that line about the girlfriend who fled to a nunnery, rather than get involved with such an ugly bugger.

'Did her husband retaliate?'

'Yes, it's in his nature. An eye for an eye, that's his philosophy, that's why I've never had a civil word from him, even though Niamh is long-since cold in her grave. He grabbed hold of her arms, and finished up breaking one of them and having to drive her to A and E.'

Kit paused to let his words sink in, but Hannah motioned for him to continue.

'The next day, I phoned to see how she was, and she told me what he'd done. I was horrified. She needed a shoulder to cry on, and I offered mine. One thing led to another, and within a week she'd walked out on Hinds and moved in with me.'

'Together with Orla and Callum?'

'Yes; my life changed overnight. She swept me off my feet, there's no other way of describing it. Niamh was a challenge, but I was ecstatic. I did everything I could to make her happy to the very end.' He swallowed, as if embarrassed. 'As for the children, their rightful place was with their mother, and staying at Lane End Farm wasn't an option. I was glad to take in the kids, but it was tough on them. Especially on Callum, who resented me for muscling in on their lives. You have to remember, the boy was young.'

'The two of you had a difficult relationship?'

'I can't pretend otherwise, no sense in rewriting history. I was an ignoramus when it came to children. I don't mind admitting, I made mistakes.'

'What sort of mistakes?' Greg had conquered his laughing fit.

'Oh, I was naive enough to expect them to be polite and well behaved. Orla was no trouble, but Callum made a nuisance of himself at every opportunity. Unfortunately, Niamh refused to let me discipline him.'

Greg exchanged a glance with Hannah. 'Discipline him how?'

'Mike Hinds thrashed Callum whenever he stepped

out of line, but the one and only time I tapped him on the backside, he ran off to complain to his father, and Mike made a huge fuss. Talk about double standards.'

'What had Callum done?'

'He found some beer – I suspected Mike gave it to him, but he refused to admit it. After knocking back the booze, he went out and broke several caravan windows. A stupid act of vandalism. Not hugely important in the scheme of things, perhaps, but embarrassing for me.'

'When was this?'

'The week before he disappeared.'

'Do you think the incident played any part in his disappearance?'

'Certainly not. The very idea is ridiculous!'

Hannah and Greg kept their mouths shut. Kit's lower lip was quivering. Perhaps he feared that he'd protested too much.

'Listen, Chief Inspector, Callum took it in his stride, I can assure you. Mike beat him countless times. I only gave him a single slap.'

'I see.' Greg made it sound as though Kit had coughed to grievous bodily harm. 'So were you really surprised when Callum went missing?'

As Kit opened his mouth, they heard the door open, and a woman's voice called out.

'Seen that husband of mine, sweetie?'

Sally Madsen swept on to the balcony. She reeked of perfume, and her white top and shorts displayed acres of orange flesh; she must spend half her life on a sunbed. 'Sorry, Chief Inspector, didn't realise Kit was busy.'

'If Gareth isn't in his office, he can't be far away,' Kit

Payne said. 'We are getting together with Bryan for a sandwich lunch to review the month's sales figures.'

'Thanks, sweetie. I only wanted to see if he needed the Merc this afternoon. My little runabout is in for repair.' Sally Madsen gave a smile so brilliant that Hannah became convinced she'd invested in cosmetic dentistry. 'Sorry to interrupt. Have fun!'

She left as quickly as she had arrived, but the dynamics of the interview had been wrecked. Sod's law. Kit had been rocking on his heels, and Sally Madsen's fortuitous arrival had given him time to regroup.

'In your first statement to the police,' Greg said, 'you admitted you'd had a disagreement with the boy, but you downplayed it. You certainly didn't mention that you had hit him.'

'It was a tap, not a beating.'

On the path below the balcony, two couples and their fresh-faced children in tennis kit were knocking a ball back and forth between them. Happy families, but who knew what tensions festered beneath the smiles and chatter?

'What made you decide Callum's uncle killed him?'

'Philip was the last person to see the boy alive, and he committed suicide after a police interrogation. What else could anyone think?'

Convenient, Hannah thought. If Philip hadn't been tried and found guilty in the court of public opinion, more questions would have been asked about Callum's relationship with his stepfather.

'Mr Hinds told us that, when they were small, Orla and Callum loved playing together in the grain. So they were close?'

'Orla told me about the grain – it stuck in her memory, poor girl. She looked up to Callum, but most of the time he regarded her as a nuisance. I hate to say it, but he was patronising and sarcastic by nature. As well as rather sly.'

Apart from that, a lovely lad, Hannah reflected. 'How did Orla react when her brother vanished?'

'She was a dreamer.' Kit drained his glass of water in a single gulp. His mouth must have been very dry. 'A fantasist. She seemed to see it all as something out of a storybook.'

'She was in denial?'

'In a matter of days she lost her brother and uncle. She found it hard to take in.'

'When did she give up on the idea that Callum might still be alive?'

'With hindsight, I'm not sure she ever did. After a year or two, she stopped talking about him. But recently, I discovered she still clung to the belief that he might turn up, safe and sound.'

The sun was grilling Hannah's forehead. She blinked in the glare, wishing she'd had the foresight to bring a hat. Greg was sprawled out in his chair, soaking up the heat like a holidaymaker. Kit had pushed his own chair back into the shade.

'How recently?'

'Oh, since she came back to Keswick. She phoned me one night, when she'd had a skinful. It was like rewinding the years, and trying to make sense of Niamh in her cups. After a few drinks, it was impossible to reason with either of them.'

'What did she say?'

'She insisted Callum wasn't dead, said she'd never

accepted that Philip was capable of harming a hair on his head.'

'Did she explain herself?'

'Not at all. She seemed to be on a high, and kept repeating, *But he's alive, you don't understand, he's alive*. She was right, I didn't understand. In the end, she rang off in disgust because I was being obtuse. Yet the next time we spoke, which was the last time I saw her, she'd changed her tune.'

'In what way?'

'She still maintained Philip was a scapegoat, but when I pressed her on why she'd said Callum was alive, she refused to give a straight answer. It was as if she'd suffered a massive disappointment. She seemed desperate to talk about something else, anything else.'

'When was this?'

Kit Payne's pale tongue passed over his lips. 'Last Friday.'

Well, well. 'As recently as that?'

'Yes, she called at my house after finishing at St Herbert's. Glenys had popped out for her weekly get-together with three old school friends; Orla preferred it when she wasn't around. That pair never found much to talk about together. I made her a pot of tea, but she didn't stop long. Twenty minutes, maximum.'

'How did she seem?'

Kit Payne contemplated his bitten nails. What caused his habit, Hannah wondered, stress or bad temper?

'Absurd as it seems, I think she had finally accepted that Callum was dead, though she still clung to her fantasy that Philip hadn't killed him.'

* * *

'Daniel! Just the man!'

A greeting that, in Daniel's experience, never spelt good news. He turned at the door to the Old Library, and saw Professor Micah Bridge walking towards him. There was an ominous quality in the principal's delight at catching his attention.

'I hate to disrupt work on your magnum opus, but I wonder if you would be kind enough to spare me a couple of minutes?'

Plainly he meant ten minutes minimum, but Daniel believed in showing good grace when surrendering to the inevitable.

'Glad to.'

'Splendid, splendid.'

The principal accompanied him down the corridor to his suite of rooms in the wing at the far end. The charity's published accounts showed that the salary of the man in charge was pitifully low. But his accommodation was luxurious if old-fashioned, and Daniel suspected Micah Bridge was so unworldly that he might have paid for the privilege of working here.

The bookshelves in the sitting room held the principal's personal collection of first editions; oil paintings of his predecessors hung on the walls. No television, no sound system, this might have been the home of a nineteenth-century man of letters. Daniel submitted to the leathery embrace of a voluptuous old armchair while the principal rang a bell to summon Jonquil, a student who worked in the restaurant, and ordered Turkish coffee for two before making small talk about the challenges of preserving the De Quincey manuscripts in the Old Library. He was building up to something. Perhaps he'd got wind that Fleur had invited Daniel to become a trustee, and wanted to recruit an ally against the balance sheet barbarians knocking at the gates of Rome.

Turkish coffee was one of the principal's vices. Jonquil served it piping hot, with glasses of water to freshen the mouth, and slabs of Turkish delight. As they took a taste, the principal murmured, 'Did I ever mention that, traditionally, the grounds are used for fortune-telling?'

Only three or four times, but Daniel mustered an expression of polite enquiry.

'It's a form of tasseography, a discipline we associate more commonly with reading tea leaves. It's bad luck to interpret grounds from the coffee you have been drinking yourself. An upturned saucer is placed on the cup, and . . . but you didn't spare your valuable time to listen to an old man showing off his knowledge of trivial superstitions. As for fortune-telling, I am at present struggling to interpret events of the recent past, let alone look into the future. Daniel, I wish to seek your advice.'

Daniel inclined his head, and waited. The principal's conversational style meandered like Lakeland lanes. He always took an age to reach his destination.

'Thank you.' The principal fiddled with the knot of his tie. 'I am troubled by the death of young Orla Payne.'

'Uh-huh?' Daniel tried to fight off a wild fantasy that he was about to hear some kind of confession. Had Professor Bridge and Orla become embroiled in an affair which led to the young woman's decision to end it all in such a bizarre fashion? Even his inventive mind boggled.

'Oh, I realise it's a nine-day wonder. Suicide while the

balance of her mind was disturbed is the inevitable verdict. Yet the truth is more complex. As so often.'

'I don't follow.'

The principal took another sip of coffee. 'Orla found it hard to accept that her brother was dead. And, reflecting after her tragic demise, I have come to a conclusion which I wish to share with you before I speak to the police. If you don't mind?'

Daniel moved forward in the armchair. 'Feel free.'

'In my opinion,' the principal said, 'Orla Payne believed that her brother was not only alive, but had turned up here, at St Herbert's Residential Library.'

'Seriously?'

'It took me some time to realise what was going through her mind, and I found the notion equally unpalatable. But she was indeed serious. At least for a short time.'

'But who . . . ?'

Professor Micah Bridge stared at the stern faces of the men who had once lived and worked in this room, as if hoping for advice. After a few moments, he closed his eyes, unable to defer his revelation any longer.

'Aslan Sheikh.'

Greg slurped some water, and wiped his mouth with the back of his hand. 'Why did Orla change her mind about whether Callum was dead?'

'If I knew that,' Kit Payne asked, 'don't you think I'd have mentioned it already? She was hugging secret knowledge to herself. A habit she picked up from Callum himself, long ago.'

'The Madsens wouldn't have been pleased, would they?

The fuss when Callum disappeared was bad enough for business. Worse than an outbreak of foot-and-mouth.'

Hannah threw Greg a warning glance; Kit replied with sorrow rather than anger.

'You do Bryan and Gareth a disservice. All they cared for was Callum being found safe and sound.'

'Really?'

'Really. And for what it is worth, our takings actually rose after all the publicity about poor Callum.'

Greg stared. 'You expect us to believe that?'

'I promise you, people flocked to Madsen's that summer.'

'Like they might slow down to gape as they pass a car crash on a motorway?'

'Your analogy, not mine, Sergeant. But . . . yes.'

'All right.' Greg began to backtrack. 'I only meant that there was huge pressure on everyone when Callum went missing.'

'Stating the obvious, if you don't mind my saying so.' Kit Payne specialised in wounded dignity. 'Bryan Madsen agreed that the park should be turned upside down in the efforts to find Callum. Some of our customers were very unhappy about it, but Niamh and I couldn't have asked more of the Madsens. They knew my stepson, of course, and they did whatever they could to help. Not that I expected Callum to be found on the site. It was more likely something had happened to him at the farm.'

Hannah leant forward. 'Such as?'

'Farms are appalling death traps. And Mike Hinds was never exactly safety conscious. Slurry tanks, heavy plant, dangerous machinery.'

'Did you and Niamh know that Callum made secret visits to his father?'

Payne shuffled in his chair. 'I spotted him a couple of times, making his way over to Lane End. I didn't challenge him about it, and I decided it was better not to mention it to Niamh. If we stopped Callum seeing Hinds . . .'

'Yes?'

'God knows how Hinds would have reacted. His pride took a hammer blow when he lost Niamh, even though their marriage was dead in all but name. A father and a son ought to be allowed to see each other. I decided to turn a blind eye.'

'How did Callum and his father get on?'

'Shouldn't you ask Hinds? I doubt everything was sweetness and light. The boy was . . . difficult.'

'You thought it possible that Michael Hinds could have lost his rag with his son, and—?'

'Please don't put words in my mouth, Chief Inspector.' The edge in Kit Payne's voice reminded Hannah that he'd risen to the top in a ruthlessly competitive business. Softly spoken, yes, but nothing like as soft as he seemed. 'All I'm saying is that Callum might have had an accident at Lane End. Searching the whole farm took time, but there was no trace of him. Just as there was no sign of him in the Hanging Wood.'

'What did Philip have to say about Callum's disappearance?'

'I heard he was distraught, but whether he was worried for the boy, or in a state because of something he'd done, who can say? I didn't know him well – I'm not sure anyone did. He was a strange person, content with his own company. Nothing like his brother.'

'No temper?'

'None. Mike Hinds hated him because he was ashamed to have a brother who suffered from learning difficulties. They'd grown up together in less enlightened times, but Mike Hinds has not an ounce of compassion in his make-up. Whereas Philip was kind and generous to Orla and Callum, perhaps because he was childlike, too. As time passed, we became desperate, and Niamh was drinking herself into oblivion. The search spread out – not just police officers, but people from all around took part.'

'Where else did you search?'

'We combed the gardens of St Herbert's Library, although to the best of my knowledge, Callum never spent time there. It wasn't so easy to get permission to look round the Mockbeggar Estate. You'd think that, with a teenager missing, anyone would be glad to do whatever they could to help. Not the old man, Alfred Hopes. He was a recluse, obsessive about personal privacy. Said it was out of the question that Callum could have trespassed on his land. Patently absurd – the grounds were fenced off, but not so effectively that an active boy could be kept out if he was determined to get in.'

'Did Callum frequent the Mockbeggar Estate?'

'Not to my knowledge, but we didn't dare rule it out. The grounds were a jungle, and we were desperate to search them, just in case Callum had got in and then suffered some kind of accident.'

'Hopes didn't prevent a search in the end, did he?'

'No, but he delayed it. He was selfish to a fault. It wouldn't have hurt him to cooperate from the outset.'

'Was there any reason to believe that he had an ulterior motive for delaying the search?'

'Good Lord, no.' Kit Payne's eyebrows jumped. 'Because he lived so close, he would have been aware of Callum's existence, but I doubt their paths ever crossed. At that time, he was in his late sixties, and suffered from asthma, diabetes, and very severe hypochondria as well. A succession of housekeepers tended to his wants, as well as carers to look after his son Jolyon, who was confined to a wheelchair. They were a sad pair, father and son. They never got on, although Jolyon's accident bound them together permanently. The old man suspected his boy was a closet homosexual, and that was anathema to a curmudgeon of his vintage. The pair of them felt more at ease with their beloved dogs than fellow human beings.'

'But Fleur Madsen isn't like that?'

'Utterly the reverse, she's the most charming woman I've ever met. I've heard her say she thanks God she takes after her mother's side of the family. Of course, she made her escape from Mockbeggar Hall once she teamed up with Bryan. It was thanks to her that we finally managed to undertake a search of the estate. She persuaded Alfred to allow Gareth to lead a search party.'

'Why Gareth?'

'Alfred Hopes and Hinds never got on, and Bryan was recovering from a serious car crash, while Joseph Madsen suffered from persistent ill health. I was occupied with caring for Niamh and Orla. Hinds led a party of his workmen searching the open countryside. Obviously there was a chance Callum had fallen down a ravine or off a fell side, even though he normally kept close to home.'

'But none of the searches found him.'

'I suppose we didn't expect them to. We heard the police were interviewing Philip Hinds in connection with Callum's disappearance.'

'What was your take on that news? No smoke without fire?'

'Putting it like that, Chief Inspector, makes it sound like a witch-hunt. But don't forget, Hinds' son was missing. That is why he was prepared to think the unthinkable. That his own brother was responsible for Callum's death. And then Philip committed suicide.'

'Perhaps he was just frightened. I've read the transcript of his interview. It must have been a terrible ordeal for a man like Philip Hinds.'

'I'm sure. But when he went home to the Hanging Wood and strung himself up, people drew the inevitable conclusion. I found the body, you know. It is something I shall never, ever forget.'

Down below the balcony, a group of passing teenagers burst into laughter. Their accents were public school posh, their clothes bore designer labels. Hannah and Greg might have been gatecrashing a hideaway for the rich and powerful. Come to think of it, that was exactly what they were doing.

'According to the file, Philip's pig went missing, as well as Callum?'

'Yes. What happened to it, nobody knew.'

'Bit odd, that the pig should vanish?'

'There was a rumour that Mike Hinds slaughtered it in a rage, because it had devoured his son, but who could ever prove it?'

'There was no proof Callum died in the Hanging Wood, or that his remains had been disposed of, or eaten by the pig. This is the countryside, the animal might have gone anywhere. With the pig gone, no tests could be carried out. Forensics hit a blank wall.'

'We didn't hear quite so much about DNA evidence in those days, Chief Inspector.'

'This was only twenty years ago, not the Dark Ages. Genetic fingerprinting was in its infancy, but the detectives who investigated weren't idiots. They couldn't find any evidence of what happened to your stepson.'

A weary sigh. 'The likelihood that Callum was dead shocked me, and devastated my wife. She never properly recovered. If you ask me, three people died in the Hanging Wood, not two.'

'Yet we don't know for sure that Callum did die there.'

'Philip may have buried the body somewhere, but it wasn't practical to excavate the whole of the Hanging Wood.'

'Did Philip strike you as a potential killer?'

Kit Payne spread his arms. 'What do killers look like, how do they behave? Did Philip have the instincts of a paedophile? With hindsight, I simply can't be sure.'

'Presumably neither you nor Niamh thought he was a risk, or you wouldn't have allowed the two children to visit the cottage in the Hanging Wood?'

Kit frowned. 'One possibility was that Philip put his arm round Callum in a clumsy gesture of affection, or did something else that my stepson misconstrued. Another was that Callum caught him masturbating in the cottage, and said something cruel. If there was a struggle, Callum's head might have banged against a wall or something. Philip would be terrified by the prospect of trying to explain why the boy was hurt, or even dead. Maybe feeding him to the pig seemed like the easiest solution.'

Quite a long speech, and it sounded rehearsed, as if Kit had his narrative of events ready and waiting for the day when he was questioned.

Hannah stretched out her legs and treated him to a saccharine smile.

Time to rattle his cage.

'Who else had a reason to harm your stepson?'

CHAPTER TEN

So Orla believed Callum Hinds had metamorphosed into Aslan Sheikh? Daniel would have been less startled if the principal had proposed a bonfire of every rare book in St Herbert's. He gulped down half a cup of coffee, heedless that it scalded his tongue.

'You're joking.'

The principal squinted in disapproval. 'This is no laughing matter.'

Daniel swallowed more coffee. The revelation was all the more bizarre because it came in such august surroundings from the lips of a mild-mannered exponent of civilised understatement.

'Let me explain,' Micah Bridge said, in tutorial mode. 'Starting with the hiring of Aslan, a task I undertook against my better judgement.'

Daniel nodded. The principal was wont to complain that he possessed no experience in human resource management, yet the trustees expected him to mastermind recruitment, performance and discipline of the entire workforce at St Herbert's.

'I have to tell you that his CV did not suit him ideally for the role I had in mind. Orla was struggling with her work, and she was keen to have support. In truth, she was ill-matched with her job, but she was the stepchild of a director of Madsen's – what could I do?'

'Did they pressure you into appointing her?'

'Goodness me, no, that isn't the way the world works, is it? You spent years in academe, Daniel, you are familiar with nods and winks, the currency of power in every senior common room in Oxford and Cambridge. St Herbert's is an institution with a modest endowment, and running costs that we can barely meet. We rely on the goodwill of our principal donors; in other words, the Madsen family. Their gifts over the years have been munificent.'

'I glanced over the accounts,' Daniel said. 'The donations column looks healthy.'

'Several generous individuals support us, but contributions from the Madsen family dwarf the rest. At one level, they are eminently fair and reasonable. They do not insist on disfiguring the library with sponsorship banners, or that their name is writ large on our occasional learned publications. It suits Bryan Madsen – I do not wish to sound churlish – to point to this little oasis of "cultural calm", as he describes it, on the fringe of his holiday park.'

'You felt you had to offer Orla the job?'

A grim-faced nod. 'Just as I recruited the daughter of Gareth and Sally Madsen when she wearied of working at a suntan salon in Keswick. Fleur mentioned her brother- and sister-in-law were keeping their fingers crossed that Sham's interview would go well, and I took the hint. I had little confidence that Orla could transform our promotional efforts, but I knew enough of her personal history to feel sorry for her. She was genuinely enthusiastic about our archive of fairy tales and historical materials. Not as a scholar – I'm afraid she had a distinctly second-class mind – but as someone who loved reading. I found that rather touching.'

'Don't reproach yourself,' Daniel said. 'She cared for St Herbert's, and you did a good deed.'

'She can't have enjoyed it so much, or she wouldn't have ended it all. Perhaps if I'd turned her down, if I'd given her more support when she worked for me . . . she might be alive to this day.'

So guilt was gnawing at the old man. Daniel drank the rest of his coffee, leaving just the sediment in the bottom of the cup. God knows what a tasseographer would make of the grounds.

Sometimes it was better not to know.

Kit Payne's eyes widened. 'For heaven's sake, Chief Inspector, the boy was only fourteen. Who would want to murder a child?'

'You were aware of the incident involving Callum and a girl from one of the caravans on the park? Her name was Briony, according to the old file.'

'You've got the wrong end of the stick; that business was something and nothing. The girl made a fuss, the father became agitated. These things happen. At Madsen's, we pride ourselves on customer care.' Kit paused, perhaps reading Hannah's mind: *spare me the commercial, please.* 'Both Gareth and I spoke to the family, and the matter was put to bed. The father didn't pursue his complaint, and it had no bearing on Callum's disappearance.'

'You were satisfied the father didn't decide to take matters into his own hands?'

'Of course not.' Kit sounded as though he couldn't believe his ears. 'The man was a police officer.'

And police officers can do no wrong? Hannah thought. Hmmm, thanks for your confidence. 'Did Callum upset anyone else, to your knowledge? Or become involved with anyone unsuitable, anyone who might have had an unhealthy interest in teenage boys?'

'No, no, no.' His voice trembled. 'For God's sake, he was only a kid, he didn't have a line of enemies queuing up to harm him.'

'Orla spoke to me, the day before she died,' she said. 'She wanted justice for her brother.'

'Meaning what?'

'That's why I'm asking you these questions, Mr Payne. Because of Orla.' Hannah looked him in the eye. 'When did she lose her hair?'

The change of tack seemed to knock him off balance. 'I can't recall. After she left home, when she was studying for her degree.'

'It's a stress-related disorder, isn't it?'

'Yes, but there's a genetic component. Niamh suffered from the same condition.'

'I didn't know that.'

'There's a lot you don't know, Chief Inspector.'

The retort stung like a whiplash, but as soon as he saw

Hannah's expression, his face fell, as if he realised he'd said too much.

'I'm sure that's right,' she said. 'So how did Niamh cope with her alopecia?'

'By pretending it didn't exist. Her hair fell out when she was in her early twenties, and it never grew back, so she wore a hairpiece. She carried it off so well that I never even realised until the night we slept together. Nobody else did, either. She called it her little secret. Orla dreaded the same thing happening to her, and sure enough, it did. But her case was more severe than her mother's. She lost all her body hair too. She drew on a pair of eyebrows, and often wore tinted glasses so people wouldn't see that she had no eyelashes. For a young woman, looks matter a lot.'

'She chose to wear headscarves rather than a wig.'

'Yes, and she looked fine, though she could never bring herself to believe it. She was attractive, but lacked Niamh's confidence and vivacity. I think she found it hard to build relationships. Although she had a few boyfriends, none of them lasted long. She once told me that men she met tended to assume from the scarves that she was a cancer survivor. To her, the truth was more depressing. After she moved back to Keswick and started work at St Herbert's, she started seeing someone, but it soon fizzled out.'

'Did she tell you who she was seeing?'

'No, and I didn't like to poke my nose into her private life. Although we kept in touch, inevitably we saw less of each other once I found happiness with Glenys.'

'Was she upset when you remarried?'

'She understood I needed to move on after the difficult years when Niamh was so ill. I hoped Orla would find someone she could share her life with. I'm afraid she was lonely, Chief Inspector, and that is why she loved to retreat into the world of fairy tales.'

'This love of fairy tales, where did it come from?'

'Oh, it dated back to her childhood. A form of escape. Her parents' marriage was unhappy, and the real world held little appeal for her. She liked to imagine herself as Gretel, with Callum as Hansel, when they roamed the Hanging Wood and visited Philip in his tumbledown cottage.'

'St Herbert's has a good stock of obscure books of old fairy tales, I hear.' Hannah's lips felt dry in the heat. Who needed the South of France, when you had weather like this in the Northern Lakes? 'I suppose she was thrilled to be offered a job. Were you able to pull a few strings?'

'As it happens,' Kit Payne said, 'I didn't even know she'd applied for the post. The first I heard of it was when she rang to say that she was leaving Newcastle and coming back to Keswick.'

'So you were reunited again?'

Kit Payne shrugged. 'Is the heat bothering you, Chief Inspector? We can move inside if you wish.'

Hannah got to her feet. 'Good idea, it is very warm out here.'

'A suntrap, isn't it? Pity I can't take advantage when I'm slaving over a hot computer. Now, I need to meet some important visitors from Bulgaria before long, but would you like to stretch your legs for a few minutes before you go, take a look around our wonderful park?'

'Thanks.' She glanced at Greg, who gave a nod. Might as well see what all the fuss was about. 'Why not?'

* * *

As he led Hannah and Greg downstairs, Kit Payne hailed his secretary, an overweight woman in her late fifties who was waddling towards the typists' room with a sheaf of invoices clutched in a shovel-like hand.

'Won't be long, Shirley. Just taking our visitors for a quick tour of the park.'

A beam lit up the woman's face, transforming her in a moment into someone pretty and looking younger than her years. She was one of those secretaries who don't disguise their devotion to her boss. While escorting the detectives to Kit's office, she had boasted that he was always first into work, and the last one to leave at night. Kit Payne had risen to the board of Madsen's through working hard and making no enemies, but taking on a ready-made family is tougher than the most demanding job, and Callum Hinds had got under his stepfather's skin. Kit admitted his patience had snapped on one occasion. Had it happened again, with fatal consequences?

Kit opened the door with his security tag, but as he marched out, he cannoned straight into Bryan Madsen, who wasn't able to limp out of the way in time to avoid him.

'Sorry, sorry, my fault.'

Kit didn't quite tug his forelock, but only because he didn't have a forelock. Years of sitting together around the boardroom table hadn't left any doubt about who called the shots.

'Not to worry, my old friend.' Bryan slapped him on the back to show no hard feelings. 'Chief Inspector, grand to see you again. We must stop meeting like this, or people will talk!'

'This is DS Wharf,' Hannah said, and the vigour with which Bryan pumped Greg's hand reminded her that twice in the Nineties he'd stood for Parliament in rock-solid Labour seats. Perhaps he'd never got out of the habit of canvassing for votes in an unpromising constituency.

'Pleasure to meet you!' Bryan gestured towards a bed packed with red begonias, and the fountain beyond. 'Having a gander at the park?'

'Everything looks very impressive.' The ACC would have been proud of Hannah's diplomacy.

'Though I say it as shouldn't, we really have created something special, and a good deal of the credit goes to this man here.' Kit blushed like a virgin receiving her first proposition. 'My father established the business on a sound footing, but once we appointed Kit as head of operations, the park really took off into the stratosphere. He leaves nothing to chance, you know.'

The man who left nothing to chance coaxed a modest expression out of his uneven features. 'I always maintain it's a team effort.'

'True, but a successful team needs high-quality leadership, and Kit is the best leader in the business. You know, Hannah my dear, this park has become the ultimate holiday destination in the Lakes – it says so on our promotional DVDs, so it must be true! See for yourself, and I dare you to tell me you aren't impressed!' Bryan resembled a belted earl, throwing open his castle to sightseers who have paid their shillings for a peek at how the other half live. 'Who knows, you may feel tempted to invest in one of our lodges yourself. A perfect destination to escape from the cares of police work – and I'm sure Kit can cut you a favourable deal with no site fees for the first eighteen months! But seriously, what brings you here?'

After all the bullshit, Hannah thought, the question he wanted to ask. Greg's smirk revealed how much he'd enjoyed Bryan describing her as his 'dear'. She'd suffer for that.

'We were asking Mr Payne about his stepson's disappearance.'

Bryan nodded. 'I'm sure he is giving you every assistance. We understand that you have to tick the boxes. I only hope it doesn't waste too much valuable police time.'

It was on the tip of Hannah's tongue to tell him to mind his own business. But even if Bryan Madsen was a boring old fart, he was a boring old fart with a shedload of influence. Unwise to get on the wrong side of someone who could pick up the phone and sound off to Lauren Self the minute his nose was put out of joint. If he wanted to believe she was simply going through the motions, fine. She'd take as long as she needed.

Employing her sweetest smile, she said, 'We're grateful for your understanding, Mr Madsen.'

'Bryan, please,' he chortled. 'Anyway, lovely to see you again. And to make your acquaintance, Detective Sergeant.'

As Kit updated him on the shifting-around of some paintings in Mockbeggar Hall, Greg murmured in her ear. 'Should we bow and curtsey?'

'Show some respect for your elders and betters,' she whispered.

'Butter wouldn't melt in my mouth, ma'am.'

'Lying toad.'

* * *

'Micah, listen,' Daniel said. 'You mustn't beat yourself up, it's pointless. If Orla was suicidal, she would have killed herself somewhere, somehow, sooner or later. But when did you find out that she thought Aslan was Callum? She never mentioned it to me.'

'Nor to me, not directly.' Micah Bridge coloured. 'Let me explain. As I say, she wanted someone to help her through the summer. It was tantamount to an admission that she couldn't cope with her job, but I thought that if I said no, Fleur Madsen would take it amiss.'

'Did Fleur imply that?'

'In fairness, no. If anything, Fleur gave the impression that she was put out that Orla had come back to her old stamping ground. But I didn't want to take a chance, so I advertised the support job at the minimum wage, assuming there would be no candidates with suitable qualifications, and the matter could be quietly dropped.'

'Instead, Aslan showed up.'

'And to clinch it, he made me an offer I could scarcely refuse. He was so keen, he was prepared to work as a volunteer, so the charity didn't have to dip into its coffers to fund the post.'

'I never knew he's a volunteer, I assumed he was on the payroll.'

'Pride, perhaps? Unemployment among the young is far too high, and he may have been afraid of being out of work, who knows? Whatever the motive for his proposal, it was remarkably generous.'

'Why was he so eager to work here?'

'I presumed he was spellbound by the magic of the place.' It was part of the principal's charm, Daniel thought, not to see anything odd in a young man offering his services to St Herbert's for free. 'If you love books, where on earth could you be happier?'

Yet in his conversations with Daniel, Aslan often moaned about life at St Herbert's; his recurrent gripe concerned the need to skulk out of doors for a fag break. The principal had asked no questions; mustn't look a gift horse in the mouth.

'But he doesn't actually seem to have any interest in literature.'

The principal shook his head. 'So it seems. Quite inexplicable. But from the outset, Orla took a shine to him, and I heard they went out for a drink in Keswick together. I couldn't help congratulating myself on a job well done. The chair of trustees could hardly complain, and I'd avoided incurring unnecessary expenditure. What I never bargained for was this complication about Aslan's supposed identity.'

'How did you find out?'

A flush of embarrassment darkened the principal's features. 'I happened to overhear a conversation between Orla and Aslan.'

'Here?'

'Yes. I happened to be on the first-floor corridor, after a conversation with the librarian in her office up there. On my way back to the staircase, I passed Orla's room, and I heard voices. The door was ajar, and she was talking to Aslan. I would have paid no attention, but it seemed Orla was in distress. I believe she had been drinking.'

'What did she say?'

'She was apologising to Aslan, and asking if they could

still be friends. She sounded tearful. I heard her say, *I was so sure you were Callum.*'

'And he said?'

'He was trying to calm her down. I had the impression he was trying to talk sense to her, but she kept rambling and wouldn't let him get a word in edgeways.' The principal frowned, groping in his memory for the words. '*The walls have ears, that's how I heard about Callum, and Castor and Pollux.*' As she said that, it occurred to me I'd better move along. They might notice the door was open, and I didn't want to appear to be listening to a private conversation between two members of staff, with one in such an emotional state.'

'What was all this about Castor and Pollux?'

'Heaven only knows. She wasn't making any sense. Even Aslan probably could make neither head nor tail of it.'

'Orla once told me her brother liked to be cryptic and mysterious, but I doubt he was in her league when it came to talking in riddles.'

'She was a troubled young woman. I moved along the corridor not a moment too soon. She came out of her room and dashed past me without a word. I could see she'd been crying.' The principal toyed with his coffee cup. 'Daniel, I do not make a habit of poking my nose into the business of others. I simply did not know whether I should offer help or behave as though I was unaware of the conversation.'

'What gave her the idea that Aslan was her long-lost brother?'

'I heard her say he looked rather like Callum. The shape of his head, the colour of his eyes, the same beaky nose.'

'But Aslan's ethnicity . . .'

'He is half-English, don't forget.' The principal sighed. 'I have been unsure whether the conversation I heard has any bearing on her suicide. Hence my decision to consult you. I am aware of your involvement with that matter of the De Quincey Festival.'

Daniel said slowly, 'I'm beginning to see what happened. How about this? Orla meets Aslan, and takes a shine to him. Then she persuades herself that he is really Callum, but when she puts this to him, he disillusions her with the truth.' He kept thinking aloud. 'The relationship fizzles out, and in her distress, Orla decides to end it all.'

'The truth being, that Aslan is not Callum?'

'Unless . . . Aslan lied, and Orla's idea was right all along.'

The principal chewed on a piece of Turkish delight. 'You once wrote that all historians are detectives. I am sure your guess is better than mine.'

To call Madsen's a caravan park was, Hannah realised as they walked around the site, akin to describing Windermere as a long strip of water. The country club boasted a brasserie that wouldn't seem out of place on the Riviera, plus a couple of bars, a gym, a climbing wall, a badminton court and a tenpin bowling alley. Beyond vivid rose beds and the large gushing fountain lay a fishing lake, sports arena, and a nine-hole golf course. Hannah had expected the place to be swarming with unruly kids and harassed parents, but everywhere she looked there were smart and sprightly senior citizens, and clean-cut families with offspring who answered to names like Justin and Minette, and who had no doubt travelled here in the freshly washed SUVs that lined the car park.

Kit showed Hannah and Greg round a luxury lodge that put Undercrag to shame with its triple glazing, underfloor heating, solar panels, spa and hot tub. You could laze in the sunshine on the decking and admire the view of Blencathra. With vaulted ceilings, exposed wooden beams and floor-to-ceiling windows, the atmosphere inside was less like a mobile home, more like a place of worship. Sun worship, at least.

When they moved out in the sunlight again, Greg pointed to a camera fixed high up on the wall of the lodge. 'That makes a round dozen cameras I've counted so far, Mr Payne. You take security pretty seriously here.'

'Our customers pay good money to enjoy the park, DS Wharf. We have a duty to make sure they are kept safe and sound.' Kit indicated a squat single-storey building on the other side of a tennis court. 'Come and take a look at our site security.'

Inside the control centre, two men in shirtsleeves kept a watchful eye on a bank of screens. Kit Payne made Hannah's eyes water by explaining how much the Madsens spent on park security, before rattling off the technical specifications of the surveillance equipment. She wondered how long it would be before his favourite phrase cropped up: *state of the art*. The answer turned out to be a minute and a half. As he talked, one of the men waved him over.

'We seem to have a trespasser in Mockbeggar Zone 3.'

Hannah and Greg moved forward to peer over Kit's shoulder at the screen in question. The rear view of a tall man was visible. He was making his way towards a small copse. The undergrowth was dense, and as they watched, he stumbled and lost his footing. Kit and the security men groaned in unison.

'Tripped over a tree root,' Kit said, with a touch of malicious satisfaction. 'I suppose he fancied taking a short cut to see how the Hall looks in the run-up to the official opening. You see why we discourage people from accessing areas of the site that we haven't cleared and upgraded yet. Health and safety is core to our vision, and our insurers insist we take every precaution. That chap could easily sprain his ankle, and ruin his holiday.'

'He's one of your residents?' Hannah was sure she'd seen the man before. Where was it?

'Presumably.' Kit sighed. 'You've seen for yourself, we provide every possible facility in the public areas. But some people you could give gold, and it wouldn't be enough. He's wandered into a part of the Hall grounds that we haven't cleared and opened to the public in the first phase of the park expansion. Of course, there's always someone who doesn't understand the meaning of "no entry". We'll send a warden from our security team to make sure he's all right, and have a quiet word to remind him of park rules.'

'Why am I reminded of *The Prisoner*?' Greg muttered as they moved outside again.

'Behave,' Hannah whispered. 'At least the bloke wasn't squashed by a giant balloon.'

Kit Payne pointed to a shiny new road and bridge, leading to a mansion visible in the distance through a group of copper beeches. 'This is the route we created, to cross the beck and connect with Mockbeggar Hall. The official opening isn't for a fortnight, but you are welcome to have a quick recce if you like.'

'It's kind of you, but—'

'Won't you take the full tour, Hannah?' Gareth Madsen stepped out from behind the fountain. 'The Hall was disintegrating through lack of maintenance, you could put your foot through the floorboards. Fleur would be the first to admit that her father could never afford to look after the old place. Now we've transformed it into a conference complex with leisure facilities and spa. The water centre is the last word in quality. Whirlpools, jacuzzi and sauna, you name it. Rainforest shower, steam grotto, salt chamber and ice igloo, not forgetting the children's fun pool. Something for everyone.'

'Wow,' Hannah said. 'Sounds utterly state of the art.'

If Gareth thought he was being sent up, he didn't let on. 'If you can spare the time, I'll take you round myself, and let Kit get back to work. He has some visiting Bulgars to see, would you believe, any minute now.'

'Thank you, but no. We just have a few more questions to put to Mr Payne about his stepson.'

'Poor Callum.' Gareth bowed his head. 'I'll never forget the day we heard that he'd disappeared. It still seems incredible.'

'I gather you helped with the search party?'

'First around this site, later in the grounds of the Hall. Things were different then. The Mockbeggar Estate was very much out of bounds. Alfred Hopes had a passion for keeping himself – and his property – to himself. I remember having to cut through a barbed wire fence to save time before the search began. The very thought of the hoi polloi trespassing sent Alfred into a lather.'

'But this was an emergency. A child was missing.'

'Yes, we needed to rule out the possibility that Callum was on the estate, even though the chances were negligible. We were clutching at straws. Poor Kit had his hands full with Niamh. They were desperate to find the lad. We all were.'

'Eventually Alfred Hopes relented, and allowed you in.'

'Fleur persuaded her grandfather that we couldn't waste any more time. If the boy was lying somewhere, injured and unable to move – well, it didn't bear thinking about. Sadly, we found what we expected to find. Nothing.'

'Meanwhile, Mike Hinds was pointing the finger at Philip. Not much brotherly love there, then?'

'The two of them were chalk and cheese,' Gareth said. 'They were never close.'

'But to suggest that Philip was a murderer?'

'Mike's son was missing, remember? He was beside himself.'

'Why did he detest Philip?'

'He hated the idea of having an inadequate brother depending on our family for his home and a few pounds to live on. Whenever I saw them together, poor Philip managed to get on Mike's nerves. It usually ended in a shouting match. Or rather, a mismatch. Mike ranted until he was hoarse, Philip just let it wash over him.'

'And then Philip Hinds hanged himself.'

Kit flinched. 'I need no reminding of that, Chief Inspector.'

Gareth said quickly, 'It was a difficult time for everyone, especially Kit and Niamh. I always had a soft spot for Philip, and so did my father. The day Callum went missing, I'd asked Philip to do some work, repairing a damaged fence. When Niamh raised the alarm, Philip joined in the search. At first, none of us dreamed that...'

'You believe he killed Callum?'

'I'm sure it wasn't deliberate. My guess is that Callum was injured in some kind of horseplay, causing Philip to do something completely out of character.'

Kit muttered, 'The simple explanation is usually right.'

'Thank you for your help,' she said.

'Is that all?'

'For the moment, yes.' She shared a tight smile with Greg Wharf. 'Now, can you direct us to the Hanging Wood?'

CHAPTER ELEVEN

'Fancy an ice cream?' Greg asked.

A kiosk built into the back corner of the country club sold ices and cold drinks. Upmarket ices and cold drinks, naturally.

Hannah gave him a sidelong look. 'We're working, don't forget.'

'Yeah, might as well enjoy it.'

'All right, mine's a 99.'

'Easily persuaded,' he said. 'Excellent, I knew it wasn't true what they say.'

She halted mid stride, unable to resist rising to the bait. 'What do they say?'

'That you are a workaholic.' He showed sharp white teeth. 'A perfectionist who drives herself too hard.'

'Then just to prove I know how to have a really good time, you can buy me a double 99. Sod the cholesterol, live for the moment.'

He pretended to clap. 'That's the spirit, ma'am. Throw caution to the wind.'

As he vaulted over a low railing to join a natty septuagenarian couple in the queue at the kiosk, she caught herself assessing his sinewy physique. Must be a touch of the sun – how long since she last checked someone out like this? Not that she had any intention of succumbing to Greg Wharf's macho charm. It was just a relief to take any interest in a man again; the nonsense with Marc had torpedoed her morale at the precise moment when she'd started shunting her career out of the siding and back on track.

Greg's short sleeves revealed powerful forearms. He kept himself fit and was a permanent fixture at the top of the division's squash ladder. Macho men weren't her type, and when Greg first joined the team, she'd been wary of his reputation for making trouble. Not least because of his womanising. But so far he'd managed to keep his hands off Linz Waller, to Hannah's surprise and Linz's barely concealed disappointment. After a few initial skirmishes ending with honours even, he'd given Hannah support in team meetings; all the more useful because everyone knew he was nobody's yes-man. As a detective, his cussed refusal to settle for easy answers had helped him bond with Les Bryant. They made an odd couple: a grumpy old man and a Jack the Lad, moaning each winter Monday about the football refereeing they'd witnessed over the weekend. Hannah enjoyed their dry wit, even though she scarcely knew a late tackle from an offside trap. Les lived alone these days – on one extraordinary occasion, he'd had a blind date with Terri, but that particular match was made in Hell, not Heaven – and as far as Hannah knew, Greg wasn't seeing anyone. Not in the force, at least, or news would have sped along the county's busiest grapevine.

'Don't say I never give you anything,' he said, presenting her with the double 99. 'You deserve a bit of sin in your life.'

He'd invested in a Diet Coke for himself, a sardonic nod to virtue, and they planted themselves on a bench overlooking a duck pond carpeted in red cup lilies with maroon foliage. A plaque on the bench recalled a deceased caravan owner *who loved this park for 30 years.*

'So what do you reckon to Madsen's?' she asked.

'Give me Tenerife any day. Thirty years in a holiday park? Sounds like a life sentence to me. Fuck me, it's nearly half a lifetime! Probably two-thirds in my case, given how much I like the ale, and that I only packed in smoking last year.'

No beer belly, though, she couldn't help noticing. 'I never knew you were a smoker.'

'Twenty-a-day man.' He held up a neatly manicured hand. 'Forensics wouldn't find it difficult to spot the nicotine traces. On the morning my decree absolute came through, I decided to make a fresh start. Threw my packet of Player's in the bin, and I've never touched one since.'

'You must have needed self-discipline to manage that.'

'Believe it or not, ma'am, I am capable of it.' He lifted his eyebrows a fraction. 'If the moon's in the right quarter.'

Hannah pretended to absorb herself in her ice cream and chocolate flakes. Greg's knack of making her feel he could read her mind was unsettling.

'What I meant was, how do you see Kit Payne? Grieving step-parent or a man with something to hide?'

'Bit of both, shouldn't wonder.' He ripped the ring pull off his can and took a swig. 'I told myself not to be prejudiced, just because he looks like the Elephant Man's love child. But he's twitchy about the cold case. I reckon Bryan and Gareth Madsen are, as well, but they are too streetwise to show it.'

'Scarcely a surprise.' She waved towards the septuagenarians, who were tucking into their cornets as they moaned to each other about the cost of private health insurance. 'Any bad vibes might make the caravan folk pause before frittering their kids' inheritance on another year's site fees.'

'I say it's worth nosing around in the Madsens' lives as long as the ACC stays on board. Payne's life too. It suited everyone for Philip to take the rap. Along with his pig.'

'The pig couldn't answer back, either. Especially after it ran off.'

'Everything was made so easy for Will Durston to wind down the investigation. He was given all he needed to close the file.'

'Except a corpse,' Hannah said.

'Makes you wonder why Mike Hinds didn't kick and scream, with his boy left unburied. If it was my son, I wouldn't rest until the kid had a proper burial.'

'But if he believed there was no corpse to find?'

'We can't take it as read that Hinds had nothing to do with the boy's death.' Greg's tone was mulish. 'Suppose they had a row, and Callum got hurt?'

'You really didn't take to him, did you?'

'Did you?'

'No, he could use some coaching in anger management. But now he's lost both his kids. We ought to cut him some slack.'

Greg wrinkled his nose. 'He was scarcely the perfect father.'

'Even so.'

'All I'm saying is, Durston's team took the soft option. If it had been my case, I wouldn't have given up so quickly.'

'If it had been yours, you'd have had the brass telling you not to throw more money at an open-and-shut case. There was a reason why no body was found. Perhaps Durston was too ready to blame it on the pig. But there's nothing new about investigations being affected by cash constraints. Even twenty years back, there were budget limits.'

'Not that you were around so long ago, ma'am, of course.' He grinned. 'Might there be another explanation why the body was hidden or disposed of? Did something about it reveal what happened to him, and who was responsible?'

'Or even if it didn't, perhaps forensic evidence could have proved Philip didn't kill him.'

He nodded. 'And Kit Payne is the man who leaves nothing to chance, we're told.'

She finished her cone and clambered to her feet. 'Shall we head for the Hanging Wood?'

'Sure.' Greg sprang up. 'And talking of the way things look, ma'am . . .'

'Yes?'

'You have a smear of ice cream on the tip of your nose.'

'Is Aslan around?' Daniel asked. 'He left a message on my voicemail asking for a word.'

Sham glanced up from her computer. She'd perfected the expression of an upwardly mobile young executive interrupted in the midst of a life-or-death task, but a glance at the screen revealed she was catching up on the latest gossip from a soap opera website.

'Waltzed in this morning, on time for once, and announced he'd only be in for an hour or so today. And then he spent all his time in the library, rather than in his own office. Never known him do that before; he once told me he's not much of a reader. Sure enough, inside thirty minutes, he was tearing out again. A man in a hurry.'

'Why the rush?'

'Dunno, he didn't say a word. The bloody librarian was asking me a question and he just waved as he dashed past. Didn't even shut the front door. I saw him stop by the flower bed and take a knife from his pocket. He cut off two red roses and took them with them. The principal would go mental about it, if only he knew.' Daniel recognised an admiration for Aslan's effrontery, mixed in with disgruntlement. 'He didn't present the roses to me, that's for sure.'

'He's keen on flexible hours, isn't he?'

'Another way of saying that he works as little as possible.' Sham sniffed. Dark rings under her eyes suggested a late night. 'Not that I blame him. Wouldn't I just love a job like that? Events organising? A real skive, if you ask me.'

'Doesn't he enjoy it?' Daniel was all innocence. 'I assumed everyone here would be highly motivated.'

'Are you kidding?' Sham allowed herself a lavish sigh. 'Aunt Fleur suggested I might fill in here for a few weeks, until Mockbeggar Hall opens to the public.'

'So you're joining the family business?'

'Dad told me they want me to run the welcome desk. He came for one of his weekly meetings with Aunt Fleur in her office here, discussing the plans for the Hall. Apparently they like the idea of having a member of the family working in the Hall full-time, and there's no arguing with that pair once they've made up their minds.' She groaned. 'No escape, is there? I meant to make a break, strike out on my own. My sister Purdey is the business-minded one, not me. I'm not really cut out for the nine to five. Maybe I should travel the world. Aslan has never settled down, and it hasn't done him any harm.'

'What brought him to St Herbert's, if not love of the job?'

'I suppose it's a pretty place to pass the summer. He's a volunteer, and in his opinion, that gives him the right to get away with murder. Mind you, the rest of us might as well be working out of the goodness of our hearts.' As if bored with whingeing, she dazzled him with a sudden smile. 'Never mind, one thing I'll say about this place is that you do meet some interesting people. Television stars, for instance.'

'I was never a television star.'

'Aunt Fleur never missed a programme. She's one of your biggest fans; she has all your books in hardback. I'm surprised she hasn't demanded your autograph yet. Maybe she will at dinner tonight.'

'You'll be there?'

'Wouldn't miss it for anything.'

'I assumed you'd have better offers.'

'Are you kidding? Keswick isn't exactly alive with excitement for people my age. And in case you're wondering, Aslan and I aren't seeing each other, not seriously. Yesterday evening was only the second or third time we've even been out for a drink.'

'Uh-huh.' He wondered why she was bothering to tell him.

'I never intended to put poor Orla's nose out of joint. I mean, Aslan is pretty fit, but she'd have been welcome to him.' So was she feeling guilty at having tempted Aslan away from the dead girl, or trying to explain away her failure to captivate him? 'Anyway, I'm looking forward to tonight. Couldn't let Purdey get one up on me through having dinner with a media celebrity, could I, now?'

An earnest vicar approached the reception desk, flourishing the St Herbert's annual programme of events. His demeanour suggested he was about to ask complicated questions to which Sham was unlikely to have answers. Daniel seized the opportunity to sidle away.

'See you tonight, then,' she called.

Climbing to his eyrie in the library, his thoughts drifted back to the principal's report of that fraught conversation between Orla and Aslan Sheikh. What connected Callum in her mind with Castor and Pollux – surely not the fact that the two siblings had different fathers?

A red squirrel dashed into the undergrowth as Hannah and Greg approached the Hanging Wood. The wood was separated from the holiday park by a barbed wire barrier which ran behind a group of low buildings where maintenance equipment and backup generators were kept, and which lay behind eight-feet-high waney-lap fences covered with health and safety warnings and signs saying *Private*. A security man had let them through a locked gate; this was no place for casual visitors. The ground was rough and potholed, and the narrow track was overgrown and surrounded by tall clumps of stinging nettles. The sweet smell of cow parsley hung in the air.

According to Kit Payne, the Madsens had abandoned the Hanging Wood after Philip Hinds' death, and the disappearance of his nephew. Philip's cottage was demolished, but there was no question of developing the land, even if it hadn't been inconceivable that the Parks Authority would allow it. The Madsens owned more than enough land to expand their site, Kit explained; two-thirds of the Mockbeggar Estate remained untouched and out of bounds to visitors.

Greg began to whistle, and Hannah recognised the opening bars to 'The Teddy Bears' Picnic'.

If you go down to the woods today, you're sure of a big surprise.

'What do you reckon to the guy on the CCTV, wandering into the Forbidden Forest?' Greg asked.

'Surely he can't have become so bored with his luxury holiday home that he went in search of adventure?'

'Naughty not to heed the notices telling him to "keep out".' Greg shot her a glance. 'He must be as keen to get into the Mockbeggar Estate as the Madsens are to warn off intruders.'

They reached the outer fringe of the Hanging Wood. As they moved between the trees, the temperature seemed to drop two or three degrees. Wych elms towered above them, along with rowan, ash and oak. Coarse grass, heather and spiky brambles obscured the old path, ivy tendrils smothered the bark.

'Did you think the chap seemed familiar?' she said at last.

A brisk nod. 'Hard to tell from that camera angle, but he reminded me of the bloke we saw outside Mike Hinds' farm.'

So she hadn't imagined it. 'Me too.'

They pushed on along the half-hidden track, ducking their heads under low and heavy branches. A foetid stench wafted from a small stagnant pond. Greg trod on a fallen branch, and the snap of wood sounded like a pistol shot.

Out of the blue, he said, 'I read up about wych elms last night.'

'You did?' He had this knack of setting her back on her heels.

He kicked the broken branch out of his way. 'Idle curiosity, that's all.'

Hannah guessed he wanted to understand the environment in which Philip Hinds had lived and died. He'd never admit it; he didn't want to seem touchy-feely. She remembered Ben Kind preaching the importance of getting under the victim's skin. Do that, he maintained, and you were halfway to getting under the killer's skin. Not that anybody thought of Philip as a victim. Except for Orla.

'Disease killed a lot of elms,' Greg said. 'Even so, some trees survived. Turns out there's something macabre about wych elms. They feature in a lot of folklore. Traditionally, they were associated with melancholy and death.'

'Why was that?'

'Nobody knows for sure. Perhaps because they drop old branches that can crack your skull, like the one I just tripped over. Possibly because they look like they are weeping. Or because elm was used to make coffins.'

His thirst for finding things out reminded her of Marc.

Daniel Kind, too. This energy and enthusiasm for stockpiling scraps of knowledge, she couldn't help finding it attractive, although she never quite understood why. They walked on in silence, their route carpeted by ferns and moss. Greg was right about the mood conjured up by the wych elms. The sun was barely visible through the canopy of leaves, and there was an earthy primitive smell in the air. Even on a day like this, the Hanging Wood had the odour of decay. Purple foxgloves supplied a scattering of colour, but for Hannah, the flowers conjured up sinister memories. They were poisonous, and when she was small, a thoughtless uncle warned her that nibbling the stems in his garden would kill her. She'd spent the rest of the day in a state of terror. She remembered his nickname for foxgloves: dead man's bells.

She'd seen photos of Philip Hinds in the files. A bulky shambling man, whose eyes looked anywhere but straight at the camera. He'd felt at home in this melancholy wood, where nobody bothered him. Inside the big body was someone small and frightened, unable to cope when his world was invaded. How must it feel to live like Philip, encircled by tall forbidding trees, with only a fat smelly pig for company? The Hanging Wood covered a tiny area, yet the bright world outside seemed as remote as a faraway land. Philip's brother had no time for him, and for the Madsens he was no more than a backup handyman. Yet even a man who craved solitude must sometimes yearn for someone to talk to. No wonder he'd welcomed fleeting human contact when his young nephew and niece came to play. You wouldn't need to be a closet paedophile to relish their zest, their innocence, their lust for life.

Durston had found no evidence that Philip had harmed

Callum, far less that he was responsible for his death. The case against him was hopelessly circumstantial. But convenient.

The track sloped gently into a dip where the trees thinned, and soon they reached a clearing. Fir cones were scattered over the ground; they'd been chewed by the squirrels. Sycamores had seeded, but too few to block the sun, which blazed down on a thick tangle of brambles and grass.

'So this is where the cottage stood,' Greg said.

Nature had reclaimed the site of Philip Hinds' home; every trace of his existence had been erased from the Hanging Wood. The undergrowth was so thick that you couldn't see where the foundations of the cottage had stood, or any sign of a pigsty. In the middle of the clearing, grass and brambles had been hewn back around a small sandstone tablet. The letters had worn, but the inscription was perfectly readable.

In Loving Memory of Callum Hinds.

A single rose lay at the foot of the table, a splash of crimson amidst the green and brown.

'Well, well,' Greg said. 'You reckon that bloke on the CCTV came here and left the rose, before he wandered into the Mockbeggar grounds?'

'But why?' She inhaled the perfume of the luscious bloom. Rich and strong, a contrast with the dank foliage. 'What reason could he have for taking an interest in a boy who disappeared twenty years ago?'

'If he's staying at the holiday park, we should be able to track him down.'

'As for poor old Philip, not a mention. Far less a floral tribute.'

'Can you wonder?'

She sighed. 'Not really, though this was his domain, the place where he lived and died. With Callum, nobody knows for sure where he died. According to the file, his mother wanted some sort of memorial to the lad placed here, as well as a stone in the local cemetery. Joseph Madsen insisted on paying for it himself. The Paynes, Mike Hinds, the Madsen family, none of them wanted to think about the man they blamed for Callum's death. He was the bad guy, he deserved nothing.'

Greg looked around. 'Did they chop down the wych elm he hanged himself from?'

A cloud of midges buzzed around Hannah's head, persistent as paparazzi. She swatted them away. 'Of course. The tree and the cottage, they both had to go.'

The detectives contemplated the sandstone memorial. Everything was still; no birds sang in the trees, no breeze rustled the leaves. People supposed a savage murder had taken place in this quiet and lonely spot, but you would never guess.

'Are you thinking what I'm thinking?' Greg asked.

She managed a smile, still trying to make sense of the strange idea. 'Depends on what you're thinking.'

'It seems crazy,' he muttered.

'Go on.'

She felt tense, expectant.

Greg took a breath. 'We're assuming the man at the farm, the man in the wood, the person who left the red rose, were one and the same?'

'Agreed.'

She was sure he'd had the same idea, and she found

it thrilling. Detective work did this to you, if you cared enough about your job. She'd learnt as much from Ben Kind. Solving a mystery was a turn-on, he said, and he was right. In her excitement, she had to force herself not to give Greg a hug.

His eyes were shining, and she knew he was excited too.

'What if we've just seen Callum Hinds?'

'It was something and nothing,' Kit Payne said. 'When you run a large holiday park, there are a thousand and one issues to deal with every day. That's the price of working in the service sector, dealing with Joe Public. Our insurance premium costs rise year on year, and don't get me started on legal fees.'

Hannah and Greg had bumped into him on their way back, as he said goodbye to the visiting Bulgars. Hannah asked whether the security wardens had found the man spotted wandering around the grounds of Mockbeggar Hall. Kit said that by the time the wardens turned up, he had vanished, and he might have headed off in any number of directions. Back to the holiday park, most likely, but he could just as easily have walked to Mike Hinds' farm, along the lane that ran from the Hall, or over towards St Herbert's Residential Library. Kit said his sole concern was to make sure the chap wasn't at risk of coming a cropper on Madsen property, and claiming compensation for personal injury.

'Back with us already, Hannah?'

Hannah looked up and saw Bryan Madsen on the balcony outside his first-floor office. A broad smile of greeting did not quite disguise his irritation that the police were still present in his holiday park.

'They wanted to know if we found the chap who was trespassing in the Hall grounds,' Kit said.

Bryan frowned. 'He's a nosey holidaymaker, not a criminal on the run.'

'He reminded me of someone, that's all,' Hannah said.

Kit stared. 'Who did—?'

She gave them a sweet smile. 'I must have been mistaken.'

Louise was fretting over which dress to wear for dinner at Mockbeggar Hall, while Daniel checked his mobile for messages. The signal in Brackdale, and especially in and around Tarn Fold, was unreliable, and he found he'd missed a call. When he dialled voicemail, he heard the voice of Aslan Sheikh.

'Daniel, it's Aslan. Sorry to miss you, but it's not important. Catch up with you next time you're at the library.'

'I'm off to have a shower,' Louise announced. 'Be honest, I can take it – don't you think the black dress is a bit too revealing? Even a bit tarty?'

He made reassuring noises, knowing that she'd make her own choice in the end. No doubt she'd decided hours ago on the red gown with the high neckline, but felt the need to indulge in the formality of consultation, like a politician wanting to be approved for doing the right thing.

When she padded upstairs, he took his mobile out into the lane that petered out at Tarn Fold. As soon as he was clear of the trees, he dialled Hannah's number. For once he got straight through, and he heard her excuse herself to a companion and step out into the street.

'Sorry, I'm up in Keswick, at the police station.'

'I wondered if you'd like to get together?'

A pause. He could hear traffic noise.

'Love to.'

'I'm tied up this evening. The Madsens have invited Louise and me to dinner at Mockbeggar Hall, would you believe?'

'My sergeant and I called in at the caravan park today. You'll probably have to listen to them complaining about our wasting their valuable time on a fool's errand.'

'Look, I wanted to talk to you about Orla. One or two things I've gathered from her colleagues at St Herbert's. You wouldn't be free tomorrow, by any chance?'

'It's Saturday, and the budget doesn't allow for overtime. When and where?'

His spirits lifted. He liked Hannah's directness, and the absence of fuss about needing to check her diary. 'The weather forecast is fine, and I've an unfulfilled ambition to explore Derwent Water. How about meeting in Keswick and then we can go on the lake? Unless you'd prefer somewhere closer to Ambleside?'

'Keswick suits me fine. Shall we say ten-thirty? I fancy taking a look at the market, so if we meet outside the Moot Hall?'

'Perfect.'

'So Callum Hinds might still be alive?' Mario Pinardi said.

Hannah and Greg were debating the case in The Forge Brow, a tiny pub backing on to the River Greta. Half five on Friday evening, and the place was packed with people who had finished work and were getting in the mood for the weekend. Mario had bagged a table outside, on a small paved patio that separated the saloon bar from the river.

'I have to admit, it's the longest of long shots,' Hannah said.

During the afternoon, her initial excitement at the possibility that Callum might have staged an audacious comeback had waned. She and Greg hot-desked at Keswick police station for a couple of hours, catching up on emails and chewing over their theory. The longer they talked, the more unlikely it seemed that Callum was back in town.

'If Callum is alive, it would explain a few things,' Mario said.

'And raise plenty more questions,' she said. 'Like where he disappeared to, and what he's been playing at all these years.'

'Explains why you saw him at Lane End – looking out for his long-lost father. Maybe plucking up the courage to say, *Hello, remember me?*'

Hannah found herself playing devil's advocate. 'Why would Callum leave a rose at a memorial to himself? I mean, narcissistic, or what? And why would his reappearance coincide with Orla's suicide?'

Mario took a swig of orange juice. 'It might explain Orla's suicide, don't you think?'

'How?'

'Suppose she met this bloke and got an inkling he was Callum. So she became insistent that her brother hadn't died at the hands of Philip Hinds. But for some reason, things turned nasty. Did she discover he had some dark secret that explained why he'd stayed away so long?'

'Must have been very dark for her to dive into a silo full of grain.' Greg drained his glass. 'Same again?'

He strode into the saloon bar, leaving them to watch the river rushing over stones set in shallow mud. Hannah found it hard to imagine that, only months before, the Greta had smashed through its banks during freakish floods that drowned large areas of Western Cumbria, claiming lives and wrecking homes. Scaffolding still shrouded houses along the riverside, and flood defences were being built in an attempt to make the buildings safe in case the waters ever swelled again.

'Where are you up to with the enquiry?' she asked.

'Orla was a pisshead,' Mario said. 'She never settled to anything; jobs and relationships, none of them lasted. The most exciting thing that happened to her was that her brother was supposedly a murder victim. She was bright and not bad-looking, and Kit Payne did his best by her after her mother died. Decent education, she was a long way from destitute. But she wasted her opportunities.'

'Callum's disappearance defined her,' Hannah said, almost to herself. 'How life-changing must it be, to lose your brother in those circumstances?'

'She moved away to make a fresh start, but it didn't work out. Once she took the job at St Herbert's, the old memories came flooding back. I'd say that in the end, they killed her.'

'You're still certain it was suicide?'

'Her father's farm and the Hanging Wood were just around the corner from St Herbert's. There was no escaping the past. She persuaded herself that Callum was alive, then changed her mind, and couldn't cope with the grief. End of.'

'Is that what you really think?'

Mario flashed the smile that sent so many women weak at the knees. 'Dunno. It's a job for an ace detective, I guess.'

'But where do you find one of them?' Greg demanded as he returned bearing drinks. 'Solved it yet?'

Mario tilted his glass. 'Cheers, mate. Might be worth my having another word with the feller that Orla palled up with at St Herbert's. He says they were casual acquaintances, no more than that. But the word is, she saw it differently. Perhaps he has something to hide.'

'Hasn't everyone?' Greg said. 'What was his name?'

'Aslan Sheikh,' Mario said.

Hannah almost choked on her lemonade. '*Aslan?*'

The two men stared at her.

'What?' Greg asked.

'Did you never read C.S. Lewis?'

'*The Lion, the Witch and the Wardrobe?*' Mario asked.

Greg made a face. 'Wasn't that the film with Tilda Swinton? Saw it on Sky by mistake. Not my cup of tea.'

'But *The Chronicles of Narnia* were Callum Hinds' favourite books.' Her voice was unsteady. 'Aslan was a Christ-like figure who came back from the dead.'

CHAPTER TWELVE

'The Hall dates back to the seventeenth century,' Fleur Madsen said, 'but it needed to be rebuilt after being burnt down the year Victoria came to the throne.'

'I read about that when I looked up the Hall's history this afternoon,' Louise said. 'Arson, wasn't it?'

Fleur moved her head to one side, allowing a pretty waitress to refill her glass with a fine red Bordeaux plucked from the newly refurbished climate-controlled wine cellars that lay beneath their feet. There were ten for dinner, sitting around a mahogany Chippendale table large enough to have accommodated twenty; Fleur sat beneath a portrait of her great-grandmother's great-grandmother. The woman in the painting wore a green velvet-and-satin evening gown, whereas Fleur contented herself with a simple black dress and necklace of pearls, but like her long-dead predecessor, she radiated the self-assurance that came with being chatelaine of Mockbeggar Hall.

'One of my ancestors dismissed a servant on a whim, and the man set fire to the place in revenge.'

Her wry smile gave no clue to her thoughts. Daniel felt a sudden urge to step inside her mind. How must it feel to belong to a house like this, where your family had lived for so long? Hard to understand for someone who had grown up in a nondescript semi on the outskirts of Manchester. When he was a boy, to live here would have seemed a dream come true. But real life was no dream. The Hall's makeover had been planned and executed with respect for the past, and many of its original features had been restored and retained, but the historian in him could not help cringing at the metamorphosis of a grand family home into an offshoot of a caravan empire.

Beggars couldn't be choosers, but was Fleur as happy about the Hall's fate as she claimed? For whatever reason, discontent lurked beneath her surface calm, he was sure of it.

Kit Payne smiled. 'Thank goodness there are employment tribunals nowadays where disgruntled staff can ventilate their grievances without resorting to acts of vengeance.'

'Not that we like to think we have any disgruntled staff,' Bryan Madsen announced, sneaking a not very surreptitious glance down the waitress's top. 'Kit does a first-rate job of keeping everyone motivated. Ably assisted by Glenys, I might add.'

Kit beamed, a spaniel relishing a pat from his master. Further down the table, his wife Glenys simpered, prompting Sham and Purdey Madsen to exchange glances that implied shared scorn of long standing. Twenty years her husband's junior, with a Geordie accent and a generous bosom, Glenys had met Kit while working in the office as a trainee personnel officer, and now she was in charge of Human Resources. Her principal topic of conversation was their son Nathan, who was currently in Tanzania on an educational holiday organised by his very expensive private school. *Just as well in the circumstances*, she'd said. Orla's name didn't pass her lips; her main concern about the suicide at Lane End Farm was clearly that it should not disrupt the equilibrium of the Payne household.

'What happened to the arsonist?' Louise asked.

Fleur shrugged. 'I believe he was executed.'

Purdey Madsen made a face. 'Gross.'

'Darling,' her aunt said, 'they knew how to deal with criminals in those days.'

'But he didn't even kill anybody!'

'He made the greatest mistake of all.' Fleur allowed herself a faint smile. 'He was careless, and so he got caught. Why risk doing wrong if you don't make sure you get away with it?'

Bryan coughed. 'When we started renovating the place, Daniel, it was hardly in a better state than it was back in 1837.'

Daniel made admiring small talk as the waitress served him with venison accompanied by a generous helping of cranberry Cumberland sauce, wild mushrooms, and a head of sweet caramelised roast garlic. The catering was handled by a firm run by a celebrity chef; nothing but the best for the Madsens. An honoured guest, Daniel sat in pride of place, between Bryan and his wife. Before the meal, his host had taken him and Louise on a tour of the Hall, a chance to show off the lovingly restored silk hangings in the drawing room, the intricate carvings and fine plasterwork in the pastiche Elizabethan gallery.

This huge dining room had been reimagined as one more facet of the Madsen money-making machine, available for hire by elite dining clubs, business magnates, and politicians in search of an awayday with a touch of class. Bryan had hinted that a committee of cabinet ministers was booked in for late August for a private meeting over dinner to discuss the next round of spending cuts. The focal point of the room was a magnificent fireplace bordered by twisted columns carved from wych elms cut down, Bryan said, from the Hanging Wood. There was a Japanese lacquered chest, a small table on which huntsmen once breakfasted, and a long case clock with a moon dial and an engraved motto, *Time flies, pursue it, Man, for why the days are but a span*. A couple of dozen Victorian portraits depicted three generations of the Hopes family: stern fathers, demure wives and assorted children, cats and horses. The Hopes undeniably thought of themselves as animal lovers, even if hunting foxes to death was their favourite sport.

Daniel tasted the meat. Tender and lean, with a tangy aroma. He tried not to think of the deer from which it came.

'What happened to the pooches, Aunt Fleur?' Sham asked, waving her knife at a pair of landscapes, each of misty heather-clad fells, which were interspersed between pictures of Fleur's forbears and their domestic menagerie.

Before his sister-in-law could answer, Gareth said, 'We're trying out different ideas for exhibiting some of the contents of the Hall, darling. The insurers might kick up a fuss if we keep all Millais' work in areas accessible to the public.

Or at least increase their already extortionate premiums. Thank God so much stuff survived – we're spoilt for choice as to what to display. The Hopes may have fallen on hard times, but at least they didn't flog every last piece of the family silver.'

Sham was about to ask another question, but was interrupted by Fleur exclaiming in admiration about her niece's bracelet. Talk of the family silver had Daniel glancing at the cutlery. Old, heavy, and no doubt absurdly valuable, it bore the same Hopes monogram as the napkin rings and the tiles of the fireplace, an elaborately curling letter H. Fleur might have become a Madsen, but the Hopes hadn't quite been airbrushed out of Mockbeggar Hall. Their monogram spoke of power and possession, a reminder to visitors of how the other half once lived. Mind you, the other half continued to live very well, to judge by this meal served with such swift and silent efficiency, albeit no longer by flunkeys born into service, but by freelancers on agency contracts. Impossible not to be impressed. And yet, like the sumptuous furniture and fittings, the food was too rich for Daniel's taste.

Hannah stayed at The Forge Brow longer than she'd intended. When Mario left for home, Greg suggested another drink and she found herself saying OK. By the time the Friday crowd thinned and the evening grew chilly, she was ready to leave, but she'd enjoyed his company far more than she'd expected. As a drinking companion, he was funny without being crude – at least, not very – and knowledgeable without being tedious. He'd arrived in the Cold Case Review Team with a very dodgy reputation, but she was glad she'd given him the benefit of the doubt. He even claimed to share her enthusiasm for the music of Diana Krall.

'Back to Ambleside, then?' he asked as they reached the car park.

'With any luck I'll be home before it gets dark.' She was seized by a sudden dread that he might invite her back to his place. Not what she wanted at all. 'Anyway, I'll see you on Monday.'

'Take care, Hannah.'

He hesitated, as if for once in his life he was unable to make up his mind about something, but then he gave a brisk nod of farewell, and strode off to where he'd left his car.

She shook her car key out of her bag. Her heart was beating faster, but her overriding emotion was relief, rather than excitement. In a strange way, it was as if Greg had passed a test by not trying it on. He'd treated her as a trusted colleague, not another potential notch on his belt.

And tomorrow, she'd see Daniel again. Things were looking up.

Orla's name wasn't mentioned until halfway through the dessert course, yet Daniel had become conscious of her presence the moment he and Louise walked through the imposing front doors of Mockbeggar Hall. She was the ghost at the feast.

It was Sally Madsen who brought Orla into the conversation – no surprise there. You only had to be in the company of Gareth's wife for ten minutes to hear her saying the first thing that sprang into her head, relying on her good looks and charm to compensate for any offence caused. Tall, tanned and tactless, she wore a short magenta evening dress meant for a woman half her age; yet somehow she got away with it. After they were introduced over pre-dinner drinks, Louise had whispered something disobliging about hair extensions and silicone implants, but whatever Sally's style secrets, they worked. For a man, anyway.

Daniel was intrigued by the contrast between the Madsen brothers, and between their wives. What did their different choices say about them? Gareth had married a woman who might otherwise have decorated the arm of a football player. Bryan had gone for the local squire's daughter. Sally's voice grew louder each time she gulped down a mouthful of wine. Fleur watched her with an indulgent smile that gave nothing away. She'd covered her wine glass with her hand the last time the waitress came round, and was now confining herself to Bowland Spring Water.

'So when is poor Orla's inquest, Kit?' Sally asked.

She'd seized a moment when Glenys Payne paused in a lengthy account of young Nathan's trip to Africa to swallow a truffle. Kit cast an anxious glance at his wife's reddened face. She must hate to be reminded that her husband had a life before she arrived in it. A life including an alcoholic wife with a suicidal daughter, and a son who was missing, presumed murdered. You could hardly blame her for wanting Nathan to be the main topic of conversation.

'I'm told it will be opened when the coroner returns from holiday next week, but she will adjourn it for twelve weeks to allow time for post-mortem reports. In a case like this, there have to be toxicology tests, and God knows what else.'

'They don't think she was under the influence of drugs when she jumped, do they?' Sally was agog; in another age, she'd have been a tricoteuse. 'It would explain things, I suppose. Such a terrible way to go.'

'Alcohol was her drug of choice,' Kit said. 'The sad thing is, people can say anything about her now, and she can't defend herself. What happened is traumatic enough, frankly, and it doesn't help to have the cold case people noseying around.'

'Pity they can't let Callum rest in his grave,' Sally said.

'That's rather the point, sweetheart,' Gareth told his wife, with exaggerated patience. 'The kid never got a proper grave, did he?'

'You'd think the police would have better things to do, with the crime figures sky-high,' Glenys complained. 'Two senior officers, Kit told me, going for a ramble around the Hanging Wood! Hard to beat that for a ridiculous waste of time. And they make such a fuss about being short of resources; any excuse for not putting enough bobbies back on the beat!'

'I suppose they need to justify their existence,' Kit said.

'That's the public sector for you.' Bryan fixed his gaze on the waitress as she topped up his glass yet again. 'Thank you very much, my dear. Yes, the police force is far too politically correct these days. Scared stiff of litigation, so they waste time and effort on trivia, for fear of someone complaining. That's the trouble with this country, if you ask me.'

'What did you make of DCI Scarlett?' Gareth asked.

Kit's brow furrowed. 'She didn't give much away.'

'She does realise she's on a wild goose chase?'

'Never going to admit it, is she?' Bryan demanded.

Daniel saw Fleur exchange looks with her brother-in-law. Presumably Fleur had spent her married life listening to Bryan pontificating, when he wasn't leering at attractive young women. Over an aperitif, Bryan had recounted his plucky attempt to stand for Parliament in an unwinnable seat; no doubt Fleur was relieved not to have spent the past twenty years small-talking with the constituency hoi polloi.

'Nobody can seriously believe that Philip didn't murder Callum,' she murmured. 'It's an absurd notion.'

'There's no proof about what happened,' Purdey said. 'We can't be certain.'

'For Christ's sake, don't you start.' Gareth usually left the tetchiness to his elder brother. 'Bad enough that Orla made her own life a misery, imagining Callum might still be alive and kicking. None of this rumour and innuendo is good for the business. If the bloody media get hold of it, my job will become ten times more difficult.'

'Just saying.' His daughter's voice was plaintive, though a gleam in her eye suggested she was more than capable of standing up to her father.

'Sorry, love, didn't mean to snap.' He gave Purdey's bare shoulder an affectionate squeeze. The gift of a daddy's girl, Daniel thought, that knack of twisting him around her little finger.

'Orla was a dreamer,' Sham pronounced in a voice loud enough to indicate that she'd overindulged in the wine.

Whenever Purdey said something, Daniel had noticed, her sister butted in a few moments later. Purdey's cool contrasted with Sham's stridency, just as her little black dress only showed off her long legs, whilst Sham's lacked any subtlety. 'No wonder she was crazy about fairy tales. Let's face it, she lived in a fantasy world.'

'She wasn't off her head,' Purdey said.

Damning with faint praise, Daniel thought.

'Orla was bloody hard work, you must admit,' Sham said. 'You're not telling me you were a member of her fan club?'

'She could be a pain, but I did feel sorry for her,' Purdey said.

If Kit Payne was troubled at the talk about his dead stepdaughter, he contrived not to show it. One advantage of possessing such unlovely features was that they masked his emotions. A useful asset for a man who depended on the Madsen family for his living. When he'd talked about grievance and employment tribunals, was that a reminder not to push him too far?

'At least she is at peace now,' Kit said.

If he intended this as a conversational full stop, Sham didn't take the hint. 'What I don't get is – why? I didn't have a clue what was going on in her head. She must have been disappointed that Aslan didn't take her seriously, but even so . . .'

'Who didn't take her seriously?' Gareth asked.

'Aslan Sheikh, you know, from St Herbert's. Orla had the hots for him. But he wasn't interested.'

'She wasn't the only one who fancied him, was she?' Purdey smirked.

Sham, determined not to rise to the bait, turned towards Daniel. 'So, did you manage to track him down in the end?'

'Yes, we spoke on the phone before Louise and I left home.'

'You were looking for Aslan?' Fleur asked.

'He left me a message, wanting a word about something, but when I caught up with him on the phone, he said not to worry, it wasn't important.'

'He's an oddball.' Fleur frowned. 'I don't expect Micah Bridge will keep him on when his contract comes up for renewal.'

'But he's not costing St Herbert's a penny!' Sham protested.

'Just because he's a volunteer, that doesn't give him the right to come and go as he pleases.' The corners of Sham's mouth turned down, but she didn't argue. 'The bottom line is, he's not pulling his weight, and that's bad for morale in any organisation. Wouldn't you agree, Daniel?'

'Yes, Fleur tells me she'd asked you to become a trustee of St Herbert's,' Gareth interrupted. 'Congratulations.'

'I haven't actually accepted yet,' Daniel said. 'But I'm flattered by the invitation.'

'Very diplomatic,' Bryan said. 'But my advice to you, old man, is to face up to the inevitable. What my wife wants, she makes sure she gets, you can take it from me.'

He leant back in his chair, and guffawed with laughter at the precise moment that the pretty waitress began to pour his coffee, with the result that she spilt some over his crisp white dinner jacket. A malevolent gleam lit her eyes even as she apologised, and mopped ineffectually at the spreading brown stain. Payback for incessant ogling. Gareth couldn't hide his amusement, but Fleur Madsen's face was as unreadable as a rune stone.

So Fleur always got what she wanted, did she? Daniel could scarcely contain his curiosity. He would love to find out what she really did want.

Daylight was fading as Hannah arrived back at Undercrag. She was back in Ambleside later than planned. The moment she'd switched on the engine of her Lexus, her mobile had sung. Terri, at a loose end and in the mood for a chat. When Hannah let slip that she'd spent the evening in a pub with her sergeant, her friend insisted on being told all about him. It had taken ten minutes to persuade Terri that Greg wasn't a candidate to replace Marc in her bed. At least she didn't make the mistake of announcing that she was due to see Daniel Kind again tomorrow morning. She'd never have heard the last of it.

As she closed the door of the Lexus, the back of her neck prickled. She froze. She wasn't alone here. Someone was watching her every move.

With agonising care, she craned her neck to look at the front of the house.

A dark figure detached itself from the shadows.

Panic surged inside her. She swallowed hard.

Keep calm, keep calm.

'Hannah,' a familiar voice said. 'I wondered how long you would keep me waiting.'

'Have you and Daniel always been close?' Sally Madsen asked Louise, as Purdey and Sham squabbled over who had devoured the most truffles. 'I wish the girls would grow out of this rivalry. I can't understand it. I'm an only child, and I always longed for a brother or sister.'

Bryan had sent for another dinner jacket. Naturally, the man who had everything could, in the space of five minutes, rustle up a spare that looked even more expensive than the one the girl had drenched.

Louise took a sip of coffee. 'Not always close, no. Our father left home when we were still at school, and the two of us made the mistake of taking sides. I backed Mum to the hilt, Daniel missed his dad. It took us years to get past that. But there was never any rivalry between us. From my point of view, it would have been crazy. Everyone always said how brilliant Daniel was. How could I possibly compete?'

Daniel had never thought of it like that. Trying to cover his embarrassment, he said to Fleur, 'So how did you get on with your brother?'

Fleur's expression gave nothing away. 'You might be surprised how little Jolyon and I saw of each other. He was older than me, and very different in every respect. I was sent away to school in Yorkshire from the age of seven. I only came home for holidays, and even then, I often stayed with friends for weeks at a time. He broke his neck in a riding accident twenty-one years ago, it was tragic. But although we made sure he had the best care money could buy, I can't say we were close.'

'You must have grown up with Bryan and Gareth,' Louise said. 'They lived only a stone's throw away.'

'We knew each other, of course. But my father and theirs didn't really see eye to eye. Old money versus new,

I suppose, coupled with resentment that we'd been forced to sell a large chunk of our land to people who had to work for a living. Not that there was any of the old money left by this time. The Hall was falling to bits, and I didn't know what the future held. Lucky for me that, one summer holiday, Bryan plucked up the courage to ask me out. And the rest is history.'

'Lucky lady,' Gareth said. 'Sally drew the short straw. The younger brother. The minority shareholder.'

His wife blew him a kiss. 'Never mind; you may be the poor one, but you're still a hunk as far as I'm concerned.'

Sham winced at the ostentatious display of mutual affection. 'Mum, please.'

Paying no attention to his niece, Bryan sniggered. 'Fleur's father almost choked on a glass of gin when I asked for his daughter's hand.'

'But like you said,' Gareth murmured, 'Fleur always gets what she wants.'

Daniel was conscious of Fleur's body brushing against his for a moment, as she reached for the cream jug. The contact was probably unintentional, but he worried that his cheeks might turn pink. Shifting in his chair, he turned to Gareth.

'So you and your brother have managed to work closely together all these years. Never a cross word?'

Gareth grinned. 'Bryan is the public face of the company, my job is selling pitches, and persuading people who have bought a cheap caravan to keep trading up, year after year. I come up with the wacky ideas, he approves or vetoes them as he thinks fit. We avoid getting in each other's way, and we don't disagree that often. When we do, I remind myself that Bryan has the voting control, and that keeps me on the straight and narrow.'

'It's all about achieving consensus.' If Bryan was trying not to sound smug, he wasn't trying hard enough. 'Same as in any family.'

Sure, Daniel thought, but it helped to have the whip hand. He was conscious of Fleur's perfume, a honeysuckle fragrance. Underneath the table, her knee touched his for an instant. Again, perhaps an accident, but he swung his leg away, just to make sure.

He wrenched his thoughts back to Hannah. If only he could learn something about Callum Hinds' disappearance to pass on to her.

'And your neighbour at Lane End Farm?' he said. 'How did Mike Hinds cope with the fact that his brother was supposed to have killed his son?'

Gareth shook his head. 'I hate to say it, but it was just as well Philip hanged himself. I was afraid Mike might take the law into his own hands.'

'And harm Philip?'

'I'm afraid so. Look at how he used to rough up poor Niamh.'

'He's an animal, frankly.' Bryan's languid tone didn't disguise his contempt. 'But what do you expect of a man who cares more about beasts on his farm than his own flesh and blood?'

'That's a bit harsh, Bryan,' Sally said.

Bryan rolled his eyes. 'I can only speak as I find. Philip was useless, but even if Mike had his suspicions, he didn't need to be the one to point the finger. Not at his own brother.'

'I hope you remember that if I ever run into trouble with the police,' Gareth said lightly.

'Did you all like Philip?' Louise asked.

'We felt sorry for him,' Bryan said. 'My father let him live in the wood for nothing, in return for a few odd jobs. The cottage wasn't much, but to be honest, we got the worst of the bargain. Not that we minded, really. My father saw looking after Philip as an act of Christian charity, and so did we.'

'My husband likes to do good,' Fleur whispered in Daniel's ear. 'As long as it doesn't cost too much.'

'He was harmless,' Bryan continued. 'Or so I thought. You may say that shows I'm not such a good judge after all, but my guess is, he never intended to kill Callum.'

'What do you think happened?' Louise asked.

'I'd say there was a bit of horseplay between them, and then things got out of hand. And the upshot was that Hinds lost both a son and a brother.'

'Now he's lost his daughter as well,' Sally said.

'You don't know for sure that he lost his son,' Purdey said.

She'd been yawning, a young woman wearied by the dinner table chit-chat of her elders. She reminded Daniel of students he'd taught with a low boredom threshold. They liked to spice up their tutorials with an occasional bit of melodrama.

'What do you mean?' Sally asked.

'Suppose Mike Hinds' son is still alive?'

'Darling, it's not a joking matter.'

'I'm not joking.' Purdey gave an elaborate yawn. Lapping up the attention, Daniel could tell. Everyone's eyes were on her, and he was sure that was what she'd aimed for.

'Purdey, what are you talking about?' Gareth demanded.

'What I said, Dad. Mike's son is alive and well.'

'Don't be silly.'

'I'm not being silly.' Purdey's silky smile made it clear she was about to play her ace. 'In fact, I've met him.'

'Marc, for God's sake!'

The instant Hannah recognised him, her panic was lost in a surge of fury. He stood next to the front door of Undercrag, hands in pockets, his demeanour expectant yet tinged with irritation, as if she had no right to come home this late. She had to stifle the urge to rush up and throttle him.

'Not the warmest welcome,' he said. 'I've been hanging around here for two hours, wondering where you might be.'

Deep breaths.

'You've still got a key. Your name is still on the title deeds. It's not as if I changed the locks.'

'I would have felt like a trespasser. It's your place at present, not mine. I meant to do the right thing, by not going inside and making myself at home without permission. I thought you'd understand.'

Aaaaagh! He hadn't lost his flair for sidestepping her wrath, and putting her in the wrong. She knew him well enough to be aware that he'd see his behaviour as eminently reasonable – sensitive, even. Must it always be like this in a relationship between a man and a woman? Two different views of the world, because the two of you were never standing in precisely the same place?

'What do you want?'

'Hannah, we need to talk.'

'It's Friday night. I've been working all day.' Well, a permissible exaggeration. 'I'm knackered. All I want is to have a soak in the bath and then climb into bed. On my own, Marc, before you get any ideas.'

He waved away the gibe, as if swatting a bunch of midges, and took a stride towards her. The smell of his aftershave mingled with the fragrance of lavender in a large stone tub outside the living room window.

'I may be crass, Hannah, but I'm not quite that crass. Listen, we can't go on like this. We had something special together, and I fucked up big style. How many times do you want me to apologise? Not a problem, I'll grovel as much as you like. We just need to move forward, that's all.'

'You don't have to grovel,' she said. 'For what it's worth, I've forgiven you. That isn't the point; the question is what I want to do with the rest of my life.'

'Spend it with me.'

He reached out an arm, but she skipped out of reach. 'No, Marc, I'm not ready.'

As soon as she said it, she regretted her choice of words. *Not ready* implied that one day she would be ready. In the light from the halogen lamp fixed under the house eaves, she saw a spark of hope in his eyes, and cursed herself.

'All right. It will take as long as it takes, I guess.'

'Marc, you need to get over me.' Horrible cliché, but what else should she say? She forced a smile. 'Terri was asking after you. You could do worse than give her a call.'

'Terri?' He was hoarse with amazement. 'Is that meant

to be funny? How many times has she wrinkled her nose when she talked about my *musty old books*?'

'I didn't realise she carried a torch for you either. Seems we were both wrong.'

For a few moments, a look crossed his face that she recognised, as he weighed up pros and cons.

'No,' he said. 'She's your friend. This is about you and me. Not Terri.'

'Up to you.'

'I'd better go.' He took a couple of paces away from her, before halting, as if he half-expected her to call him back. Typical man, Hannah thought. Hope sprang eternal. 'I parked down the lane.'

'Goodnight, Marc.'

She fished out her keys and walked up to the front door. Not trusting herself to speak, far less to look back over her shoulder.

'You may not believe this, but I've changed.'

Oh yeah?

'I'm sorry about your miscarriage, Hannah, more than I ever said. Heartbroken. But we can start again.' He paused. 'Try for a baby.'

Jesus.

She caught her breath.

I don't believe I'm hearing this.

'Hannah.' His voice was clear as he walked away; in the quiet of the evening, it seemed unnaturally loud. 'Don't forget one thing. I love you.'

The key rattled in the lock. She felt clumsy and juvenile. Her hands began to tremble.

* * *

'*Aslan Sheikh?*' Fleur repeated. 'I don't believe it!'

'You don't have to,' Purdey said. 'I'm telling you what he told me. And I happen to believe it's true.'

'You're making it up!' Sham blurted out. 'He never said anything about it to me!'

Purdey shrugged. 'So?'

Gareth said, 'I think you'd better tell us the whole story.'

For once, he sounded stern and humourless, like the Victorian paterfamilias who stared down from the opposite wall. Daniel snatched a glance at his fellow diners. Kit and Glenys looked bewildered, Bryan displeased, Sally agog and open-mouthed, hungry for fresh revelations. Hurt and angry, Sham had turned the colour of beetroot. Louise was frowning with concentration, keen not to miss anything. Only Fleur's expression – or lack of it – gave nothing away. Perhaps her studied indifference was a clue; why make such an effort to appear unfazed? Daniel found himself admiring her gift for hiding what she really thought.

'Yes,' Purdey said. 'Mike Hinds was his father, and Aslan had come back to check him out.'

'Check him out?'

'Correct. They'd never met, and Aslan was afraid he wouldn't be welcome if he turned up on his father's doorstep and introduced himself.'

'Never met?' Bryan was bewildered. 'But if you're trying to say that this man is Callum Hinds, then—'

'I'm not saying that!'

She was dragging it out, Daniel thought, relishing her fifteen minutes of fame in the family circle.

'What, then?'

'Aslan wasn't Callum. His mother met Mike Hinds in a bar. They had a fling, and Aslan was the result. By the time he was born, his mother had left Keswick for Carlisle, and before long she went back home to Turkey. Mike Hinds never knew anything about the child.'

'This is bizarre.' Gareth shook his head in disbelief. 'I know Mike was a womaniser in his younger days, but . . .'

Sally said, 'How on earth did you find this out?'

'I met Aslan when I called in at St Herbert's. Aunt Fleur asked me to drop off some financial statements for the principal. Aslan and I got talking. He invited me to meet up for a drink at a bar in town that night, and since I had nothing better to do, I agreed. That was when he told me his story; it only took a few drinks to loosen his tongue. He swore me to secrecy, but I think he wanted to impress me with his exotic life story. An illegitimate son of a Keswick farmer, raised in Istanbul, who has roamed the world for years and is now back in Cumbria in search of his roots. Fascinating if you like that sort of thing, but he wasn't my type. When he invited me back to his flat, I made it clear I wasn't interested.'

'I bet,' Sham muttered.

'What do you mean?' her mother asked.

'Oh, come on, Mum, don't tell me you haven't worked it out. Why do you think she was so upset when Dad's secretary Lily went back home to Australia?'

Purdey said quietly, 'Keep your nose out of my life, Sham. It's nothing to do with you. Besides, you ought to be grateful. I told Aslan he'd stand a much better chance with you. If he fancied easy pickings.'

'You cow!' Sham banged her spoon on the wooden

tabletop. Her lower lip was thrust out, making her resemble an infant losing her temper at mealtime.

'Purdey, Sham, you're not teenagers any longer, behave!' Gareth was seething. 'I'll speak to you both later, when our guests have gone home. Your private lives aren't for public consumption. All I want to know right now is whether there's any truth in this incredible story that Mike Hinds has an illegitimate son he knows nothing about.'

'He had no reason to lie,' Purdey said sulkily. 'Everything he told me seemed perfectly believable. He hadn't contacted Mike Hinds at that time; he'd heard from his mother, and also by asking around, that Mike has a vicious temper. I told him he needed to choose his moment carefully if he wanted a reunion. Time it wrong, and Mike would be getting out his shotgun. I said I wasn't sure Mike would be thrilled to discover he had a long-lost son.'

'But he'd lost Callum,' Sally said.

'I don't think he'd see Aslan as a straight swap, Mum,' Purdey said with exaggerated patience. 'It's not as simple as happy ever after.'

'The real question is whether this tale he told you is true,' Bryan said. 'It seems extraordinary, like something out of one of Orla's fairy stories.'

'It could be true,' Kit Payne said. 'Niamh told me about some of Mike's affairs. The ones she knew about, anyway. A girl from Eastern Europe was among his conquests, I remember.'

'So Aslan really is Mike's son?'

As Gareth lingered over the question, his brain seemed to be stepping up a gear. Like everyone else, Daniel thought, he must be computing what he'd learnt, trying to figure out the implications.

'Well, well,' Bryan said. 'The prodigal has returned, after all.'

'But not the prodigal everyone hoped for,' Fleur Madsen said.

CHAPTER THIRTEEN

Saturday morning in Keswick, and Market Square was crammed with bargain hunters swarming around stalls that sold pies and paintings, clothes and crafts, and pretty much everything else you could wish for. Traders' raucous cries punctuated the hum of a hundred conversations, smells from the fishmonger's wafted through the warm air, mixing with those of home-made preserves and pungent cheeses. Marooned in the pedestrianised area was Moot Hall, with its sturdy tower and one-handed clock. Over the years, it had served as a courthouse, a prison and a town hall. Now it housed a tourist information office, with posters, leaflets and videos extolling Keswick's various delights: Derwent Water, the Theatre by the Lake, Skiddaw, Blencathra – and a pencil museum.

The temperature was rising as Daniel smeared a dollop of sunblock on his face and neck. He'd arrived early, but he was hopeless at waiting, and found himself inventing a dozen reasons why Hannah might not show up. At last he spotted her through the crowd, handing over money at a stall that sold belts and bracelets. The bag under her arm bulged with purchases. A single woman with a busy job didn't have much time for shopping, and she'd made the most of the market. A short-sleeved blue top and denim jeans clung to her. Since their last encounter, she'd lost weight, he thought, even though she'd never had much to lose. From a distance, she looked scarcely old enough to have left police college, let alone take charge of a cold case squad. His spirits rose as she caught sight of him, and gave a wave before hurrying over to him.

'Thanks for sparing me an hour or two,' he said. 'I'm sure your Saturdays are precious.'

'Glad to.' She smiled, showing even white teeth. 'This is a treat.'

He dropped a light kiss on each cheek. She wasn't wearing make-up – no need. He liked the fresh smell of her hair and her skin. The Madsen women were sleek and gorgeous in a no-expense-spared way, but give him the natural look any time.

'Derwent Water, then?' The lake was only five minutes away. 'So how is your book going?'

'The question all writers dread,' he told her. 'No matter what target or deadline you set, it always turns into a frantic race against time. Coupled with the need to dream up increasingly unlikely excuses for slow progress whenever your agent calls. Ensconcing myself in the library at St Herbert's seemed like a smart idea at the time. Allegedly, it's an oasis of peace, where nothing ever happens, the only disturbance an occasional snore from an adjoining table. But what happens the minute it becomes my second home?

Orla Payne decides to make me her confidant, and next thing I know, all hell breaks loose.'

Hannah laughed. 'You're fated.'

'My own fault.'

'She must have found you sympathetic.'

'Nosey, more like. I've never been able to get rid of this urge to find things out. Very useful in academe, but in the real world, sometimes it's easier not to know. When I was a kid, Dad used to tell me I was too curious for my own good, and he was dead right.'

'He usually was,' she said.

'I overheard him talking to Cheryl on the phone when he thought the house was empty, so I knew about his affair a week before he broke the news to Mum.' He aimed a kick at a scrap of litter on the pavement. 'Looking back, that may just have been the most agonising seven days of my entire life.'

'I'm sorry, Daniel.' Her hand brushed his. 'It's such a shame you never spent enough time together before he died. He was thrilled by your idea of history as detective work. It showed you were a chip off the old block, he said.'

'Hardly. When Orla told me about her missing brother, and that she didn't believe he was dead, I tried to winkle more information out of her. But she clammed up on me. It was obvious she was unhappy, but I didn't know why.'

'She never hinted at suicide?'

'I keep asking myself if I should have spotted what was in her mind.' His tone was as bleak as Blencathra in winter. 'There were subtle clues, just as with Aimee. But I didn't spot them.'

'You did all you could, you told her to talk to me.'

'Passing the buck, to be honest.'

'It was the right advice. Don't beat yourself up about it.'

'Easier said than done, Hannah.'

'Listen.' She seized his arm, forcing him to stop in mid stride. 'I spoke to her, so did my DC the day she died. She was drunk and depressed. We are supposed to be the professionals, and we couldn't get any sense out of her. How do you help someone who won't let you help? I'm sure you couldn't have saved Aimee, and you're certainly not to blame for what happened to Orla, OK?'

'OK.' They started to walk again. 'You know, I could never make out whether she wished she'd kept her mouth shut, or whether she'd discovered something that changed the complexion of things.'

'What do you think she might have discovered?'

'Your guess is as good as mine. Perhaps it was all in her mind. She was seriously mixed up, and the booze didn't help. The last couple of times I saw her, she reeked of it. The principal wasn't happy, and one or two colleagues started to keep their distance.'

They had reached Hope Park. Hannah said, 'Which colleagues?'

'Sham Madsen, for one; she was never a fan of Orla's. And a chap who worked with her, and took her out a time or two, started avoiding her. Or so she thought.'

High in the sky, a gaudy yellow-and-red kite caught their attention, and they watched it gust along before starting a jittery descent towards Derwent Water.

'Not Aslan Sheikh, by any chance?'

'You know him?'

'I know the name. We haven't interviewed him yet, but he's top of the list for Monday.'

'Good plan.' In front of them lay the slate and roughcast stone exterior of the Theatre by the Lake, blending in with the landscape so that it looked as though it had been part of the scenery for ever, not for just ten years. A poster advertised *What the Butler Saw*. Daniel couldn't resist the temptation to ham up the suspense. Lowering his voice, he said, 'But . . . do you know his real identity?'

The park and the paths around it were busy. Elderly couples reminiscing, children squealing, mothers scolding. A gull wheeled overhead, a couple of geese honked messages to each other. Hannah took no notice, eyes widening as she concentrated on him, pupils dilating, lips slightly parted. He felt a thrill of excitement, knowing he had something she wanted badly, even if it was only gossip that he'd gleaned from a drunken girl at a dinner party.

'Tell me,' she breathed.

The window of Aslan's poky bedsit looked out to the steep and sweeping curves of the saddleback mountain. The view was the only good thing about the place, the reason he'd decided to rent it. That, and the fact he could afford nothing better.

He wanted money; he was pissed off with years of living hand to mouth. It shouldn't be necessary. Not for a kid of his class.

Shame about Orla, but her death wasn't his fault. He'd wanted her to give him an insight into the Hinds family, it was part of his plan to survey the ground before approaching his father with the truth. He hadn't checked how the inheritance laws worked, but surely one day he'd be entitled to a stake in the farm at Lane End? What he hadn't bargained for was Orla deciding that he was Callum, because he'd adopted a Turkish name that happened to feature in a story his mother had read him when he was young. He'd never have guessed that his half-brother loved C.S. Lewis. Orla was so distraught when she found out he wasn't Callum that he'd not wanted to admit that there was a blood tie between them, until he was clear how she would take the news. With hindsight, he should have come clean. If she knew she had a half-brother, she might not have jumped into the grain. Better sweep the thought to one side. The roses had been an impulsive acknowledgement of the half-brother he'd never known; he wasn't even sure why he'd made the gesture. He didn't do sentimentality.

Anyway. The one positive he could take from this whole shitty situation was that he might never be poor again.

This encounter needed to be face-to-face, nothing else would do. Yet he couldn't turn up out of the blue, and drop such a bombshell.

He'd found the right number.

Now he reached for his phone.

Hannah yanked a straw hat and dark glasses out of her bag as Daniel pushed off from the shore of Derwent Water. Rather than take a round trip by motor launch, they'd hired a small rowing boat for half an hour, so they could talk without being overheard. The sun shone on the surface of the water, in patterns chopped and changed by the motion of the oars. Canoes and kayaks drifted by, the motor launch was chugging back towards the jetty. He watched Hannah rubbing sun oil into her bare arms. She was gazing absently towards the wooded slopes of Friar's Crag. Lost in thought, mulling over what he had told her.

If Aslan Sheikh was Orla's half-brother, what bearing did it have on her death? He and Louise had tossed the question back and forth while the taxi took them home to Tarn Cottage, and he'd slept fitfully because his mind kept working overtime, but he hadn't come close to an answer. If anyone could unravel the knots, it was Hannah.

'Ruskin said this was one of the three most beautiful scenes in Europe,' he said.

'I can believe it.' She pointed towards the fells flanking the lake. 'Got your bearings? That's Cat Bells to the west, Castlerigg Fell to the east. Behind you is Derwent Isle. And the biggest island, over there in the middle of the lake, is St Herbert's, where the hermit of Derwent Water lived. One summer when I was a student, a couple of friends and I rowed out there. The plan was to stay overnight in a tent.'

'I never knew you liked life under canvas.'

'Once was enough. We'd had too much to drink, and the tent collapsed an hour after we landed. Before we could put it back up again, there was a violent storm, with thunder and lightning. We were scared to death as well as soaked to the skin. These days, people camp on the island for corporate team-building events. I hope they have more joy than the three of us – we were barely speaking to each other by the time we made it back to dry land. St Herbert could keep his island hermitage, as far as I was concerned. I've never even explored the library they named after him. Next week, I'll put that right when I have a chat with Aslan

Sheikh. Or Michael Hinds' son, if that really is the truth of it.'

'Purdey Madsen seemed confident of her facts. Mind you, none of the Madsens are lacking in confidence.'

'That's how they got to be filthy rich. I guess dinner at Mockbeggar Hall was a memorable experience?'

'You bet. The Madsens never do things by halves, and Purdey Madsen is no exception. As if it wasn't enough to be dragged out of the closet in front of her nearest and dearest, she dropped her bombshell about Aslan Sheikh, and made Sham spit with jealousy for good measure.'

'Can we rewind a few weeks, to when you befriended Orla Payne?'

'She was pleasant, rather naive, without a trace of ego or self-consciousness. Even though she wore a scarf to cover her baldness, she didn't mind talking about her alopecia. Her enthusiasm for history, like her love of fairy tales, wasn't sophisticated. Much of the time, she lived in a dreamworld. After she told me about her childhood, I understood why.'

'She talked about her parents?'

'Yes, she was close to her mother. Overawed by her father. One day when she did something to annoy him, he threw a rag doll of hers on the fire in the inglenook. Once the marriage collapsed, she stayed in her mother's camp. The two of them had a lot in common, including the taste for booze and the mood swings. When she took Kit Payne's name, her father was furious. I suppose he felt betrayed and let down, but she just saw the red face and heard the raised voice.'

'He hasn't mellowed, trust me.'

'A dangerous man to cross – that's how she described her own father.'

'Sad.' Hannah pictured the farmer's fist, clutching the scythe. 'Yet she was right.'

'Callum was closer to Hinds. Not that he wanted to follow in his father's footsteps. He wasn't cut out for farming. But he had plenty in common with his dad. Orla implied that her brother had inherited that nasty streak.'

'Was she in awe of Callum, too?'

'I'd say so. She made him sound smug and superior. A clever boy who exploited the age gap between them, and treated her as a lackey. Literature was the only bond between them. They both read voraciously, and their tastes ran to fantasy. Callum was into C.S. Lewis and Tolkien, she was hooked on the fairy tales.'

Hannah trailed her hand in the water. Her fingers were slim, with nails cut short and not painted. She wore no rings. 'What did Orla tell you about Philip Hinds?'

'She was fond of him, they both were. Callum loved to escape from home and explore the Hanging Wood, and she often went along with him. For two kids with vivid imaginations, it was the perfect playground. Especially for Callum. Orla found it spooky, she didn't like to go in on her own. Of course, she was only a child.'

'Spooky is right, believe me. I went with my sergeant for a reconnaissance yesterday.'

'Yes, I heard.'

She narrowed her eyes. 'Did the Madsens gripe about it?'

He grinned. 'Bryan did mutter something about public

servants with nothing better to do with their time. Question is, did you learn anything?'

'We weren't hoping for forensic evidence twenty years on. Perhaps it was an indulgence, but I wanted to see for myself the place where Philip was supposed to have killed Callum. Your father taught me the importance of thinking yourself into the minds of the people you wanted to investigate, and part of it involves understanding their environment. Where they work and live and play. The snag with cold cases is the passage of time. But sometimes, the distance of the years helps you see more clearly.'

'And how do you see the case against Philip Hinds?'

'Purely circumstantial. Doesn't mean he didn't kill the boy, of course.'

'But you believe he was innocent?'

'I'd say he loved the Hanging Wood, it was the one place he felt at home. To me it felt like a dank and dismal prison, but I'm sure he'd hate to desecrate it. But that's guesswork. Police officers work on the basis of evidence, not gut feel.'

'Is that really what my father believed?'

She smiled. 'That sceptical glint in your eyes reminds me of him.'

He was conscious of the sun scorching his cheeks. What had she felt for Ben? Liking, of course; respect, certainly. Anything more?

Her gaze settled on Derwent Isle again. They had rowed round in a circle, as he followed a course back to the shore.

'Orla must always have hoped that a fresh explanation for Callum's disappearance would emerge. Something that exonerated her uncle.'

'Wishful thinking?'

'She was keen on happy endings. If her hopes were dashed, that could have sent her into a tailspin. There must be a reason why she committed suicide.'

'I suppose there is no doubt that she killed herself?'

'Very little. Hypothetically, if she came across evidence suggesting someone other than Philip murdered Callum, that someone had a motive to get rid of her. But what evidence, which someone, and above all why? It's speculation piled on speculation, and I don't suppose historians approve of speculation any more than the Crown Prosecution Service does.'

'True, but we all speculate sometimes.'

He eased off on the oars and leant back to take in the view of the forbidding bulk of Skiddaw to the north of the town. Hannah followed his gaze, the breeze ruffling her hair. He was seized by an urge to stroke and smooth it, to feel its silky texture and the warmth of her skin. Bad idea. He needed to be patient. The moment was too precious to spoil.

Aslan crushed the phone against his hand.

'You killed Callum.'

Silence.

'And then you killed Orla.'

'Not true.'

Aslan laughed, incredulous. 'You expect me to believe you?'

'Believe what you want. She jumped.'

'I believe you murdered both of them.'

'I don't have to listen to this.'

'Do you want the police to listen, instead? I'll ring them now, if you want.'

'They will think you are mad.'

'I'm angry, actually, not insane. You killed my half-brother, and then my half-sister.'

'Why on earth would I want to do that?'

Aslan paused. This was his weak spot. He hadn't filled all the gaps in his knowledge, there were things he didn't fully understand.

'I know about Castor and Pollux.'

A long silence. Surely a killer would not hang up?

'What do you want?'

Aslan felt a wave of relief wash through him. He had won.

'I called in at Marc's shop last weekend,' Daniel said. 'Bought a set of Wainwrights, much to Louise's disgust. She says I ought to throw out at least two books for every one I buy. I had new bookshelves put up in the cottage after moving in, but already the to-be-read pile is mounting on the floor of the spare room.'

'Marc and I had the same conversation a dozen times,' Hannah said, 'but I never made any headway. Once a bibliomaniac, always a bibliomaniac.'

Lunch in the light and airy cafeteria at the Theatre by the Lake. Hannah savoured a mouthful of her open sandwich: smoked Borrowdale trout with lemon-and-dill dressing. Until now, they'd steered clear of personal stuff, which suited her fine, but Daniel knew Marc had moved out back in January, and was bound to be curious.

'Marc told me you and he were due to meet up this week,' he said.

So Marc had talked about her to Daniel, even though

he'd been jealous of their relationship. Another sign that he might be growing up; pity it was too late.

'He wants us to get back together again, but I don't think it will work.'

'Perhaps you both need more time.'

'We've had six months.'

'It may take longer.'

'I've had long enough to get used to living on my own. It's sort of liberating.'

'I know what you mean. The endless compromises when you share with someone are hard work. Ask my sister.'

He showed his white teeth in a grin. A good-looking man; strong features, clear brown eyes, she couldn't be blamed for finding him attractive. Plenty of women would, even if he'd never appeared on television. But what drew him to her was that she was sure she could trust him absolutely – as she had his father.

'And how are things with Louise?' Grabbing the chance to change the subject.

'She's good. That bastard who gave her such a rough time is a fading memory, thank God. Now she's looking round for a place of her own up here. Not that I'm pushing her out; she's someone else who likes to have her own space. At least the sparks don't fly between us the way they did when we were teenagers.'

'Sibling rivalries, eh?' She swallowed the last morsel of trout. 'There's no escaping them in this case. The Hinds brothers, the Madsen sisters, Callum and Orla. Perhaps it's just as well my sister emigrated years back.'

'Speaking of siblings, there's a question about Castor and Pollux.'

He gave her the gist of what Aslan had told him. 'Let's suppose Orla resorted to playing the detective. She'd fantasised that Aslan Sheikh was Callum, larger than life. When he disillusioned her, she was forced to accept that her brother was dead after all. But she was sure Philip was incapable of murder – so she tried to fathom what did happen to Callum.'

'If she decided that he was killed by someone she cared for, that could have driven her to suicide.'

'Kit Payne? He'd done his best for her, as he did for her mother.'

'And we do know that Callum didn't hit it off with Kit.'

'Did she talk to you about Kit?'

'Not much, but she seemed to like him.'

Hannah savoured her camomile tea. 'After so many years, she is hardly likely to have found any evidence that Kit was responsible for Callum's death. But if she confronted him . . .'

'Would he admit his guilt to her, do you think?'

'Only if she caught him off guard. He's a streetwise businessman, don't forget. I'd expect him to deny it. Perhaps prey on her fears, say that she needed psychiatric help. Which might explain why she jumped into the grain.'

'I've never met him, but even hard-nosed executives aren't always natural-born killers. Do you think he's capable of murdering a young boy?'

'Depends on the provocation. If they had a fight, and Callum died by accident, Kit might have panicked and hidden the body. Once he'd done that, he was trapped. No going back.'

'So he sat back and watched an innocent man persecuted for a crime he didn't commit?'

'You'll be amazed what people will do when the self-preservation instinct kicks in. Besides, he might be able to salve his conscience on the basis that there was no evidence to prove Philip's guilt, and that the storm would soon blow over.'

'It was Kit who found Philip's body.'

Hannah nodded. 'I hadn't forgotten.'

'If that's how it happened, it may never be possible to prove Kit's guilt.'

'No.' Hannah fiddled with her teaspoon. 'Unless – something else happens.'

'Such as?'

'If we finally find Callum's remains.'

Taking risks didn't faze Aslan. How else could you make something special out of your life? The mistake he'd made so far in his life was that the risks he'd taken had never earned a proper reward.

The butterfly knife lay on his bedside table. He traced a finger along the blade, so gently that the skin did not break. He liked danger, that was the truth of it. It turned him on more than any woman.

Looking through his window, he spotted distant walkers, tiny dots of colour on the grey slopes. His eyesight was keen, his body muscular and strong; he needed to make more of his life before he grew lazy and old. Since arriving in the Lakes, he'd spent time climbing. Once, he'd nearly found himself stranded on Helvellyn when the mists closed in. He was alone, and nobody knew where he was. He'd got away with it, suffering nothing more than bruises as he scrambled down the scree as if his life depended on it. Perhaps it had. He was accustomed to getting away with things; some days he could persuade himself he was invulnerable, and like a denizen of Shangri-La, he would live for ever.

The sun was high, tonight his star would be in the ascendant. His life was going to change, no question. He wasn't a planner – he was too disorganised a thinker to bother with tactics or strategy. Sometimes you just had to play a card, and see where it fell. In returning to the Lakes, he hadn't worked out a plan of action. Curiosity had pulled him back. Mum had talked of the Lakes for years after she left Turkey. When he was older, he'd asked about his father, but she hadn't told him much. Perhaps there wasn't much to tell. She'd spent a couple of years in England on a student visa, earning a few quid behind a bar to help fund her studies. Mike Hinds came in for a pint one night, and swept her off her feet; almost literally, she told her son. He was a farmer, big and strong as well as intelligent. Enough virtues for her not to mind too much about his temper. For a few weeks, she was in seventh heaven, until a fellow barmaid told her he was married, and forty-eight hours later a pregnancy test came out positive. She plucked up the courage to tell Hinds, fearing a volcanic outpouring of rage. But all he wanted was to solve a problem, and he gave her the money for an abortion, along with plenty of cash to pay for the plane home.

Thank God she was determined to keep me.

Mum stayed in England until after he was born. It seemed strange that she'd given him the name of the man who had let her down, but she said that, in the hospital crib, his newborn face was the image of his father's.

He was half-English, and Mum remained a passionate Anglophile until the day she died. She'd deserved so much more than the hand-to-mouth existence she'd led. She kept in touch with news from Britain, and she knew all about Callum's disappearance. It made the national newspapers, and she said she'd thought about contacting Mike Hinds, and letting him know that he still had one son, but she was afraid her child would be rejected, as she had been.

He was intrigued by Callum's disappearance and wondered if his half-sister knew more about it than had been made public, but he'd never returned to the land of his birth until this year. It wasn't a conscious avoidance, it was just how it happened. You had to trust to fate. In the States, he almost came a cropper when he sold some drugs to a pretty customer who turned out to be a female cop. A quick getaway saved him, but he was ready for a change of scene. And, for a man who never did things by halves, why not a change of ID as well?

So Aslan Sheikh was born.

The small room was stuffy, even with the window thrown open. He kicked off his shoes and padded off to stand under a cold shower, relishing the jets of water as they smacked against his chest, buttocks and legs.

It was almost a metaphor. Washing away the wrongs of the past. Shutting his eyes, he pictured his mother's face, and saw a slow smile creep across it.

'How are you spending the rest of today?' Daniel asked, as they leafed through the pamphlets in the theatre shop.

'Praying for an excuse to put off mowing the lawn,'

Hannah said. 'Occasionally, I remember Marc did have his uses.'

'Why don't we take a walk around the lake? Not enough time for a full circuit, obviously, but we can catch the launch back from one of the jetties.'

'Don't you have a book to write?'

'I'm in search of inspiration.'

'You're writing about the history of murder, aren't you; De Quincey and all that? I'm not sure I'm flattered.'

He laughed. 'While I'm at it, why don't we come back here for dinner this evening and then watch the play, if they have a couple of tickets left? *What the Butler Saw*, it's my favourite by Orton. It's the one where a character says, *We must tell the truth!* To which she is told that's a thoroughly defeatist attitude.'

'Sounds like a lot of defence lawyers I've met.'

'Can I take that as a yes, then?'

'So why did you want to meet here?' Aslan asked. 'A bit risky, I thought.'

His companion's eyes settled on the farm buildings. The day was over, and the roaring tractors had fallen silent. Aslan had arrived in good time before his appointment, and he'd caught sight of the farm labourers clambering into the van that would take them to their accommodation in the town. In the old farmhouse, a light shone behind a curtained window.

'There's a very good reason, believe me.'

'Want to share it with me?'

Aslan leant against the side of the slurry tank, as if he'd paused for a casual chat. Not for the first time in his life, he was finding it hard not to sound cocky. So far, so brilliant. The bag at his feet bulged with banknotes. This was a highly professional transaction. A pleasure to do business.

'Don't you want to count the money?'

Aslan smiled. 'Shouldn't I trust you?'

A shrug. 'It's up to you.'

'Oh well, you're right. It's sensible to take precautions.'

Aslan grinned. Crushed in his hand was his tiny mobile. Any messing, and he'd dial 999. And the butterfly knife was sticking out of his jeans pocket, backup if he needed it.

As he bent down, he heard the knife fall to the ground and before he could pick it up, he felt a searing pain in the side of his head. He fumbled frantically with his phone, but the agony was unbearable, and he couldn't think straight.

His last conscious thought took him back all those years to when he used to watch the cruise ships sailing away from Warnemünde. Sailing beyond the lighthouse and into the unknown.

'It's years since I've seen an Orton play,' Hannah said, as they joined the crowd streaming out of the theatre. 'The last one was *Loot*. I seem to remember it features a bungling police inspector.'

Daniel cleared his throat. '*I'm innocent till I'm proved guilty. This is a free country. The law is impartial.* To which Inspector Truscott replies, *Who's been filling your head with that rubbish?*'

She laughed and mimed applause. 'Do you have an encyclopaedic recall of loads of British literature?'

'Only enough to get me through the pub quiz at the Brack Arms.' They stopped outside the front entrance, letting people bustle past on their way to the car park. Darkness had fallen, but the night was still warm. 'Speaking of pubs, how about a drink before we head back?'

'Thanks, but I'll say no.' She smiled. 'It's been a lovely day, Daniel. I've enjoyed seeing you again, and thanks for filling me in on your conversations with poor Orla Payne.'

'Any time.'

As he bent forward to kiss her cheek, a ringtone pierced the chatter of the passing theatregoers. *Hill Street Blues.*

'Shit, that's me,' Hannah murmured. 'Lousy timing, as ever.'

She plucked a phone out of her bag and took a few paces to one side as she listened. He watched as her expression changed from annoyance to alarm.

'What is it?' he asked as she finished the call.

'That was Mario Pinardi,' she said hoarsely. 'He's investigating Orla's death. And now he has another corpse on his hands.'

CHAPTER FOURTEEN

'Unbelievable.' Mario Pinardi yawned as he took a weary swig from the polystyrene coffee cup, and spilt as much as he drank. Lucky the carpet tiles were the colour of mud. 'Two bodies found on the same farm inside a week. I mean, what are the odds on that being a coincidence?'

'When the deceased are a woman and her long-lost half-brother? When they both worked together? When the farm belongs to their father?' Hannah bit into the Cox's Orange Pippin she'd stuffed into her bag before driving out to Keswick. 'A zillion to one, I'd say.'

After a night without sleep, Mario's face was as grey as the fells in winter. His eyes had a haunted look, as if he kept replaying in his mind the vision of the crime scene at Lane End. Big mistake. The first time Hannah ever saw a butchered body, Ben Kind advised her that some sights are best forgotten, if you want to stay sane. One horror was all it took to send some people into a tailspin. And it didn't get any worse than watching as a corpse with a crushed skull was dredged out of a slurry tank.

Mario tossed his cup towards the waste-paper basket. Short by a clear six inches. 'The stench soaked into my sinuses; it feels like I'll never breathe fresh air again,' he muttered. 'Christ, what a way to go.'

'You could do with a couple of hours' kip,' she said. 'Must be twenty-four hours since you last saw Alessandra.'

'No time.' Mario gritted his teeth. 'Got to keep going.'

She didn't try to talk him round; he had to show a lead. Keswick's incident room scarcely ever buzzed like this, let alone at one o'clock on a summer Sunday, but all available staff had been hauled in at short notice to help out. An admin assistant chewed her biro as she listened to a voicemail message from the coroner's officer; the fingers of her colleagues raced across keyboards, inputting data from the crime scene. A printer spewed out pages of typescript; in the corner, a scanner whirred. They were already more than halfway through the crucial first twenty-four hours of the murder enquiry, and nobody was agonising about the overtime bill. Yet.

Hannah and Mario perched on plastic chairs either side of a whiteboard on which he'd scrawled a crude map of the farm with a red marker pen. This morning the brass had confirmed Mario as SIO in the Lane End murder enquiry. A no-brainer, given his involvement in the Orla Payne case, and the absence through holidays and sickness of more senior officers, even though he was only a DI. He'd feel the pressure of overpromotion, nagged by the knowledge that if he didn't achieve a quick result someone was bound to be brought in over his head. When she'd called to suggest they share intelligence, Mario didn't think twice before saying yes.

'Sheikh had a bedsit in Crosthwaite. So far, we've found two separate sets of ID. Fake papers in the name of Aslan Sheikh, which he used to get into this country. Another has his first name as Nuri Michael Iskirlak.'

'*Michael?*'

'Yeah, seems like his mum named him after Hinds, even though the feller dumped her.' Mario sighed and said again, 'Unbelievable.'

Why is life so often one unbelievable thing after another? Hannah wondered. Aloud, she said, 'Any leads from Crosthwaite?'

'Not a lot. Plenty of stamps in both his passports, real and false. We've established that he grew up first in Turkey and then in Germany. He travelled light, and he didn't give much away about himself to anyone. His landlady lives on the ground floor, but she's a turn-a-blind-eye sort who thinks he's brought one or two women back since he moved in, but doesn't know if any of them stayed overnight. She can't help us with his movements yesterday, and her other tenant is off trekking across Europe. Thanks for nothing, eh?'

'Anyone talking to the people he worked with at St Herbert's?'

'My DS is there now – apparently the library is open seven days a week. I'd no idea people still read so much. What we'll learn, God knows. Sheikh doesn't sound the bookish type to me. There are no books at Crosthwaite except a battered copy of one of the Narnia books and a paperback of *On the Road*. His iPod holds some crap music and no photographs. Thirty years old, but never settled down. Bit of a chancer, if you ask me.'

'Last night he took one chance too many.'

Aslan had made two 999 calls. The first cut off after three seconds, with nothing said. In the second, moments later, a man had shouted something. It was wild and unintelligible and on the recording it sounded to Hannah like a bitten-off yelp. A crashing noise was followed by a low groan that reminded her of the air hissing out of a punctured tyre. Another crash, then the line went dead. By identifying the mobile phone mast which picked up the strongest signal from the phone, the call had soon been tracked to the vicinity of Lane End Farm. The same area from which Michael Hinds had called earlier in the week to summon the emergency services after he discovered his daughter's corpse in a tower of grain. But the call had not come from the same phone.

Mario was finishing his shift when he was alerted, due to his familiarity with Lane End Farm. He'd decided to call there himself, along with a young DC. The lights were on behind curtained windows, but Hinds and his wife took an age to answer the door. When they did, it was clear they'd been interrupted in the middle of a drunken sex session. They denied any knowledge of a 999 call, and insisted they'd heard nothing. The Polish workers had long since finished for the day and headed back to their rooms in Keswick in Hinds' van. Leaving Lane End to just the farmer, his wife and their animals.

Hinds wasn't happy about being disturbed, but he didn't have his scythe to hand, and it's difficult to get too stroppy when you're naked under a grubby old dressing gown. Mario insisted on taking a look around outside, and after a short argument, Hinds bowed to the inevitable. When Mario climbed a ladder to shine a flashlight into the slurry tank, he saw that the crust on top of the slurry had been smashed through.

'When I realised there must be a body in the tank,' Mario had said, 'I watched Hinds, to study his reaction. Fear, horror, shock, guilt? Not a muscle in his face moved, I swear. Not so much as a twitch. He might have been the Man in the Iron Mask, for all the emotion I saw.'

They'd needed to summon support and special equipment to fish the body out of the tank, and it wasn't recovered until the early hours. By then, Mario had obtained a provisional ID. There had been some sort of struggle on the cobbles close to the slurry tank, and a bank debit card had slipped out of the dead man's pocket. It bore the name of Aslan Sheikh.

'Would have been nice if the killer had dropped a credit card instead, but life's never that simple, is it? We also found a butterfly knife nearby.'

'You think the victim took it with him for protection?'

'I guess so, given that it's not the murder weapon. Sheikh must have dropped it when he was attacked, and either the killer didn't see it in the dark, or wasn't bothered about it.'

'Any sign of Sheikh's mobile?'

'In the slurry tank, along with its owner.'

Hinds had insisted on taking a look at the body once it had undergone some rudimentary cleaning up, so that the bloodied features were discernible. He claimed he'd never seen the dead man before in his life. Nor did he have the faintest idea why an unknown corpse should have turned up at Lane End, days after his daughter had chosen the farm as the place to end her life.

Either he was guilty, or very, very unlucky.

Events moved fast following the discovery of the corpse. Hinds called Gareth Madsen for a recommendation to a shit-hot lawyer, and when his old friend heard that the body probably belonged to Aslan Sheikh, he dropped the bombshell that Aslan had told Purdey of his true identity. At that point, even the iron mask crumpled with shock. But Hinds refused to say anything more until the legal eagle showed up.

Mario had interviewed Hinds for a second time that morning, this time in the presence of a sharp-suited criminal solicitor from Carlisle, to be met with flat denials that Hinds knew his son was in the country, far less that he called himself Aslan Sheikh and that for the past few weeks he'd been working at the library across the fields from Lane End. Despite tough questioning, Hinds gave nothing away. He'd never had any further contact with the boy's mother after he'd paid her to have an abortion and leave the country. He said she and her pregnancy were a nuisance that had cost him an arm and a leg to dispose of, and that he'd not given her any further thought from that day to this. Let alone imagined that his son was back in the Lakes.

'Hinds is a hard man,' Mario said. 'No doubt who is the real bastard in that family, for sure, but is he hard enough to have murdered his own flesh and blood?'

'Forensics reckon Sheikh was killed at the farm?'

'Looks that way. There are bloodstains and clothing fibres close by the slurry tank, plenty for us to work on. This looks like a crime of desperation. The head wounds were severe, and it seems unlikely he was transported from somewhere else.'

'Was he dead when he went into the tank?'

'Not sure yet. He was hit on the head several times, hence the blood splatter – a single blow wouldn't have done it.'

Sunday, very bloody Sunday. 'So the culprit and the victim arranged a rendezvous at or close to the farm?'

'Apparently. Assuming a prearranged meet, it looks like we're not talking about a crime carefully planned out to the last detail.'

'Cause of death?'

'We're spoilt for choice at present. Whether the blows to the head killed him straight off, or he died after he was inside the tank, we won't know until the PM results are available. Just our luck it's Sunday. Seems he had a thin skull, but if by any chance he wasn't dead when he was bundled into the slurry, he'll have inhaled the slurry into his lungs and drowned, or found it impossible to breathe under the weight of the stuff and suffocated.' Mario grimaced. 'I thought dying in a mountain of grain was bad enough, but . . .'

'No sign of the murder weapon, you said?'

'No, our culprit may have missed the things that the victim dropped, but he wasn't considerate enough to leave his weapon lying around for us to fall over. The preliminary view is, it was a dumb-bell or something similar. Maybe from a gym.'

'Plenty of people exercise with them at home. I do myself,

though much less often than I ought to. Do Hinds and his wife have a set of dumb-bells?'

'That isn't how they get their exercise, apparently. The living room stank of booze and sex when we arrived. We found pornographic DVDs, and Deirdre was wearing a basque. She had a yellowing bruise around her left eye. When I asked about it, she said she'd walked into a door on Friday night. She'd shoved a mask and a couple of nipple clamps under the cushions on the sofa and I found them as soon as she asked me to sit down. I'm still trying to figure out whether she meant me to see them or not.'

'So they were too busy to realise what was happening – literally in their own backyard?'

'That's their story, and if the legal eagle has anything to do with it, they will stick to it like limpets. A middle-aged married couple enjoying themselves on a Saturday evening in the privacy of their own home, too preoccupied with connubial bliss and a Swedish movie about orgies in a convent to hear someone being battered to death in the dark outside.' Mario gritted his teeth. 'Somehow the nipple clamps seem like a detail which make it just about credible.'

'Or is that what we are supposed to believe?'

'Yeah, for all I know, the sexy set-up was concocted in the space of five minutes to give Hinds an alibi.'

Hannah lobbed her apple core straight into the bin. Greg Wharf would have had a lot of fun with the vision of Deirdre wearing nipple clamps. Just as well he wasn't here. Time to push him out of her mind.

'And what do you believe, Mario?'

'Wish I knew.'

'Would Deirdre protect him if she thought he'd killed a man?'

'He's her husband.'

Hannah made a face. She wouldn't lie to save Marc in similar circumstances. But what if their relationship hadn't hit the buffers, what if she had nothing else in her life but him?'

'She's frightened of Hinds, but I'd say there's still a spark between them too. God knows what she sees in him.' Mario winced. 'Terrible what some men do to women. Would she perjure herself on his behalf? You bet. All the same, the thought of a man killing his own son . . .'

'He might not have known Aslan was his son.'

'Isn't that stretching things too far? The question remains – why murder him? And why ignore the oldest rule of all – don't shit on your own doorstep?'

'Suppose Aslan turned up at the farm, and announced himself as son of Hinds. Maybe he wanted to soak his dad for cash. Payback for leaving his mother in the lurch. Hinds would have been stunned. What if he lost the plot?'

'And beat his own boy to death before tossing him into an iron box full of shit? You really think he's capable of that?'

A picture came into Hannah's mind of the sun catching the blade of Mike Hinds' scythe. Never mind that he didn't have a criminal record; he was no stranger to violence. Niamh had felt the rough edge of his temper, and so had Deirdre. Maybe he'd even hurt Callum, the boy who kept his name. What chance for a swaggering stranger who threatened to turn his life upside down?

'I'd say he's capable of pretty much anything.'

* * *

'You haven't told me if you've arranged to see Hannah again,' Louise said.

Daniel blinked. 'She took a message about the discovery of a dead man at a farm linked with a cold case she's investigating, and she had to shoot off home. For all I know, she's needed to go into work today. Not the ideal moment to consult our social calendars.'

'Excuses,' she snorted.

With a lavish sigh, she started to attack her dessert. Vanilla panna cotta with gooseberries. Daniel had found himself unable to resist the sticky toffee pudding, with toffee sauce and clotted cream. You might as well be hanged for a sheep as a lamb; at least he'd had a green-leaf salad to start.

Sunday lunch at The Tickled Trout, a welcome respite from a morning spent house-hunting for Louise. A cottage in Elterwater had looked perfect, with roses clambering around the door, but the rising damp would cost a fortune to eradicate. A swish apartment in Ambleside boasted every labour-saving gadget you could wish, but the block had been shoehorned in between a microbrewery and a garage, and if the exhaust fumes didn't poison her, the smell of beer would make sure she had a permanent hangover. With houses, as with people, appearances deceived.

The Tickled Trout was an upmarket pub-restaurant down the road from Ambleside. Last January, in the car park on the other side of the window he was facing now, Daniel had kissed Hannah for the one and only time. He hadn't planned it, and neither had she. But Marc found out about their meeting, and soon all hell broke loose, and Hannah found herself personally ensnared in a case of multiple murder. Louise didn't know the full story about Marc and Hannah, and at times she seemed to take it personally that her brother was testing her patience. In her black-and-white lawyer's mind, Daniel was wimping out of the chance of happiness when he should have moved on from Aimee's death and the mistake that had been Miranda.

Must it always be this way between siblings? He cared for Louise more than anyone in the world, yet sometimes he wondered why sororicide was rare. Probably she was tempted to fratricide once in a while. Now their adolescent arguments were a fading memory, they would fight to protect each other, but prolonged exposure to each other's company sometimes stretched their nerves to breaking point.

Daniel savoured the taste of toffee. Clearly Aslan had taken the job at St Herbert's with a view to getting to know his sister, and picking the right moment to introduce himself to his father. Lane End Farm was a good size and located in a beautiful part of Britain. It must be worth plenty, even in these straitened times, and Aslan would be more interested in money than orchestrating a sentimental family reunion. But Michael Hinds' reputation was as Cumbria's very own Mr Angry. Had Aslan provoked his father to such rage that he'd committed another of those rare – you might be tempted to say, astonishingly rare – crimes: filicide?

Louise put down her spoon and narrowed her eyes. 'You look as though you've wandered into a different country. What's going on in that brain of yours?'

'I'm thinking about families, what holds them together, what drives them apart.'

She dabbed at her mouth with a napkin. 'We're hardly

experts on family life, you and me, after what happened with Dad.'

'Or maybe we are. We've seen the ups and downs, more than most.'

'I don't remember that many ups after Dad walked out on us.' She frowned. 'Yet Hannah cared for him. I bet she sees something of you in him.'

'I'm nothing like him. He was a hardened cop, spent his life turning over stones and seeing what lay beneath. Dangerous work. Academe is cosy, you know yourself – the main risk is RSI from writing too many articles in learned journals that hardly anybody wants to read.'

'You are absolutely like him,' she said. 'Neither of you could ever let go without finding what you were looking for. My only question is this – have you any idea what you *are* looking for?'

St Herbert's was open to residents and Friends of the Library and their guests on Sundays, and when Daniel said that he wanted to call in, Louise insisted on coming along for the ride. Whatever she said, she was every bit as nosey as him. Driving past the narrow reservoir of Thirlmere, he listened to the news on local radio. The main story was the discovery of a man's body at a farm near Keswick, but he was not named.

'You think you know who it is?' Louise asked.

The road was clear, and he put his foot down. 'Hope to God I'm wrong, but . . .'

Soon they were parking at St Herbert's. As they jumped out of the car, Daniel spotted Micah Bridge trudging towards the front entrance. The principal's stoop was more pronounced than ever, and as they came up to him, a defeated look clouded his watery eyes. Daniel felt a gnawing sadness. Aslan may not have matched the profile of the typical habitué of St Herbert's, but he'd been young and full of life. Less than a week ago, he'd shinned down that drainpipe from the parapet up on the first floor, seemingly without a care in the world. To picture him lying on a mortuary slab made Daniel's stomach churn. No matter what Louise said, he could never have done his father's job. How had the old man coped, dealing with violence as a way of life?

After introducing Louise, he said, 'This latest death at Lane End Farm . . .'

Speaking in little more than a whisper, the principal said, 'The victim is Aslan Sheikh, he was murdered. Daniel, I can scarcely believe what is happening. My God, two members of staff dead within a few days of each other.'

'What have you heard?'

'Very little.' The principal mopped sweat off his brow with a handkerchief. 'The policeman wanted me to tell him about Aslan. What work he did, the people he dealt with. Whether he had any enemies.'

'They aren't suggesting an accident or suicide this time?'

Micah Bridge shook his head. 'Surely you are not implying that Orla was murdered as well?'

'I'm not implying anything, but hatred isn't the only motive for murder.'

'What do you mean?'

'Perhaps Aslan was killed because of something he found out, or witnessed.'

'Such as?'

'He was here on Friday morning, wasn't he? Sham told me he spent time in the library. She thought he was looking something up.'

The principal stared. 'I find that hard to credit. He showed so little interest in our collections.'

'Looks as though he stumbled across a reason to take an interest.'

'For heaven's sake, what could it be? This library is a place for quiet, scholastic research. We have nothing to do with the grubbiness of murder.'

Some have grubbiness thrust upon them, Daniel thought.

'Are the police still here?'

'They left an hour ago, once they had finished speaking to Sham.'

'She's working today?' Daniel was surprised. 'I thought she only—'

'Works Monday to Friday, and then with the utmost reluctance?' The principal sniffed. 'She claims her aunt sent her, saying she ought to be here to lend a hand, given that the press may turn up at any moment with their flashbulbs and their prying questions. I'm not sure I believe her. It's almost as if she's . . . gloating over Aslan's death.'

To spite Purdey, because Aslan had confided the truth about his identity to her and not to Sham? Daniel wondered.

'Where is she now?'

'On reception, as usual. Checking her lipstick so as to present her best face to the arriving media, no doubt.'

The principal couldn't conceal his bitterness. He seemed to take the deaths of Orla and Aslan as a personal attack on himself and St Herbert's. Come to think of it . . .

'When were you first appointed principal, Micah?'

'Seventeen years ago. Though for some years before that, I regularly gave lectures and undertook academic work here.'

'Were you around when Orla's brother went missing?'

The principal pursed dry cracked lips. 'As a matter of fact, yes. It was a dreadful time; that poor young boy who disappeared, never to return. Not that I ever met the lad. And to this day, I've barely exchanged a dozen sentences with his father. I made the mistake of seeking a donation to our funds on one occasion.'

'So you know Fleur from way back?'

'We were barely acquainted in those days. I knew her father better. He wasn't a man of letters, but he did support the library. *Noblesse oblige*, I suppose. He was keenly aware of Sir Milo's legacy, and that after Jolyon's accident, the Hopes name would soon be dead. He was bitter that the money had run out, and that the only reason his daughter lived so well was that she'd married for money, rather than love. It wasn't just that she married into a family that sold caravan pitches to the common herd. She picked the brother who held the purse strings, even though her father disliked him.'

'Alfred Hopes was a snob, then?'

Micah Bridge coloured, and Daniel realised he'd struck a nerve. The principal's academic elitism was as snobbish as Alfred Hopes' condescension about class. 'You might say so, but at least he wasn't ruled by profit-and-loss accounts and balance sheets. But why do you ask?'

Daniel waved the question away, realising he didn't

have a sensible answer. He'd become lost in a maze, taking one wrong turning after another in trying to make sense of the fates of Orla and Aslan. Time to start thinking like a historian again. Gathering all the scraps of evidence, seeing if they contradicted assumptions he'd already made. How often had he preached to students the importance of asking the right questions? He believed with a passion that understanding history helped you to make sense of the present, and so it must be with murder. The reasons for the deaths were rooted in the past, he was sure of it. Ask the right questions about what happened twenty years ago, and he'd find the right answers.

A squeal of brakes made him swivel round. An open-top sports car was screeching to a halt at the end of the drive. Fleur Madsen was hunched behind the wheel, dark glasses masking her eyes. The wind had tangled her hair; he'd never before seen her looking a fraction short of elegance personified. The principal, looking as though the arrival of his chair of trustees was all he needed to make his misery complete, dragged himself forward to greet her.

With a wave to Fleur and a nod to his sister, Daniel opened one of the double doors and came face-to-face with Sham Madsen, admiring her reflection in a compact mirror.

'Didn't expect to see you today, Daniel!' Her eyes opened very wide. He thought she'd overdone the mascara. 'Or you, Louise! Have you heard the dreadful news?'

'I don't know any details.'

'Apparently,' Sham lowered her voice, as if imparting a state secret, 'poor Aslan's head was bashed in and he was dumped in a slurry tank. Yuck, can you imagine? Dad is worried sick about Mike Hinds. He wants to make sure he has the best defence.'

'Why? Does he think Hinds is guilty?'

'No, I'm not saying that, but it stands to reason the police think so. What if Aslan turned up at Lane End and demanded money? Old Mike would go apeshit.'

'Killing his own son would be a bit of an overreaction, wouldn't it?' Louise asked.

Sham made a throat-slitting gesture. 'Hey, you don't know Mike.'

'What was Aslan researching on Friday morning?' Daniel asked.

She frowned. 'Search me.'

He'd do better to search the archives instead, but before he could head off for the library, Fleur trotted through the door, Micah Bridge trailing in her wake. She had taken off the sunglasses; her eyes lacked their usual sparkle and her make-up didn't disguise the pallor of her cheeks. She was wearing a plain white blouse and black trousers, and an expression as severe as her outfit. As they exchanged greetings and shock-horror exclamations about Aslan Sheikh's death, he remembered Aslan describing her as a cougar. Had she flirted with him? Or even gone further? Today, for sure, she wasn't in flirtatious mood.

'What brings you two here on a Sunday?' she asked. Unspoken was the rider: *I didn't have you down as a rubbernecking sensation-seeker.*

'The day before he died,' Daniel said, 'Aslan checked something out in the library. I was curious about what it might be.'

Fleur looked at him in bewilderment. He'd never before noticed the faint worry lines around her eyes. 'I simply cannot imagine.'

If she was feigning ignorance, she didn't merely look a little like Audrey Hepburn, she was a better actor. Yet Daniel was gripped by a conviction that she could help him to unlock the mystery, even if she didn't know where to find the key. He was tempted to cross-examine her. But did she really want the truth to come out?

His mind was made up by the roar of a car racing down the drive outside. Micah Bridge glanced through the open door and winced.

'It seems that the first journalists have arrived.'

Sham said, 'Are you sure they aren't just Friends of the Library?'

'These men do not look as if they have ever read a book in their lives.'

'Ouch.' Fleur raised her eyebrows. 'Micah, I've never once heard you say anything bitchy before. You must be stressed. We all are, of course, but we must put on a brave face with outsiders. What happened to Aslan and Orla is nothing to do with their work at St Herbert's.'

'We'd better leave you to it.' Seizing his chance, Daniel beckoned his sister to follow him down the corridor.

'What exactly are you looking for in these archives, then?' Louise asked as soon as they had closed the doors of the Old Library behind them.

He contrived an expression so inscrutable that she couldn't resist the urge to giggle.

'I want to find out about Castor and Pollux.'

* * *

It took less than thirty minutes for Daniel to trace what he was after. He spent another ten at his favourite desk, gazing at the yellowed sheets he'd borrowed from the archive downstairs, turning what he had discovered over in his mind. Testing hypotheses, in the way he'd once taught to students new to deductive reasoning, searching for answers that were not only valid but sound. After browsing for a while through the crammed bookshelves, Louise came up to join him, but soon she became bored by his reverie, and started drumming her fingers against the iron railing. She'd never been afraid to bring him back down to earth.

'So was that a eureka moment, or not?'

He leant back in his chair. 'You bet.'

'Go on, then. Surprise me.'

'John Everett Millais was a regular visitor to Keswick as guest of the Hopes family,' Daniel said. 'According to Sir Milo Hopes' memoir, Millais repaid their hospitality by making them a present of this painting.'

He pointed to an old photograph of a painting in a heavy gilt frame similar to others they had seen at Mockbeggar Hall. Two labradors with huge brown eyes stood side by side, as if awaiting a command. The sunlit turrets, seen through the trees behind them, made the Hall seem like a palace from a fairy tale. Daniel suspected Millais had dashed the painting off as a thank you; he'd sought to convey the dogs' unyielding loyalty and fidelity, yet the effect was cloying and sentimental, so that the picture was a long way short of a masterpiece. Hadn't William Morris dismissed his fellow Pre-Raphaelite as *an artist bought and sold and thrown away*? He'd overdone the hasty hack work, and this was an example. But Morris's sneer meant nothing to Milo Hopes, who wrote in his memoir that he would always owe a debt to his distinguished guest for immortalising his beloved animals, and vowed that Millais' gift should always have a place of honour in Mockbeggar Hall.

The painting bore a caption so blurred it was barely legible.

Castor and Pollux.

'Well, well,' Louise murmured. 'Go on, break it to me gently. What on earth connects a Victorian painting of family pets with Aslan Sheikh?'

Daniel lifted a lined sheet covered in tiny copperplate. 'Milo Hopes loved his labradors. In his writings, he gives the impression they meant much more to him than his servants. Eventually, first Castor, and then Pollux, died at ripe old ages, and he established a graveyard in the Hall grounds. That's where they were buried, and it became a family tradition for the Hopes' dogs to be laid to rest alongside, with headstones recording their names and dates.'

'Aaaaagh!' Louise couldn't contain her frustration. 'Come on, Daniel, enough of the history, what's the link with the here and now?'

His eyes flashed with amusement; for an instant, he was a teenager again, relishing a half-forgotten pleasure, the chance to tease his impatient sister.

'Seriously? You still don't see it?'

CHAPTER FIFTEEN

'Utterly gorgeous.' Hannah waved towards the sun-soaked cipher garden and the slope of the fell beyond. 'You'll find it a wrench to leave, Louise.'

Louise, in cropped top and denim shorts – the severe business suits that used to be her uniform had been consigned to the charity shop – was bustling around the table at the back of Tarn Cottage, filling their tumblers with cranberry juice. She'd produced a chicken salad they could eat outside while Hannah and Daniel discussed what he'd found in the library. When he'd called her, she said at once she was free to come over. The invitation was Louise's idea; hopeless as she was with managing her own love life, the control freak in her relished matchmaking for her brother.

'I've inflicted myself on Daniel for long enough. He doesn't need a sister cramping his style. It was my fault he started spending time at St Herbert's.'

'Just as well you did,' Hannah told him. 'I bet you're right about Castor and Pollux.'

'I'd have got there sooner,' he said, 'but the painting has been moved during the renovations of Mockbeggar Hall. It hung in the dining room until recently. Purdey Madsen mentioned it when we were there on Friday night – she asked where were the pooches – but I didn't realise what she was talking about.'

'So you reckon Callum's body is buried in the old pets' graveyard?' Louise asked.

This was Daniel's theory, the only explanation that fitted the facts. Why else would two dogs dead for more than one hundred years mean anything to Orla, and consequently to Aslan?

Hannah nodded. 'While we were interviewing at the caravan park on Friday, the CCTV picked up a man in the grounds of Mockbeggar Hall, an area closed to the public. They assumed he was a caravan-dweller whose curiosity had got the better of him, but he looked very much like someone DS Wharf and I had seen loitering around the entrance to Lane End Farm.'

'Aslan Sheikh?' Louise asked.

'I've seen Aslan's passport photos, two of them, one for each of his identities. Those little snaps are hardly ever good likenesses – least I hope not, mine makes me look like Rosa Klebb – but I'm sure it's the same bloke. Orla had told him about Castor and Pollux, and he wanted to see the pet cemetery for himself.'

Daniel chewed on a celery stick. 'I wonder what else Orla told him? Did someone decide they had to kill him, to preserve a secret?'

'Looks that way,' she said. 'So, what secret could be so dangerous?'

The three of them ate without speaking for a minute or two. The atmosphere was heady with the scent of potted lavender and roses scrambling over the trellis nailed to the cottage's rear wall. Daniel was conscious of Hannah's presence beside him, and her long slim legs an inch away from his. Wearing a short, semi-floral, belted summer dress, she was displaying much less flesh than Louise, but in sitting down, he'd brushed against her, and the contact sent a jolt of excitement through him, as if he'd touched a live fence at a farm.

At this time of evening, they no longer needed to shield their eyes from the glare. Barely a thread of cloud lingered over Priest Ridge, and the fell was bathed in a mellow light. The cipher garden was alive, and never wholly quiet, but the only sounds were the scurrying of squirrels in the undergrowth and up the trees, and the piping call of a redshank concealed by reeds beside the tarn.

'When I lived in the city,' Louise said, 'I took crime pretty much for granted. The month before I moved out, my next-door neighbour was mugged on a tram, and a woman who lived half a mile away was dragged into a park and raped by a teenage thug with a knife. But the Lakes should be different. A place so lovely shouldn't be disfigured by cruelty and violence, it feels like an offence against nature.'

'There's nothing gentle about nature.' Hannah blinked at the tartness of the cranberry juice. 'It's wild and unsentimental. Ask any farmer.'

'Speaking of farmers,' Daniel said softly. 'I can't get out of my mind what has happened to this man Hinds. If I ever had children, it would break my heart if one of them were to suffer pain. But to have three, and lose them to violent death, one by one . . .'

'He lost his brother, too.'

'You don't suppose someone hates him so much, they want to make him suffer?' Louise asked.

'Over the space of twenty years?' Daniel spread his arms. 'Who could hate a man that much?'

'And you are assuming Callum did die a violent death.'

'What's the alternative? Whether or not he was buried in the same grave as Castor and Pollux, he must be dead. In the end even Orla lost hope that he was still alive. If he was killed accidentally, somebody covered it up. Why do that, if they weren't afraid of being arrested, or if they weren't responsible for his death?'

'All right, but as for Mike Hinds, it's unthinkable that he was the culprit. Surely?'

They turned to Hannah, who was leaning back in her chair while her eyes followed the flight of a buzzard over the trees on the lower reaches of Tarn Fell. She dabbed at her lips with a paper napkin.

'Of course you're right. A father, murdering his offspring? Straight out of a Greek tragedy.' She toyed with a slice of lettuce she'd speared with her fork. 'But it was your father who taught me that being a detective means being ready to think the unthinkable.'

Louise paled. 'I hear the man has a foul temper, but even so . . .'

'Let's not run ahead of ourselves,' Hannah said. 'Aslan was murdered, but Callum might have been the victim of some kind of accident, and there's still a strong likelihood that Orla committed suicide. Daniel, I've been mulling over what you said about getting a handle on the sequence of events.'

'It begins twenty years ago, with Callum's disappearance,' he said. 'The past colours the present.'

His sister feigned a yawn. 'There goes the historian again.'

'The snag is,' Hannah said, 'we know much more about what's happened over the last week. Not one, but two prodigals returned to their roots and finished up working side by side at St Herbert's.'

Daniel nodded. 'Coming back set Orla thinking about Callum again. She spotted a family resemblance in Aslan – it wasn't a neurotic fancy. But when Aslan denied that he was Callum, her last hope of finding her brother alive went up in smoke. Hard to take.'

'And Castor and Pollux?' Louise asked.

'She was familiar with the Hopes archive, she must have been aware of the pet graveyard. In fact, given that she spent the first eighteen years living a stone's throw away from Mockbeggar Hall, first at Lane End, then with Kit Payne in his home in the caravan park, she almost certainly knew about it for years. Yet she never mentioned the dogs to me until that last time we talked.'

'There may be something else in the archive that we didn't have time to read,' Louise said. 'Some clue that set her on a fresh track.'

'Such as?' Daniel shook his head. 'How could a memoir a century old explain what happened to her brother? Orla picked up new information, for sure. But where from, God knows.'

'Whatever the new information was,' Hannah said, 'it

must have pointed to whoever was responsible for Callum's disappearance.'

A crow's wings flapped above the roof of the cottage. Daniel put down his knife and fork.

'It's all about history; the answer lies in what happened twenty years ago. Understand that, and you understand why Aslan finished up in a tank of slurry.'

The sunset was glorious, a soft reddish-orange glow above the silhouetted fells. Once they'd drained their cups of camomile tea, Daniel asked Hannah if she'd like a stroll around the garden before the drive home. As they walked, they talked about a hundred and one things while Louise, tactful for once in her life, disappeared on dishwasher-loading duty.

'Your dad would have been thrilled,' Hannah said, ducking beneath a low oak branch, 'to imagine talking to you about a case. It grieved him that he missed out on your growing up. His choice, Louise would say, but it cost him dear. I suppose you don't remember much from the days when he was still at home?'

'I have more memories than you might imagine. Vivid, too. The big cases, when he was out all night, the stuff that got in the newspapers. It excited me, his detective work, I was proud to be his son. Even if he didn't know it, even though the job screwed him up. He cared too much; he was often stressed to the eyeballs.'

'That never changed, till the day he retired. It's the nature of police work, you can't be left untouched by it. If dealing with crime and catastrophe doesn't stress you out from time to time, you aren't paying attention.'

She caught her foot on a tree root, and stumbled. He grabbed her arm to prevent her falling to the ground. Her flesh was firm and warm. As she steadied herself, he released his grip and she halted by an old yew tree, resting her back against the trunk.

'Thanks. I ought to look where I'm going.' She smiled and said lightly, 'It's so easy to trip up and make a fool of yourself, when you least expect it.'

'I can't imagine you making a fool of yourself.'

She put her head to one side, considering him. 'We all do it sometimes, don't we?'

He cleared his throat. 'I like it, that you tell me about your work. Reminds me of life with Dad. He offloaded occasionally, perhaps not as much as he should have done. But I realise there's plenty of stuff you can't discuss.'

'You're helping a lot. The tip about the dogs' graveyard is terrific, a real breakthrough. We'll take a look there tomorrow. See how Bryan and Fleur react when we announce that the missing boy may not have been gobbled up by that much-maligned pig after all, but could have lain in their own backyard for the past two decades.'

Daniel winced. 'Wear your body armour. The reopening of the Hall may need to be put on hold and Bryan will hate that.'

'My heart bleeds. It won't leave the Madsens destitute. The lovely Fleur will still be able to spend more on one pair of shoes than the budget for my entire wardrobe.'

His eyes travelled over her. 'I'd say you're doing fine.'

It wasn't soft soap; give him the natural look any day. Fleur's glamour was too self-conscious, too expensively contrived. Micah Bridge's words sneaked back into his mind. *She married for money, rather than love.* No doubt the match suited both husband and wife. Bryan acquired an attractive woman to take his arm at business and social gatherings, Fleur was free to spend as though there were no tomorrow.

A pink tinge coloured Hannah's cheeks. 'It helps, talking things through. I've never—'

'Yes?'

'Sorry, I was about to say that, even though I talked to Marc about the cases I was working on, it wasn't quite the same. You have first-hand experience of life in the police, and that removes a barrier.'

'How are things with Marc?'

'You mean, between Marc and me?' She cracked a twig in her fist. 'Last week, I'd have said it was over and done with. And yet . . . one or two doubts are creeping in. Or at least, I can't quite make the break. Too soft, you see. Ben would have been cross with me; he had no time for dithering.'

'Give it time.'

'I dunno, maybe I'm not suited to living with someone else. Since January, I've never once been bored with my own company. All the same, it's good to have someone to discuss stuff with.' She grinned. 'You make an excellent sounding board. Most detectives need someone on the outside to lend an ear, every now and then. A spouse, a partner, someone discreet they can trust to keep stuff confidential.'

'Don't worry, I know how to keep my mouth shut.'

'Of course you will. You and Louise were a detective's kids. It's almost like talking to family.'

His turn to blush. Hannah didn't give her trust lightly,

he was bound to feel flattered. To cover his embarrassment, he said, 'I have a confession to make.'

She laughed. 'Oh yes, Daniel?'

'I've been wondering about Callum. As you said, there isn't much hard information, just a few clues, scattered around like crumbs. Looking at the photo of the Millais painting made me think of Giovanni Morelli.'

'Never heard of him.'

'Morelli was an art historian who argued that you can recognise the hand of an artist from tiny details in their work better than from a signature. The way the folds of a background character's ears are painted is more distinctive than the theme of the picture or the stuff that's more obvious and likely to be imitated.'

'The importance of unconsidered trifles, huh?'

'Exactly. And the Morelli technique isn't confined to attributing works of art correctly. Sigmund Freud took a similar line with scientific method, finding hidden meaning in small details. Freud admired the detective work of Sherlock Holmes, who believed that inconspicuous bits of apparent trivia helped you find the truth, if only you interpreted them correctly. So if we apply that to what we know about Callum Hinds . . .'

'Yes?'

If he ever talked like this to Louise, she groaned and urged him to get on with it. Hannah was different; fascinated for some reason by how his mind worked. She leant closer to him, more like a first-term student than a seasoned cop. The wind blew a strand of her hair against his cheek. It was like being stroked with silk. He was seized by the urge to put his arm around her, and draw her to him. Here they were out of sight of the cottage, and masked by the trees from people walking up on Priest Ridge. For once in his well-ordered life, he was in danger of losing control, and finding himself swept away like a stick in a stream.

He stepped backwards, creating a space between them, and ticked the points off on his fingers. 'One, even Orla said that Callum was sly. He'd listen behind doors to rows between their parents, and boast about it to his sister. Two, he was a peeping Tom who spied on a girl in a bikini who was staying at the caravan park, and on his father making out with his new lady friend. Three, he enjoyed nursing secret knowledge, it gave him a sense of power. Little scraps of information, but they help us see a picture of Callum. So what do we make of a kid like that, half-eavesdropper and half-voyeur?'

'Go on.'

'Suppose he heard something he wasn't meant to hear, saw something he wasn't meant to see.'

'Such as?'

'Quite; that's the sixty-four thousand dollar question. Answer it, and I'd guess you have the answer to everything.'

She nodded. 'Makes sense. Callum caught somebody doing something they shouldn't, and he dropped hints to his kid sister, but held back the full story?'

'Yes, but my guess is that recently, she stumbled across the truth, or part of it. That's why she wanted to talk to you. Only by then, she was too drunk and depressed to make any sense.'

'She made it clear she wanted justice for Callum,' Hannah muttered. 'I owe it to her not to let them down.'

'Don't beat yourself up about her call,' he said sharply. 'I know what she was like. You couldn't have saved her.'

'Well, that's a matter of opinion, Daniel.' Hannah gritted her teeth. 'Anyway, you can apply the Morelli technique to another snippet. When Orla called me, she said: *How could you do that to your own brother?* What kind of narrative can we fashion from that?'

'She enjoyed being mysterious, if you ask me. I think she believed it made her seem more interesting. Poor Orla, she was mixed-up and naive. And she may have been nicer than Callum, but they had plenty in common.'

'That remark – you reckon she was talking about Callum?'

'Either him or Michael Hinds doing the dirty on Philip, I thought. But another idea crossed my mind this afternoon. A long shot, but . . .'

'Try me,' she murmured.

He took a breath, struggling to focus his thoughts on the children of Michael Hinds instead of on the woman standing in front of him, just out of reach.

'Jolyon Hopes was left paralysed after a riding accident. He was gay, and had no children. Although he lived for another ten years or so, he died relatively young. Leaving the way clear for his sister to inherit Mockbeggar Hall.'

Hannah raised her eyebrows. 'You think she might have caused her brother's accident?'

She couldn't quite mask the scepticism in her voice, and he felt his cheeks reddening. 'As I say, it's a very long shot.'

'Thanks, I'll find out how Jolyon came to have his fall.'

Letting him down lightly. 'There are other possibilities.

Orla might have been talking about Bryan doing the dirty on Gareth Madsen. Or even about Philip Hinds, rather than Michael. Suppose Philip did something cruel to his brother. That might explain why Michael took revenge by blaming Philip for Callum's disappearance.'

'Mike Hinds didn't need a special reason to stitch up Philip,' Hannah said. 'He's just an angry selfish bully.'

'Hey, don't sit on the fence,' he said with a grin. 'Tell me what you really feel about the man.'

She laughed. 'You've gathered, we didn't bond. Then again, I didn't care for the way he threatened to decapitate my sergeant.'

'Surely he wouldn't have used the scythe?'

'I don't know. There's something untamed about him. Frightening. No wonder Orla was scared by him.' She shook her head. 'Should we be getting back? Louise must be wondering what on earth we are getting up to.'

He managed to stifle the flirtatious joke that sprang to his lips. And he was rewarded when, without a word, she linked her arm in his as they followed the path back through the twists and turns of the strange dreamlike garden to the sunlit cottage, and reality.

'Isn't she lovely?' Louise said, when they were back inside after waving Hannah off from Tarn Fold. 'She could do a lot better than a second-hand bookseller with a roving eye, that's for sure.'

'Don't start. She hasn't finished with Marc, far from it.' Daniel kicked off his sandals and flicked the hi-fi remote. Barber's *Adagio for Strings* filled the living room. 'But I think she fancies living on her own.'

'She fancies you.' Louise tapped the side of her nose. 'Trust me, a woman senses these things. But even if she is still hooked up with the bookman – you will call her?'

'Tomorrow.'

'Excellent!'

'Don't get too excited. I'm back at St Herbert's in the morning; there's something about this case that I want to check and let her know.' He thought for a moment. 'In fact, there's more than one question I'd like to ask.'

Her eyes narrowed. 'She's the detective, Daniel. You're not, and you're not Dad, either.'

Stretching out on the sofa, he closed his eyes, letting the lush music wash over him.

'You really think I'd forgotten, that, Louise?'

Hannah listened to Jamie Cullum singing a mix of standards and newer stuff on the drive home. She liked his voice, it usually took her out of herself, but tonight she couldn't help fretting about what she should do with her life. Leaving Marc to Terri's tender mercies had to be an option. She might even try her luck with Daniel. But something bugged her about Ben's son. He was a very bright guy, and incredibly personable; he had the world at his feet. It was taking a long time for him to get over the death of Aimee, but when he finally did so, she was sure he'd find life in the Lake District wasn't satisfying enough. Tarn Cottage would become a rural pied-à-terre, while he spent most of his time jetting around the world on lecture and book tours. He had a first-class brain; he'd get bored with her if they spent too long together. And even if he didn't, how could he fit in a partner whose life revolved around police work?

A rabbit ran across the road and she slammed on her brakes at the last moment to avoid squashing it. An SUV following too close behind did an emergency stop and finished a couple of inches short of her back bumper. The driver took out his anger by hitting his horn. He'd have thought better of it if he'd realised she was a cop, but Hannah didn't want to make a scene. As the rabbit disappeared into the hedgerow, she set off again, and the SUV overtook at the first opportunity, horn blaring again in disgust as it disappeared into the night.

She needed to concentrate on the road. Driving in the dark was never easy on the Lakes' narrow byways, and she shouldn't allow herself to become distracted. Most of the men Hannah knew were skilled at compartmentalising – how else had Marc indulged himself with Cassie Weston while setting about building a new life with her after the move to Ambleside? She'd never been much good at filing her emotions in neatly separated folders, but she wished she could learn the knack.

'Our Day Will Come', Jamie was promising, as she pulled up outside Undercrag. Better hope he was right. At least Marc didn't seem to be lurking around the house again like a ghost. Her mobile chirruped as she was climbing out of the car. Terri again. She'd seen a couple of missed calls from her, made during her stop at Tarn Cottage. Before setting out, Hannah had called Terri and made the mistake of telling her she was going to see Daniel Kind. Obviously her friend was agog for an update.

Ignoring her wouldn't work; Terri never took no for an answer, and if she was determined to talk, there would be another call, and then another. Hannah checked her watch.

Must have been about this time last night that a desperate murderer hit Aslan Sheikh on the head and threw him into the slurry tank. She pressed *answer* and said, 'Hi, kid.'

'Been trying to get hold of you all evening.' Terri sounded breathless. 'Are you still . . . with Daniel?'

'No, I'm back home.'

'You'll have to tell me about it some other time.' This might just be the most unexpected thing Hannah had heard Terri say. 'Hey, listen, I need to talk to you.'

She gripped the phone in her palm. 'What is it?'

'This bloke who was murdered at the farm near Keswick?'

'Yes?'

'I was talking to Stefan this evening. He told me about this mate of his, who works at the farm.'

'One of the Polish labourers?'

'Yeah, really fit bloke, name of Zygmunt. He's a witness; you need to talk to him.'

'My colleagues at Keswick have spoken to people at the farm. I can't just muscle in on their patch.'

'Listen, Zygmunt has decided he's not going back to the farm, he's a free agent now. These two deaths have spooked him, and no wonder. A woman suffocated in grain, and a man chucked into a slurry tank? You couldn't make it up. Anyway, he told Stefan he saw something the other day, when that woman jumped into the grain tower.'

Hannah felt as though an icy finger had traced a pattern down her spine. 'What did he see?'

'Someone was watching her. Even followed her towards the grain tower.'

'Seriously?'

'Zygmunt swears it's the truth. I've met the feller, he isn't a liar.'

'Why didn't he speak up before?'

'Everyone reckoned the girl killed herself. And he didn't want to get anyone into trouble. Or draw too much attention to himself. It's not easy for migrant workers, you know; they worry that if they are in the spotlight, they might risk being asked to leave Britain. We're not such a welcoming country as we used to be, Hannah.'

'OK, point taken, but is he willing to talk now?'

'Only to you.'

'Hang on a moment—'

'No arguments, sweetie. I've explained that you're completely trustworthy. How are you fixed tomorrow morning?'

Shit, this was becoming complicated. But how could she say no?

'All right. I'll call you first thing.'

CHAPTER SIXTEEN

It was sweltering inside St Herbert's, the atmosphere sauna-like and oppressive. All the windows in the Old Library were open, but it made no difference. Daniel could almost feel the pounds dripping off him in sweat. Much more of this, and he'd look like a wraith. But a change was on its way; the Radio Cumbria weathergirl had warned of a build-up of pressure, and thunder and lightning were forecast for late morning and the afternoon. Everyone Daniel saw seemed heavy-legged and sluggish, as if the humidity had drained their last drops of energy. The Old Library was deserted apart from the librarian, whose footsteps sounded squeaky and unnaturally loud as she trudged to and fro between her desk and the catalogues. Casual readers and residents alike had fled, as though fearing the epidemic of death among members of staff might prove contagious. Even the journalists had abandoned St Herbert's; Daniel suspected they were circling Lane End Farm like vultures, but at a safe distance, in case Mike

Hinds lost it once and for all with his scythe or his gun.

For the first time in their acquaintance, even Professor Micah Bridge had loosened his tie. There was a moist glistening in the deep furrows of his high forehead, and he leant against a bookcase for support. His breathing was an unhealthy rasp; he sounded like a candidate for an imminent stroke. The deaths of Orla and Aslan had diminished him; he seemed to have shrunk, and become infirm before his time. How much more could the principal take?

'Jolyon Hopes?' The high scratchy voice echoed in the silence. 'He was a reckless rider, by all accounts. I heard he took a chance too many with a young and nervous horse.'

'On the estate?'

'Goodness me, no. The accident occurred in Cheshire, I believe.'

'So he was away from home at the time?'

'He loved horses. The Hopes were renowned as a family of animal lovers, although that did not stop them hunting foxes. I gather he went hunting all over the north of England. His father was devastated by the calamity, of course. Not least because it ruled out any chance of the Hopes name continuing into the next generation.'

'Was Fleur with him at the hunt?'

'No, if memory serves, she was on holiday with her husband on a cruise in the West Indies at the time. She flew back to be at her brother's bedside. In the end, he pulled through, although his vertebrae were smashed beyond repair. He was never able to look after himself again.'

'Fleur was out of the country at the time of the accident?' Another theory shot down in flames. Hannah was right to be sceptical.

'Indeed.' Micah Bridge pursed his papery lips. 'Dare I enquire as to the reason for your curiosity?'

Daniel contrived an enigmatic smile. 'I'm fascinated by stories about families. Like the Hinds and the Paynes. Or the Hopes and the Madsens.'

'Ah, a true historian of England; those families' stories concern the perennial struggle between land and trade.' The principal's moist eyes locked on him; could he really be as other-worldly as he seemed? 'Alas, we both know that trade always wins. But your current researches are much more targeted. This book of yours about the history of murder. You are not by any chance suggesting—?'

The double doors leading to the corridor swung open behind them. Daniel did not need to turn round to know who was there. The fragrance was unmistakable.

'Daniel!' Fleur Madsen's voice had an uncharacteristic tremble. 'I saw your car outside, and guessed you were here. Can we talk?'

'Sorry, Hannah.' For once in her life, Terri sounded uncomfortable as she placed the mobile down on the table. Her tan was tinged pink with embarrassment. 'Zygmunt has changed his mind; he's wetting himself at the prospect of getting involved.'

Hannah swore under her breath, her shoulders stiffening with anger and frustration. They were sitting opposite Stefan at a table on the pavement outside the Windermere pub where he worked. The stop-start of noisy car engines as the traffic snaked past them, heading lakeside, was making her temples pound, and in the sticky atmosphere the stench of petrol made her throat constrict with nausea.

The farm labourer had been due to arrive three-quarters of an hour ago, but he'd failed to show. Stefan finally tracked him down on his mobile, but when Terri took the phone and spoke to the man, the conversation didn't go to plan, and within a minute, he'd cut her off.

'He doesn't have a choice.' Hannah rapped the table's metal surface to make her point. It made her feel better, even if her knuckles stung. 'If he has information that would help our enquiries, he has a duty to share it. He's not at risk, and even if he were, we could look after him. If he'd rather speak to someone other than me, fine. No way can he put his head below the parapet now.'

'It's just that—'

'Listen, Terri, I'm not pissing about. If he tries to melt away into the landscape, we'll dig him out. If he keeps his mouth shut, there's every chance he'll finish up in a cell, looking at a one-way ticket home. He needs to cooperate, and tell us whatever he knows.'

Terri stared as if Hannah had stepped out of an alien spacecraft. 'All these years we've been friends, you've never talked to me like a detective chief inspector before.'

'Yeah, well, I'm not in the mood for games.' Hannah didn't often raise her voice, but she was past caring about making a scene. 'Mario Pinardi found a body dripping in slurry on Saturday night. He won't forget the stink of death and shit in a hurry. As for Orla Payne, I spoke to her less than forty-eight hours before she died of suffocation. Two people, laid out on mortuary slabs long before their time, do you wonder I'm not prepared to let this bloke wimp out?'

Terri put up her hands, like a boxer on the ropes warding

off a flurry of punches. 'All right, all right, I'm only trying to help.'

'Give me the phone.' Stefan stretched out a beefy arm tattooed with a picture of a mermaid with bee-stung lips, and breasts the size of beach balls. 'I will talk to him.'

'I'd be grateful,' Hannah said, as Terri slid the mobile across the table to him.

Stefan was a man of few words, many of them heavily accented and hard to interpret, but that didn't faze Terri, who talked enough for two. He seemed to be a man of simple pleasures, content to gaze with quiet approval at Terri's cleavage, even if it wasn't quite a match for the mermaid's.

He redialled and spoke with quick-fire fury in Polish to his friend. Whatever he said left no room for argument. Inside a minute, he rang off and thrust the mobile into his trouser pocket as though he never wanted to see it again.

'He changes his mind, he will come soon.'

'Thanks, Stefan,' Hannah said.

It crossed her mind that it would be a mistake to underestimate Stefan. For all his taciturnity, he seemed strong in temperament as well as in physique. Not in the same league as Mike Hinds, no doubt, but cross him, and sparks would fly. Did Terri know what she was getting into? A question for another day.

'Perhaps you can spare me five minutes in my office, Daniel?'

Fleur Madsen set a brisk pace across the floor of the Old Library, not waiting for an answer. Shaken she might be, but she had a nervous energy that the heat hadn't sapped, and she took it for granted that Daniel would follow her lead. Her pallor made a striking contrast with the black trouser suit; she resembled an exquisitely tailored ghost. She'd made it clear she wanted to speak to Daniel in private, and Micah Bridge needed no encouragement to make himself scarce; he seemed to find her very presence intimidating.

As she made a few noises about the awfulness of Aslan's death, and the insensitivity of so many journalists, she took him to the back staircase. It led to her office, but so did the main staircase, up from the corridor by the reception desk, and it would have been quicker to go that way. He suspected Fleur didn't want Sham to know they were having a conversation. And he was beginning to think that he could guess why.

Reaching the first floor, Daniel found himself looking down a narrow passageway that ran the length of the building. Halfway along he saw the landing of the main staircase. Doors spaced at irregular intervals opened off the left-hand side of the passage; on the right, windows looked out on to the drive and car park; beneath them were bookshelves crammed with modern first editions. Fleur pointed out a complete run of Graham Swift first editions as she took out a key for the door marked *Chair of Trustees*. For a few moments, it rattled clumsily in the lock; her hands were shaking, but at last the door opened and she waved him inside.

The room was spacious, with a dedicated workspace, plus a large leather sofa and occasional table for informal one-to-ones. Everything was predictably neat and well organised; Fleur didn't strike him as a woman who could bear clutter. Was that why she'd never bothered to complicate her life with kids? Her desk was immaculate, with pens, paper clips and rubber bands stored in the compartments of a bronze tidy, and a sleek wireless laptop. A solitary photograph showed her and her husband shaking hands with Margaret Thatcher. The shot must have been taken long ago; Bryan's hair was still dark and plentiful. Yet Fleur's appearance had scarcely changed. She looked steely-eyed enough to have been the Iron Lady's daughter.

As he took a seat at one end of the sofa, she indicated a door set in the side wall. 'I even have my own bedroom. A bit of a waste, frankly. My predecessor lived in Whitehaven, and often stayed over. But Bryan and I live so close to the Residential Library, I never need to stay the night. I could walk home, if I was in the mood, but that would mean schlepping through the Hanging Wood, unless I made a twenty-minute detour. So I bring the car, and try not to worry about my carbon footprint.'

You're talking too much. The torrent of small talk must be down to nerves; she was unfamiliar with not being in control of events, and unsure how to cope with a sense of helplessness.

'So – you wanted a word?'

'Yes, um, that's right.' She turned round the chair at the desk, and straddled it. 'The librarian tells me you and your sister were researching my family's records. I wondered—'

'Orla Payne said something to Aslan about Castor and Pollux. I think he checked Sir Milo's memoir and found those were the names of two dogs, buried in the grounds of Mockbeggar Hall. They were painted by Millais, in thanks for the hospitality he'd received.'

'That's right.' Fleur swallowed. 'The painting is a family heirloom.'

'I believe it usually hangs in the dining room at the Hall.'

She nodded. 'We moved it during the renovations. It needs to be sent away for cleaning.'

'So, not moved simply in order that I shouldn't see it?' Her jaw dropped, as much at his insolence as in denial that the Madsens might be so Machiavellian. 'Doesn't matter. I reckon Orla discovered, or guessed, that her brother Callum was buried along with the dogs.'

A rictus grin. 'You can't be serious?'

'Sorry, Fleur, but I am.'

'And your friend, DCI Scarlett, I presume you've discussed your theory with her?' He inclined his head. This was why Fleur had asked him up here, he felt sure. To get an understanding of what he'd shared with Hannah. 'So what does she think?'

'She'd like to take a look at the pet graveyard.'

'The Hall estate is private property,' Fleur said. 'We have only opened up a part of it to the holiday park's residents. Dead animals deserve a dignified resting place, as much as dead people. I doubt Bryan would be willing to allow the police to dig up the grounds on a wild fancy.'

'Much more than a wild fancy, to be fair. At first, Aslan was unclear how Orla had learnt about Castor and Pollux. After all, it wasn't long ago that she thought he was really Callum. Because she'd locked the door to her room here, he shinned up the outside drainpipe to break in via the window. Hardly any of them shut perfectly, as you know.'

Fleur stared. 'Aslan did?'

'I saw him with my own eyes. He pretended to me he'd simply climbed up on to the parapet on a whim. It took him a while to figure out how Orla might have learnt the truth about Callum. As it did me.'

'What do you mean?'

'Orla and Callum had plenty in common.' He exhaled. 'Just as Callum was a voyeur, so Orla was an eavesdropper. She heard enough to work out the rest.'

'Heard from whom?'

He smiled, even though he felt genuine sorrow. 'From you, Fleur, or from someone you were entertaining here.'

'Is this some kind of macabre joke, Daniel? If so, I have to say it's in very poor taste.'

'No joke,' he said. 'A summer's day, and with your window and hers next door both open, she must have listened to your conversation. My bet is that she heard enough to be sure that she knew not only that Callum was buried in the dogs' grave, but also who put him there.'

Zygmunt proved to be one of the labourers Hannah had seen when she and Greg Wharf visited Lane End Farm. He'd seemed keen to avoid them, but within five minutes of his arrival in Windermere, he'd relaxed sufficiently for her to start asking questions. Stefan had poured him a pint of bitter, which he downed in a few gulps, and it helped loosen his tongue.

'You're sure this was on the day Orla climbed up the grain tower?'

'Uh-huh.' He wiped the froth from his mouth. 'But I didn't see her. Not then.'

Terri said, 'Ziggy was with Hinds the farmer when they found Orla Payne's body. A horrible experience – you must have had nightmares ever since.'

'It was not good.'

Hannah said, 'Was this in the morning or the afternoon?'

'Two o'clock, maybe half past.'

'And you saw someone around the farm, someone who didn't work there?'

'Uh-huh.'

Hannah leant forward. *Now for it.*

'Can you give me a description?'

Dark clouds were gathering as Fleur and Daniel pushed through thick clumps of nettles in the wilderness beyond the formal gardens of St Herbert's. They were heading for the Mockbeggar Estate. Sweat stuck Daniel's shirt to his chest. He kept mopping his brow with a handkerchief, but only a storm could freshen things up. The weather was about to break, and he'd be soaked to the skin long before he regained the sanctuary of St Herbert's. But Fleur had promised to take him to see the pet graveyard, an offer he was far too curious to refuse.

A holly hedge thicker than the walls of a mediaeval fortress barred off the Mockbeggar grounds, but the stream at the boundary was low after the long dry spell, and they clambered along its edge like mountain goats. At the bridge carrying the new road from Madsen's to the Hall, instead of following the road, they kept straight on, through an avenue of lime trees with trunks gnarled in elaborate and beautiful patterns.

'There it is.' Fleur pointed to the tall elms in the distance. 'The Hanging Wood.'

So that was the place where Orla and Callum had loved to play with Philip Hinds. Two children and a childlike man, all destined to die before they grew old. Daniel's heart thudded with anticipation. Soon he would know the truth about their fate.

Fleur spoke a little about Gareth Madsen and Michael Hinds. Garrulous no longer, she chose her words with as much care as counsel delivering a considered opinion on a finely balanced point of law. Every now and then, she threw him a quick glance, as if to gauge his reaction. No teasing now, no provocative smile.

'Gareth always liked Mike, not only because of the time they spent as students together, drinking heavily, playing sport and chasing women. Two strong, very masculine men.'

He wasn't sure whether she meant this as a compliment. 'But very different from each other?'

'Yes, but they did have some things in common. Whereas Mike and my husband were chalk and cheese. I'm afraid Mike never cared for Bryan.'

'And is the feeling mutual?'

'Bryan never forgave Mike for heckling him once at a political meeting, when Bryan said farmers expected too many handouts from government. A silly argument, but the animosity festered for years. Mike was furious that Bryan invested so much trust and responsibility in Kit Payne. He even blamed Bryan for the break-up of his marriage.'

'A bit harsh, surely?'

Fleur cast him a curious glance. 'More than harsh. I'm afraid Mike sometimes seemed . . . unbalanced.'

'Presumably, if Niamh hadn't run to Kit, she'd have found somebody else.'

'Precisely. She was too much of a free spirit to be a farmer's wife for ever. Second time around, he married a doormat. Deirdre suited him much better than Niamh. She didn't mind him wiping his feet on her.'

'You speak of Mike in the past tense.'

'Did I?' For a moment she was flustered. 'It's just that . . . it feels as though nothing will ever be the same again. The deaths of Orla and Aslan have changed everything. Poor Mike, I don't know how he'll cope.'

'You think he might choose to kill himself?'

A long sigh. 'God, I don't know. I'm not sure I know anything anymore. I suppose . . . it's possible. Farmers have the means of death ready to hand, and Mike might decide he can't go on any longer.'

'Because of his grief, you mean?'

'Grief?' She shrugged. 'Guilt, as well, I suppose. Here we are. The animal graveyard.'

Between a couple of the lime trees were a row of unevenly spaced slabs of moss-covered York stone. Each bore an inscription, most of which were so weathered as to be illegible. Daniel bent down over the largest stone; it was the size of a small coffin lid. A child's coffin lid. Next to it lay a fading red rose. A tribute from Aslan, he guessed. Peering hard, he managed to decipher the words.

Castor and Pollux, semper fidelis.

'Always faithful,' she murmured. 'That's why we love dogs,

isn't it? They are so much more loyal than human beings.'

Now for it. On the way here, he'd shied away from pressing her, but he needed to know what she knew.

'How did Callum die, Fleur?'

She took a breath. 'It was an accident. Mike told Gareth that they had a row about the girl Callum had spied on. Callum had called in at the farm after being with Philip at his cottage. I don't know the details, but Mike lost his rag and thumped Callum, and the boy lost his footing. They were out in the cobbled yard, and Callum fell on to a saw. It ripped open his throat; Mike said the blood spurted like a geyser.'

'So why didn't he call an ambulance?'

'The boy died almost instantly, Mike said, and so he panicked. His son had been killed in horrific circumstances, and it was his fault. He was sure Niamh would seize on the chance to destroy him. He'd be prosecuted for manslaughter, and was bound to lose the farm. His life would be over. His only thought was to save himself.'

'So he buried his own son's body in a dog's grave?'

Fleur's features were frozen into a mask. 'Yes, when we stand here and discuss it, Mike's cruelty seems unimaginable. And yet I don't suppose it seemed like that for him. Nothing he could do would bring Callum back to life.'

'Why not hide the corpse on his own land?'

'I simply don't know, but I guess he thought that, if it were ever found, the finger of suspicion could only point at him. Although he was in a panic, he knew better than to risk his own neck.'

'And then he put the blame on his own brother, and drove him to suicide?' Daniel had never met Michael Hinds, but the man Fleur described sounded like a monster.

'I suppose he was afraid Philip would tell people that Callum had gone to Lane End and he'd fall under suspicion himself.'

Daniel felt drops of rain moisten his hair.

'And when did you find out about this?'

'Gareth told me shortly before Orla died. He and Mike had a few drinks one night, and the alcohol loosened Mike's tongue. He was in a bad way, because Orla's return to the Lakes had spooked him. She'd developed an obsession about Callum, she kept raking up old ground. And I suppose his conscience kept plaguing him.'

'Why confide in Gareth, after keeping his mouth shut for twenty years?'

'It's a long time to keep such a dreadful secret. Perhaps there was nobody else he trusted, perhaps it was simply a cry for help. Not that there was much Gareth could do.'

'But he told you Callum was buried along with Castor and Pollux?'

'Yes, he came to St Herbert's one day for a private chat. It wasn't something we could discuss at the caravan park, in case someone interrupted us. He was desperate to make sure that Bryan didn't know.'

'Because Bryan would go straight to the police?'

She nodded. 'He'd see it as a civic duty. Never mind what it meant for Mike Hinds.'

'You like Mike Hinds rather more than your husband does?'

'No, I don't much care for him. But he was Gareth's friend, and he'd suffered a good deal.'

Again the past tense, he noticed. 'Gareth told you the

story in your room on the first floor, and Orla, who was next door, overheard because the windows were open?'

'Stupid of us, but we didn't think. Frankly, I was so stunned by what Gareth said, it knocked me sideways. All those years, I assumed Philip was responsible for Callum's disappearance. Gareth made me swear that I wouldn't breathe a word about Mike. It was desperately difficult to keep it to myself, but before I could work out what to do, Orla killed herself. I've been haunted by guilt ever since.'

'How exactly did Orla come to die?'

She wiped a raindrop from her cheek. 'I suppose she was mortified by what she'd heard. Not just that Callum was unquestionably dead, but their father had concealed his body here. I feel awful about it. That simply because I lent my brother-in-law a listening ear, a young woman was driven to commit suicide.'

'It was a symbolic gesture to go to Lane End Farm to end it all?'

'Presumably. Heaven only knows what dark thoughts go through such a troubled mind. Poor girl, perhaps she wanted to talk to her father; perhaps she actually did.'

'And Aslan Sheikh?'

'Orla didn't tell him the whole story, as I understand it, but she let enough slip for him to work out that Mike had something to hide. Again, I can only guess at his reaction. I suspect he was more interested in Mike's money than in a family reunion.'

'You think Aslan tried to blackmail his father, and Mike's response was to hit him over the head and throw him in a tank of slurry?'

'How can I know what to think, Daniel?' The mask

splintered, and she gave him an imploring look. 'All I know is that there have been too many deaths. It really has to end.'

'And how do you expect it to end?' he asked softly.

Was that a tear in her eye, or simply another splash of rain?

'I dread to think,' she whispered. 'I dread to think.'

His throat constricted. 'By Mike Hinds . . . doing the decent thing for once in his life?'

She stared at the ground. 'Gareth doesn't think Mike can take any more. He's urged him to make a clean breast of everything, to set the record straight. But I don't know if he's up to that.'

The rain was spattering on the leaves above them. Soon they would be drenched.

'He has no choice.'

'I hate to say it, Daniel, but you're wrong.' Her voice was no more than a whisper. 'Things have gone too far.'

'Mario, where are you?'

'In the incident room. What's up, Hannah?'

'I'm on my way to Keswick.' She was talking hands-free as she sped along the main road from Windermere, only a couple of miles from Ambleside. 'I have a witness who saw someone lurking around Lane End Farm, the afternoon Orla Payne died. You need to get over there. I'll tag along, if it's OK by you.'

'Be my guest, it's always good to work with you. But what's the hurry?'

'Enough people have died already. We don't want any more bodies on our hands.'

Mario's voice was taut. 'You think the murderer might kill . . . someone else?'

'Or himself,' she said.

Daniel and Fleur parted at the bridge. She said she wanted to go back to the Hall, and check that the maintenance work was on schedule. He suspected it was an excuse. She wanted time to herself, and privacy.

The rain whipped him as if he were a galley slave. He heard a rumble of thunder. Time to move fast, and get away from the trees during the storm. But something made him linger on the bridge's parapet, watching Fleur's retreating back as she hurried towards her ancestral home.

There was no doubting her horror at everything that had occurred to the children of Michael Hinds. No doubting, either, that she was afraid. But afraid of Hinds topping himself? He wasn't sure. If she was right, and the man had caused the deaths of all three of his children, it might seem the best way out.

He fished his mobile out of his pocket. Better speak to Hannah, and let her know everything Fleur had told him.

Fleur had become a tiny doll-like figure, blurred by the slanting rain as she scurried along towards the Hall's front entrance. Oblivious to the downpour, he fastened his eyes on her again, wondering what thoughts were swimming round inside her head.

Wondering why the story she had spun sounded to his ears like one of Orla's favourite fairy tales.

He couldn't believe it.

CHAPTER SEVENTEEN

'God, is that the storm I can hear?' Hannah asked. She was driving past Rydal Water, and it wasn't pelting down yet, but the first flecks of water splashed on to her windscreen even as she spoke.

'Yeah.' Over the microphone, Daniel's voice was muffled. 'You've seen drowned rats less sodden than I am right now. Not sure I'll ever feel dry again. But I needed to tell you what Fleur said.'

'Thanks, but you need to find shelter fast. Not under the trees, too dangerous if lightning strikes. You could be killed.'

'I'll make a dash for it in a second. On your way to Keswick?'

'Yes, no time to lose. Especially if what Fleur told you is true.'

'But you don't think it is?'

'Do you?'

'No.'

'She's found an answer for a lot of questions, hasn't she?' Hannah said. 'But not all of them.'

'Do you believe Mike Hinds is a murderer?'

'Wish I knew.'

'Come on, Hannah.' Even as the rain lashed him, he found it impossible to contain his impatience. 'We've found a witness who saw someone spying on Orla just before she climbed up the grain tower.'

'Really? And do you have an ID?'

'From the description,' Hannah said slowly, 'the man bears a strong resemblance to Gareth Madsen.'

'I knew Ben Kind,' Mario Pinardi said. 'He was a bloody good copper.'

'The best.' Hannah took a swig of Diet Coke from a can. The incident room was as noisy as the Saturday market, and she had to raise her voice to make herself heard above the gabble of phone talk and the rattle of keyboards. 'His son is no fool, either.'

'So I hear.'

Mario dodged her eyes, and she guessed he'd heard gossip about her and Daniel. Every force brimmed with rumour and innuendo, and she was an easy target. People knew she and Marc were no longer living together, and no doubt her sex life was the subject of endless lascivious guesswork. If only they knew the truth. This last six months, she'd been as pure as any nun, for Christ's sake.

'Fleur Madsen didn't convince Daniel that Hinds killed Aslan Sheikh.'

'Suppose Gareth spun his sister-in-law a line . . .'

'And covered his tracks by putting the blame on Hinds?'

'Who was supposedly his bosom buddy, yes.'

Hannah clenched her fist. 'It's an absolute bugger. Bryan Madsen is pretty odious, but I rather liked Gareth. He's not like Hinds.'

'He's a salesman, isn't he? Maybe he can talk his way out of it.'

Mario bared his teeth in a fierce grin, but for all the show of resilience, his shoulders were rigid with nervous tension.

'Sir!' An admin assistant who was in the middle of a phone conversation shouted over from the other side of the room. Her face was bright with excitement as she gestured to Mario's phone with her free hand. 'You need to hear this. The caller is Mrs Birt. I'll transfer her right now.'

He picked up the receiver and put on the loudspeaker. 'DI Pinardi. Can I help you?'

'I was just telling your colleague, I saw a photo in the newspaper of that poor girl who died, and I saw you were appealing for information.'

The woman was well spoken, but sounded breathless and apprehensive. A touch of nervousness was a good sign; this wasn't someone likely to call the police on a whim.

'Thanks so much for taking the time to help us.'

He did the PR stuff so well, Hannah thought. If only she'd been able to tease out Orla Payne's story . . . no, better not go there.

'I saw her, it was on the day she died. That very morning.'

'Uh-huh?'

'We have a caravan, you see. We've been going to Madsen's for six years, ever since the children were young.'

'And you saw Orla Payne?'

'Yes, I go out jogging each morning before breakfast. Trying to lose a few pounds, you know?'

'I do know, Mrs Birt.' The woman must think Mario was so pleasant, so unhurried. Surely she would be put at ease and tell them what she knew? 'Now, what exactly did you see?'

'This was near the new bridge that leads to the old Hall. They've done the area up, you know. It's still cordoned off, but I go round the edge. It's quiet there, and I like it best when there aren't too many people around.'

'I understand.'

'I caught sight of the young woman. She was crying. I don't know why she was distressed, but I thought she must be someone who worked at the holiday park, and perhaps had done something wrong. I changed my course, to keep out of their way. I'm sure they didn't spot me, they were too wrapped up in their conversation.'

'They?'

'I told your colleague, Stacey, he took her into one of the old caravans by the new road. Half a dozen of them are empty, they are waiting to be refurbished, I think. I supposed he just wanted a word in private with her. He put an arm round her shoulder, as if he was trying to calm her down.'

'Did you recognise him?'

'Of course I did, I've already explained. It was Mr Madsen.'

'Which Mr Madsen?' Mario asked.

Hannah held her breath.

'Why, Gareth, of course. He's the one you see around

the park, he's much more hands-on than Bryan.' The woman paused. 'Don't take that the wrong way. I'm sure there was no funny business going on with the girl. He was just trying to comfort her, that's how it looked.'

'Did you hear what they were talking about?'

'Not a word.' She sounded virtuous. 'I kept my distance.'

Mario exchanged a look of frustration with Hannah. 'Of course, Mrs Birt. I'll hand you back to my colleague now, if you don't mind, so we can take one or two details, just in case we need to speak to you again. Thank you so much, it's so good of you to take the trouble to call.'

'I hope it helps.' Mrs Birt was pleased with herself. 'And don't worry about the fact I didn't hear anything. You can always ask Gareth, can't you?'

'We certainly can,' Mario said.

He transferred her back to Stacey, and clenched his fist in triumph.

'Gareth will need a brilliant line in chat to wriggle out of this. He never mentioned talking to Orla on the day she died. If he followed her to the farm . . .'

Hannah swivelled on her chair. 'Say Orla challenged him about Callum's death, and whether he was responsible. He might have threatened her – or simply laughed in disbelief. Either way, it was an unequal contest, a young woman with a history of mental health problems up against a rich and powerful businessman.'

'Yeah, she could never prove anything, not after twenty years, even if Callum's remains were dug up from the pet cemetery at Mockbeggar Hall.'

'The chances of forensic evidence establishing who was

responsible for putting him there are close to nil. If that conversation left her in despair, she might have been ready to end it all. Her brother was never coming back, and she'd made a deadly enemy of the man who employed her stepfather.'

Mario nodded. 'Time to give Gareth a ring?'

He lifted his phone and called the holiday park. Impatiently negotiating the automated answering service, he demanded to be put through to Gareth Madsen the moment he made it as far as a human being. He got no further than Gareth's PA. Hannah saw him wince at her response as he banged down the receiver.

'Shit, shit, shit.'

'What's up?'

'He left ten minutes ago, and didn't say where he was going.' Mario snapped his fingers. 'We just missed him.'

'You could have caught your death,' the principal said.

Daniel was ensconced in one of Micah Bridge's armchairs, clad in an ancient and moth-eaten dressing gown that must have represented a fashion crime even in the 1970s. The rich smell of Turkish coffee filled his nostrils, the taste of it lingered on his tongue. While he'd recovered from his drenching in a hot bath, the principal had asked one of the staff who doted on him to set about the task of drying the sodden clothes. Thank God St Herbert's was equipped for emergencies. A tumbler containing an inch of whisky squatted at his feet.

Racing back from the Mockbeggar Estate had felt like something out of a low-budget horror movie. Even by Lake District standards, the storm had been hellish. A falling branch missed fracturing his skull by inches, and although he managed not to be struck by lightning, the rain whipped him with a sadist's glee. As he squirmed around the holly hedge boundary, he tripped and fell into the stream. Scratched and bruised, he picked himself up and struggled on in the face of wind and rain, but the wildness of the weather drove out of his mind all thoughts of Mike Hinds and his dead children.

Only as he relaxed in the steamy bathroom did he contemplate an alternative scenario to the one Fleur had conjured up. An explanation fitting all the facts, not merely those that suited her. When he finally clambered out of the vast old claw-footed bath, he wiped away the mist from the mirror, and saw the beginnings of a smile on his face. His mind was clearing, too.

'Fleur showed me her office upstairs. I never realised there was a bedroom attached. Not that she needs it, of course, living so close by.'

'She does not need to sleep here, that is true.'

As with a lawyer or a politician, it was what Micah Bridge didn't say that counted for more than what he did say.

'But she did use the bedroom?'

The principal's face turned traffic-light red. He folded his arms, as if to repel further interrogation. 'I can say no more.'

'Hey, Micah, we're both grown men. Don't fret about telling tales out of school.'

'This is a most delicate business.' The older man hesitated. 'We are speaking in the strictest confidence?'

'You have my word.'

'Very well.' The principal lowered his voice, as though the walls had ears. And in St Herbert's, of course, they did. If Orla hadn't eavesdropped, she and Aslan might still be alive. 'This morning I was provided with certain rather distressing . . . intelligence.'

'About Fleur?'

A nod. 'I'm afraid so.'

'Who told you?'

The principal looked over his shoulder, as if checking for eavesdroppers. 'The librarian. She came to me in a state of considerable anguish, having kept her own counsel for some little time. But after the two deaths, and the unpleasantness of press intrusion, she felt I had to know. She fears for the very future of St Herbert's if we fall prey to scandal.'

'What scandal?'

'It involves muffled cries coming from the chair of trustees' room – her bedroom, the librarian thought. Sounds of a . . . shall we say . . . unequivocal nature.'

Daniel gripped both arms of his chair. 'She overheard Fleur having sex with someone?'

The principal's Adam's apple bobbed in distress. He might have been a bishop, contemplating the desecration of a cathedral by heretics. As for Daniel, he didn't know whether to laugh or cry.

'The librarian was passing along the first-floor corridor one evening. It's a quiet area, hence her amazement at what she heard. Naturally, I questioned whether Fleur Madsen might simply have been exercising vigorously on her own, or something of the sort.' Daniel fought the urge to giggle. 'I have to say that the librarian was adamant. The chair was up to no good of a very particular kind.'

'She couldn't have been mistaken?'

'Daniel, the librarian may be sixty-three and rather . . . um . . . rotund. But she was married once, long ago, and I believe she now has a . . . shall we call it an understanding . . . with a gentleman who keeps pigeons in Maryport. I can assure you, she is by no means as unworldly as she may seem.'

Daniel tried not to be distracted by images of the librarian disporting herself in a remote pigeon loft. 'Any idea who her companion was?'

'No doubt whatsoever about his identity, Daniel. The librarian happened to see him leaving the first floor a few minutes after the . . . um . . . sounds died down.'

Daniel pictured her lurking within eyeshot of Fleur's door, holding her breath, flabby jowls trembling with a mixture of outrage and glee. The principal lowered his gaze.

'He wore a cheery smile, needless to say. And the librarian noticed that his shirt was carelessly buttoned.' The principal's frown lines deepened. 'He has a reputation as something of a ladies' man, but even so – fornicating with his own brother's wife!'

'Gareth Madsen?'

'I am afraid you are correct. Ghastly even to think of it. In all candour, I do not care for Bryan Madsen, but nonetheless, it is a shocking business. Such a sordid betrayal.'

Daniel swallowed a mouthful of whisky. Glenmorangie, from the St Herbert's cellar. It seemed sinful to sit here in the shabby comfort of Micah Bridge's rooms, and savour its tang, while Hannah and her colleagues were striving to find the truth about the savage murder of Aslan Sheikh. And self-indulgent to want to satisfy his curiosity about the strange relationship between Fleur and Gareth Madsen. But it wasn't prurience. He had the makings of a theory about Callum Hinds' death, and the historian in him could not resist testing it against the evidence.

'You told me before that you don't know Bryan well, but did you come across him all those years ago, when you first came to St Herbert's, around the time that Callum Hinds disappeared?'

The principal considered. 'I think not. Of course, I was aware of him, given that he had married the daughter of Alfred Hopes of Mockbeggar Hall, and was the heir apparent to Joseph Madsen. My recollection is that he was incapacitated, following a road accident. He sustained very bad injuries, by all accounts, though obviously he lived to tell the tale.'

'He told me he crashed his car not long before Callum went missing, hence his limp. Do you recall the circumstances?'

'I'm afraid not. He was supposed to have been lucky to have escaped with his life, that's about all I can remember. Presumably he was driving too fast and spun off the road.' A wrinkling of the nose. 'Gareth, of course, was once a racing driver, and I seem to recollect some rather distasteful gallows humour to the effect that Bryan was trying to emulate his younger brother. I'm sorry I cannot be of more assistance.'

'Please don't apologise, Micah,' Daniel said. 'You have helped, more than you can know.'

'He might be anywhere,' Mario said.

A burly young DC was easing their car through queuing traffic on the way out of Keswick. His hands, resting on the steering wheel, were the size of coal shovels. He was a broken-nosed rugby player, sixteen stone of muscle, and his nickname was the 'Brick Shithouse', but nobody was silly enough to call him that to his face. Handy man to have around if things turned nasty.

They were heading for Lane End Farm. Hannah's idea. Mario still wasn't convinced, but he was struggling to make decisions. And someone needed to make a decision. Ben Kind used to say that you never regret what you do in life half as much as the things you don't do.

'Gareth won't make a run for it.' Her voice was calmness itself, despite the blood pounding in her temples. 'Take it from me, that isn't his style. He may never have made it to Formula One, but you need nerve to race fast cars. He's a daredevil, a risk-taker. A fighter, not a quitter.'

'But why would he go to Lane End?'

'My guess is, he wants to stage a confrontation with Hinds.'

Mario swore. 'I should have left an officer stationed at the farm. But the staff cuts . . .'

'Don't beat yourself up, it would make no difference. Gareth knows all the short cuts and ways in from the site of the holiday park to the farm. How else did he manage to keep Orla under surveillance before she jumped into the grain?'

In the quiet of the car, the back-and-forth thrashing of the windscreen wipers sounded unnaturally loud. Pools were forming on the road surface, and the downpour had slowed the cars to a crawl. The DC revved his engine and rapped on his horn, before squeezing the car past a rusty Fiat full of pensioners out on a shopping trip. Wrinkled faces stared out through the misty windows in dismay, as if they feared being pulled over and arrested for tiresome driving.

'You still think Orla jumped?'

'Maybe Gareth pushed her, maybe after their conversation that morning, he just wanted to keep an eye on her to make sure she did get out of his hair by committing suicide.'

'Bastard.'

Hannah was breathing hard. Trying not to imagine what a man like Gareth Madsen might do if he became desperate.

'Yes.'

So Fleur and Gareth were lovers. How long had that been going on? Daniel sat in the deserted restaurant of St Herbert's, wearing an old T-shirt and jeans borrowed from Jonquil's brother, who worked in the kitchen, and savoured the peppermint taste of a slab of mint cake. He needed energy after the ordeal of the storm, and hadn't Hillary and Tenzing famously consumed Kendal mint cake on top of Everest, celebrating their conquest?

Micah Bridge said he'd heard gossip that, as a teenager, Fleur dallied with Gareth before teaming up with his elder brother. The switch made perfect sense from her point of view. Gareth was the charismatic one, but Bryan was destined to inherit a controlling interest in the caravan park and was a rising star in local politics. Fleur had her head screwed on. The Hopes family might have squandered a fortune, but she was determined not to give up the good life or allow Mockbeggar Hall to fall into the hands of creditors. Presumably, she and Gareth had reached an understanding.

They could have their cake and eat it. Everyone would be happy. Now and then Fleur would flirt with a much younger man like Daniel or Aslan, simply to cover her tracks.

But where to have their fun? There wasn't much privacy around a caravan park, and a hotel room might seem a bit tacky for the lady of the manor. The tumbledown cottage tucked away in the middle of the Hanging Wood offered an ideal solution. What it lacked in luxury, it more than made up for with back-to-nature atmosphere. Gareth could shift poor Philip Hinds out of the way whenever he wanted, by giving him a string of time-consuming menial tasks, and they'd have the place to themselves. Everyone gave the Hanging Wood a wide berth, what could possibly go wrong?

A sly inquisitive boy called Callum Hinds, that was what went wrong.

Daniel took a gulp of spring water. The way he pictured it, Callum turned up at the cottage one day and spied on Gareth and Fleur in flagrante. So much more exciting than ogling a teenager in a bikini. Full-on sex between two of the most important people in the neighbourhood – shock-horror stuff! No wonder Orla saw he was excited just before he disappeared. He'd have hugged his secret to himself, relishing the taste of power. Two grown-up lives in the palm of his hand.

Or perhaps he'd simply eavesdropped, and heard the couple talking. It wouldn't take much to figure out they were having an affair. And what if they'd discussed some other guilty secret that they shared?

The rain hammered at the windows, frantic as a convict on the run, desperate to be let in to a place of sanctuary.

Daniel digested the last morsel of mint cake. He could make a pretty good stab as to what that other guilty secret might be.

From the lane, the farm appeared to be at peace. The rain had relented, but there wasn't a glint of light in the sky and Hannah supposed that this was just a lull before another storm. The tractors and muck spreaders were motionless, there wasn't a soul in sight. Presumably Zygmunt's colleagues had jacked in their jobs as well. A silent earthquake was ripping apart Mike Hinds' world.

'Ready?' Mario asked.

Was Gareth Madsen here, and how would Hinds respond to their arrival? Only one way to find out. She yanked her hood up over her head as she scrambled out of the car. Above the drumbeat of the rain, she heard in the distance the mournful bleating of neglected calves.

Mario, a couple of strides ahead of her and the DC, stopped in his tracks.

'What's that?'

Yes, there was something else. Hannah strained her ears.

'Someone sobbing?'

'Sounds like a woman.'

'Deirdre?'

'Who else?'

Mario broke into a run, side by side with the young DC. The crying came from behind the farmhouse. All the curtains were closed, an old-fashioned mark of respect for the dead. Last time she was here, Hannah hadn't clocked the paint peeling from the door-frame or the fact that the lavender in the pot outside had died. You could be forgiven for believing the Hinds had abandoned their home.

As she rounded the side of the house, she saw Mario and the DC standing over Deirdre Hinds. She had screwed herself up into a foetal ball, crouching on the cobbles. From head to toe, she looked a sodden mess, with her cheap and scruffy clothes drenched through, and her hair tangled like a ball of coarse wet wool. What little Hannah could see of her face was blotchy, and it looked as though someone had blacked her eye. No prizes for guessing the culprit, but thank God he'd done nothing worse to her. Hannah had feared he was about to lose it big time.

Mario stood at the woman's side. 'Where is he?'

Shoes slapping on the cobbles, Hannah came closer. Deirdre's grey eyes were cloudy with tears. She tried to answer Mario, her lips moved, but no sound came. It was as if she'd been struck dumb.

Hannah knelt down so that she and the other woman were face-to- face.

'What is it, Deirdre?' she asked.

The woman stared at her.

'Did he hurt you?'

Deirdre Hinds shook her head. In denial about her husband's abuse, or was something more shocking on her mind?

'Tell me where Mike is,' Hannah said.

Deirdre clamped her eyes shut.

'Please, Deirdre, talk to me. Is Gareth Madsen here?'

Deirdre took a deep breath and let out a long shriek of pain. She might have been one of the animals in the shippon, waiting to be fed. But Hannah heard the truth in the horror of her cry. It was not hunger that drove the woman to despair. Nor even a smack from her husband's heavy hand. What tormented her was something she could not bring herself to describe.

'*How could you do that to your own brother?*'

Orla Payne's words echoed in Daniel's head as he walked out of the restaurant. She'd quoted Callum, quoting someone else. If he was right in believing Callum had spied on Gareth Madsen having sex with his sister-in-law, chances were that he'd been fascinated by their post-coital chit-chat.

Bryan had been seriously injured in an accident shortly before Callum disappeared. What if Fleur suspected Gareth of fixing Bryan's car so that he would crash? If she'd challenged Gareth about the accident in the boy's hearing, there would have been boundless scope for blackmail. Callum might not have taken it seriously, but if he'd dropped so much as a cheeky hint to Gareth that he knew about Gareth's affair with Fleur, and his attempt to kill his brother, so that he could take both Bryan's inheritance and his wife, he'd have placed himself in serious jeopardy. A man willing to murder his own flesh and blood wouldn't scruple at disposing of a teenager who threatened his comfortable existence. The risk-taker in him might have relished it. Killing Callum in the Hanging Wood, burying his body in the pet graveyard nearby, liberating the pig, and encouraging Mike Hinds to put the blame on his own brother. Cruel and conscienceless, but very neat.

And where did this leave Fleur? She'd known about the car crash, probably known or guessed about Callum.

Even if Gareth denied everything and protested that she was imagining things, she was smart enough to see through the salesman's patter. Yet she hadn't uttered a word, and Callum's remains were left to rot alongside the skeletons of the dead dogs.

Worse than that, she'd not been able to bring herself to give him up. Was love a drug for her, did he give her something no other man could? So that not even Orla's death, or Aslan's, drove her to come clean?

How could the woman live with herself?

'Daniel, there you are!'

For Christ's sake, it was unbelievable. Fleur was back at St Herbert's. Turning at right angles into the main corridor, he saw her heading towards him from the reception area. He could see Sham Madsen at her desk, a troubled look on her pretty face, and guessed that neither of them knew where Gareth was or what he was up to.

'I had to come and see how you are,' Fleur said. 'I wanted to make sure you were all right after that awful storm.'

The colour of her cheeks might be snow-white, but she'd composed herself and put on fresh lipstick, a vivid splash of crimson. The note of concern in her voice was nicely calibrated. Fleur might have no conscience, but she remained a class act. Having gathered her strength at the Hall, she needed to check what he knew, and what he suspected, so she could rehearse her defence. One look at those compressed crimson lips told him she would never surrender.

'That's good of you,' he said. 'As a matter of fact, there are one or two questions I meant to ask.'

* * *

'Tell us where they are,' Hannah said. 'Mike and Gareth, or either of them.'

Deirdre was mute, but she managed a feeble nod of the head. In the direction of the long line of outbuildings. Hannah and Mario exchanged glances.

'Will you wait here?' Mario asked her.

'No chance. I want to find them.'

'All right.' Whether or not he thought her stupid to take the risk, Mario had too much sense to argue or try to be protective. He turned to the DC. 'Stay with Mrs Hinds, make sure she comes to no harm. We'll holler if we need assistance.'

The two of them sloshed through the puddles, past one steel-framed structure after another, casting a glance inside each one to see if they could catch sight of their quarries. Nothing, nothing, nothing.

As they approached the last of the outbuildings, an unmistakable stench greeted them. Hannah felt sick in the pit of her stomach.

Nothing for it but to take a look. If she wasn't able to hack it, she should never have come to Lane End Farm.

Mike Hinds was sitting on his haunches inside the building. Flecks of rain plopped through a gap in the roof, down on to his weathered face, but he did not move an inch. His eyes stared through the two police officers. Hannah dared not imagine what he was seeing. He did not flinch as they approached, gave not the faintest indication that he was aware of their existence. She felt sure they were not in danger from him. His rage was spent. Orla had wanted justice, and her father had contrived the wildest justice: revenge.

The log-cutting machine was still and silent, its work done. Something was strapped to the conveyor belt, remnants of someone who once lived and breathed. The wicked blade was invisible, embedded in what was left, and this must have caused the machine to crash to a halt, but too late – far too late – to save Gareth Madsen.

The basket placed on the floor to collect the sawn logs was overflowing with a chaotic mess of segments spewed out by the log cutter. Slices of the man responsible for the deaths of Mike Hinds' three children.

'Aaaah . . .'

Mario groaned, then made a dreadful retching sound and turned to throw up on the ground. Hannah felt hypnotised, out of herself, paralysed by the savagery of what she saw. A human being, transformed into offal.

Blood, blood everywhere. Sticky viscous blood, staining Mike Hinds' clothes and fingers, coating the severed remains of the murderer. Flowing in rivulets, mixing with pools of rainwater, streaming out of the building and on to the cobbles.

Thunder rolled and clattered in the distance. Soon the rain would teem down again. In time it would cleanse the farmyard of Gareth Madsen's blood, washing it down the drain like so much sewage.

CHAPTER EIGHTEEN

A gust of wind sent leaves fluttering along the beck in Tarn Fold. Daniel felt a momentary chill on his neck, for all the warmth of an August Saturday. He and Hannah had spent the past hour walking to the top of the fell and returning by way of the wooded slopes of Brackdale. With excruciating tact, Louise had insisted on staying at home to pore over her finances as she decided whether to put in an offer for a picture postcard cottage in the heart of Hawkshead.

'Fleur is sticking to her story, then?' he asked.

They'd talked about the case when Hannah arrived earlier in the afternoon. Mike Hinds was still undergoing psychiatric assessment. Deirdre had been discharged from hospital, still adamant that her husband was a victim, not a wrongdoer. When the medics examined her, they'd found old scars on her ribcage and buttocks that she claimed were the legacy of years of consensual rough sex. Nobody believed her, but what could you do? Her cousin, who farmed in Borrowdale, had agreed to keep

Lane End Farm ticking over, until it could be put on the market.

'Like superglue.'

'For God's sake, what a woman.'

'You said it, Daniel.'

'How has Bryan Madsen taken all this?'

'His upper lip is so stiff, you'd think it was injected with novocaine.' Hannah shook her head. 'Got to hand it to him. His brother was a murderer, with whom his wife had a long-term affair, but you'd never know to listen to him. *Life must go on*, that's what he says. Of course, he's right, but easier said than done, eh? I'd hate to think what's going on beneath the surface, probably better not to know. The company's PR people issued a press release saying that Bryan's thoughts are with Deirdre Hinds "at this difficult time".'

'I caught Kit Payne reading a statement on the television. The message from Madsen's Holiday Park is *business as usual*.'

'Yeah, can you imagine? But Kit says that bookings and enquiries reached an all-time high over the last seventy-two hours. Everyone loves a good murder, even better with lashings of sex and gore thrown in. The bad guy is dead, the man who turned him into mincemeat is under twenty-four-hour guard. We have uniforms outside the farm to turn back sightseers and journalists with zoom lenses, desperate for a glimpse of the log cutter. Talk about a money shot. Pity finances didn't stretch to us having a constable at Lane End when it really mattered, but I don't suppose it would have made any difference.'

'So all's well that ends well?'

'Yes, if all you care about is a cheap frisson.' Hannah tore a leaf from a sycamore branch and screwed it up in her fist. 'Mario Pinardi is on sick leave. I visited him again last night, he's in a poor way. It's heartbreaking; he simply can't deal with what we found at the farm.'

'Not surprising.' Every time he pictured the scene in his own mind, his gorge rose. How had his father handled this kind of stuff, how did Hannah cope? They stared at each other. Her expression gave nothing away. 'And how are you doing?'

'The welfare people offered me counselling, and I spent an hour with a nice lady from Kendal, but now I've found my diary is mysteriously booked up for the foreseeable future.' Hannah gulped in the soft woodland air. 'Never thought I'd say this, but I'm with Bryan Madsen. It's best not to dwell on these things. That way madness lies, huh?'

'Nobody can be strong all the time, Hannah.'

'I used to say the same to your dad, but he took no notice. I thought he was invincible, but no one is, are they?'

'No,' Daniel said in a whisper.

'When he died, I thought I'd never get over it. Heaven knows how you handled it, I was only his protégée.' Locks of hair had fallen over her eyes, and she flicked them back. 'What I'm trying to say is, I know you're right. That first night alone at home, after we found . . . what we found . . . at the farm, I won't pretend it was easy. I hardly slept a wink. But that was almost a week ago. I'm over it.'

He leant back against the nearest tree trunk. 'It'll take a lot longer than a few days to forget what you saw.'

'I'm not sure I want to forget it, not entirely. It's a reminder of what human beings can do to one another.

Makes me remember why police work is worthwhile. We can make a difference, even working in a backwater like cold case reviews.'

'Don't keep underselling yourself.'

She laughed. 'You sound just like Ben. How many times did I hear him say that? But you're wrong, I don't undervalue myself. Specially not after Lauren Self told me what a great job I was doing yesterday. Stuck in her gullet to say it, but she's recovered from the shock of seeing the Madsens' sponsorship go up in smoke, and she has a vested interest in looking on the bright side if she wants promotion. We may not have saved Gareth Madsen's life, but at least they've avoided the cost of the trial, and my money is on Hinds being unfit to plead. Given all the cutbacks, it might mean a net gain to the bottom line. Budget calculations were scrawled all over her face. But even Lauren couldn't quite bring herself to claim a glorious victory.'

Daniel exhaled. Cost pressures and internal politics, these were the reasons he'd fled from academe. 'Will Fleur's nerve crack, do you think?'

'We're not banking on it. Her class aren't short of self-assurance, and Bryan is sticking by her. She's intelligent enough to have settled on her story – it's a subtly revised version of the one she rehearsed with you. She's determined enough to recite it, word-perfect, until we run out of difficult questions.'

'Remember that lecture we attended in the spring?' he said. 'The stuff about women who commit serious crimes? How women learn "good-behaviour narratives" early in life, and mitigate consequences of their actions by accessing "good" narratives. It's the power of storytelling. All of us do it. Orla, Aslan, Fleur, you and me. Anyone can rewrite their story to make a horrendous experience seem strangely positive.'

'Fleur maintains her fling with Gareth was something and nothing. Even though they evidently went at it hammer and tongs whenever the opportunity presented itself. She excuses herself on the basis that the car crash left Bryan impotent, and a woman has to take her satisfaction where she can find it.'

'Wasn't Bryan supposed to be a randy old goat?'

'That was his narrative. All part of the image for a successful entrepreneur. His relationship with Fleur sounds more like a business partnership. He confirmed that what he calls his "wedding tackle" was mangled in the accident. My sergeant interviewed him, though he spared me the grisly details.'

'What about Sally Madsen?'

'Fleur says she was having an affair with the bloke who runs her suntan lounge, the latest in a long line of toy boys, so she won't find it too easy to clamber on to the moral high ground. At least Fleur and Gareth kept it in the family, eh? Sally plans to move in with her lover while she fights Bryan and Fleur over who gets Gareth's shareholding. Even if she does, it's a minority stake. Bryan and Fleur will keep control of the business. And Mockbeggar Hall.'

'Does Fleur still deny that Gareth caused Bryan's car crash?'

'Categorically. A wicked invention. Slanderous. Not a shred of evidence to back it up, et cetera. She's even talked about consulting m'learned friends to protect her reputation. Attack is the best form of defence.'

'You don't believe a word of it?'

'When she says the car crash was a genuine accident? No, Daniel, your theory that Gareth wanted Bryan dead feels right. Who knows, maybe he got the idea from Jolyon's accident. A convenient mishap leading to a valuable inheritance. The first night I met the Madsen brothers, in Mancini's bar, Fleur made a flip comment, comparing Gareth to an actor in an old film, *The Postman Always Rings Twice*. Isn't that the one where the bloke kills the husband to get hold of his wife? I can't help wondering if it was some sort of private joke between them. But none of that will wash in court, and we'll never know for sure. Just as we'll never know whether Gareth pushed Orla, or she jumped. Makes no difference; either way, she's cold in her grave. My take is that she wanted to die, and so she did his dirty work for him.'

'Fleur knew Gareth had killed Aslan – and Callum. The boy's bones have been dug up from the dogs' grave. No wonder he was keen to lead the original search of the Mockbeggar Estate. Fleur must have known the remains were there. She can't possibly hope to get away scot-free.'

'Want to bet? Fleur claims she challenged Gareth about Callum's death, and under pressure he said something about Castor and Pollux. Fleur says that was what Orla overheard. But she also maintains she had no proof Gareth was a child-killer, and it's a serious thing to accuse your own brother-in-law. She was wrestling with her conscience about whether to talk to us when Aslan died. Again, her line is that she couldn't know for sure that Gareth was responsible. He cooked up a story throwing all the blame on

Mike Hinds, and she swallowed it, hook, line and sinker.'

'So Fleur claims to be squeaky clean?'

'Absolutely. All part of her narrative, you see. She has cast herself as the loyal mistress, denied her conjugals by an act of God, standing by the man she married for better or worse, then seduced and woefully misused by a charming rogue. At one point, she actually said, *I'm not looking for pity*. As if.'

'You believe she knew Gareth killed the boy?'

'My best guess is that she leapt joyfully on to the idea that Philip was responsible, like everyone else. Shut her mind to the possibility that Gareth might be involved. We all do denial when it suits us, don't we?'

'I suppose.'

'When Orla started sniffing around, I think Fleur became suspicious, hence her conversation with Gareth. She must have guessed Gareth killed Aslan after luring him to the farm. It looks as though he planned to lay all the blame at Mike Hinds' door.'

'Which is why Fleur wanted me to believe that Hinds was guilty.'

He closed his eyes, taking in the fragrance of the woodland. A mix of earth and fern and wood and wild flowers. So far removed from the stench of death.

'Spot on. I'm sure they were in cahoots, though there's no chance of a conspiracy charge now. Gareth went to talk to Hinds, pretending to help him out by footing his legal bills. He meant to take Hinds by surprise and kill him, just as he'd done with Aslan. Make it look like suicide. Hinds hasn't made much sense during the limited time we've had to interview him, but we've pieced things together by talking to Deirdre as well. It seems that Hinds started to wonder if Gareth had something to do with Aslan's death. He knew he was innocent, though he had no idea why Gareth would want to kill anyone. When the conversation didn't go as Gareth planned, he lunged at Hinds. At that moment, Deirdre came out of the house and screamed, and Hinds took Gareth off guard and knocked him out. When he woke, he was trussed up and lying on the log cutter, waiting to be turned into sausage meat. He pleaded for his life, but Hinds wasn't in the mood for mercy. Deirdre begged him, too, but he smashed her cheekbone and she crawled away in case he decided to slice her up for good measure. Hinds didn't switch on the machine at once, that we do know. He let Gareth sweat for a good ten minutes. Christ, it must have seemed like an eternity. And when he saw Hinds reaching for the lever to start the saw . . .'

For a few seconds, neither of them spoke.

'It can't be right,' Daniel said. 'Fleur didn't lay a finger on anyone, but morally . . .'

'The police avoid getting too hooked up on morality,' Hannah said gently. 'Ben must have told you that. Upholding the law is difficult enough as it is.'

'But if Fleur gets away with this . . .'

'Tough shit, she gets away with it. Orla has had justice, sort of, and that makes me feel marginally better about messing up when she called me. But justice is always messy, ask any lawyer.'

In his frustration, he punched the tree trunk. Stupid, really. It hurt his hand, for no good reason, but somehow he didn't care.

'It's so wrong.'

'You know what they say, Daniel.' Hannah's smile was wan. 'History is written by the survivors.'

'I almost forgot.'

Hannah wound down the driver's window of her car. Daniel was seeing her off after she'd declined an offer of dinner. Things to do back at the house in Ambleside. It was true, yet it wasn't the whole truth. She wasn't ready to insert herself any further into his life.

'Yes?'

'Marc gave me a present.' She lifted the copy of *Hidden Depths* from the passenger seat. 'I've read one poem every night before going to bed.'

'Oh God, my juvenilia.'

'Hey, I like poetry. Everything from John Donne to Thom Gunn. Not every police officer is a philistine, you know. I'll let you into a secret – I wrote a few verses myself, when I was a student. But they were lousy, not like yours.'

'So Marc tracked the book down for you? It's pretty scarce. Deservedly so, I'm afraid.'

'He wanted to surprise me. For once, he succeeded.'

Daniel shoved his hands deeper into the pockets of his chinos. 'What's the latest with the two of you?'

She shook her head. 'That's the most difficult question you've asked me all day.'

'Sorry, I don't mean to pry.'

'I'm not trying to be evasive.' She ground her teeth. 'My mate Terri thinks it's about – you know, the miscarriage. I don't agree; that was ages ago, but she reckons I still haven't got over it.'

'A loss like that,' he said, 'you don't get back to normal any time soon.'

'And you lost Aimee. To say nothing of Miranda.'

'You're right there, let's say nothing of Miranda. That was a mistake, pure and simple. My fault, not hers – I dived into another relationship far too fast after Aimee killed herself.'

Hannah blushed. 'I wondered if you'd sign the book for me?'

'Love to, but I didn't bring a pen out with me. Hang on, and I'll nip back to the cottage.'

'Don't worry, it will do another time. I'm sure we'll see each other again before long.'

'I'd like that – if you're sure?'

'Why not? We're friends, aren't we?'

She watched his face fall. 'Well, yes. Of course.'

'Fine. And – thanks again for a lovely afternoon.'

'The pleasure's mine.'

She thought he would kiss her goodbye; instead he took a step backwards, and waved. She raised her hand as she put her foot down and accelerated out of Tarn Fold.

A mile later, Terri rang. It took five minutes for her to get to the point. She coughed nervously, and the timid build-up was so out of character that Hannah guessed what she was about to say.

'I just wanted to mention . . . I bumped into Marc last night. There was a book signing at his shop, and I was at a loose end, with Stefan working. Marc and I went for a quick drink later on. I mean, that's absolutely all there was to it. He talked about you the whole time; he's still besotted, you know.' She paused. 'Honest, it was totally innocent. You don't mind, Hannah?'

'Course not.' Why was her upper body rigid with tension?

'Thanks, Hannah. I knew you'd understand.'

Half a minute later, she'd rung off. It might have been the shortest phone chat she and Terri had ever had.

On the radio, Carole King sang 'It's Too Late'. Hannah remembered Marc, turning up at their home the other night, and the hard time she'd given him. The lane was narrow and winding, and Hannah realised she was taking the bends too fast. She stamped on the brake just in time to avoid a collision. The drystone walls were a hazard, the lane barely wide enough to take a single vehicle, let alone offer latitude for careless driving. If you encountered a car coming in the other direction, you had no choice but to reverse until you came to a passing place. Trouble was, Hannah hated going backwards.

At last she reached the main route through Brackdale that would take her out of Daniel's valley and home to Ambleside. As she drove through the small settlement of Brack, her phone rang again. She hadn't been this popular in years. Unless it was Terri, determined that, having dug herself into a hole, she would keep digging.

'What is it?'

'Blimey, Hannah. Not like you to sound so tetchy.'

Greg Wharf – how about that for a turn-up for the book? Surely not a call about work on a Saturday evening?

'You still there, Hannah?'

'Uh-huh.'

'Everything all right?'

'Yeah, yeah, of course. I'm in the car, on my way back home after a day out.'

'OK, it's just that . . . I'm in Kendal at the moment. I was planning to call in at Westmorland General, and see Mario Pinardi. I wondered if you wanted to come along too.'

Hannah tightened her grip on the steering wheel. 'Actually, I'm less than ten minutes away.'

'Well, then!' Greg brightened. 'We don't need to stay long. I mean, visiting time finishes at eight and Alessandra is sure to be there anyway, along with all the little Pinardis. I just want him to know he's in our thoughts.'

'Good plan.'

'We could have a quick drink afterwards, if you have half an hour to spare.'

'Sure,' Hannah said. 'Why not?'

ACKNOWLEDGEMENTS

St Herbert's is described by Daniel Kind as the only residential library in England, and, like the other organisations and businesses that feature in the story (other than Cumbria Constabulary, my version of which is very highly fictionalised), it does not exist. There is, however, a splendid residential library just over the border in North Wales. St Deiniol's Library in Hawarden, venue of a marvellously enjoyable launch of *The Serpent Pool*, inspired my creation of St Herbert's and I am grateful for the help and information given to me by the staff of St Deiniol's. I hasten to add that St Herbert's is not a thinly veiled equivalent of St Deiniol's. I recommend it warmly to anyone fascinated (as I am) by the concept of a residential library. All the people who appear in this novel, and not only those associated with St Herbert's, are my inventions, and do not have, and are not meant to have, counterparts in real life.

Similarly, Madsen's Holiday Park is a product of my imagination, though again I benefited greatly from talking to James G. McAllister, a client and expert in the caravan and holiday home business. His parks are based in North Wales, and Madsen's is not meant to represent either them or any equivalent in the Lake District.

Many other people have assisted me in various ways during the writing of this book. Stephen Knowles and Ted Brown gave me a start with the set-up of the opening chapter, and Damien Culshaw offered a good deal of practical assistance on farming matters. I found a visit to the Culshaw family's farm in Lancashire fascinating, and I'm most grateful to Damien's parents for allowing me to explore. I only hope I haven't misrepresented the realities of farming life beyond the extent required by crime fiction. David Ward gave me useful insight into the origins of the Theatre by the Lake in Keswick, and Rachel Swift took my family and me on a tour backstage which formed part of a memorable birthday on a beautiful day in the Lakes. Ian Pepper helped with information on forensic science, while Roger Forsdyke gave me expert guidance on issues affecting police officers nationwide, a subject I also researched through various publications; Roger's police force is not based in Cumbria, and my account of the working lives of Hannah and her colleagues is not a portrayal of their real-life equivalents. To reinforce the fictional nature of the story, I have introduced a number of changes on matters of detail, as well as some aspects of local topography . . .

I'm indebted to my agent, Mandy Little, my publishers, and my family for their support through difficult times. Whilst I was writing this book, my mother died, and I am proud to dedicate it to her memory, knowing that I owe my passion for reading and writing above all to her.